FiNALEonline.de

FiNALEonline ist die digitale Ergänzung zu deinem Abiturband. Hier findest du eine Vielzahl an Angeboten, die dich bei deiner Prüfungsvorbereitung zusätzlich unterstützen.

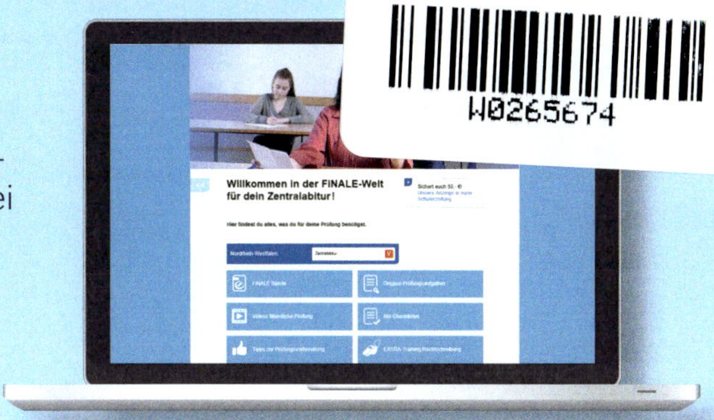

Das Plus für deine Vorbereitung:

- Original-Prüfungsaufgaben mit Lösungen (bitte Code von Seite 2 eingeben!)
- EXTRA-Training Rechtschreibung
  So kannst du einem möglichen Punktabzug bei deinen Abi-Klausuren vorbeugen.
- Videos zur mündlichen Prüfung
- Tipps zur stressfreien Prüfungsvorbereitung
- Abi-Checklisten mit allen prüfungsrelevanten Themen

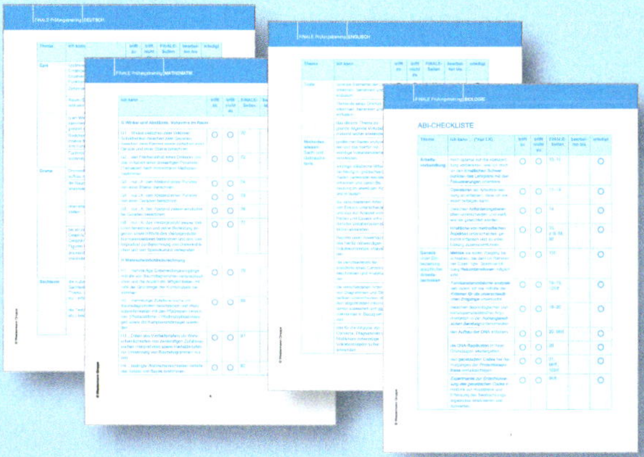

Abi-Checklisten

Sie helfen dir, den Überblick über den Prüfungsstoff zu behalten.

FiNALEonline.de

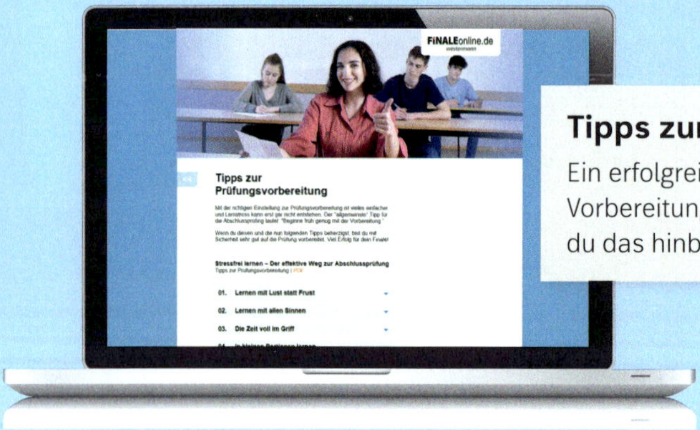

Tipps zur Prüfungsvorbereitung

Ein erfolgreiches Abitur erfordert eine gezielte Vorbereitung ohne unnötigen Lernstress. Wie du das hinbekommst, erfährst du hier!

Videos zur mündlichen Prüfung

Nur wenige Abiturienten wissen genau, wie sie abläuft, die „Mündliche". Die Videos geben dir Einblick in den Ablauf der Prüfung und Tipps für die richtige Vorbereitung.

Die Kombination aus FiNALE-Buch und FiNALEonline bietet dir die optimale Vorbereitung für deine Prüfung und begleitet dich sicher zu einem erfolgreichen Abitur 2023!

www.finaleonline.de

westermann

FiNALE
Prüfungstraining

Niedersachsen

Zentralabitur 2023
Englisch

FiNALEonline.de

Liebe Schülerin, lieber Schüler,

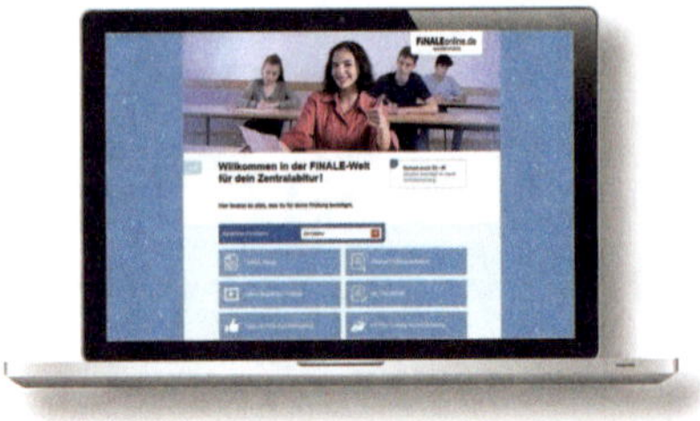

sobald die Original-Prüfungsaufgaben zur Veröffentlichung freigegeben sind, können sie unter **www.finaleonline.de** zusammen mit ausführlichen Lösungen kostenlos heruntergeladen werden. Gib dazu einfach diesen Code ein:

EN9K2X3

Einfach mal reinschauen: www.finaleonline.de

Autorinnen: Isabel Wagemann-Steidel und Ortrud-Christine Rotzoll sowie Lara Jost

westermann GRUPPE

Bildnachweis:
|Peter Wirtz Fotografie, Dormagen: Titel. |toonpool.com, Berlin, Castrop-Rauxel: Popa Matumula 159.1.

Druck A[1] / Jahr 2022
Alle Drucke der Serie A sind im Unterricht parallel verwendbar.

Redaktion: Federlese GbR – Christina & Boris Kühne, Grevenbroich
Kontakt: finale@westermanngruppe.de
Layout: LIO Design GmbH, Braunschweig
Umschlaggestaltung: Gingco.Net, Braunschweig
Umschlagfoto: Peter Wirtz, Dormagen
Druck und Bindung: Westermann Druck GmbH, Georg-Westermann-Allee 66, 38104 Braunschweig

ISBN 978-3-7426-**2337**-9

Inhaltsverzeichnis

Arbeiten mit FiNALE

FiNALE Prüfungstraining Englisch möchte Ihnen eine praxisnahe Hilfe zur Vorbereitung auf die Abiturprüfung sein. Im Praxis-Teil finden sich daher – neben den Original-Prüfungsaufgaben 2021 – zu allen geforderten Themenbereichen weitere authentische Aufgaben, die in ihrer Form den Vorgaben entsprechen. Wir verzichten hier auf eine Differenzierung nach Kursen mit grundlegendem beziehungsweise erhöhtem Anforderungsniveau. Im Abitur unterscheiden sich die Aufgaben einerseits durch den Textumfang, andererseits durch den Schwierigkeitsgrad des Textes. Auch als Schülerin oder Schüler in einem Kurs mit grundlegendem Anforderungsniveau sind Sie durch den Englischunterricht mit längeren und komplexeren Texten vertraut. Als Schülerin oder Schüler eines Kurses mit erhöhtem Anforderungsniveau können Sie eine Textanalyse auch an kürzeren, einfacheren Texten üben.

Zwei Aufgaben im Kapitel „Beispiele für Prüfungsaufgaben" werden kleinschrittig erarbeitet und schließen mit einer Musterlösung. Dies soll für Sie eine exemplarische Hilfe sein auf dem Weg vom Ausgangstext über das Textverständnis, die Methodik der Textanalyse und die Evaluation hin zur Gliederung und sprachlichen Darstellung des Zieltextes. Den weiteren Aufgabenbeispielen folgen Bewertungskriterien ganz in der Form, wie Ihre Lehrerinnen und Lehrer sie zur Korrektur der Abiturarbeiten an die Hand bekommen. Sie dienen Ihnen zur Selbstkontrolle in Ihrem fortschreitenden Prüfungstraining. Geschrieben wurde dieses Buch im Jahr 2022, damit es frühzeitig zur Vorbereitung auf das Abitur 2023 beitragen kann. Die zu diesem Zeitpunkt aktuellen Abituraufgaben 2021 werden jeweils mit Musterlösung angeboten. Sobald die Original-Prüfungsaufgaben des Jahres 2022 freigegeben sind, können Sie sie unter www.finaleonline.de abrufen.

Das Kapitel „Basiswissen" bietet Ihnen eine kompakte Übersicht über die für das Zentralabitur vorgegebenen Themen. Es hilft Ihnen, das im Unterricht erworbene Wissen zu strukturieren und in seinen Grundzügen abzurufen. Um den Umgang mit dem thematischen Vokabular zu vertiefen, ist dieser Teil in englischer Sprache geschrieben und wird durch Glossare zum thematischen Vokabular ergänzt.

Die sprachliche Leistung spielt in der Fremdsprache bei aller inhaltlich-thematischer Kompetenz immer noch die herausragende Rolle. Ein sicherer Umgang mit den Strukturen und Wörtern der englischen Sprache ist also unabdingbar. Deshalb haben wir in FiNALE ein ganzes Kapitel zur sprachlichen Leistung aufgenommen.

Wir wünschen Ihnen viel Erfolg!

Informationen und Tipps zur Prüfung

Das Kerncurriculum (KC) für die Sekundarstufe II

Mit der Einführung des neuen Kerncurriculums für die gymnasiale Oberstufe entwickelt sich der Englischunterricht auf moderne Weise weiter – so, wie es mit dem entsprechenden Kerncurriculum für die Klassen 5–10 bereits angelegt wurde. Das KC für die Oberstufe führt die im KC für die Sek I angelegten Grundlagen fort, sodass ein nahtloser Übergang in die Qualifikationsphase erfolgen kann. Grundlegend ist auch in der Sekundarstufe II der Gemeinsame Europäische Referenzrahmen *CERF (Common European Framework)*.
Im Zentralabitur **2023** wird die Prüfung aus folgenden **drei Bestandteilen** bestehen (s. auch S. 8 ff.):

1. Hörverstehen (30 Minuten),
2. Sprachmittlung (60 Minuten), sowie
3. einer Textaufgabe (auf erhöhtem Niveau: 240 Minuten, auf grundlegendem Niveau: 210 Minuten). Für die Textaufgabe besteht weiterhin die Wahlmöglichkeit zwischen zwei Vorschlägen; die Auswahl der Textaufgabe ist in der Prüfungszeit inbegriffen.

Die folgende Zusammenfassung der wichtigsten Anliegen des neuen KC gibt Ihnen eine Orientierung über die im Abitur von Ihnen erwarteten Kenntnisse und Kompetenzen.

Die Kompetenzorientierung

Kompetenzen

Das Abitur in Niedersachsen ist nicht nach Inhalten ausgerichtet, sondern es wird eine kompetenzorientierte Prüfung abgenommen. Inhalte sind selbstverständlich immer noch wichtig, sie ergeben sich aus den im Unterricht verpflichtend zu behandelnden Materialien. Die inhaltliche Grundlage sind die Themenfelder, die das Kerncurriculum für die Sekundarstufe II ausweist.

Der Englischunterricht soll es ermöglichen, Fremdes und Anderes zu erfahren und durch Perspektivenwechsel andere Weltsichten zu verstehen, um Perspektiven zu koordinieren und Empathie zu entwickeln.

Hierzu müssen die Inhalte „meaningful", also für die Lernenden von Bedeutung und außerdem in einem interkulturellen Sinne relevant sein. Hierbei wird ausdrücklich von einer erforderlichen Verstehensanstrengung ausgegangen, sodass Aufgaben nicht einfach nur mit bereits vorhandenem Weltwissen oder Allgemeinbildung gelöst werden können. Gefordert sind somit interaktive fremdsprachliche Prozesse, die sinnvolle diskursive Handlungen notwendig machen. Auf diese Weise sollen Reflexion und Selbstreflexion ermöglicht werden.

Um kompetent sprachlich und interkulturell kommunikativ handeln zu können, müssen Wissen und Können miteinander verknüpft werden. Inhalte werden in ihrer Bedeutung relativiert, da die Kompetenzen zwar an Inhalten erworben werden, dieses jedoch exemplarisch geschieht, sodass in der Abiturprüfung keine speziellen Inhalte wie etwa „India“ oder „The American Dream“ im Mittelpunkt stehen. Gefragt sind vielmehr methodische Problemlösungsstrategien, denn die erworbenen Kompetenzen werden auf neue Situationen, Themen und Kontexte transferiert. Sprachliche, pragmatische oder soziokulturelle Strukturen müssen in den einzelnen Prüfungsteilen erkannt und im Sinne eines kompetenten Umgangs mit der Fremdsprache beherrscht werden.

Wichtig ist hierbei der Hinweis, dass laut KC der Erwerb interkultureller Kompetenzen nicht mit der erfolgreich bestandenen Abiturprüfung endet, sondern ein Leben lang fortgesetzt wird.
Für Schülerinnen und Schüler bedeutet dies, dass sie laut KC nicht nur auf vorhandenes Wissen zurückgreifen müssen, sondern dass sie sich weiterführendes Wissen selbst beschaffen und entsprechende Zusammenhänge erkennen können. Weiterhin sollen sie in der Lage sein, Handlungsschritte zu planen und Lösungen auf kreative Weise zu erproben. Die verfügbaren Kenntnisse, Fähigkeiten und Fertigkeiten sollen dabei zum Einsatz kommen, das gewonnene Ergebnis soll anhand angemessener Kriterien selbst überprüft/evaluiert werden.

Diese Erweiterung der Kompetenzfelder wird nicht nur in den Unterricht, sondern vor allem auch in die Abiturprüfung einfließen.

TIPP Further reading

1. *Kerncurriculum für das Gymnasium – gymnasiale Oberstufe*
   Herausgegeben vom Niedersächsischen Kultusministerium (2009 und 2017), 30159 Hannover, Schiffgraben 12
   Das Kerncurriculum ist auch als PDF-Datei auf dem niedersächsischen Bildungsserver abrufbar: http://www.cuvo.nibis.de
2. *Gemeinsamer Europäischer Referenzrahmen für Sprachen: lernen, lehren, beurteilen*
   Autoren: John Trim/Brian North/Daniel Coste in Zusammenarbeit mit Joseph Sheils. Langenscheidt, ISBN: 978-3-126-06520-7
3. Materialien für kompetenzorientierten Unterricht, hrsg. vom Niedersächsischen Kultusministerium (2010), und Materialien zur Sprechprüfung (2014) auch online unter www.nibis.de
4. Bildungsstandards für die Allgemeine Hochschulreife, als PDF zu finden unter http://www.nibis.de/uploads/1gohrgs/files/englisch/Bildungsstandards_allg_Hochschulreife.pdf (Zugriff: 01.04.2022)

Kompetenzerwerb

Der Erwerb der für die Abiturprüfung erforderlichen Kompetenzen wird bereits in der Sekundarstufe I grundgelegt. Dennoch ist es ratsam, sich in Bezug auf die Abiturklausur rechtzeitig mit den strukturierten Kompetenzanforderungen vertraut zu machen. Das erworbene Wissen soll in der Abiturarbeit abgerufen und in verschiedenen Zusammenhängen genutzt werden können. Am Ende der Einführungsphase soll hier das Niveau B1+ nach dem Gemeinsamen Europäischen Referenzrahmen erreicht werden. Im Folgenden werden die wichtigsten Kompetenzen kurz dargestellt.

Abitur 2023

In der Abiturprüfung wird es zwei Prüfungsteile geben:

1. a) Hörverstehen (30 Minuten)
1. b) Sprachmittlung (60 Minuten)
2. Textaufgabe (210 Minuten gA / 240 Minuten eA)

Hörverstehen

Im Abitur 2023 wird es einen Hörverstehensteil geben, der 30 Minuten in Anspruch nehmen wird. Sie sollten dabei imstande sein, wesentliche Inhalte eines authentischen Hörtextes zu verstehen.

Als Material für die Prüfung können Hörvorlagen z. B. aus Radiosendungen, Reden, Interviews oder Gesprächen herangezogen werden. Die Länge der einzelnen Vorlagen wird fünf Minuten in der Regel nicht überschreiten. Das Hörverstehen wird mittels geschlossener und halboffener Aufgabenformate überprüft, denkbar wären also diese Aufgabenformate:

- Multiple Choice (mit drei oder maximal vier Alternativen pro *item)*
- Zuordnungsaufgaben
- Kurzantworten (mit 1–5 Wörtern)
- Gelenktes Notizenfertigen (Vervollständigung von Sätzen, Tabellen, ...)

Richtig/Falsch-Fragen zum Ankreuzen wird es nicht geben, die Ratewahrscheinlichkeit wäre zu groß.

TIPP zum Punktesammeln

Wichtig: Sollten Kurzantworten gefordert sein, zählen Rechtschreib- und Grammatikfehler nicht, solange erkennbar ist, was ausgesagt werden soll! Die geforderte Wortzahl ist unbedingt zu beachten!

Die Datei mit den Höraufgaben läuft bis zum Ende, ohne angehalten zu werden. Sie enthält daher auch alle Zeitintervalle, die zum Lesen der Aufgabenstellung benötigt werden. Die Texte werden zweimal angehört.
Um 5 Punkte zu erreichen, müssen 45 % der items richtig gelöst werden, für 11 Punkte mindestens 75 %.

Sprachmittlung (Mediation)

Im Abitur 2023 wird im ersten Prüfungsteil auch die Kompetenz Sprachmittlung geprüft. Hier kommt es darauf an, den Inhalt eines deutschsprachigen Textes sinngemäß, zielgruppengerecht und kontextgebunden in englischer Sprache wiederzugeben. Die entsprechenden Merkmale der geforderten Textsorte müssen beachtet werden. Die Adressatin bzw. der Adressat muss in die Lage versetzt werden, den Text für ihre/seine Zwecke nutzen zu können. Je nach Text kann es sinnvoll sein, kulturelle Besonderheiten zu berücksichtigen, indem man zusätzliche Erläuterungen anfügt. Unbekannte Wörter und Wendungen müssen gegebenenfalls umschrieben und sprachliche Strukturen vereinfacht werden. Die Mediationstexte beziehen sich häufig auf Alltagserfahrungen bzw. kulturelle Besonderheiten aus dem deutschsprachigen Raum.
Sprachmittlung (*mediation*) darf also keinesfalls mit Übersetzung (*translation*) verwechselt werden. Entscheidend ist für die Sprachmittlung allein die korrekte Wiedergabe wesentlicher Inhalte in sprachlich angemessener und idiomatisch richtiger Weise.
Für den Prüfungsteil Sprachmittlung gilt als Bewertungsgrundlage: Der Inhalt wird mit 40 %, die Sprache mit 60 % bewertet.
Das Beispiel auf Seite 9 bis 11 zeigt eine mögliche Aufgabenstellung. Zusätzlich finden Sie im Kapitel „Beispiele für Prüfungsaufgaben" weitere Sprachmittlungsaufgaben (S. 149 ff., 161 ff., 166 ff., 169 ff.).

Beispielaufgabe Mediation

Your English partner school is doing a school project on child poverty. You are asked to write a text for the project's website, presenting the current German debate. You found the article printed below. Write the part of your article that summarises in English the most important aspects of von Bullion's text, about 250 words.

„Kinder verdienen ein bedingungsloses Grundeinkommen"

Constanze von Bullion

[...] Alarmierend, inakzeptabel, unerträglich – jedes Mal, wenn in Deutschland Zahlen zur Kinderarmut präsentiert werden, kennt die Empörung kaum Grenzen. Zwischen 1,9 und 2,7 Millionen Kinder und Jugendliche leben in der Bundesrepublik mit einem Armutsrisiko. [...] Bei Kindern Alleinerziehender ist das Risiko, abgehängt zu werden, mehr als doppelt so hoch wie in Zwei-Eltern-Familien. Und wer bei Eltern groß wird, die beide keine Arbeit finden, lebt in einer biografischen Hochrisikozone. [...]

Was das bedeutet, hat die Bertelsmann-Stiftung zusammengetragen. Solchen Kindern fehlt neben dem Markenschuh und der Wertschätzung meistens auch das Selbstbewusstsein, Chancen zu ergreifen. Sie erleben mehr Streit zu Hause als andere, neigen öfter zu Risikoverhalten, müssen häufiger Klassen wiederholen. Die Tür zur Zukunft fällt da nicht ins Schloss, sie ist gar nicht erst aufgegangen.

Schlimm? Schlimm. Nur dass es eben kaum jemanden so aufzuregen scheint [...]. Sicher, man will mit allerlei Maßnahmen helfen. Aber es stehen sich da zwei Denkschulen gegenüber wie Supermächte im Kalten Krieg. [...]

Die erste Denkschule heißt: Kinder sind arm, weil ihre Eltern es sind. Nur wer Erwachsene besser in den Arbeitsmarkt integriert, gerade Mütter, wird Kinder aus der Armut holen. So argumentiert die SPD.

Die zweite Denkschule heißt: Kinder müssen unabhängig werden vom Erfolg ihrer Eltern. Seit Jahren fordern Sozialverbände, Linke und Grüne deshalb ein Grundeinkommen für Kinder von etwa 500 Euro im Monat. Familien mit geringem Einkommen sollen die Summe ganz bekommen statt anderer Leistungen. Besserverdiener dagegen müssten auf einen Teil des Geldes verzichten, so der Vorschlag. Je mehr sie verdienen, desto weniger bezuschusst sie der Staat.

Es wäre immerhin ein Versuch, das Gestrüpp staatlicher Familienleistungen zu lichten und vor allem: es gerechter zu machen. Denn so, wie es jetzt läuft in Deutschland, werden Besserverdiener klar bevorzugt. Es geht schon mit dem Kindergeld los, das jedem Kind in gleicher Höhe zusteht, egal, was die Eltern verdienen. Die Prämie ist für gut situierte Familien oft verzichtbar, zumal wenn beide Eltern verdienen. Egal, man nimmt halt mit, was man kriegen kann. [...]

Familienförderung in Deutschland ist oft ineffektiv und grundungerecht. Hauptnutznießer dieses Systems aber sind die ohnehin Privilegierten [...]. Und die CDU, einst die Familienpartei? Will jetzt ein Baukindergeld, das Mittelstandsfamilien beim Wohnungskauf unterstützt. So nach dem Motto: Genug kann nie genügen.

Wer das alles nicht mehr mit ansehen mag, muss raus aus alten Denkgebäuden. Gerade bei ärmeren Kindern wächst die Chance gesellschaftlicher Teilhabe erheblich, wenn beide Eltern Geld verdienen statt nur ein Elternteil. Das Armutsrisiko sinkt dann von 16 auf fünf Prozent. Soll das gelingen, müssen viel mehr Mütter entschlossener auf den Arbeitsmarkt zurückdrängen, in Vollzeit. Weiterführende Schulen müssen konsequent in die Lage versetzt werden, Schüler nachmittags zu betreuen und zu unterrichten, damit Armut – die im Kopf – sich nicht vererbt.

In einem Land, das im vergangenen Jahr einen Überschuss von 23 Milliarden Euro erwirtschaftet hat, muss das drin sein. [...] Das Geld daraus sollte in einen Feldversuch wie den in Finnland gesteckt werden. Dort bekommen 2000 Erwachsene jetzt zwei Jahre lang ein bedingungsloses Grundeinkommen. Am Ende wird geschaut, ob es ihnen hilft, auf eigenen Beinen zu stehen.

Das Gleiche sollte Deutschland mit einem Grundeinkommen für Kinder ausprobieren. Es würde Eltern statt anderer sozialer Leistungen ausbezahlt. Stellt sich heraus, dass sie von dem Geld nur Zigaretten und Flachbildschirme kaufen, ist die Idee gescheitert. Zeigt sich aber, dass das Modell Türen aufstoßen kann in ein selbstbestimmtes Leben, ist Umdenken gefragt, hin zum Kindergrundeinkommen. [...]

Source: Constanze von Bullion, "Kinderarmut: Kinder verdienen ein bedingungsloses Grundeinkommen", in: *Süddeutsche Zeitung*, 02.05.2017, https://www.sueddeutsche.de/wirtschaft/kinderarmut-kinder-verdienen-ein-bedingungsloses-grundeinkommen-1.3453867 (accessed on 14 February 2022, abridged).

Beispiellösung

We need an unconditional basic income for children

Germany is a very rich country looking at the economy as a whole but not if you consider children or teenagers. An estimated 1.9 to 2.7 million live in or close to poverty, especially those coming from households of single- or unemployed parents, according to an article by Constanze von Bullion, published in the German newspaper "Süddeutsche Zeitung" on 2 May 2017.

She presents findings by the Bertelsmann Foundation that – for poor children – poverty does not only result in a lack of products such as branded shoes but also a lack of self-confidence.

Every now and then, Germany discusses these issues, but a solution has not been found so far. One position argues that poor children come from poor households. Hence parents with well-paid jobs would change this. Others want children to be treated independently of their parents: they demand a guaranteed and unconditional basic income for children. The less their parents earn, the higher this amount should be.

Currently, all children receive monthly child benefits, regardless of their parents' income. Parents with a high income usually do not need this money but take it anyway. Hence supporting families this way is ineffective and unjust.

Bullion argues that organising schooling in a way that allows both parents to work full-time is a far better way of ensuring that poverty will not be inherited. She also states that Germany should try out the Finnish model of an unconditional basic income for children. If this money is wasted, the idea will have failed. But it may also contribute to increasing children's social mobility.

Bewertung für die Aufgabe zur Sprachmittlung

Diese Übersicht ist ein Auszug aus der Bewertungskala des Niedersächsischen Kultusministeriums.[1]

Punkte	Sprache (60 %)	Inhalt (40 %)
15–13	Die Zielsprache wird nahezu durchgängig korrekt und treffsicher verwendet: – Geringfügige sprachliche Mängel beeinträchtigen die Verständlichkeit nicht. – Thematischer und funktionaler Wortschatz werden idiomatisch und treffend verwendet. Die Darstellung enthält alle durch die Aufgaben geforderten charakteristischen Textmerkmale. Bei der Gestaltung des Textes werden die sprachlichen Anforderungen der Situations- und Adressatenorientierung nahezu vollständig umgesetzt.	– Alle Aspekte der Aufgabenstellung werden beachtet. – Alle im Sinne der Aufgabenstellung wichtigen Informationen werden präzise und situations- bzw. adressatenorientiert wiedergegeben. – Ggf. werden relevante kulturspezifische Erläuterungen präzise formuliert, wie z. B die Erklärung von Eigennamen oder kulturspezifischen Begriffen. – Die Darstellung und die Gliederung sind klar und logisch.
06–04	Die Zielsprache wird in Teilen korrekt verwendet: – Die sprachlichen Erfordernisse der Aufgabenstellung werden teilweise beachtet und umgesetzt. – Zahlreiche Mängel beeinträchtigen die Verständlichkeit so, dass einzelne Aussagen nicht erfassbar sind. – Thematischer und funktionaler Wortschatz werden nur lückenhaft verwendet. Die Darstellung enthält wenige durch die Aufgabenstellung geforderte charakteristische Textmerkmale. Bei der Gestaltung des Textes werden die sprachlichen Anforderungen der Situations- und Adressatenorientierung in Teilen korrekt umgesetzt.	– Die Aspekte der Aufgabenstellung werden teilweise beachtet. – Wenige im Sinne der Aufgabenstellung wesentlichen Informationen werden wiedergegeben; der Situations- bzw. Adressatenbezug wird nur ansatzweise beachtet. – Die Darstellung und die Gliederung sind in Ansätzen logisch und zusammenhängend.

[1] Niedersächsisches Kultusministerium, ANLAGE 1 Bewertungsskala Sprachmittlung Erlass vom 02.11.2015 – 33-82102-03/15 i. d. F. vom 16.2.2017, https://www.nibis.de/uploads/redriedl/moderne_fremdsprachen/20151102_Erlass%2BAnlage_Moderne_Fremdsprachen.pdf (Zugriff: 14.02.2022, gekürzt)

Schreiben

Ausschlaggebend beim Schreiben ist die sogenannte kommunikative Absicht; es muss deutlich werden, welchem Zweck der Text dienen soll. Es wird erwartet, dass die Schülerinnen und Schüler selbstständig Texte verfassen, die zielgruppengerecht und sinnvoll strukturiert sein sollen. Die Abiturklausur wird aus einer großen Bandbreite möglicher Themen ausgewählt, die sich auf fachliche oder auch persönliche Fragestellungen beziehen können. Hierbei müssen Planungsstrategien, beispielsweise die Mindmap, ebenso bekannt sein wie Vorgehensweisen zur Gliederung, Bearbeitung und kritischen Beurteilung der eigenen Texte. Die Grundlage der schriftlichen Abiturprüfung können auch sogenannte mehrfach kodierte Texte sein. Hierzu zählen zum Beispiel Karikaturen, Bilder, Statistiken oder Diagramme.

Auf die Bewertung der sprachlichen Leistung im Rahmen der sogenannten **integrativen Sprachentwicklung** wird später noch eingegangen (s. S. 131).

Leseverstehen

In der Abiturprüfung 2023 wird es keine Aufgaben zum Leseverstehen geben, da man sich bundesländerübergreifend auf das Aufgabenformat „Sprachmittlung“ verständigt hat. Dennoch müssen die erworbenen Kompetenzen auf der Niveaustufe B1+ während der Qualifikationsphase dahingehend erweitert werden, dass das Niveau C1 erreicht wird, um selbstständig einen längeren, anspruchsvolleren fiktionalen oder nichtfiktionalen Text zu verstehen, ihm gezielt Detailinformationen zu entnehmen und unbekanntes Vokabular zu erschließen. Die Arbeit mit einem Wörterbuch muss also beherrscht werden, ebenso wie die unterschiedlichen Arbeitstechniken etwa des intensiven und extensiven Lesens. Sie müssen außerdem in der Lage sein, sprachliche und gestalterische Merkmale eines Textes zu erfassen und somit die Wirkungsweise eines Textes analysieren können.

Den Erschließungstechniken wie *skimming* (globales Leseverstehen, Erkennen der Hauptaussage des Textes), *scanning* (detailliertes, genaues Lesen) und *careful reading* (Suchen nach spezifischen Informationen) kommt dabei große Bedeutung zu. Weiterhin sollten unbekannte Wörter auch ohne Zuhilfenahme eines Wörterbuches erschlossen werden können.

Sprechen

Die Kompetenz „Sprechen“ ist für die schriftliche Abiturprüfung ohne Bedeutung. In einer P5-Prüfung (oder mündlichen Nachprüfung im schriftlichen Prüfungsfach) werden hingegen sowohl monologisches als auch dialogisches Sprechen geprüft. Beim monologischen Sprechen muss man über einen Zeitraum von ca. zehn Minuten frei und zusammenhängend über ein vorgegebenes Thema reden, das auf der Grundlage von Prüfungsunterlagen, zumeist einem Text, zu erschließen ist. In der Regel wird zunächst eine kurze Zusammenfassung des Textmaterials erwartet, bevor die weiteren Aufgaben abgearbeitet werden. Hierbei soll laut KC korrekt und flüssig gesprochen werden. Der/

Die Schüler/-in soll im anschließenden Prüfungsgespräch zeigen, dass sie/er flexibel und spontan auf die prüfende Person reagieren und eigene Argumente begründen kann.

Insgesamt soll das Prüfungsgespräch so natürlich wie möglich und idiomatisch korrekt geführt werden, wobei der/die Schüler/-in zeigen soll, dass sie/er Verständnisschwierigkeiten in der Zielsprache ausräumen und Wortschatz- und Grammatiklücken überbrücken kann. Die mündliche Prüfung dauert in der Regel mindestens 20 Minuten.

INFO Mündliche Abiturprüfung als Präsentationsprüfung

Innerhalb des Abiturs kann Englisch als mündliches Prüfungsfach gewählt werden (P5). Die Prüfung kann auch als Präsentationsprüfung abgehalten werden. Das Thema der Prüfung wird den Prüflingen von Seiten der Prüfenden vorher mitgeteilt. Die Prüflinge erstellen eine Präsentation zu dem Thema und reichen diese vor dem Prüfungstag ein. Neben der auf Englisch zu haltenden Präsentation erfolgt am Prüfungstag ein längeres Prüfungsgespräch zu dem Prüfungsthema in der Fremdsprache.

Verknüpfung der Themenfelder und Lektüren

Die curricularen Vorgaben für die Oberstufe sehen die Behandlung von **verpflichtenden Themenfeldern** vor, die im jeweiligen Abiturdurchgang durch verpflichtend zu behandelnde Materialien ergänzt werden. Die verpflichtenden Materialien sollen vor einem thematisch breiteren Hintergrund erarbeitet und in diesen eingebettet werden.
Die folgende Übersicht hilft, dies zu veranschaulichen.

Verbindliche Themenfelder für 2023

Auf alle genannten Themenfelder muss im Laufe der vier Semester eingegangen werden. Aufgrund von Corona wurde für das Abitur 2023 entschieden, für das Fach Englisch der Behandlung der verbindlichen Materialien sowie der verbindlichen Unterrichtsaspekte Vorrang vor der Behandlung weiterer Themen der Themenfelder zu geben.

Beliefs, values and norms in society: Tradition and change	**Individual and society**	**Globalisation**
– Britishness – the American Experience – postcolonial/neocolonial experiences – migration effects on the world of work	– identity – ethnic, cultural and linguistic diversity – gender and sexual diversity	– effects on the world of work – impact on personal lives – global responsibility concerning e.g. politics, the environment, economy – English as a global language

Erhöhtes Niveau (eA) **Shakespeare** – the world that made him – modern adaptations	**Die Lektüren/ Materialien müssen mit diesen Themen verknüpft werden.**	**Science and technology** – chances and risks – visions of the future – the media, e. g. the influence of the media on public opinion and personal life – the digital revolution

Das Curriculum ist vor allem auf eine Vernetzung der Themen ausgelegt, wie sie sich durch die jeweiligen literarischen Texte, Sachtexte, Songs, Filme oder Dokumentationen ergibt. Im Folgenden werden die verbindlichen Texte für den Abiturdurchgang 2023 aufgelistet und thematisch verortet, sodass Sie in der Lage sind, die sich anbietenden Vernetzungen nachzuvollziehen. Die jeweiligen Niveaustufen werden mit gA (grundlegendes) und eA (erhöhtes) Anforderungsniveau abgekürzt.

Verbindliche Materialien für 2023

Die Reihenfolge, in der die Materialien behandelt werden, ist nicht festgelegt. Auch gibt es keine feste inhaltliche Bindung der Lektüren an die Themenfelder. Die hier genannten Verknüpfungen sind daher nur Vorschläge.

Material	**inhaltliche Schwerpunkte**	**thematische Verknüpfungen**
Roman: Sindiwe Magona, *Mother to Mother*	*apartheid in South Africa, ethnic and cultural diversity, justice, personal guilt and accountability*	Individual and society
		Beliefs, values and norms in society
Short Story: Andrea Levy, “Loose Change” (2005)	*belonging and identity, postcolonial experience, ethnic and cultural diversity*	Beliefs, values and norms in society
		Individual and society
Short Story: Shereen Pandit, “She Shall Not Be Moved” (2005)	*belonging and identity, postcolonial experience, ethnic and cultural diversity, racism*	Beliefs, values and norms in society
		Individual and society
		Globalisation
Film: *Gran Torino*	*search for values and beliefs, personal life and happiness, second generation immigrants, gang culture in the USA, violence, cultural clashes*	Individual and society
		Beliefs, values and norms in society
		Globalisation

zusätzlich für erhöhtes Anforderungsniveau		
Short Story: Jhumpa Lahiri, "The Third and Final Continent" (1999)	*belonging and identity, displacement, postcolonial experience, ethnic and cultural diversity, migration*	Beliefs, values and norms in society Individual and society Globalisation
Short Story: Qaisra Shahraz, "The Escape" (2009)	*belonging and identity, displacement, postcolonial experience, ethnic and cultural diversity*	Individual and society Globalisation Beliefs, values and norms in society
Drama: William Shakespeare, *Hamlet* (~1600)	*questions of morality, the role(s) of women, fate vs. free will*	Shakespeare Individual and society
Roman: Mary Shelley, *Frankenstein* (1831)	*ethics of science, the role of nature, dreams of happiness, questions of human identity*	Individual and society Science and technology

Hinweis
Die Lektüren werden in diesem Band an der Stelle thematisiert, an der sie inhaltlich am naheliegendsten zu verorten sind. Grundsätzlich bietet jedes der Materialien verschiedene Zugangsmöglichkeiten an, sodass es unter unterschiedlichen Gesichtspunkten behandelt werden kann. Dies wird im Folgenden exemplarisch verdeutlicht.

Beispielhafte Verortung von Materialien

Anhand des folgenden Beispiels soll deutlich werden, dass keines der Materialien nur einen einzigen thematischen Zugang zulässt, sondern vielseitige Diskussions- und Interpretationsanlässe eröffnet. Allen Materialien ist gemein, dass sie interkulturelles Verständnis und das Bewusstsein für globale Probleme schärfen können. Diese übergeordnete Betrachtung bildet den Schwerpunkt in diesem Band. Eine inhaltlich detaillierte Thematisierung erfolgt im Unterricht und kann mithilfe von Sekundärliteratur oder Informationen aus dem Internet vertieft werden. Hier soll in erster Linie der Blick für den größeren Zusammenhang geschärft werden, in dem die Texte zu verorten sind.

Material	Mögliche thematische Erarbeitung
Film: ***Gran Torino*** (gA + eA)	**Individual and society:** Der Film *Gran Torino* (2008, Regie: Clint Eastwood) spielt in einem vom wirtschaftlichen Niedergang gezeichneten Viertel in Detroit.

Grundlegende Kenntnisse zum Verständnis des Films: – individual and society	Der Hauptfiguren sind der Koreakriegsveteran Walt Kowalski, ein ehemaliger Ford-Mitarbeiter, der ein von rassistischen Vorurteilen geprägtes Weltbild pflegt, und Thao, der zu den aus Südostasien eingewanderten Hmong in seiner Nachbarschaft gehört. Im Verlauf des Films entwickelt sich der rassistische Walt Kowalski zu einem ungewollten Helden, der auf seine Art Thao als Vaterfigur dient und ihm letztlich bei der Identitätsfindung und Integration in die US-amerikanische Gesellschaft hilft. Walt Kowalskis ganzer Stolz ist sein 1972er Ford Gran Torino, ein letzter Beweis für die einst blühende Wirtschaft Detroits. Als Thao im Rahmen eines Initiationsritus versucht, den Wagen zu stehlen, verhindert Kowalski dies mit Waffengewalt. Auf dieselbe Weise schützt er später Thao und seine Familie vor einer Gang. Walt Kowalski lässt während der Filmhandlung zwar nicht vom Waffengebrauch ab, aber sein Verhalten gegenüber Thao, der die bisher von Walt Kowalski verachtete asiatische Minderheit symbolisiert, wandelt sich zum widerwilligen Helfen.
– beliefs and values – cultural and ethnic diversity – the role of gang culture and violence	**Beliefs, values and norms in society:** Der Katholik Walt Kowalski übt seinen Glauben nicht aktiv aus und lässt Pater Janovich dies auch unmissverständlich spüren. Erst zum Ende des Films geht Walt zum Pater, um die Beichte abzulegen. Er tut dies, weil er seinen Tod plant. Dass er einen Maßanzug bei seinem Tod trägt, zeigt, dass er trotz aller Rauigkeit doch an gesellschaftlichen Wertvorstellungen festhält. Sein gewaltsamer Tod durch die von ihm provozierte Schießerei der Vorstadt-Gang, die Thaos Familie und das Viertel tyrannisiert, lässt sich als Sühne für seine Schuld, die er am Tod eines koreanischen Teenagers trägt, deuten.
– globalisation	**Globalisation** Das Thema der Globalisierung lässt sich in den Aspekten der Auswirkungen des Koreakrieges und der Wirtschaftskrise von 2008 finden. Die Teilnahme Walt Kowalskis am Koreakrieg und seine ihn prägenden Eindrücke wie das plagende Schuldgefühl, eine am Kriegsgeschehen unbeteiligte koreanische Jugendliche getötet zu haben, sowie die Auswirkungen für die pro-amerikanischen Hmong sind Folgen der globalen Vernetzung. Die ethnische Gruppe der Hmong, die auf Seiten der USA gegen Nordvietnam gekämpft hatten, fanden Zuflucht in den USA, wo sie oftmals Ausgrenzung erfuhren. Die Wirtschaftskrise von 2008 traf Detroit, zuvor ein industrieller Ankerpunkt der US-amerikanischen Autoproduktion, hart. Massenentlassungen und Rückbau der Automobilproduktion erfolgten, was den wirtschaftlichen und sozialen Niedergang der Region bewirkte.

Basiswissen

Das folgende Kapitel gibt einen Überblick über die curricularen Themenfelder des Oberstufenunterrichts ohne konkrete Semesterzuordnung. Das Ziel dieses Vorgehens ist es, einen Gesamtüberblick über die inhaltlichen Kenntnisse zu bieten, die im Zentralabitur z. B. auch für Hörverstehen und Mediation vorausgesetzt werden. An geeigneten Stellen wird darauf hingewiesen, wie die verbindlichen Lektüren thematisch im größeren Kontext verortet werden können. Die Zuordnung in fünf große Themenfelder entspricht den Vorgaben für das Abitur 2023 (s. S. 14). Fast alle Unterkapitel in diesem Buch entsprechen dem geforderten Basiswissen für beide Jahrgänge. Darüber hinaus wird auf weitere Lektüren, Filme und andere Materialien hingewiesen, die in vorherigen Abiturdurchgängen relevant waren und/oder sich als „Klassiker“ zur näheren Auseinandersetzung mit dem Thema eignen.

Beliefs, Values and Norms in Society

Britishness

People outside of Britain often refer to the British as the English – two terms which are often falsely regarded as being synonymous. This stereotypical perception may have its roots in the history of the British Isles as well as the history of the British Empire. Here, the dominance of English culture can certainly still be seen. In the following chapter a general overview will be given with regard to the correct terms to use when speaking of “the British” as well as the main cultural values and norms which have shaped British society.

Common Stereotypes

British people, but in particular the English, are considered to be well-mannered and polite. A common example named in this context is that British people apologise both when they accidentally run into someone and when they are run into. The British are also renowned for their sense of irony and for their small talk, which they usually begin by talking about the weather, especially when they meet someone they don’t know. Some consider the English to be snobbish and arrogant but also very hospitable. Both the British and the Irish are famous for their pub culture. More stereotypes could be listed, but being what they are – clichés –, all of them must be carefully examined.

TIPP Further reading

The peculiar ways of the English are humorously depicted in *Watching the English* by Kate Fox (2004), a sociological approach to (stereo)typical English behaviour and “Englishness”.

Geographical and Political Distinctions

There are several phrases commonly used to refer to the English-speaking area in Europe. They are explained here.

- **Great Britain:** refers to the main island including England, Scotland and Wales
- **The United Kingdom** (of Great Britain and Northern Ireland): the political term meaning England, Scotland, Wales and Northern Ireland; the terms "Britons" and "The British" are commonly used synonymously to describe the nation and its people
- **Scotland, Wales and Northern Ireland** were and are centrally governed by London but have all gained rights of self-government (S & W: 1999, NI: 2006)
- the **Republic of Ireland:** independent from the United Kingdom since 1921; as a result of the independence treaty, the island of Ireland was divided into Northern Ireland (which still belongs to the UK) and the Republic of Ireland

English Cultural Dominance and its Historical Roots

- The **name "England"** is derived from the Angles, a Germanic tribe which settled the island during the 5th and 6th centuries.
- On the island of Great Britain, England gained dominance over Welsh and Scottish territories, which had been settled by Celtic tribes; over the centuries, all three parts of Great Britain became a political union which still bears traits of its cultural diversity (this can be observed in language, cultural heritage and political concessions).
- At the beginning of the 16th century, England gained worldwide influence during the **Age of Discoveries:** English merchants followed the great explorers; English settlers founded colonies in North America and other newly-discovered parts of the world, while the British East India Company set out to exploit the wealth of the newly established Asian colonies economically.
- The growing territorial expansion during the 16th and 17th centuries led to the development of the **British Empire,** which – at its height – included approximately one quarter of the world's land.
- The Empire lost its influence as the former colonies began to seek independence.
- The earliest colonies to obtain independence from Britain were the thirteen northern American colonies, which in 1776 formed the United States of America.
- During the 19th and 20th centuries, most of the other colonies gained independence by peaceful or violent means (the most important ones being India, South Africa, Australia and the Republic of Ireland); some former colonies joined the Commonwealth of Nations – an organisation which promotes trade and cultural relations between its members.

Because of the long history of Britain as the world's ruling colonial power, British culture has influenced societies worldwide. Its cultural effects can be observed in many nations: Australia recognises Queen Elizabeth as Queen of Australia, represented by the Govenor-General; driving on the left is the rule in many former colonies and many still use English as their official language, etc.

Democracy and Monarchy

Despite being a monarchy, the United Kingdom has a long history of parliamentary structures (first attempts to assert popular power date back to the Magna Carta of 1215 and the Bill of Rights of 1689). Britain has no written constitution, and its legislature is based on laws passed by parliament. Parliamentary sovereignty is the leading norm and the monarch no longer plays an active role in legislative processes. Parliament constitutionally consists of the Crown (the monarch formally heads Parliament), the House of Lords (the aristocracy) and the House of Commons. Parliament, however, is controlled by the Prime Minister and his or her cabinet. The Prime Minister and his or her government have gained the executive powers of the monarch and act in his/her name.

The Issue of Class

Britain is considered to be an extremely class-conscious society. The definition of "class" can very generally be put as a distinction in social standing which developed in feudal times and became more diversified during the Industrial Revolution. Social differences can be defined in terms of heritage (aristocratic vs. common birth), educational, professional and financial standing. Class distinctions into upper, middle, lower and, since the Thatcher Era of the 1980s, a new upper and an underclass have their origins in the emergence of new working and entrepreneur classes during the Industrial Revolution.

The British class system is no longer "closed", meaning that it offers chances for upward or downward movement (social mobility). Education or professional success allows members of lower classes to move upwards on the metaphorical "social ladder". Thus, people are no longer bound to the class they were born into.
Class is generally associated with certain stereotypical traits. The various classes differ with regard to habits and attitudes, as can be observed in everyday life, for instance, in where people live, what they eat, the way they dress, spend their free time, which newspapers they read and which TV programmes they watch, which schools their children attend, the vocabulary they use and what accent they speak with. British people are very aware of these class differences.
Class differences are most easily observed in the British educational system, which is still divided into public schools (which in fact means "private") and state schools. British public schools control admission by means of tuition fees and application procedures, but grants and scholarships can be applied for. Attending one of these schools is still to some extent a requirement for admission to the so-called "Oxbridge" universities. Thus, social mobility is essentially a matter of financial and educational background.

Britain and the EU

The UK was a member of the EU from 1973 to 2020, but during this period the scepticism of certain political and public circles towards Europe never ceased.
On 23 June 2016, a referendum was held about Britain's membership in the EU: 51.9 % voted to leave the EU, 48.1 % to remain. The UK finally left the EU after long and complex negotiations on 31 January 2020. Brexit is the UK's attempt to break free from unwanted EU rules and regulations in order to re-establish national sovereignty. Its supporters hope the UK will shed what they see as its EU-regulated and hampered shell in order to negotiate free trade agreements with other countries that will provide it with a better economic and social future.
Others fear that there will be significant economic drawbacks, as the UK is no longer a member of the European single market. This may lead to higher prices of goods on both sides of the Channel, despite the new EU-UK Trade and Cooperation Agreement.
Another problem is the question of Northern Ireland. The Republic of Ireland is still part of the EU, but the Brexit deal avoids a "hard border" between the Republic and the six counties of Northern Ireland and establishes a de facto customs border between the two islands. This is a major problem for the anti-EU Protestants in Northern Ireland. Peace-threatening conflicts between certain elements in the Republic of Ireland and Northern Ireland have rekindled, though such conflicts had been settled by the Good Friday Agreement in 1998. Brexit has partially aroused feelings of insecurity in Northern Ireland concerning its future. A well-wrought solution to Northern Ireland's special situation is yet to come.
In the Brexit referendum Scotland voted with a significant majority to "remain". Some politicians – and many Scottish people – would now like a second referendum on Scottish independence, i. e. to leave the UK in order eventually to rejoin the EU. This is unlikely, however, to be agreed by the present government in London.
In the course of time, Brexit may turn out to be a success story, but the people's will in the referendum vote was strongly influenced by populist politicians. Many British people do not like the new regulations and consequences of Brexit, as they bring changes for the worse, such as visa requirements, export restrictions, reduced research funding or the UK's withdrawal from the Erasmus study programme.

Internationally, Britain has established a strong connection with US foreign policies (for years it had or has been engaged both in Afghanistan and Iraq), which partly results from its alliance with America during the Second World War and the subsequent formation of NATO. However, unlike former American administrations, which often regarded the United Nations as a weak institution, Britain regards the UN as an important framework for promoting international foreign policy. Like the United States, Britain is a permanent member of the UN Security Council.

Glossary of Common Political Terms (BE)

administration	Verwaltung (im AE auch: Regierung)
Act (of Parliament)	(verabschiedetes) Gesetz
bill	Gesetzesvorlage
chamber	Kammer (z. B. House of Commons)
checks and balances	Gewaltenteilung (in der Politik)
constituency	Wahlkreis
constituent	Wähler/-in
domestic/foreign policy	Innen-/Außenpolitik
Foreign/Home Secretary	Außen-, Innenminister/-in
election	Wahl
electorate	Wählerschaft
representative	Volksvertreter/-in
MP (Member of Parliament)	Abgeordnete/-r
Speaker	Vorsitzende/-r des Unterhauses
(hereditary, life) peer	(erbliches, lebenslanges) Mitglied des Oberhauses
in office	im Amt
to hold office; to take office	amtieren; ein Amt antreten
to stand down	zurücktreten
universal suffrage	allgemeines Wahlrecht

The American Experience

The United States of America came into being as a reaction to a lack of political influence. As colonies of the British Empire, the original thirteen states, which had been settled by British citizens, had to pay taxes to the motherland. Yet their interests were not represented in parliament; hence the famous slogan "No taxation without representation". Instead of granting their overseas citizens a say in their own affairs, the British crown continued to impose taxes, which led to several uprisings that eventually turned into outright war between the colonies and their motherland. The imbalance of power led the American settlers to declare their independence in 1776. The famous document, originally written by Thomas Jefferson and signed by representatives of the American people (today called the "Founding Fathers"), questioned the rights of the British King, George III, and included the following statement, which would later become the basis of democratic thought and popular emancipation from the ruling aristocracy: "We hold these truths to be self-evident, that all men are created equal, that they are endowed by their Creator with certain unalienable Rights, that among these are Life, Liberty and the pursuit of Happiness."

This concept of equality and equal opportunities became the key to America's self-perception and national identity and led the US to emerge from the War of Independence (1771–1776) as the world's first modern democracy. In its time (and long before the French Revolution), the concept of equality, as expressed in these lines, was revolutionary.

The American Constitution

- written in 1787
- new ideas of a democratic state stated in the **preamble** of the constitution: "We the People of the United States, in Order to form a more perfect Union[1], establish Justice, ensure domestic Tranquility, provide for the common defense, promote the general Welfare, and secure the Blessings of Liberty to ourselves and our Posterity, do ordain and establish this Constitution for the United States of America."

The Bill of Rights

- the first ten amendments to the American Constitution
- written because some delegates feared that the new American government would threaten everyone's chance of achieving personal freedom and the pursuit of happiness
- The First Congress of the United States originally proposed twelve amendments in 1789, ten of which were added to the constitution as a preamble.
- amendments known as the Bill of Rights
- guarantee America's citizens certain unalienable rights, e. g. freedom of religion, freedom of speech and the press as well as the right to bear arms

The American Dream / American Nightmare

Keyword

"The American Dream": There is no single definition of what the American Dream actually is, as it varies for each and every American. The term was first used by James Truslow Adams, an American historian, in his book *The Epic of America*, in 1931: "[The] American Dream [is] the dream of a land in which life should be better and richer and fuller for every man, with opportunity for each according to his ability or achievement."

In order to understand how people who had grown up in a monarchy and were used to being subjects of a king or queen could come to the conclusion that they possessed equal rights, one must consider the motives which led the early settlers to leave Britain.

1 Barack Obama took up the idea of "a more perfect union" in a speech he delivered on 28 May 2008, in which he elaborated on the issues of race and inequality in the USA.

The Puritans, religious values, New Canaan

- The first English settlers to arrive on American soil were religious outcasts, Protestants who had wanted to cleanse the Anglican Church from remaining Roman Catholic influence. These **Puritans**, as they called themselves, were persecuted in England and thus left for the colonies. Other religious sects like the Quakers, Baptists and Methodists followed.
- In September 1620, a group of 102 people left England for America, sailed on a ship called the Mayflower, which arrived 65 days later in a bay they called Plymouth Bay.
- Between 1620 and 1640 thousands of Puritans emigrated to New England and founded the first settlements in Plymouth and Massachusetts Bay. To them, America was God's promised land, a **"New Canaan"**, a reference to the biblical country to which Moses led his people to free them from slavery in Egypt. In America the Puritans hoped they would be able to follow their religious beliefs and live freely.
- Puritan values such as integrity, virtue, the right to education, individual freedom and communitarianism still constitute central aspects of American self-perception.
- At the same time, the Puritans imposed strict moral rules on their communities, and today "Puritan" is a term associated with extreme conservatism and prudishness.

American values and beliefs

The key to the image of the United States as the country of unlimited opportunities, where each and every person can turn from "dishwasher to millionaire", from rags to riches, lies in these early visions of individual freedom, opportunity and self-reliance which led millions to emigrate to the former British colonies. These ideals shape the American Dream, which is not one single concept but a combination of individual goals and general values.

- **Individualism/self-reliance:** The underlying belief is that everyone is responsible for their own fate and has the liberty to determine their way of life.
- **Opportunity:** If a person is given the chance to take matters into his or her own hands, he or she will prosper. If that person fails, however, he or she has not worked hard enough.
- **Freedom:** This has two faces. On the one hand, it allows all individuals to pursue their own vision of happiness without being controlled by a central government. On the other, this belief also led to a general scepticism towards any kind of federal interference in individual affairs. Even today, Americans still tend to be sceptical of decisions made by the central administration in Washington, D.C., suspecting it of limiting their communal, state or personal rights.
- **Community:** Individual hardships such as unemployment are seen as personal failures, yet the local communities readily offer help to those in need. Because of this communal spirit, federal programs of social welfare and common health care often meet with opposition as they are seen as an intrusion into personal rights.

The American Dream is still alive, and each year many people come to the United States to pursue it, although the number of people able to obtain a "green card" has always been limited and many immigrants today arrive illegally. After the original settlement

period, the main waves of immigration entered the US between the middle of the 19th until the beginning of the 20th century, when the United States was in need of workers and a sufficient number of people to settle new territories in the west. Millions of mostly European immigrants arrived at Ellis Island, New York, were inspected and continued on to the city of New York and later to places across the entire country. German immigrants, for example, settled mostly in the Midwest, as can still be observed when looking at city names on a map.
The first thing many immigrants saw when they came by ship to New York City during the 19th and the first half of the 20th century, was the Statue of Liberty, which is located on Liberty Island.

The Statue of Liberty

- given to the USA as a gift by France in 1886 to celebrate the first 100 years of American independence from Britain (the centennial)
- a robed woman, holding a lighted torch in her right and a tablet in her left hand, showing the date of the Declaration of Independence (4 July 1776)
- underneath her right foot the remains of broken shackles can be seen
- one of the most famous American icons, symbolising enlightenment, independence, liberty and freedom
- the theme of Emma Lazarus's famous poem "The New Colossus" (1883), which can be seen on a bronze plaque inside the statue

Ellis Island

- the place where most immigrants first set foot on American soil
- an island of hopes but also an island of tears for a number of immigrants, as some of them were detained there for legal or medical reasons or even sent back to their home countries; for the majority the gateway to a new – better – life
- a federal immigration station from 1892 to 1954

The American Dream today

- The American Dream itself has come to be seen more critically.
- A considerable number of critics regard the American Dream as an illusion, as not everyone has access to the opportunities usually associated with it.
- Examples of American nightmares include the Vietnam War, 11 September 2001, and the financial crisis starting in 2008.

The Frontier Experience

Since its independence in 1776, the country had continually acquired larger territories to the west. To put it simply, both the Pacific and the Atlantic coast had been settled and explored, yet the middle of the vast continent was still mostly open territory which remained unknown. The fringe between the settled and unknown territories, more commonly called the "Wild West", not only refers to the geographical border between wilderness and civilisation but also to the social and political aspects which characterised these areas.

The **westward movement** of the early settlers was not a federally organised enterprise. Instead, the federal government simply assigned the right to obtain land in the west to people who were willing to take on the challenge of discovering these unknown lands. While the **pioneers** moved westward in covered wagons, law enforcement and legal order were slow to follow. This left the frontier zone, which was already inhabited by the Native American tribes, in a state both of lawlessness and seemingly unlimited opportunity. This sense of entitlement, combined with the idea of Manifest Destiny (see below), led to the brutal treatment of the Native Americans. The Indigenous nations were initially taken full economic advantage of, often via Christian missionaries and by fostering alcoholism. From the early 19th century onward, Native tribes were forced to relocate from their ancestral homelands reservations (most notably, "Trail of Tears").

The Turner Thesis (1893)
Frederick Jackson Turner defined the "frontier experience" as the key which determined the American belief in freedom and unlimited opportunities. The abundance of land in the west and the experience of unlimited space provided the psychological basis for the American conviction that anything can be achieved. Once the west had been explored, the US sought to overcome new frontiers. Thus, the frontier experience was later also considered an explanation for American endeavours to overcome frontiers in a much broader sense (be it in areas of technological advancement or by landing on the moon).

Manifest Destiny

The term "Manifest Destiny" was coined by the American journalist John L. O'Sullivan in 1839.

- stands for the belief that America is the one nation ordained by God to expand across the North American continent
- according to John L. O'Sullivan: "[America is] the nation of progress, of individual freedom, of universal enfranchisement"; according to him, the American people had been chosen "to establish on earth the moral dignity and salvation of man – the immutable truth and beneficence of God."[2]
- America = a country that is superior to all other countries
- stresses the virtue of the American people, as they are the ones to establish moral rules and values across the globe; American patriotism is deeply rooted in the concept of "Manifest Destiny"

  A picture that illustrates the idea of the "Manifest Destiny" is the allegorical representation of the new west in the painting *The American Progress* by John Gast (1872).

[2] Source: John L. O'Sullivan, "The Great Nation of Futurity," *The United States Democratic Review*, Volume 6, Issue 23, pp. 426–430.

Gran Torino (Film, gA, eA)

Directed by Clint Eastwood, the film *Gran Torino* was released in 2008, at the beginning of a major financial crisis which brought dramatic changes in economies worldwide. Banks collapsed and people lost their homes, jobs and hope. The film is set in a run-down part of Detroit, once the proud and wealthy centre of the US motor industry, now dominated by poverty and shattered dreams.

The protagonist of the film, Walt Kowalski, a disillusioned, racist veteran of the Korean War, is played by Eastwood himself. After the death of his wife, Walt has become an outsider in his part of town. The sole object of his pride is his Gran Torino, a big muscle car, built at the beginning of the 1970s, when Walt still worked at the Ford Motor Company in Detroit. Walt is a Catholic but does not go to church any more. His neighbours, a family of Asian immigrants, belong to the ethnic group of the Hmong. Walt despises these people, but when the son of the family, Thao, tries to steal Walt's car because he is under pressure from a gang, Walt resolves to help the boy. He also helps Thao's sister Sue against three young men. The family is so grateful and friendly that Walt reluctantly begins to change his behaviour towards them. He becomes a friend and father figure to Thao. When the family is attacked by the gang and Thao and Sue are injured, the victims do not go to the police (there are no witnesses). Thao wants revenge, but Walt wants to prevent Thao from becoming a killer. Walt himself faces the gang unarmed, provokes them and gets shot, sacrificing himself in order to protect the family. He leaves his Gran Torino to Thao.

Eastwood weaves several complex topics into a moving story: migration, racism, gang culture and violence, war trauma, a dying city and culture, the loss of religious beliefs and the collapse of the American Dream on the one hand, and an individual's alternative to growing racism, hatred and isolation on the other.

Main characters and their profiles

In the following the three main characters are described with ten adjectives each to give you a short yet descriptive overview of their personality.

Walt	lonely, conservative, masculine, racist, self-reliant, practical, conscience-stricken, determined, considerate, caring
Thao	insecure, soft, torn, lost, weak, a push-over, persistent, willing, self-confident, positive
Sue	strong, assimilated, friendly, self-confident, open, considerate, courageous, intelligent, emancipated

Background information

Motor City ("Motown") Detroit – from boom to bust

Several factors led to Detroit's fate and its fall from being "Motor City" to a broken shell of its former glory (cf. https://archive.nytimes.com/www.nytimes.com/interactive/2013/08/17/us/detroit-decline.html, accessed on 1 April 2022).

reliance on single industry	– by 1950, the population figures had reached almost 1.85 million – the "Big Three" auto companies Ford, General Motors and Chrysler attracted many workers – decentralisation halted the boom: strikes led by the unions, refusal by black and white Americans to work side by side – automation (replacing assembly-line jobs with machinery) cost tens of thousands of jobs – foreign competition threatened profit – lack of industrial diversity made Detroit suffer more than other cities
racial tension	– 1950: population was 16 % black – 1967: population was approx. 33 % black – today: population is about 82 % black – fear and hatred have remained since the 1967 riots and have hindered growth
failed leadership	– city leaders supposedly involved in corruption, others ignored deep-rooted structural problems (e. g. Coleman A. Young, Kwame M. Kilpatrick)
no efficient transit system	– the focus was on the car industries, investments went into roads and highway construction rather than public transportation
consequences of poverty	– 36 % of the population is below the poverty level – fewer taxpaying residents leads to reduced social services – city's unemployment rate is approx. 19 % – plans to cut pensions – growing gang violence

Angry white men

In the first half of the film, the protagonist Walt Kowalski is shown as a typical "angry white man". This stereotype refers to a group of white males without higher education, who were once blue collar workers but face unemployment or minimum wage jobs. Especially in the so called "rust belt" (former industrial region in the north east, covering Ohio, Pennsylvania, Wisconsin and Michigan, which was hit hard by the financial crisis in 2008 und suffered economic collapse), many feel abandoned by the government and overwhelmed by the changes that are taking place throughout society. They believe in a strong national identity, the concept of American masculinity as personified by Clint Eastwood in *The Man with No Name* or *Dirty Harry*. Globalisation, emancipation, mul-

ticultural society and gun control laws are not part of their favoured lifestyle. Instead they direct their anger often towards immigrants, African Americans, and LGBTQ individuals.
Deindustrialisation had a massive negative impact on the lives of the working class (see table on Detroit, above) and their fear of identity loss. Their anger, ignored or underestimated for years, finally led to a wave that helped carry populist Donald Trump into the White House in 2016.

Keywords
Angry white male: a politically reactionary white man, especially from the dispossessed US working classes, who is angry about his (real or imagined) loss of status or position in life: *the simple, knee-jerk reaction of the angry white male*

Blue-collar mentality: of or relating to wage-earning workers who wear work clothes or other specialised clothing on the job, e.g. mechanics, dock workers, miners

American masculinity

For many years the concept of American masculinity seemed to consist of the following traits:
- the strong-and-silent type
- being a protector and provider
- being stoical and brave at all times (not expressing emotions)
- using violence to deal with problematic issues

Many "angry white men" still strongly believe in this concept, but its current crisis becomes more and more apparent. Mark Green, executive editor of "The Good Men Project", believes that the predicament can only be addressed if society realises that American culture has turned its masculinity into a "narrow, conformist, violent, bullying version" of itself.[3]

Gran Torino focuses on two very different concepts of masculinity: the old concept as desribed above and a more reflective, caring version that includes a sense of responsibility for past and present actions.

Keywords
Incel movement: online subculture of predominantly white men failing to find romantic and/or sexual partners („**in**voluntary **cel**ibate"); statements and discussions are often informed by resentment, hatred and self-pity; several murders and mass shootings attributed to incel ideology over the past two decades

[3] Source: https://goodmenproject.com/featured-content/the-american-man-is-in-crisis-snsw/ (accessed on 1 April 2022)

History of the Hmong

The story of the Hmong people is a tragic story that is seldom openly discussed in the US Here you can find information about their origin and why the Hmong came to the States.

- one of the most recent Asian immigrant groups to come to the USA
- they originate from the northern mountain regions of Laos
- during the Vietnam War, Hmong villagers fought for America against the North Vietnamese in what has been called a "secret war" in Laos
- after the war, Laos was taken over by Pathet Lao communists
- Hmong were persecuted due to their support of US involvement
- Hmong and other Laotian exiles escaped to Thailand
- Hmong achieved refugee status because of their war efforts on behalf of the US as well as their need to escape the communist regime in Laos

The trauma of war or PTSD

Keyword

Post-traumatic stress disorder (PTSD): A condition of enduring anxiety after experiencing – or being close to someone who has experienced – shock, acute danger or other frightening or threatening ordeals. PTSD can occur in adults or children and is more common in female than male victims of violence. It may be associated with subsequent narcotics or alcohol dependency.

Many war veterans suffer from PTSD. War veterans from the Korean War (1950–1953), also known as the "The Forgotten War" or "The Unknown War" because World War II or the Vietnam War overshadowed it, frequently suffer not only from PTSD but also from lack of recognition for what they sacrificed and endured while serving their country.

Background information and *Gran Torino*

Background Information	*Gran Torino*
Detroit	– Walt worked for the automobile industry – he experienced the better times of Detroit – he is now stuck in a multicultural, impoverished neighbourhood – his neighbourhood is being bullied by a gang
angry white man	– first half of the movie: Walt's world has collapsed completely, but he refuses to move house – his anger is directed toward his coloured neighbourhood – Walt frequently uses racial slurs and exhibits racial stereotypes
blue-collar mentality	– Walt: used to be hard-working, well-paid member of car industry and proud of his job: still keeps his Gran Torino

American masculinity	– the Grand Torino expresses Walt's masculinity – Walt was a soldier in the Korean War – in the first half Walt represents the typical angry white man, believing in traditional American masculinity – in the second half he represents more progressive traits: being a mentor to Thao – the main traits remain till the end: being protective, brave, solving an issue with violence – Thao represents the opposite: he likes gardening, lets his sister "boss him around" – Thao's journey into American masculinity: gets a job as a constructor (considered typically male), has a girlfriend (dates Youa) and finally inherits Walt's Gran Torino (complete American identity)
the Hmong	– Walt's neighbours are Hmong – culture clash becomes obvious in the first half
PTSD	– Walt fought in the Korean War – he killed 13 people, among them an innocent Korean teenager – most likely suffers from PTSD – his Asian neighbours trigger old memories and guilt

Main themes

family	Walt Thao and Sue Walt → Thao	– estranged from his own family – his sons show a lack of respect towards him – part of extensive Hmong family – Thao has a difficult position in his female-dominated family, no male role model – Walt becomes a father figure for Thao
racism in multi-cultural society/ cultural clash	Walt Sue and Thao	– "white flight" from Highland Park – uses racial slurs – social norm of staying with one's own people (Sue is an exception: she is dating a white boy)
guilt and redemption	Walt	– killed 13 people in the Korean War, among them an innocent teenager – responsible for the spiral of violence and its impact (drive-by shooting, rape) – sacrifices his life in order to atone for past and present guilt

American masculinity	Walt	– stereotype of angry white man – develops another kind of masculinity, although certain traits remain
	Thao	– almost opposite to the concept of American masculinity – is "manned up" by Walt (job, girlfriend, car)
(gun) violence		– Walt has at least two guns – Latino and Hmong gangs use guns

Symbols and motifs

the Gran Torino

- represents conservative American values
- the muscle car stresses Walt's (American) masculinity
- symbolises its owner's status as "outdated model"
- represents the growing bond between Walt and Thao

lighter and silver star medal

- stands for Walt's Korean war experiences
- symbol of his ever-present guilt
- at the end Walt uses the lighter to provoke the gang into shooting him, thus changing the symbol of guilt into one of redemption

cross

- symbol of Walt's salvation

motif: life and death

- are juxtaposed (funeral vs. birth ceremony, Walt's death vs. peaceful life for Thao and Sue)
- the film is framed by two funerals
- Father Janovich often focuses on "life and death"
- Walt's war experience
- final shootout

dilapidation vs. refurbishment

- street in disrepair symbolises the loss of values and traditions
- Thao's job of refurbishing houses symbolises the gaining of self-confidence
- Thao and Walt working together and helping each other with repairs: symbolises their friendship

The US as a World Power

The United States of America became the foremost world power after the end of the Cold War with the Soviet Union. Because of once having been a colony ruled by a foreign nation, it chose to stay out of global politics for over a century. Its involvement in two world wars in the first half of the 20th century led to a change in its foreign policy from isolationism to interventionism.
When, after WW II, the US and its allies found themselves in a worldwide struggle for influence and power with the Soviet Union, the American ideal of freedom and democracy turned into an outright ideology opposing the communist system. In 1947, President Truman formulated the so-called **Truman Doctrine,** which would define US foreign policy: Truman stated that it was "the policy of the United States to support free peoples who are resisting attempted subjugation by armed minorities or by outside pressure". The main aim of the US in the years 1947–1989 was to restrict the expansion of the Soviet Union. This period also shaped post-Cold War US policy and led it to develop new concepts of preemptive intervention to protect its national security (as in the wars in Afghanistan and Iraq). The key to American foreign policy is its self-image as a nation offering the promise of freedom and democracy; a promise whose roots lay in the concept of Manifest Destiny (see p. 26).
US foreign policy has repeatedly been criticised as being hypocritical in the sense that the nations and peoples the US military supposedly sought to set free from oppressors were then in fact subjected to American interests. Indeed, some overt and covert international interventions, especially in Central and South America and the Middle East, can be seen as mainly motivated by commercial interests and matters of national security (by securing natural resources, controlling the influx of drugs into the US, etc.) rather than the altruistic aspiration of bringing peace and democracy.
From a German perspective, however, the role of the US and its allies during the Second World War must be considered as that of a liberator without whom our nation might never have grown to become an internationally accepted democracy.

Glossary of Common Political Terms (AE)

amendment (to the constitution)	Zusatzerklärung zu der Verfassung; die ersten zehn *amendments* sind in der *Bill of Rights* verfasst
constitution	Verfassung
unalienable/inalienable rights	unveräußerliche Rechte
civil rights movement	Bürgerrechtsbewegung
Declaration of Independence	Unabhängigkeitserklärung
equality, emancipation	Gleichheit, Befreiung/Emanzipation
freedom (of speech, of the press, religious freedom)	(Rede-, Presse-, Religions-) Freiheit
from rags to riches	Redewendung: vom Tellerwäscher zum Millionär

the Founding Fathers	die Gründungsväter, die Unterzeichner der Unabhängigkeitserklärung
“In God we trust”	offizieller Wahlspruch der USA: „Wir vertrauen auf Gott.“
the Promised Land the land of milk and honey God’s own country the New Canaan	das gelobte Land das Land, in dem Milch und Honig fließen Gottes eigenes Land das neue Kanaan alles Bezeichnungen für Nordamerika (später die USA)
pioneer	Pionier
pioneer spirit	Pioniergeist
pursuit of happiness	das Streben nach Glück
to attain self-fulfilment	sich selbst verwirklichen
success	Erfolg
failure	Misserfolg, Versagen
to pledge allegiance to the flag	den Fahneneid leisten Ausdruck des amerikanischen Patriotismus, wird u. a. in Schulen an offiziellen Feiertagen gesprochen: “I pledge allegiance to the flag of the United States of America, and to the Republic for which it stands, one nation under God, indivisible, with liberty and justice for all.”
to prosper	Erfolg haben, gedeihen
to settle	(be)siedeln
settler	Siedler
settlement	Siedlung
to be persecuted	verfolgt werden
religious/political persecution	religiöse/politische Verfolgung
to immigrate	einwandern
immigrant	Einwanderer
immigration	Einwanderung
influx of immigrants	Zustrom von Einwanderern
Immigration Act	Einwanderungsgesetz
multiculturalism	Multikulturalität
naturalisation	Einbürgerung
assimilation	Assimilation, Angleichung an Bestehendes

Postcolonial/Neocolonial Experience

This chapter will outline the main aspects of two issues:
- How did Great Britain influence other nations as an empire? What consequences does its role as a former empire have for the UK?
- What consequences does its role as a former colony have for the US? How does its society deal with its minorities?

Keywords

Postcolonialism: term first used in the middle of the 20th century; refers to the time after the British had left the colonies, i. e. after their formal rule over the colonies had come to an end

The withdrawal of the British often caused fresh complications or laid bare problems they sowed during their rule. Many countries thus faced difficulties in setting up a functioning government. In addition, political independence did not necessarily lead to economic independence.

The Commonwealth: a group of 54 states; many former British colonies joined at the end of the decolonisation process; aims at racial equality and national sovereignty; British Queen is head of the Commonwealth

From Empire to Commonwealth

- At the beginning of the 17th century, Britain started to expand its empire worldwide.
- In most cases, the British colonisers ruled with brutal force, seizing land at will, ending rebellion in bloodshed, causing widespread famine as well as implementing slavery and exterminating whole ethnic groups.
- After the Second World War the British Empire changed rapidly.
- Most British colonies had become independent from Britain by 1970, but a large number of them stayed closely connected with their former coloniser by joining the Commonwealth.
- While the British ruled the colonies, they regarded their culture, values, traditions and language as superior to those of the colonised. Cultural identities and boundaries were thus often disrespected.
- Now, after independence, they faced the difficult task of recreating their own identity, bridging the gap between their country's native traditions and values and British ones.
- As people from member countries of the Commonwealth were allowed to emigrate to Britain, many people did so in the second half of the 20th century. First they were welcomed, as workers were needed after the Second World War, but in the 1970s, when more and more workers faced unemployment because of the economic crisis, immigration came to be seen more critically.
- Much postcolonial writing – both from the former colonies and Britain – deals with the issue of being caught between two cultures or of trying to find one's identity.

Minorities in the UK

Nationalisation and Immigration Acts

Imperial Act (1914): People from the colonies were given British citizenship.
British Nationality Act (1948): New status of Citizen of the United Kingdom and Colonies (CUKC) came into effect for those living within the Commonwealth. This preserved their existing status as British subjects whilst allowing them national citizenship of their own country of origin. However, this did not apply to countries that had gained independence by that date.
Immigration Act (1962, 1971): These acts, passed to counter increasing immigration, tightened the law on immigration of British subjects from other parts of the Commonwealth. Immigrants had to prove strong links to the UK (partiality) in order to be allowed to live and work in Britain.
British Nationality Act (1981): Today's nationality law differentiates between several forms of citizenship, in particular for those living in the overseas territories. Only those with British citizenship and some Commonwealth citizens are still automatically entitled to reside in the United Kingdom.

- About 12.4 % of the population in the UK were born abroad (2013). The non-UK born population decreased from 9.4 million in 2017 to 9.2 million in 2020, and the non-British population decreased from 6.2 million to 6.0 million. Poland remains the most common non-UK country of birth, taking over from India in 2015 (which reflected longer-term migration trends); Polish has been the most common non-British nationality in the UK since 2007.[4]
- Between the 1960s and 1980s, many Indians, Pakistanis and Bangladeshis immigrated to Britain. They now form the largest immigrant communities.
- Many of them settled in the Midlands or in towns in Lancashire, Yorkshire and Strathclyde, where they worked, for example, in the textile industry.
- The highest percentage of ethnic minorities can be found in the London area.
- In recent years, the UK has constantly tightened its laws on immigration.
- The main immigrant groups to Britain – from India, Pakistan, the Caribbean, Africa, Southeast Asia and Eastern Europe – differ widely in culture, religion and language.
- **Ethnic diversity** enriches Britain, not only when it comes to music, fashion and food.
- Many embrace the opportunities and advantages of ethnic diversity (such as the former Foreign Secretary Robin Cook, who said that chicken tikka masala " is now a true British national dish"[5]).
- Others fear that "Britishness" will eventually be lost; they interpret multiculturalism as meaning that various cultures coexist peacefully but without having a common basis of shared values.

[4] Source: https://www.ons.gov.uk/peoplepopulationandcommunity/populationandmigration/internationalmigration/bulletins/ukpopulationbycountryofbirthandnationality/2017 (accessed on 1 April 2022)

[5] Source: https://www.theguardian.com/world/2001/apr/19/race.britishidentity (published on 19 April 2001, accessed on 1 April 2022)

- **Second-generation immigrants,** i.e. children born to parents who immigrated to Britain prior to (or shortly after) their children's birth, faced and still face a variety of problems:
  - They often experience a clash of cultures. Outside their parents' home they adopt a western lifestyle similar to that of their friends and classmates. At home, however, they live according to values, beliefs and traditions typical of their parents' home countries, which many of these children and teenagers have never visited. Quite often they do not speak their parents' language any more either. For some, the transition between these two different lifestyles is not easy.
  - They face difficulties when it comes to living up to the expectations of their parents, friends, teachers, etc.
  - They often have to face discrimination and overt racism.
  - According to a 2007 poll, about a third of British Asians felt it necessary to "act and think white" in order to fit into British society. About the same number did not feel British but believed they needed to be a "coconut", meaning to be "brown on the outside but white on the inside"[6].
  - Therefore, defining one's identity and becoming confident in both cultures has been a central issue for most second-generation immigrants.

Today, the third or fourth generation slowly but surely become more integrated into British society and have arrived in British politics and public positions like the mayor of London Sadiq Khan.
The large number of immigrants from the EU, mostly coming from Eastern Europe after the opening of the borders in 2004 and subsequent years, have had less problems to adapt to British society. However, their existence in Britain remains the subject of public scrutiny and was one reason for the Brexit vote in the 2016 referendum. In 2022, it is still unclear what their status in Britain will be in the future.

In literature, this clash of cultures is portrayed most prominently by British writers such as Hanif Kureishi, Farrukh Dhondy, Zadie Smith and Salman Rushdie.

> **Keyword**
> **Postcolonial / New English Literature:** the literature which deals with the consequences of the British Empire is called postcolonial literature or New English literature. Its authors reflect their nations' history as parts of the former British Empire and the role of the individual in these contexts.
> The main issues which are addressed in postcolonial literature are: social and cultural changes/conflicts, exploitation and the misuse of power, cultural alienation and integration of the individual torn between the values of the former colonisers and his or her traditional values and beliefs.

[6] Source: BBC poll, http://news.bbc.co.uk/2/hi/uk_news/6921534.stm (published 30 July 2007, accessed on 1 April 2022)

Examples of Postcolonial Societies: India, Australia, South Africa

At its height, the British Empire encompassed about a quarter of the world's land mass and dominated its crown colonies politically, economically and culturally. One must distinguish two types of colonies:

- those which were mainly colonised by the British with a relatively small indigenous population (such as Australia), sometimes also called the "white" colonies
- those colonies with a large indigenous population (such as India).

The decline of the British Empire resulted from internal demands for more independence from the Crown (the earliest colonies to leave were those in North America, see chapter I). In most cases this progression from colonial rule to independence was achieved peacefully. But in those countries with a large indigenous population, the way to independence was often paved with rebellion and violent conflict. In the following, the route to independence of three former colonies of the British Empire will be described briefly.

India

India became independent in 1947 and was the first non-white colony to gain complete independence from Britain.

- British influence in India started as early as the 16th century with the founding of the British East India Company. Because of its spices, cotton and tea, India was mainly a trading colony.
- 1858: The British Crown took over the areas ruled by the British East India Company, and in 1876 Queen Victoria became Empress of India. The time of British rule is also called the "Raj" (Hindu for "reign").
- 15 August 1947: The Indian Empire became independent but was divided into the Union of India and the Dominion of Pakistan.

The case of India is unique in the way it gained complete independence from the British Empire at a rather early date and by non-violent means. In India, the British rulers were by far in the minority, and dissatisfaction with British rule led to a national independence movement headed by Mahatma Gandhi. At first, he demanded equal civil rights for Indians in their own country and accused the British of mistreatment and oppression of the Indian people. Gandhi's struggle sparked a nationwide independence movement. His key to achieving independence was the revolutionary concept of civil disobedience. Being in the majority, the Indians were able to halt all social and economic life by simply refusing to comply with the British. Gandhi's aim was to achieve independence by non-violent means. After many years of struggle and several years spent in prison, Gandhi achieved his goal. Being unable to rule the country any longer, the British complied with India's demand for independence and thus lost one of their most important colonies.

Gandhi's concept of non-violent resistance became a role-model for other leaders of oppressed peoples and minorities. Leaders like Nelson Mandela (in South Africa) and Martin Luther King (in the US) considered him to be their inspiration to fight peacefully for racial equality and civil rights.

Australia

- dominion status in 1901, formally independent in 1931
- Australia's eastern half was claimed by the British in 1770 and most of the original settlers were prisoners shipped from England to the colony of New South Wales, which was founded in 1788.
- Australia's history as a penal colony for Britain resulted from the fact that the country was relatively poor in resources and from the overflow of criminals in British prisons.
- The Australians did not seek independence from Britain by violent means and indeed kept close political and constitutional ties to the United Kingdom until the last century. Australia gained the rights to self-government in 1901 and is a fully independent nation today although the British Queen is formally still head of state; she is represented by the govenor-general of Australia.
- Most of the Australian population is white and of European descent (mostly British and Irish), but after World War II, Australia opened its borders to immigrants and experienced a large influx of nationals from Europe and Asia. Today, nearly two out of seven Australians were born overseas.

Keyword

The Aboriginals / The Stolen Generation(s): Australia's Aboriginals (or: Aborigines) settled the continent 40,000 years ago. Their number was comparatively small, and the white settlers regarded the indigenous people as inferior and barbaric. Their semi-nomadic way of life and the absence of large settlements made it easy for the settlers to take away their land in order to build their own settlements and farms and raise cattle. The Aboriginals found it increasingly difficult to maintain their traditional way of life. For centuries to come they were oppressed and discriminated against by the white population. This oppression reached its climax in the racist ideology which led to the implementation of a child removal programme executed between about 1880 and 1960. This state-supported programme allowed the abduction of Aboriginal children from their families, supposedly to protect them from bad living conditions. These children were put under church or social care and raised according to white values and traditions, thus eradicating the indigenous traditions. It is estimated that more than 100,000 children were put under such guardianship. Not until 2008 did the Australian government, headed by Prime Minister Kevin Rudd, apologise for these actions, and several redress schemes were initiated by the Australian government to compensate those taken from their families.

South Africa

The Republic of South Africa is a parliamentary representative democratic republic and a multi-racial southern African country with a population of more than 50 million. After transition from white minority rule under apartheid, a system of state-enforced racial segregation and socio-economic discrimination, the nation held its first free elections in 1994.
South Africa has the largest, most diversified and most highly industrialised economy in Africa, which has achieved moderate economic growth in recent years.
Due to its political and commercial ties across Africa and its active role within the African Union, South Africa has a considerable influence on the continent, especially in southern Africa. As a strategic partner of the USA, it plays a leading role in trade and investment, in democracy and youth leadership development as well with regard to peace and international security.

The following **issues** are **of high importance:**
- bilateral political, trade and investment ties
- development cooperation
- conflict mitigation and development across Africa
- anti-apartheid struggle
- HIV/AIDS, COVID-19 and other health challenges
- education and skills shortage
- corruption
- poor rural infrastructure
- pollution

Social issues – poverty, inequality and unemployment

Although the post-apartheid era has seen some national socio-economic gains, South Africa remains a highly unequal society with respect to wealth and income distribution as well as access to jobs, social services and land ownership. Most people of colour are poor, have limited access to education and suffer high unemployment, with average incomes far smaller than those of the historically privileged white minority.
In townships – the vast, high-density housing settlements where many of the poor live –, social and political tension is fuelled by shortages of quality housing, utilities and social services. Other key problems include public corruption, widespread violent crime and dissatisfaction among the country's black youth, who face particularly high unemployment rates.
In order to change the dissatisfying status quo, the government is investing billions of dollars to upgrade infrastructure and improve public services, while facing continuing challenges in meeting popular expectations.

Politics and history

More than three times bigger than Germany, South Africa has a population of approximately 58.5 (2019) million. The country has important metal and mineral deposits as well as gas, diamond and rare earth mines. Further key exports include machinery and equipment. Altogether there are 11 official languages, of which English, Afrikaans, Zulu and Xosa are the most widely spoken. Nearly 80 % of the population is Christian (with Protestants as the largest group). The literacy rate is 95 % (2021, age over 15). Life expectancy at birth is roughly 60 years for males and 63 years for females – relatively low for a developed country. The high HIV adult infection rate of more than 19 % (2018) is one of the reasons.

The COVID-19 pandemic 2020 and 2021 has struck South Africa heavily with a rising unemployment rate and a collapse of the important area of tourism. Infection rates were strong but then went down in spring 2021.

The Cape region was formerly a Bantu tribal area. In 1488, the Portuguese seafarer Bartolomeo Diaz became the first European to set foot on South African soil, and in the second half of the 17th century, German and Dutch (Boer) settlement started, combined with a first wave of expulsion or enslavement of indigenous peoples. However, in the late 18th century the Zulu tribe developed territorial power. After occupation by the British in 1806, the Cape region became a British crown colony in 1814, causing aggravation among the Boer population, especially because of the racial equality aspired to by the British. This initiated the "Great Trek", in which Dutch settlers moved up-country in order to find independence and uninhabited grazing land. Instead they came into collision with the Zulu, resulting in a number of battles.

By 1856, the Boers had sufficiently established their control of the Transvaal territories to found the first Transvaal Republic. Annexation of these territories by the British in 1877 triggered the first Anglo-Boer War – or "War of Independence" as it was called by the Boers, who eventually prevailed. In 1880–81, the second Transvaal Republic under President Paul Kruger was proclaimed and remained independent until the end of the Second Boer War in 1902. South Africa received dominion status in 1910. In the following decades the first racial discrimination laws were passed, and in 1931 South Africa was given complete independence within the British Commonwealth. After World War II the apartheid system was installed. In 1961, it became a republic.

In the later 20th century, increasing international pressure and national opposition initiated a process of dismantling apartheid on the basis of negotiations. The African National Congress (legitimised by President F. W. de Klerk), Archbishop Desmond Tutu and the future president Nelson Mandela, known to the people as "Madiba", were essential players in the struggle for freedom and equality. In 1997, the new constitution of South Africa came into force, Thabo Mbeki succeeded Mandela, and in 2003, the Truth and Reconciliation Committee handed over its final report to president Mbeki. He was followed by Jacob Zuma, who stepped down in 2018 after many years office and numerous accusations of corruption. The current president is Cyril Ramaphosa.

Present challenges

Today's national governance challenges include health issues, corruption, crime and increasing labour unrest. The government has admitted that corruption is a problem, and Zuma has taken strong public stances against it. There have been reports, however, that prosecutions of suspected corrupt officials have been selective and that cases reported in the press are not always officially investigated.

South African rates of violent crime are high, and criminals often aggravate crimes like robbery by violent assault, rape or murder. Explanations for such brutality vary. Women's rights activists and others have long denounced the lack of stronger public and state responses to sexual violence. According to many media reports, police misconduct incidents, ranging from serious human rights abuses – including torture and targeted killings – to high-level corruption and lesser misconduct such as roadside bribery, are increasing, which does not help reinstate trust in law enforcement.

Economy

South Africa's economy is the largest on the continent. Although only about 10 % of the country is arable, and agriculture contributes less than 3 % of GDP (gross domestic product), wine, wool, maize, sugar and fruit is mainly what South Africa is famous for. The industrial sector is more significant (approx. 30 % of GDP). The largest share of GDP, namely 67.5 %, is contributed by services. There are well-developed tourism, banking, energy, transport and communications sectors.

The biggest economic domestic challenges include a poorly educated workforce and problems caused by the corona pandemic.[7]

Sindiwe Magona, *Mother to Mother* (gA)

first published 1998, South Africa

Characters

Mandisa – the narrator
Mxolisi – Mandisa's son (1st child)
Lunga – Mandisa's son (2nd child)
Siziwe – Mandisa's daughter (3rd child)
Dwadwa – Siziwe's father, Mandisa's 3rd husband
Lungile – Lunga's father, Mandisa's 2nd partner
China – Mxolisi's father, Mandisa's 1st husband
Mama – Mandisa's mother
Makhulu – maternal grandmother
Amy Biehl – an American student murdered in Guguletu

[7] Source: CIA World Factbook 2021, https://www.cia.gov/the-world-factbook/countries/south-africa/ (accessed on 1 April 2022)

Background

Amy Biehl, a young Fulbright scholar who came to South Africa to assist in the preparations for the first democratic elections, was killed on 25 August 1993 by a mob of rioting students as she drove through the all-black township of Guguletu.

Synopsis and discussion

The story is told through the voice of Mandisa. After it is revealed that her son Mxolisi is guilty of stabbing Amy Biehl, Mandisa writes to Amy's mother, hoping to strike a common chord of grief. For in her lament – mostly about her family's circumstances –, Mandisa also sees herself as a victim, without excusing her son's actions. By describing the background to her own and her family's life, she hopes to explain her son's action: how it was triggered by the relentless apartheid policy of the government. In her eyes there are always two sets of victims when a homicide occurs. The killer, in a different sense, is a victim, too.
The book takes the form of a long letter to Amy's mother, interspersed with an account of the events of the day of Amy's death (as recollected by Mandisa) and with memories from Mandisa's life. It works on at least three levels: the direct address directed to Amy's mother, the description of the day of the murder and the history of a typical young woman and her family in South Africa during apartheid and post-apartheid.

Mandisa refers to her happy early childhood and tells us that she became a mother at the age of 15, which destroyed her dreams of a well-educated future. She then became a housemaid. One day things became even worse. The Group Areas Act passed by the South African government organised neighbourhoods according to race. Moving blacks to poor and arid ghettos with inadequate housing, a bad school system and insufficient social infrastructure was dehumanising and fuelled the hatred in the communities towards the white elite.
Her son's introduction to racial violence was when he watched the killing of two older boys he knew. This shaped his view of the world and his view of good and bad. His mental picture was consolidated by the observation that school rebellions and looting were considered a rightful weapon in the fight for freedom and met with admiration within the black community. Consistent with this, Mxolisi later, at the age of 20, became a leader of the student revolutionary movement.
Black children and adolescents often grew up without much contact with their parents, who worked as day labourers in the white neighbourhoods. This increased school dropout rates and youth-related problems in the black communities. Law enforcement did not respond to black on black crime. And this was also true after the end of apartheid, when Amy Biehl was murdered. For it was only then that the police made any real effort to hunt down the killers. This made it clear that the system placed greater value on the life of a white woman than on black citizens. While some community members called Mandisa the mother of a murderer, others labelled her a freedom fighter – a divergent interpretation which shows both the difficulty of moral judgement and the complexity of the racial situation in South Africa.

Style

Magona's prose is full of figurative language. She uses metaphors and metonyms (cf. stylistic devices, p. 114 ff.) to describe crowds and their impact on an individual's free will and in this way opens another perspective on how Mxolisi was influenced to kill Amy Biehl. It becomes an example of the use of violence in freedom movements. The author's metaphorical usage of "whirlwind" to depict the effect of forced removals can be found throughout the novel.
The author does not baulk at unpleasant topics. The rawness with which she describes Mandisa's feelings towards Mxolisi's conception – Mandisa inwardly loathes her child because he symbolises the end of her dreams – touches the core of motherhood. In the same way she carefully creates Mxolisi's irreducible reality, which opens an unexpected, and at first sight unintelligible, perspective on a delinquent.
As far as form is concerned, Magona borrows from the idea of the epistolary novel[8] in order to underline the authenticity of the narrator's voice.

Main topics for discussion

- day-to-day hardships under apartheid
- dissolution of neighbourhoods and communities caused by the apartheid regime
- artificial racial hierarchy of apartheid
- racial and economic privileges
- ethnic and cultural diversity
- accountability and justice
- values of "justice" vs. "reconciliation"
- immaculate conception as a symbolic Christian reference

Reference to present-day South Africa

When Nelson Mandela led the country through a cleansing phase of "truth and reconciliation" to abolish apartheid, South Africa began a peaceful transition period. What was overlooked was the young generation of black people who were, despite being given fresh hope, unable to participate in the country's new economic prosperity. Because of a lack of education, these men and women had to struggle as unskilled workers. Becoming aware of their situation, they responded violently to societal challenges. This is one key aspect of the novel.

Social study topics

- township life
- the multilingual reality of South Africa
- anti-apartheid-related school boycotts
- the role of the police during apartheid
- the role of violence in both maintaining and fighting against apartheid
- acts of reconciliation and healing
- apartheid in South Africa

[8] An epistolary novel is a novel written as a series of personal documents such as letters, diary entries, etc.

Migration and the World of Work

Human migration means that people move from one place to another. They do this temporarily or permanently. In the history of mankind, migration has been an evolutionary necessity, as in the hunter and gatherer societies, where people were nomadic and were always looking for better places to find food, to hunt and find shelter. Freedom of mind as well as better work opportunities have always been driving factors of migration, as in 19th century immigration to the US.

Today, in a more or less fixed system of states with state borders, migration is still a huge factor in the development of a society, but in increasingly wide sections of society – especially in right-wing and nationalist political groupings –, it is also seen very critically (cf. the reference to Enoch Powell's "rivers of blood" speech in *East is East*).

In addition to the post-WW II migration to the UK from its former colonies, the past two decades, after Poland and nine other countries joined the EU in 2004, have seen a huge influx of people from Eastern Europe. People from the new EU member states have been more willing to do unskilled and low-paid jobs than their British counterparts. This has caused a political debate in Britain and can be seen as one of the many reasons for some people to favour Brexit. As this is a world of large economic differences, i.e. the so-called North-South divide, migration will remain one of the problems of our times, with societies that are better off facing huge numbers of refugees from poorer countries until a certain measure of equality is reached.

In the US, migration has been the driving factor of the nation's creation. However, attitudes towards migration differ with regard to countries of origin. The southern border of the US has been the subject of fierce political debate for a long time, as a lot of immigrants from Mexico and other Latin American countries cross this border, many of them illegally. The discussion about the so-called "dreamers" (sons and daughters of illegal immigrants to the US – the term probably originates in the abbreviation of the name of a piece of 2001 legislation) was particularly fuelled by former President Donald Trump.

Andrea Levy, "Loose Change" (gA, eA)

A note on the author

Andrea Levy (1956–2019) is of Jamaican descent. As a novelist she explored themes around British Jamaicans and questions of racial, cultural and national identity. Levy's roots included her Jewish (Jamaican) and Scottish grandfathers. Her Jamaican father came to London in 1948, where he was joined by her mother a year later. Levy grew up in a family of four children in a council estate in north London and had a typical working-class background. After finishing school she studied textile design and weaving. Her fiction has been honoured with literary prizes. Her best-known novels are *Small Island* (2004) and *The Long Song* (2010).

Synopsis

Andrea Levy published her short story "Loose Change" in 2005. The story illustrates the fate of an Uzbek refugee, Laylor, who has recently arrived in London. Its message is that being generous does not depend on your own wealth but that many people shy away from helping others because they do not want to become involved.

While it is pouring with rain outside, the unnamed first-person narrator hurriedly steps into the National Portrait Gallery in Central London looking for loose change she could use for the tampon machine in the ladies' toilet. Even though she does not usually talk to strangers, she speaks loudly into the room and gets the attention of another woman who offers her some change.

Back in the gallery, the narrator looks for this other person, Laylor, who starts to talk to her about some of the works of art. They differ about the meaning of the paintings they look at. The narrator then offers to buy the other woman a coffee in the gallery café.

Sitting opposite her, the narrator gradually notices Laylor's different attitude, language and background and realises that she is in a decidedly precarious situation. It turns out that she sleeps in a square with her brother. Even though Laylor never asks for anything either for herself or for her brother (who appears briefly), the narrator feels obliged to offer help and kindness to Laylor, even in a small act. By that point, her unwillingness to talk to strangers has been overcome by growing interest. Laylor's miserable situation dawns on the narrator, who struggles inwardly over the advantages and disadvantages of helping a refugee, connecting Laylor's story to her own family history when they first came to the UK (her grandmother is of Caribbean descent). The narrator is torn between empathy and prejudice against homeless people and refugees.

The narrator, a single mother, has a spare bedroom in the small house or flat she shares with her son; so she could, in fact, do something for the Uzbek woman. In her mind she rehearses the comfort and friendship she could – and actually resolves to – offer. Yet in the end she sees Laylor as a potential intruder into her otherwise quiet life and walks out of the café, leaving the situation and Laylor behind.

Analysis

The story unfolds in the limited perspective of the first-person narrator, a middle-aged woman, who shares her views of the situation and her growing apprehension of Laylor's true character with the reader. The setting and characters are described solely through the narrator's eyes. The woman in need seems the stronger of the two characters because she offers kindness (loose change) and her story, whereas the narrator passes judgment on her before finally leaving the café. The reader gets no idea of Laylor's thoughts. The story expresses the narrator's reflections on social behaviour and on what would happen if she helped the Uzbek woman. Despite knowing that help is necessary for people who have just arrived and are homeless in another country, and despite her own family history – her grandmother had been shown just that kindness –, she runs away from the responsibility.

Topics

- migration in Europe – displacement
- giving a chance to refugees and homeless people
- class and social conditions
- the making of identity

Shereen Pandit, "She Shall Not Be Moved" (gA, eA)

A note on the author
The British author Shareen Pandit is a political activist and lawyer of Muslim South African descent. Born in Cape Town, Pandit has always been active in fighting for the rights of the black community. Some of her stories and poems actively condemn discrimination against the black population. This brought her into conflict with the South African government of the time, and in 1987 she fled to London with her husband. She lives in London with her daughter.

Published in 2005, the short story "She shall not be moved" presents an everyday example of racism on a London bus. The scene is told in a very biased way by a narrator whose identity is difficult to grasp. However, the reader can deduce that she must be a woman and the girl at her side must be her daughter because at one point she talks about Mariam's dad, with whom she evidently lives. She mentions events like having been forced to leave her country, so she is probably not British by origin.

Synopsis

The unnamed first-person narrator reflects on a scene she and her small daughter Mariam have been involved in when travelling by bus to Mariam's dance class.
As the narrator squeezes onto the bus with her daughter, the bus driver is calling to a woman with a pram to move on. However, this mother cannot use the pram space, as two middle-aged white working-class women sitting there obviously do not intend to move. The narrator identifies the woman with the pram as probably being Somali and carries on talking about her in that way, also describing her as a "haughty queen". The "Somali woman" seems proudly unmoved by the situation; she does not react to any of the bystanders even when the black bus driver comes up to her and yells at her rather than asking the two white women to make room.
The narrator feels guilty about not standing up against the two white women or against the bus driver and then tries to sympathise and talk with the "Somali woman". The situation ends when the Somali woman gets off the bus saying in a voice of granite that the bus driver is a slave but she herself is not.
The narrator reflects that the situation must have been erupting before she even got on the bus. She feels the Somali woman's words cut into her. The day finishes with her taking her daughter to a bagel shop after dance class as if to make up for not getting involved and to make the daughter forget the episode. But Mariam still looks at her in a reproachful, disappointed way. Her attempt at education and her words about getting

involved have failed miserably in this situation. She did not follow her own code of moral conduct.

Analysis

The first-person narrator of "She shall not be moved" retells the situation on the bus, limiting the reader to her own perspective. This, however, includes an awareness of her problem with herself and specifically with her desire to educate her daughter in moral courage, as she fails to stand up against the wrongs she sees quite clearly. This awareness overlaps with her description of the journey.

As a narrator she is unreliable and biased. She comments on every action and has her own way of describing and assigning meaning: the white women are like characters from the TV series *Eastenders,* the woman with a pram seems Somali to her from her style of clothes and her height. Only on a close reading does the reader realise that the narrator is probably afraid of getting involved and that she is in "this miserable country" because she got into trouble "back home". She constantly mentions what she should do but never does, despite her daughter's expectant looks.

The narrator seems politically active and says she would normally stand up against wrongdoing and that principles like human rights have to be defended. In the story, her comments on her bad conscience about not speaking up for the Somali woman constantly break into the description of the situation on the bus. She tries to make her daughter forget the episode but realises that she herself cannot. She had to leave her country of origin, but now, in a new country, her courage seems to have left her. Like so many immigrants, she just wants to lead a quiet life.

Topics

- everyday racism
- the making of identity
- class and social conditions
- postcolonial experience
- political activism
- displacement: questions of belonging and identity

Individual and Society

The following chapter will focus on the various facets of identity – both ethnic/cultural and personal identity. How does identity affect a person's position in society?
Central issues to be tackled are:
- the different roles an individual might assume and the potential conflicts between those roles;
- the connection between one's biologically determined sex and the largely socially defined gender of a person;
- minorities and outsiders.

Keywords

Individual: The term derives from the Latin "indivisible" and commonly refers to an individual subject, i. e. a person, who can be distinguished from his or her surroundings. As such, the individual has to position himself or herself vis-à-vis the society in which they are living. The relationship between the individual and his or her society can be difficult if the former comes into conflict with the latter's norms and values.

Society: This term refers to a collective of individuals united e. g. by a shared territory, history or ways of living and thinking. In order to be effective and not to fall prey to anarchy, societies are organised according to a set of rules and regulations which can even overrule the interests of the individual for the sake of the community.

Roles and Role Conflicts

- While the individual was traditionally believed to be a unified "whole", the concept of the different roles of a person underlines the fact that one does not just have **one** single identity but actually has to fulfil a number of different roles in different situations and contexts.
- A social role consists of a certain pattern of behaviour, of rights but also of obligations. Social roles are performed in **interaction** with other persons. Roles are mostly to be seen in relation to others (child – parent; teacher – student).
- Whether one's behaviour is in line with one's particular role can be judged by society's **expectations** of that role.
- If an individual shows forms of behaviour that are considered **inappropriate** for the social role in question, he or she may have to face various forms of **punishment** (ranging from being made aware of one's improper behaviour to actual punishment); if the behaviour in question is deemed **appropriate**, there will, in return, be **rewards** from society.
- A role (e. g. doctor, teacher, bus driver) can be **achieved** by or **ascribed** to an individual (e. g. child).

- In certain situations, a person can be faced with a **conflict** between contrasting roles which he or she should take on at the same time. Thus, if a mother happens to be her own child's teacher, she would be expected to be simultaneously strict towards the child in her role as teacher and loving in her role as mother.

Gender Identity and Diversity

A central component of an individual's identities is their[1] **gender**. Unlike the biologically determined **sex** (male/female), **gender** and **gender role** (such as masculine and feminine) are often perceived as being social constructs. Accordingly, a society holds a set of certain stereotypical ideas about how a "real" woman and a "real" man should behave, what they should look like but also what they are capable of.
Traditionally, men are thought of as masculine, strong, rational and powerful, while women are considered to be feminine, weak, emotional and submissive. These assumed characteristics have also been used as a "justification" for men's dominant role in society. With the advent of the Feminist Movement in the 1960s, the validity of conventional gender roles was called into question.
However, the media especially still present largely conservative images of "typical" men and women, thereby keeping these concepts alive. If a person does not conform to the gender role associated by his or her society with his or her sex, he or she may have to face resentment. Even in the comparatively tolerant Western societies, particularly "masculine" women and "feminine" men are not universally accepted.
The aim of gender diversity is to represent people of different genders in a fair way. This concerns mostly men and women and their ratio in companies, politics or other fields of life. Traditionally, men have dominated many areas of public life such as politics, engineering, science, medicine or computing. Gender diversity has been widely discussed but progress towards having less male and more female company directors – and indeed bosses in many walks of life – has been slow.
However, after the feminist and post-feminist debates of the past decades, discussions about gender have recently become more open, including transgender and non-binary people. This has meant that more people have had the courage to come out with their particular sexuality or their gender identity.

Outsiders

- If an individual deliberately or unintentionally fails to conform to the rules of the society in which they live, they can easily become socially stigmatised **outsiders**.
- When a larger group of people rejects the conventional norms of mainstream culture, this might lead to the formation of a **counterculture** which openly propagates a set of values significantly different from those of the society in which they live.

[1] In English-language texts, the pronouns „he"/"she" and their possessives „his"/"her"/"hers" are often substituted with „they" and „their"/"theirs" in order to avoid attributing a gender.

- Such countercultures are often associated with younger generations that rebel against their parents' way of life.
- Famous countercultural movements include the "Beat Generation" of the 1950s, the "hippies" of the 1960s, the "punks" of the 1970s and 1980s and the "hip-hop" scene, which developed from the 1970s onwards, all of which included such forms of artistic expression as music, graffiti and dance.
- There are numerous ways of expressing one's dissatisfaction with mainstream culture, e.g. through the use of taboo language (as employed by writers of the Beat Generation), through the open violation of generally accepted moral standards (as in the form of "free love", practised by the hippies), through one's appearance (clothing and hairstyle of the punks), or by aligning oneself with strata of society that are far removed from the mainstream (e.g. hip-hop culture).
- Often aspects of countercultures are eventually commercialised and assimilated by mainstream culture, thereby losing their originally rebellious impetus.

Minorities in the US

Since its birth in 1776, the United States of America has been a nation of immigrants. Especially during the 19th and early 20th century, millions of people (at first mostly from Europe, later also from other continents) were allowed to enter the country, since the young nation was in need of settlers and workers. The US has therefore always been an ethnically and culturally mixed nation, which has led to discussions about how this society might deal with its diversity and how it can be defined.

Keywords

Multicultural society: a society where various ethnic groups and their cultural heritage are accepted in their own right

Salad bowl: the various ethnicities living in the United States mixing their traditions, cultural values, etc.; the various cultures do not merge into one but stay distinct ("unity in diversity")

Melting pot: The various ethnic groups do not retain their cultural heritage but amalgamate into one new nation. The term first appeared in an essay by Jean de Crèvecœur, entitled "Letters from an American farmer" in 1782.

The term "salad bowl" is now considered to be more politically correct.

One main group which did not enter the United States voluntarily but was deported to the US is the group of thousands of slaves from Africa who were shipped to the British colony and later to the newly founded nation. The descendants of these slaves form the second largest minority in the US (in recent years the number of Hispanic immigrants has exceeded the black population). Their history is one of discrimination and deprivation, which will be summarised briefly below.

African-American History

- 1619: first documented ship of African slaves bound for Jamestown, Virginia
- 17th–19th century: the **Atlantic slave trade**; by 1860 an estimated 3.5 million enslaved Africans lived in the US; another 500,000 lived freely in the (northern) states or territories
- 1861–65: American Civil War; caused by the separationist movement of eleven slave states which refused to end slavery; the North fought to prevent secession of these states and eventually won
- **Emancipation Proclamation** 1863: during the Civil War, President Abraham Lincoln declared that all slaves in the secession states (South) were free
- **Jim Crow Era**: after the Civil War, slavery was illegal; however, many former slave states passed laws which discriminated against blacks, prevented them from purchasing land and voting and segregated blacks from whites in almost all areas of public life
- racial segregation remained into the 20th century; this system of separation and discrimination was met with increasing resistance and led to the formation of the Civil Rights Movement between 1954 and 1968

The Situation of African-Americans during Reconstruction

The former slaves formally gained freedom after the North won the Civil War, but they were far from having equal rights. Especially in the South, repressive laws and regulations prevented them from purchasing land, participating in elections, etc. (see Jim Crow Era above). This led to a number of developments:

- Many former slaves left for the industrialised cities of the North, in which all-black ghettos developed.
- Freemen who stayed in the South often continued to work as sharecroppers for former slave masters. Unable to buy land, they remained dependent on white landowners and still lived in great poverty.
- Discrimination and racism continued (not only) in the South in an institutionalised form of racial segregation and state legislature. Both in the North and the South, blacks began to put up resistance against all forms of discrimination.

The Civil Rights Movement

- 1909: African-Americans founded the National Association for the Advancement of Colored People (NAACP); the aim was to call attention to discrimination in the South and the cities of the North
- 1954: landmark decision of the Supreme Court in the case of Brown vs. Board of Education, which declared the racial segregation of schools to be unconstitutional
- 1955: Rosa Parks, an NAACP member, refused to give up her seat in a bus for a white person in Montgomery, Alabama and was consequently arrested; led by Martin Luther King, thousands of blacks in Montgomery boycotted public transportation (Montgomery Bus Boycott); in 1956, the Supreme Court declared racial segregation on buses to be unconstitutional

- 1950s and 60s: protests continued on various issues, many of them led by the Southern Christian Leadership Conference (SCLC), formed by Martin L. King; following the example of Mahatma Gandhi, they organised peaceful protests and acts of civil disobedience to stop segregation in other areas of public life
- 1963: March on Washington; an estimated 250,000–300,000 people (about 80 % black) marched to the Capitol in Washington, D.C. to demonstrate peacefully for jobs, freedom and an end to racial discrimination
- During this march, the most famous leader of the movement, the Reverend Martin Luther King gave his famous speech "I have a dream", which moved millions of people and brought widespread attention to the the Civil Rights Movement. King later received the Nobel Peace Prize in 1964 and was assassinated in 1968.
- Forced by the public to take action, the government passed laws to stop racial discrimination and segregation: the Civil Rights Act of 1964 and the Voting Act of 1965.
- Racial discrimination did not end and exists covertly and overtly to this day; African-Americans still have a higher risk of unemployment, poverty and imprisonment in comparison with the white majority population.
- Systemic racism towards black people today has motivated new campaigns against violence like the movement "Black Lives Matter" in June 2013 (cf. below).
- Shortly before and after former President Trump's inauguration, a lot of new movements were started, including huge demonstrations for human rights and other issues such as women's rights, immigration reform, healthcare reform, racial equality and freedom of religion. Thousands of women wore pink woollen hats in their march on Washington to accuse Trump, among other things, of using sexist and racist language.

Black Lives Matter

Black Lives Matter is a socially motivated movement internationally known for its spectacular "die-in" actions and street demonstrations. It is a decentralised network of activists without a formal hierarchy which started its actions and protest marches in order to take a stand against racially motivated police brutality towards black people and a series of deaths in police custody.

BLM appeared on the scene in 2013 and entered public awareness in 2016 when the movement became more active in protest against Donald Trump's racist utterances. In May 2020, it gained global attention in denouncing George Floyd's death in Minneapolis (Minnesota), caused by police violence in arresting him. According to BLM, Floyd died from suffocation. The acting officer was found guilty of murder in court in April 2021; the three other policemen were found to have been violating Floyd's civil rights.

The protest marches related to Floyd's death led to lootings and rampage, resulting in curfews and deployment of the National Guard. The police violence shown there brought Amnesty International into the arena, criticising violations of human rights.

Sometimes, BLM is criticised from within its own ranks as supporting racial bias and deepening the divide between black and white people, as well as sidelining black women's experiences. So, "Say Her Name" has been created to focus attention on female victims of police violence.

Black empowerment – Amanda Gorman
Since the inauguration of US President Joe Biden in January 2021, the young poet and activist Amanda S.C. Gorman (*1998) has become globally known. Her poem, "The Hill We Climb", evokes a moment of unity and a new era for her country. However, her acclaimed work has focused on issues of oppression, feminism, race and marginalisation as well as the African diaspora. She was the first person to be named National Youth Poet Laureate and made the cover of *TIME Magazine's* February 2021 issue.

Critical Race Theory (CRT)
CRT is an academic civil rights movement that began forming in the US in the 1970s. It examines social, cultural and legal issues with regards to race and racism. It argues that racism is institutionalised and favours the interests of white people. Laws, for instance, my seem to be colorblind but still have racially discriminatory effects. Since early 2021, several US states have introduced laws that ban or restrict the teaching of CRT in schools.

Jhumpa Lahiri, "The Third and Final Continent" (eA)

A note on the author and the text
Nilanjana Sudeshna Lahiri (born 1967), called "Jhumpa" in kindergarten, was born in London to Bengali immigrants but moved to the US at the age of three. Her father had got a job at the library of the University of Rhode Island in South Kingstown. However, her parents remained committed to their East Indian culture and determined to rear their children with experience of and pride in their cultural heritage. Lahiri studied literature and published her first anthology of short stories in 1999.
In her stories and novels she focuses on the lives of Indian Americans but claims that she is largely talking about her own experience of seeking her own roots and trying to build a sense of belonging. In 2001, she married a Greek-American and in 2011 she moved with her family to Italy. Since 2015, she has also been publishing in Italian.

Synopsis

Jhumpa Lahiri's short story "The Third and Final Continent" – from her early collection *The Interpreter of Maladies* (1999) – has, like most of her fiction, a strongly autobiographical element. The career of the central character reflects that of her father and the sense of uprootedness expresses the feelings that made her leave the US.
The narrator takes us back to his beginnings in London in 1964, where he had come to study at the London School of Economics and where he shared a dismal apartment house with other poor Bengali immigrants. At the age of 36, he gets a job offer as a librarian at M.I.T. and his marriage is arranged back in Calcutta. After a week in India, he flies out to the US. Despite having a job, his budget is still very tight.
He arrives at Boston on the day the first Americans landed on the moon. His first accommodation is at the YMCA; it is notoriously small and loud, and cooking is forbidden.

Originally, he wants to stay there for six weeks till his wife arrives, but the noise from outside is unbearable, so he follows up an advert in the *Boston Globe* for a room to be 'rented to boys from Harvard or Tech' (MIT).
The owner, Mrs. Croft, an extremely old lady dressed in a long black skirt, is seated at a piano. She starts to talk about the American flag on the moon and wants him to answer "splendid". He is satisfied with the room, and she produces the key, warning him about "no lady visitors". This makes him think of his wife Mala and of their marriage, which he regards as a duty he had to fulfil.
The narrator moves in with Mrs. Croft, who seems not to have moved from her piano bench and who orders him every night when he comes home to sit down beside her and engage in the same conversation about the American flag on the moon and to answer "Splendid!". This becomes a daily routine. He meets Mrs. Croft's daughter, Helen, who tells him he is the first boarder her mother has called a gentleman; he learns that Mrs. Croft is 103 years old and that the piano had been her source of income after she was widowed. He draws parallels to his own mother and starts to worry about his landlady and to imagine her past life.
After six weeks, his wife arrives and they move into a furnished apartment. He is disappointed at Mrs. Croft's unemotional reaction to his leaving her house, but Mala now makes the apartment their home. It is strange for him to have someone at his side, and he tries to anticipate his wife's needs and to get used to having a home that smells of cooked rice and soap. Still, they talk little.
One evening, the narrator suggests they should go out. Mala dresses in a beautiful sari and makes up her hair elegantly. They find themselves near Mrs. Croft's house, where Helen answers the door and he learns that the old woman has broken her hip. When Mrs. Croft tells him that she called the police and he responds "Splendid!", Mala laughs. Mrs. Croft announces that Mala is a perfect lady. And now the narrator laughs, too, quietly but noticed by his wife. This is their first real intimacy.
From that moment on, things change between them and they start to share the experience of the new city. The narrator calls this time a sort of honeymoon. Months later, Mala consoles him when the narrator learns that Mrs. Croft has died. She is the first person he mourns in America.
The story moves into the present. The narrator and Mala have been married for decades now and can barely remember a time when they didn't know each other. Their son is at Harvard. They still live in Boston and have integrated themselves into American society.

Analysis

The first-person narrator talks about the different cultures he has faced: outwardly, he has adapted to wherever he lives, but inwardly he remains rooted in his original Bengali culture for a long time. He does a good job as a librarian and advances up the career ladder as time goes by. Overall, the reader is left with a positive impression of his immigrant experience in America.
The narrator explains his distance to Bengali traditions food and clothing, and he initially remains a stranger to his wife after she arrives, finding it awkward to eat with his hands or to speak Bengali. Only when visiting his former landlady, Mrs Croft, with Mala, his

attitude towards his wife changes slowly: for the first time he realises how difficult it must be for Mala in this strange country and remembers his first weeks in London. Their contrasting expectations and feelings are bridged over only slowly, but in the process the two become a married couple adjusting to life in a different country and enjoying new circumstances together. This makes the story one of successful immigration to the US.
After the death of his own mother, the aged widow Mrs. Croft, deeply rooted in another century and different attitudes and cultural traditions, seems like a foster mother to him. Unintentionally, she provokes a change in the couple's understanding of each other and facilitates their integration. The narrator is able to truly mourn her, which he had not done with his own mother, as he was then only fulfilling the duties of a son.
Lahiri's message is that life is unpredictable, with extraordinary turns of events bringing great sorrow and love. Her story addresses the wide Indian diaspora, especially in the West.

Topics

- the American Dream
- immigration
- the individual and society
- the making of identity

Qaisra Shahraz, "The Escape" (eA)

A note on the author
The widely acclaimed, award-winning British Pakistani novelist Qaisra Sharaz (born 1958) is also active as a screen writer and journalist. She has lived in Manchester ever since she was nine years old and has worked as a college inspector, an international teacher trainer and an education consultant, among other things. Among her central focuses are the question of race, cultural divisions and diversity and the question of gender. A short story touching on all these topics – clothing, female modesty, multiple identities and cultural clashes – is "A Pair of Jeans" (1988).

Synopsis

The story "The Escape", from 2009, features seventy-three-year-old Samir celebrating the Muslim festival Eid ul-Fitr, when he looks back on his life and the changes he and the area he lives in have gone through. He also remembers a trip he made to Pakistan, where he understood what "home" meant to him.
Samir now lives alone in his large family home, a detached house in a suburb of Manchester but only uses his master bedroom, as his wife has recently died and his children have all left the house. He does not really feel at home there any more, as too much has changed.
The story begins with Samir praying in a mosque, where he does not feel a sense of belonging either, because of different – younger – generations praying there now and because of the different cultural backgrounds the community comes from. In his now

multi-ethnic area, a mix of Pakistani, Bengali, Asian and Somali shops and mosques have sprung up where formerly there where only Catholic schools and churches and some small shops that he remembers with nostalgia.
His son Maqbool brings him home and later picks him up for the first Eid family gathering at his eldest daughter's house. Samir reflects that they used to celebrate this feast at his own house, which was filled with chatter and joy and delicious smells.
On this first Eid ul-Fitr without his wife, Samir announces, to his children's surprise, that he will be going "home to Pakistan" for a few months to be with his family there and revisit some of the places of his childhood.
But, on returning to Pakistan, he realises he's no longer sure where his real home is. Samir takes his brother's family in Lahore by surprise, too. They greet him with hospitality but are unsure what his true intentions are. Only the young children's reactions are natural; everyone else reacts awkwardly.
Samir travels to his home village and visits his parents' grave, where he takes in the experience of Pakistani life around him and reflects on his past and his possible future life. He remembers how, over 40 years earlier, he had come to London with a friend, felt uneasy there and moved on up north. He recalls the different stages of assimilating to the British workforce and of taking care to settle in good surrounding (a detached house in a good area) and to ensure the education and career of his children.
Back in the village, he visits a widow and her teenage daughters who were supported by his late wife. He is touched and embarrassed by their humility and their behaviour. He is overwhelmed by the grief for his late wife and re-establishes the sponsorship and offers to pay for the daughters' college education. On leaving the widow's home, he walks back through the village, noticing no one of his own age-group nor anyone he recognises.
Back in Lahore, he tells the family that he will be going "home" to England. His brother does not understand Samir's concept of home but is relieved that the guest is leaving.
During the flight back, Samir meets another Pakistani man of his age and they start to talk about home, the homeland and homecoming and escaping back to the UK "to a new home".
Once back, Samir decides to leave his house to his children, moves into an elderly people's home and rewrites his will in order to settle the financial support for the widow in the village. A week after arriving there, his new friend Ibrahim moves in three doors down from him and pure joy returns to Samir's life as he shows him around the house. The escape is over and both decide they have the right to enjoy their lives as "the new English babus" who, having worked enough, can now enjoy their remaining years in a home of their own choice.

Analysis

The short story is told from Samir's point of view by a third-person narrator. The question of belonging is central: torn between his memories of his old life, his upbringing in Pakistan and his present circumstances, Samir is shown to have multiple identities: he has a growing sense of loss and confusion especially after his wife's recent death.
The question of where the elderly first-generation migrants belong is a poignant one. What is their "homeland"? Is it the place of their birth or where they have spent most of

their lives? The story answers this question inasmuch as, towards the end of the story, Samir finds out that his home is in Manchester – a place changed noticably since he arrived there but richer for all its cultural variety –, despite the fact that he maintains emotional links with his country of birth. This is shown by the gestures, tone of voice and facial expressions that Samir notices but also by the distance and the lack of understanding he encounters. But he can only begin to understand what "home" means to him after he has made his escape to Pakistan. Back in England, he can escape a lonely life in his family home by making a move to a new home, with new friends, not cut off from his family but independent.

Topics

- postcolonial experience
- migration
- the making of identity
- questions of belonging
- age and memories
- the generation gap

Glossary – Individual and Society

alienation	Entfremdung (z. B. von der Ursprungskultur)
assimilation	Anpassung (Aufgabe der urspr. Kultur)
to adapt to sth.	sich an etwas anpassen
to blend in	sich einfügen, integrieren
to integrate	integrieren
immigrant, to immigrate, immigration	Einwanderer/-in, einwandern, Einwanderung
colonialism, coloniser, colonised	Kolonialismus, die/der Besiedelnde, kolonisiert
citizenship	Nationalität, Staatsangehörigkeit
naturalisation	Einbürgerung
to receive / to be granted citizenship	die Staatsbürgerschaft erhalten
refugee, asylum seeker	Flüchtling, Asylsuchende/-r
ethnic minority, ethnicity	ethnische Minderheit, Volkszugehörigkeit
indigenous	einheimisch
integration	Integration
imperialism, imperialistic	Imperialismus, imperialistisch
loss of identity	Verlust der Identität
cultural clash	kultureller Zusammenprall (Konflikt)

melting pot vs. salad bowl	„Schmelztiegel" vs. „Salatschüssel" (unterschiedliche Konzepte, die die Vielfalt der Kulturen in den USA beschreiben sollen)
mutual understanding	gegenseitiges/beiderseitiges Verständnis
open-minded vs. narrow-minded	aufgeschlossen vs. engstirnig
pluralistic society	pluralistische (vielseitige) Gesellschaft
covert/overt discrimination	versteckte/offene Diskriminierung
(racial) segregation	Rassentrennung
deprivation	Aberkennung, Entzug (z. B. von Rechten), Benachteiligung
oppression, to be oppressed by s. o.	Unterdrückung, von jmd. unterdrückt werden
racial equality	Gleichwertigkeit verschiedener Rassen
civil rights	Bürgerrechte
civil disobedience	ziviler Ungehorsam
boycott	Ablehnung etwas zu kaufen oder zu benutzen, um z. B. eine Institution zu schwächen

Globalisation

Effects on the World of Work and on Personal Lives

Keyword

Globalisation: a worldwide development involving the integration of financial, economic and communications systems; often seen as an unstoppable process, affecting people all around the globe, no matter whether they live in industrialised or developing countries, in big cities or rural villages; transfer of goods, capital and services as well as communications make life easier, but not everyone profits from the development; smaller economies may suffer

The world is said to be getting smaller, i.e. it has become a **"global village"**. The term was coined by Marshall McLuhan, a Canadian philosopher and media specialist.

Economic Challenges

As today's customers wish to buy products at the best cost-performance ratio, the global market has become very **competitive**, with the following (and related) consequences:

- More and more jobs are outsourced or offshored to cut down production costs, thereby severely damaging local labour markets.
- When jobs are outsourced to low-wage countries, the workers often work in so-called "sweatshops" for long hours at a stretch, earning only minimum wages and under working conditions that are often inhumane.
- While "global players" consider efficiency, speed, flexibility and profit most important, employees are increasingly unable to defend their rights.
- Critics like the Canadian journalist Naomi Klein accuse multinational companies of exploiting the poor and indirectly supporting child labour by only having their own profits in mind.
- People in developing countries often live in poor conditions, without a decent education or access to new means of communication. Therefore they cannot reap the benefits of globalisation.
- In order to reduce the number of sweatshops, fair trade is becoming increasingly important. Its aim is to ensure that workers and small-scale producers in poor countries are paid a fair price for their work and products.
- Despite these attempts, the gap between the rich and the poor is widening.

Aspects of the "global village"

- The development of aeroplanes, fast ships and trains has made fast transportation of goods and people from one part of the world to another possible.
- New means of communication, especially the internet, have made collaboration between business partners and private individuals easier.

- Multinational companies have branches all over the world, and cost-effectiveness is a decisive factor when new production sites are set up.

Effects on the way of life

Anyone can experience the effects of globalisation, e.g. when
- travelling (and meeting people from one's own town halfway round the globe);
- keeping in touch with friends or business partners in distant countries with the help of new means of communication, which are faster than ever before;
- buying new goods that come from or were processed very far away; or
- calling a service "hotline" of a company that uses a call-center in India.

Globalisation is not always regarded as a positive process:
- Some people fear that individual cultures will finally blend into a single global culture, thereby losing their identity and the benefits of diversity.
- Despite or because of a globalised world, millions of people in developing countries still suffer from malnutrition or die of incurable diseases.
- Others work under cruel working conditions, producing goods that will be shipped to and sold in industrialised countries at a low price.
- One of the latest financial crises, starting in the USA in 2008, has shown that such catastrophes will ultimately affect other nations as well, as businesses are linked and global trade is now the rule.
- Due to increased mobility, diseases like H1N1 ("swine flu") or the coronavirus (cf. p. 62 f.) can easily spread all around the globe, developing into a pandemic.
- The refugee crisis in Europe (peaking in 2015) can partly be seen as connected to globalisation: People from all over the world want to participate in growing economic wealth. Many people from poor countries want to find a better future and leave their homes – just like people have always done over the centuries (e.g. emigration to America in the last two centuries). At the same time, civil and other wars as well as climate change force people to emigrate. As more and more countries close their borders, problems in many regions are growing. Among these problems are huge refugee camps, pushback policies denying migrants their right to apply for asylum and people drowning and starving during dangerous journeys.
- Terrorism has become an ongoing global threat, which has led to a growing feeling of insecurity in many societies. In some countries (e.g. Israel) terrorist attacks have been a permanent aspect of everyday life for six or seven decades. In most Western as well as Middle Eastern countries, what we know as Islamist terrorism (Al-Qaeda, the "Islamic State") began with the "9/11" attacks on the World Trade Center in New York and the Pentagon in Washington on 11 September 2001. This lead to the controversial "War on Terror" on the part of the USA and its allies, most notably in Afghanistan from 2001 to 2021. Since then, the world has seen a large number of terrorist attacks connected with Islamist ideology (e.g. in France, England, Nigeria, Germany) or with the ideology of white supremacy (e.g. in Christchurch in New Zealand or Utøya in Norway).

INFO Anti-globalisation movements

Many ecological and political movements around the world criticise the levelling and disadvantageous effects of globalisation. This has led to the formation of NGOs and alliances opposing the rule of capitalism over the economy of this increasingly smaller world. In opposition to the G8 summit, these organisations formed the **World Social Forum**.

Global competition

The increasingly globalised working world demands new skills and abilities of each individual. Since not only multinational companies but also smaller firms are outsourcing parts of their production, making use of cheap and well-educated workforces abroad, people in industrialised countries will experience more competition when looking for work as well as on the job. This requires both white-collar and blue-collar workers in the West to:

- acquire skills and competencies that are either very specialised or carried out with special qualities no one else can offer;
- become more flexible; one must be able to adapt to changes on the job and learn new ways of working quickly;
- continue learning throughout one's whole life; it is no longer sufficient to learn a job and expect to stay in it for the remainder of one's career;
- be familiar and keep up with new forms of (computer) technology and communications, since these are constantly changing and improving; and to
- be able to compete with workers from all around the world who can offer the same or similar skills and abilities for lower wages.

Globalisation and the COVID-19 Pandemic

At the beginning of 2020, a highly-infectious and often lethal pandemic caused by the coronavirus started to spread rapidly across the world. Governments worldwide faced a situation threatening health and lives as never before. Harsh measures, including travel bans and stay-at-home-orders which sometimes stretched over several weeks, were imposed to keep the disease at bay, temporarily infringing fundamental rights like freedom of assembly and movement. All kinds of public services and shops were put under lockdown; night-time curfews were even decreed to prevent people from leaving their homes.

As there was initially no vaccine to cope with the virus, the pandemic had the world under control until the first vaccines were developed and administered a year after the original outbreak. The vaccination programme has unfortunately developed into a problem in its own right, with manufacture, distribution and administration obstacles arising on international as well as national and local levels.

The spread of the pandemic can be seen as a negative effect of globalisation: it has definitely been fostered by long-distance travelling from one continent to another.

In economic terms, the epidemic has severely damaged global trade and caused heavy financial losses. Even famous, financially strong brands have suffered because custom-

ers have had to stay at home. Online orders have flourished but can hardly cushion the drastic losses to local businesses. Moreover, distortions in global supply and demand – as for FFP2 masks – have demonstrated the vulnerability of global trade to unscrupulous business practices.
The various lockdowns have hit social and cultural life in particular very hard, closing entire entertainment branches like theatres, cinemas and concerts, along with museums and art galleries as well as restaurants, hotels and bars. The restrictions on even informal group and family meetings have made people very lonely. Elderly people and people living on their own who have not been allowed to receive visits or to visit other people have suffered greatly from this situation.
School – and with it family – life has also been massively affected. Teachers and students have had to adjust to digital schooling without any personal presence, and families had to get used to the new discipline of home schooling. Similar conditions have been imposed on university staff and students. Children from underprivileged backgrounds were hit particularly hard as they often lacked the necessary hardware and internet connection as well as their own study space. The natural needs of children and young people to grow up together have been disrupted, and the changing requirements imposed by governments, sometimes relaxing and then reinstating lockdowns, have done nothing to alleviate matters.
As governments and institutions struggle to deal with the COVID-19 health crisis, our globalised world has proved shockingly vulnerable to the virus, its economic effects and the spread of misinformation. Whether an effective level of immunisation worldwide can be reached, with vaccines distributed fairly to all nations, will be a real test of globalisation.

Global Responsibilities

The UN

- 24 October 1945: A group of 51 countries founded the United Nations (UN) as a replacement for / successor to the League of Nations.
- The UN headquarters is located in New York City and the current Secretary General is António Guterres.
- The UN has 193 member states.
- It defends human rights and fundamental freedoms.

Five of the six **main organs** of the UN (General Assembly, Security Council, Economic and Social Council, Trusteeship Council and Secretariat) are located in New York City, while the International Court of Justice is in The Hague (the Netherlands). There are **various programmes** and funds affiliated to the UN. Two of the best known are UNICEF (United Nations Children's Fund) and the UNHCR (Office of the United Nations High Commissioner for Refugees). The latter deals with the needs of refugees and displaced persons in post-conflict countries, e.g. Djibouti.

Aims of the UN

- to preserve international peace and security
- to promote friendly relations between member countries
- to support international cooperation with regard to economic, social and cultural as well as humanitarian issues
- Apart from **peacekeeping** and **peacemaking** operations, peacebuilding has become more and more important.
- Here the UN and its affiliated organisations work to equip national groups with the necessary skills in conflict management to ensure lasting peace.
- Currently (April 2022) the UN is involved in 12 peacekeeping operations, e. g. in Haiti, Mali and South Sudan.
- **Humanitarian aid** is also of major importance, e. g. providing relief for people affected by either man-made or natural disasters and helping refugees and displaced persons.
- Other main concerns of the UN are **international law and development** (e. g. sustainable development, agriculture, international trade).

Global political changes

International peacekeeping is one of the aims of the UN:

- Once peace has been established in a country or region, peacekeepers are sent to the country or region in question to oversee the peace process.
- This can be done by overseeing elections, providing reconstruction aid and supervising the withdrawal of combatants.
- Very often, UN peacekeepers are soldiers, but they can be police officers or other civilian personnel.
- The UN Security Council authorises peacekeeping missions, which are then carried out by the international community.
- Many of these missions are organised and led by the UN itself. There is no UN army. While the troops acting as peacekeepers are under the control of the UN, they still belong to the armed forces of their country of origin. The UN itself is controlled by the Security Council and the UN Secretariat. This reduces the risk of a single peacekeeping party following its own interests.
- Regional organisations (e. g. NATO) can be authorised by the UN to lead peace-keeping missions. These regional organisations can also arrange peacekeeping missions of their own.

Migration – A Global Challenge[1]

- Migration has been a worldwide phenomenon since the beginning of human history.
- People have had a number of reasons for leaving their places of origin: poverty and the dream of a better life elsewhere, climatic reasons, wars and civil wars or religious persecution, to name only the most important.
- One has to distinguish between migrants and refugees:

[1] Source for all figures: https://www.unhcr.org/figures-at-a-glance.html (accessed on 1 April 2022)

- **Migrants** leave their countries of origin for a limited period of time or permanently, usually for economic reasons. They might have job offers in a different country or they might have heard of good opportunities. Examples of this are emigration from European countries to the USA in the 19th century, immigrants from Poland to the Ruhr district also during the 19th century, migrant workers inside Europe today, for example to help on farms, as carers for elderly people or to work in hospitals, and people from Africa trying to find better living conditions in Europe.
- **Refugees** usually flee their homes in order to get away from immediate threats to their survival, such as persecution, wars or climate change. Examples of this at present are the Muslim Rohingya from Myanmar, Venezuelans to other South American and Central American countries, or Syrian or Afghan people to Europe. An important example from the past are the Jews from Germany and other countries who had to flee from the Nazis.
- The International Migration Report of the UN from 2019 states that most migrants worldwide go to countries in Asia, followed by Europe and North America. The countries with the most migrants are the USA, followed by Saudi Arabia and Germany. These migrants for the most part seek – and find – employment in the countries of destination. They are not refugees, but quite a large number of them are illegal immigrants. According to the UN, there were 272 million migrants in 2019.
- The UNHCR (United Nations refugee agency) states in its statistical report for 2021 that the world is now witnessing the highest levels of displacement on record. 82.4 million people around the world have been forced to leave their homes. Among them are over 26 million refugees, over 40 % of whom are under the age of 18. 48 million are internal refugees, i. e. they flee from one part of the country to another (Nigeria is one example). There are 4.1 million asylum seekers worldwide. However, 73 % of refugees stay in neighbouring countries: Syrian refugees mainly flee to Turkey, Jordan and other countries close by. Nearly half the refugees worldwide at present come from Syria, Afghanistan and South Sudan.
- In 2021, Turkey hosted the largest refugee population worldwide, with 3.7 million refugees and asylum seekers, followed by Colombia (1.7 million), Pakistan (1.4 million) and Uganda (1.4 million). Most refugees come from Syria (6.7 million), Venezuela (4 million), Afghanistan (2.6 million), South Sudan (2.2 million) and Myanmar (1.1 million).
- There are also millions of stateless people, who have been denied nationality and access to basic rights such as education, healthcare, employment and freedom of movement.
- About 1 percent of the world's population have fled their homes.
- Nearly 1 person is forcibly displaced every two seconds as a result of conflict or persecution.
- The fact that most refugees seek help in neighbouring, not always wealthy countries can cause major problems there: The population of these countries has to share access to education, healthcare and jobs with the refugees. Compared to rich countries like Germany, countries like Jordan or the Lebanon find it far more difficult to cope with the situation. Colombia is another example of these conflicts: it is a country which is

only just beginning to overcome the effects of a civil war. Recently it has also been the destination of over 1 million refugees from Venezuela.
- On the other hand, migration always also means enrichment: The destination country will, with time, integrate the new arrivals. Their culture, beliefs and customs will become part of the country, thus leading to a more diverse culture in general.
- Many migrants and refugees want to return to their home countries if the situation allows them to. Seasonal migrants, for example, usually leave their families behind and return when their work has finished for the year. Many refugees want to return to their old home after the end of a war, others would like to build a new life elsewhere.

The EU

- Currently 27 states belong to the European Union (EU). The newest members are Bulgaria and Romania, which both joined the EU on 1 January 2007, and Croatia which became a member on 1 July 2013.
- After World War II there was a desire for a united Europe in order to prevent extreme forms of nationalism. The European Coal and Steel Community (ECSC), the European Economic Community (EEC) and the European Atomic Energy Community (Euratom) were merged into the European Community (EC) in 1967.
- The EU as we know it came into existence in 1993, when the Maastricht Treaty, which, among other things, initiated the euro as a common currency, was ratified.
- The individual member states came to be regarded as one single global player.
- At present the EU faces the challenge of maintaining its unity – and indeed remaining a union at all – in the face and the aftermath of the refugee crisis. The countries of the EU have very different attitudes to solving the refugee problem.
- In December 2019 the United Kingdom (UK) left the EU, a decision taken by referendum in June 2016. There have already been numerous consequences: businesses have been burdened with significant administrational issues, supply chains have been disrupted and there is a shortage in workers, particularly in the healthcare and hospitality sector. However, it is not always clear whether these and other issues have been caused by Brexit of the COVID-19 pandemic.

Aims of the EU

- to promote prosperity and social progress with European citizenship for its peoples while still keeping their diversity alive
- to promote friendly relations between member countries
- to guarantee freedom and justice for the peoples of Europe
- to represent the member states internationally with a single voice, tackling the various challenges of globalisation, as well as respecting human rights

When it comes to defence, the individual member countries are sovereign. However, there is military cooperation in peacekeeping missions.

The three main groups which make up the EU are the Council of Ministers, the European Parliament and the European Commission.

Although the EU has no official capital, the official seat of the European Commission and the Council of the European Union as well as the second seat of the European Parliament are in Brussels, Belgium.

Global Warming and its Consequences

Environmental pollution has been growing rapidly and globally. The following factors in particular create global problems:

- Especially in developed nations, rampant consumerism is still increasing **energy consumption and waste gases** from factories.
- Over the last decades the number of **vehicles** on the roads has steadily increased. Cars are no longer found only in industrialised countries.
- The number of people travelling by plane is also greater than ever, due to the fact that plane tickets have become affordable for a larger number of people. Short-haul **flights** have become particularly popular.
- **food miles:** Whereas some years ago many people bought fruit and vegetables locally and ate seasonal products, they now want to eat strawberries and cherries in December. Hence more goods are transported by plane. Ecologically conscious customers ask themselves whether it is better to buy local product than food (even fair trade) that has been flown across continents. The non-sustainable production of meat and dairy foods is another critical factor in global warming.
- Everyone leaves a **carbon footprint** (emission of greenhouse gases from factories, transportation, food, etc), either directly or indirectly.
- **Greenhouse gases** such as carbon dioxide (CO_2) and methane cause chemical damage to the atmosphere (e. g. holes in the ozone layer) as well as global warming.
- Lots of pupils from all over Europe have left their schools on (some) Fridays and joined the movement *Fridays for Future* started by the Swedish teenager Greta Thunberg in a protest against climate change.

After years of heated discussion among scientists and (especially) politicians worldwide, it is now considered common knowledge in most nations around the globe that the world's climate is changing and that these changes are, to a large degree, man-made. This change manifests itself most dramatically in the fact that the global average temperature is rising, and this has many side effects.
The documentary *An Inconvenient Truth* and its follow-up *An Inconvenient Sequel: Truth to Power* lay out the scientific facts on global warming in detail.

Causes of global warming

- Fossil fuel emissions, so-called greenhouse gases, form a layer in the earth's atmosphere which traps the sun's heat and thereby causes the temperature on the ground to rise; this is called "global warming".
- The quantity of greenhouse gases produced worldwide is rising because:
  - more cars, planes and industrial complexes are being built and used;
  - forests are burnt to make way for agriculture, people, roads, etc.;

- growth in the number of cattle is increasing the emission of methane.
- The global rise in temperature is causing the polar ice caps to melt, diminishing their efficiency as a cooling device and mirror to reflect sunbeams and thus speeding up the heating process in the atmosphere.

Effects and consequences

There are many consequences of climate change. Some may seem rather insignificant at first but turn out to be disastrous in the long run. Although these effects are often spoken of as taking place in the future, many of them are already happening.

- Rising global temperatures are causing more water to evaporate both on land and in the oceans, changing historical patterns of rainfall and drought; many people are unable to adapt to these irregular weather phenomena.
- Oceanic warming is causing hurricanes to become more frequent and violent, as the warm water enhances evaporation and (indirectly) wind speed.
- Changes in temperature also cause natural habitats to change. Plants and animals have to adapt, and if they cannot do, so they will die out. Biodiversity is therefore endangered, limiting the natural resources on which we subsist.
- Diseases are spreading more quickly because parasites like mosquitoes and their animal hosts are affecting populations in previously safe areas.
- As polar ice caps melt, more and more of the earth's landmass is flooded, leaving people homeless.
- If enough polar ice melts, the North Atlantic current (Gulf Stream), which guarantees Europe's warm climate, might stop. In a worst-case scenario, Europe might experience another ice age.
- In other areas, desertification will continue to increase, a phenomenon which is already taking place.
- All these developments will dramatically reduce the area of land on which human existence is possible and will therefore lead to worldwide migration that we will be unable to deal with.

The effects are threatening the entire planet and the way we live today. Because of this, scientists, politicians and citizens worldwide have a duty to seek ways of reducing greenhouse gases in order to slow down climate change. Each individual can participate in reducing greenhouse gas emissions by using better insulation in houses, saving electricity, recycling waste, using public transportation instead of a private car, flying only when absolutely necessary, etc.
The key to saving the environment is "thinking globally and acting locally".

Political efforts to reduce greenhouse gas emissions are still faced with various difficulties and conflicts of interest. Each climate summit therefore only achieves small steps towards stopping or slowing down climate change. Scientists and independent organisations alike argue that these small steps are not enough to prevent the catastrophic consequences of global warming. The main goal remains to cut greenhouse gas emissions, especially those caused by the burning of fossil fuels.

INFO The Kyoto Protocol and the Paris Agreement

International efforts to stop climate change – the Kyoto Protocol and the Paris Agreement
The international political elite came together in Japan in December 1997 and issued a common declaration, the **Kyoto Protocol**, which came into effect on 16 February 2005. The protocol aimed to reduce the emission of greenhouse gases by an annual 5.2 % by 2012, taking 1990 levels as a basis.
Ever since then, numerous other summits have taken place in order to reduce and slow global warming. In Paris in 2015 a global agreement on the slowing of climate change (the **Paris Agreement**) was reached and adopted by 195 countries. Among the decisions made was the resolution to limit the long-term increase of global average temperature to well below 2°C above pre-industrial levels. The agreement came into effect on 4 November 2016, as enough countries had ratified it. In June 2017, the USA withdrew its consent to the agreement.
One of the first actions of the current US President, Joe Biden, was to announce that the US were to rejoin the Paris Agreement on Climate Change: it did so on 19 February 2021. With the US being part of the Paris Agreement again, two-thirds of the countries producing half of global carbon pollution have committed themselves to carbon neutrality. This agreement, the first legally binding global climate change agreement, has been ratified by 196 countries (April 2022).

Fridays for Future

- In August 2018, Greta Thunberg, a then 16-year-old Swedish climate change activist, started protesting outside the Swedish parliament in Stockholm in order to raise awareness of the dangers of climate change.
- According to Thunberg, politicians are not taking enough action against climate change, which is putting our planet's future at risk. Thunberg's solitary school strikes soon caught the attention of the media in countries all over the world.
- Up to May 2019, an estimated 1.4 million teenagers and young adults worldwide followed her example by going on strike from school every Friday and protesting against climate change. This movement is known as "Fridays for Future". Since the beginning of COVID-19, it has been more difficult to demonstrate for new climate change policies, but the movement has tried to find other ways of protesting.
- Greta Thunberg has delivered several public speeches in which she has put pressure on politicians and world leaders to combat climate change more swiftly and resolutely. She spoke at various important global meetings, e. g. the United Nations Climate Change Conference in Katowice, Poland in December 2018 and at the World Economic Forum in Davos, Switzerland in January 2019.
- The speed of the reaction and the immense sums of money provided by governments during the COVID-19 crisis seem to prove Fridays for Future's point: Immediate global action is possible, but the governments all over the world do not seem to regard an effective fight against global warming as a top priority.

Alternatives to Using Fossil Fuels

Recent discussions on fossil fuels and their effect on the atmosphere have supported the development of technology to make use of renewable sources of energy such as wind, water and solar power. In many European countries, national programmes to subsidise these technologies have been established. The US is also aiming to support these alternative energies more substantially, but this has not been achieved by recent administrations. The Fukushima disaster in spring 2011 led the German government to withdraw from using nuclear energy in future. Other parties urge that nuclear power should be used instead of fossil fuels (which are still the most important sources of energy). However, the use of nuclear energy has always been controversial.

Natural alternative energy sources

In general, the use of wind, water and solar power seems far less risky and also less expensive in the long run. The challenge engineers face is to make these technologies more efficient and find ways to store the energy produced. One main hindrance is posed by companies investing more money in fossil fuel exploration and exploitation and in expanding nuclear power facilities. Since these technologies are well established, their exploitation yields enormous profits, whereas investment in new, ecologically-friendly sources of energy is costly, but could create many jobs.

Non-renewable and/versus renewable energy

- Since the Industrial Revolution, Western societies have been in constantly growing need of energy resources to power industrial production and satisfy communal and household requirements for fuel and electricity.
- This increasing demand for energy has led to various developments:
  - The exploitation of natural resources such as oil, gas and coal has led to the destruction of natural habitats on land and in the oceans.
  - The use of nuclear power plants has created a seemingly safe, cheap and climate-friendly source of power. This view is, however, disproven by accidents like those in Chernobyl and Fukushima as well as the ongoing problem of where to store nuclear waste.
  - New inventions have succeeded in making use of renewable energies such as wind, water and solar power.
- The most immediate result of the use of fossil fuels since the Industrial Revolution is the amount of carbon dioxide and other pollutants emitted into the atmosphere.

Environmental sustainability

It will prove difficult to sustain usable natural resources. Industrialisation and capitalism, together with a continuously growing world population, have led to a massive exploitation of limited resources. Thus, finding ways to make our societies and lifestyles sustainable is one of the most important global challenges.

Global goals

In 2015, United Nations member states formulated 17 objectives - or „Sustainable Development Goals" - for a fairer and better world to be achieved by 2030. These included issues such as gender equality, clean water, physical and mental well-being, international peace and justice.
For example, they aim to end global poverty by ensuring that economic resources and fundamental services such as healthcare are available to everyone and by making sure that even the poor are protected from potential environmental disaster. They also seek to implement policies aimed at promoting equality with respect to income, political inclusion and opportunities, but that also allow developing nations in particular a fairer economical share. With respect to climate change, the 17 global goals commit themselves to raising awareness for this issue, protecting against disasters related to climate change and integrating measures on a national level. They also seek to reduce waste, in particular food waste, manage resources more sustainably and to combat market distortions such as tax reductions and subsidies that reward wasteful consumption.[2]
The signatory states have shown variable speed at implementing these goals in their policies. Germany was one of the first to begin this process in the shape of the „Deutsche Nachhaltigkeitsstrategie" in 2017. Whether, however, these 17 aims can be converted from words on paper to real action is yet to be seen. A first stock-taking in 2020 saw positive developments on a communal level and well as in grassroots movements such as Fridays for Future. On the other hand, the report also notes that povery is still growing, basic needs are still nowhere near being met on a global scale and natural resources and habitats continue to be recklessly destroyed. Clearly, more public pressure and political daring will be required in the coming years.

English as a Global Language

The general importance of English in the globalised world of international trade and politics, science, popular culture and travel is still unrivalled. No matter where you are in the world, a command of English will always help.
Worldwide, 1.348 million people speak English as a native speaker or as a second language, followed by Mandarin, the main language in China (1.120 million), Hindi (600 million) and Spanish (543 million).[3]
Especially in the countries of the former British Empire, English is not just a language universally understood and spoken, it is very often still an official language. In India, for example, more than 3,000 newspapers are published in English, but English is spoken by only about 12 % of the population. There are 1,652 languages and dialects in India, which makes English as a working *lingua franca* even more important. All in all, English is the official language in 55 countries today.

[2] Source: https://www.globalgoals.org/ (accessed on 1 April 2022)

[3] Source: https://www.statista.com/statistics/266808/the-most-spoken-languages-worldwide/ (published 30 March 2021, accessed on 1 April 2022)

It has been estimated that about a billion people worldwide speak English as a second language.[4] According to the EU statistical service, 96 % of all students at lower secondary level in the EU study English as a second language.[5] International organisations like NATO or OECD use English exclusively, as do many internationally operating enterprises like Airbus Industries and even Volkswagen in their Shanghai branch.
According to Bill Bryson[6], English differs from other languages in three outstanding respects that make it attractive even to speakers of other mother tongues. First, its rich vocabulary is wider than that of other languages. The latest edition of the *Oxford English Dictionary* lists 615,000 words; 200,000 words are commonly used in English, compared to 184,000 in German and just 100,000 in French. What adds to the wide range of words is the large number of synonyms. The best known collection of synonyms and antonyms, *Roget's Thesaurus*, has over 100,000 entries. Thirdly, there is an almost endless list of words that can be used both as noun and verb.

English as a *Lingua Franca*

A *lingua franca* is a language that can be used by speakers who do not have any knowledge of each other's mother tongue. It is therefore also referred to as a "contact" or "link" language. English used in this context bridges the linguistic gap for non-native speakers of English who do not share a common first language and thus serves as a means of intercultural communication. Since this happens worldwide, English has been called a "global *lingua franca*". The result of this extensive use of English is that it is shaped not only by its native speakers but also by those who use it as a foreign language. Researchers[7] have found that although speakers of English as a *lingua franca* do not always adhere to the rules of grammar and pronunciation, communication is not necessarily inhibited by this. What seems more important in this respect is language awareness, along with a command of communication strategies. Nevertheless, the more closely a person's grammar approximates to Standard English, the more readily they will be understood.

Varieties of English[8]

American English

- American English is relatively homogeneous compared to British English. About 80 % of the population speak with the same accent.– The USA contains four speech groups:

[4] Source: https://www.statista.com/statistics/266808/the-most-spoken-languages-worldwide/ (published on 25 September 2014, accessed on 1 April 2022)

[5] Source: hhttps://www.thoughtco.com/how-many-people-learn-english-globally-1210367 (published on 27 August 2020, accessed on 1 April 2022)

[6] Source: Bill Bryson, *Mother Tongue. The Story of the English Language*, London: Penguin, 1990, S. 3 f.

[7] Source: Barbara Seidlhofer, "English as a lingua franca", in: *ELT Journal* 59/4 (October 2005), p. 339 f.

[8] You can find lots of additional information as well as sound examples of these and other varieties of English on video platforms online.

Northern, Midland, Southern and New England. Midland is subdivided into North and South Midland.

- Regional variation due to geographical and historical factors: colonists on the East Coast were in touch with people from England via trade; therefore similarities with British English (e.g. the pronunciation of "Tuesday", "news"; the absence of [r] in "horse", "car").
- Social prestige is linked to pronunciation, e.g. the sound of [r] is carefully produced by upper-middle-class speakers when they want to indicate their social standing.
- There has been some rivalry between England and America as to the question whose language is more correct. On becoming independent, Americans emphasised the differences between British and American English, thus creating some sort of language nationalism.
- Immigrants often try to conceal their origins by overemphasising vowel sounds, e.g. in "coffee". This is called hypercorrection.
- The phenomenon of t-dropping is widely practised. That means that [t] is not pronounced in the middle of a word, e.g. in "winter" or "internet".
- [o] in "clock" is realised like the [a] in British English "car". A British native speaker could therefore mistake the American "clock" for the word "clerk".
- The way Americans speak is often referred to as "the American twang". This most commonly refers to "General American", which is a generalised Midwestern accent used by many TV and radio hosts. (cf. p. 75 for AAVE/Black Vernacular).

British English

- In the Middle English period, Oxford, Cambridge and London shared the same kind of English. Because of the prestige attached to it, London English became the basis for Standard English as early as the time of Chaucer's Middle English and in turn formed the national language.
- One variety of English spoken in London is called Cockney. In the sixteenth century this was not associated with the language of the East End working-class, as it is today, but it was the language spoken by all Londoners outside the court. It was only in the eighteenth century that Cockney became regarded as coarse or low English. One of the reasons for this development was that the City became the centre of commerce and trade, thereby making the old inhabitants move east to Wapping, Shoreditch and Bermondsey.
- Characteristics of Cockney include h-dropping, which means that the [h] at the beginning of a word is not pronounced, and the "glottal stop", which is the result of not pronouncing the [t] in words like "butter" or "bottle". Furthermore, the [g] in word endings is often omitted, for example in "eatin'".
- Standard English as spoken by a mere 2–5 % of the British population has also been labelled "Received Pronunciation" or simply "RP". It was until recently spoken by British middle-class people, especially in the South, and it was used by most TV and radio news presenters.

Australian English

- Like American English, Australian English is fairly uniform in pronunciation.
- Three different social accents can be distinguished: "Cultivated" (similar to British English; 10 % of speakers), "Broad" (working-class accent; 10 %) and "General" (80 %). On the whole, there is not much regional variety in dialects.
- Girls and women tend to speak General or Cultivated Australian, whereas boys and men prefer General or Broad Australian.
- Using a rising tone at the end of a statement, which has become popular with girls and women (not only in Australia), is called "rising inflection".
- Australian English contains various words from the Aboriginals, for instance "billabong", "didgeridoo", "boomerang", "koala" and "kangaroo".
- Usage is also influenced by vocabulary from American English, for example: "cookies", "station wagon", "teller", "mail", "labor" and "dollar".
- Australian English has been influenced by large numbers of immigrants, so-called "New Australians" from Turkey, Greece, Italy, Sri Lanka, etc.

New Zealand English

- It is very similar to Australian English, although New Zealanders regard their way of speaking as more sophisticated and try to be as close to British English as possible.

Canadian English

- In the wake of the American Revolution, Loyalists (supporters of the English) fled to Ontario, providing the basis for "General Canadian" as an urban, middle-class variety.
- Along the Atlantic coast there were many English-speaking settlements.

English in India

- Approximately 70 million people use English in India. About 25 million use English regularly, thus making it an important language of official life.
- English is spoken mainly by the educated ruling classes.
- Many national daily papers are in English (e.g. *The Times of India*).
- All-India Radio broadcasts in English all over India.
- English was used in the fields of government, education and imperial rule.
- In 1857, English-speaking universities were established in Bombay, Calcutta and Chennai (formerly: Madras).
- English has become the language of prestige and of nationalist opposition.
- A large number of Indian words have been integrated into English, e.g. "curry", "bungalow" or "veranda", especially by English administrators in the nineteenth century.

Pidgin

A pidgin is an artificial, auxiliary language without any native speakers. It is used by people with different mother tongues who need a common means of communication. Pidgin English was the traders' and slaves' *lingua franca*. The word "pidgin" is derived from the way the Chinese pronounced the word "business". There are French, English and Portuguese pidgins.

Creole

- If a pidgin is used as a first language, it is called a creole. This process happens gradually and it takes several generations.
- When slaves from many different African tribes with different languages were transported to America by slave ships, they needed a common language. Therefore, they spoke pidgin English, which was accessible to all of them.
- Examples are the Caribbean creole of Barbados, which is based on English, or Haitian creole, which is based on French. The creole of Papua New Guinea (Tok Pisin) has a written as well as a spoken form.

African American Vernacular English (AAVE)

- Formerly called Black English, AAVE has absorbed aspects of African pidgin and Caribbean creole and has a long and distinctive tradition. It has a distinct set of rules, although it is still often misjudged as inferior because certain grammatical structures of English are simplified or do not occur. Nowadays, however, it is considered to be simply another variety of English. It is also called "Black Vernacular".
- The verb "to be" is left out under certain circumstances („She at home.") and habitual "be" is used in place of simple present („He be watching TV every night.").
- On the one hand, AAVE is representative of a disadvantaged past, on the other hand, it is also a means of self-expression.
- Contributions from the African world to everyday English are words and expressions like "voodoo", "banana" or "high five".
- Black Vernacular probably originated even before the slave trade began.
- Due to music and popular films and series, it has achieved wide public attention. Some features of AAVE are apparently unique to this variety, but the structure is often similar to other English varieties spoken in the US and Caribbean. The number of speakers of AAVE is extremely difficult to establish.

South African English (SAE)

English was first brought to the Cape area by British settlers, fortune seekers and missionaries in the late 18th and early 19th century. The minority of about 3 million first-language SAE speakers is outnumbered by second- and third-language speakers because English is seen both as the language of communication and aspiration as well as a 'colonist' language. For many black parents English is an instrument for their children's advancement. SAE is dominant in public life for reasons of practicality, even though official documents are also translated into the other ten official languages.
In the Soweto uprising in 1976, the question of a teaching language in black schools was crucial: the students opted for English, as they did not want to study in Afrikaans, the language of their white oppressors. So English has always been seen as opposing Afrikaans, with the black population preferring to use English and the language of their own cultural origin, whereas many white people have kept to Afrikaans.
Strong influences on SAE vocabulary and pronunciation mainly come from the surrounding African languages as well as from Afrikaans or unclear sources. Due to SAE having different native tongues, the pronunciation tends to vary a lot. In general, pronunciati-

on is closest to NZE (New Zealand English), tending to become more levelled through teaching in urban schools and through modern media.

Glossary – Globalisation

anti-globalist	Globalisierungsgegner/-kritiker
backwardness	Rückständigkeit
company philosophy	Geschäfts-/Firmenphilosophie
competition; to be competitive	Konkurrenz(kampf)/Wettbewerb; konkurrenzfähig sein
corporate identity	Firmenimage
crop diseases	Krankheiten von Pflanzen/Saatgut
debt relief	Schuldenerlass, Entschuldung
desertification	die Wüstenbildung, das Vordringen der Wüste
developing countries	Entwicklungsländer
development aid	Entwicklungshilfe
driving forces of globalisation	die Antriebskräfte der Globalisierung
drought	Dürren, Dürreperioden
earth's atmosphere	die Erdatmosphäre
economic growth	Wirtschaftswachstum
economic prosperity	ökonomischer Wohlstand
emerging markets	Schwellenländer
environmental commitment	Umwelteinsatz
environmental damage	Umweltzerstörung
environmentally friendly	umweltfreundlich
expansion of capitalism	Ausbreitung des Kapitalismus
fair trade	fairer Handel
floods	Hochwasser, Überschwemmungen
global interconnection	globale Querverbindungen
global marketplace	globaler Marktplatz
global player	Weltfirma
global superpower	globale Supermacht
global warming	Erderwärmung
going global	*umgangssprachlicher Ausdruck, der ursprünglich für die globale Expansion von Firmen verwendet wurde*
greenhouse gases	Treibhausgase

human rights	Menschenrechte
increase profit margins	die Gewinnspanne erhöhen
Industrial Age	das Industriezeitalter
industrial nations	Industrieländer/-nationen
international stock markets	internationale Börsenmärkte
labour laws/market	Arbeitsgesetze/ Arbeitsmarkt
lingua franca	eine Sprache, die von Personen mit unterschiedlichen Muttersprachen benutzt wird
low-wage countries	Niedriglohnländer
mass tourism	Massentourismus
microcredits	Kleinkredite
NGO (non-governmental organisation)	Nichtregierungsorganisation
outsourcing	Produktionsverlagerung
political turmoil	politischer Aufruhr, politische Turbulenzen
pollution	Verschmutzung
population overshoot, overpopulation, excess of population	Überbevölkerung
poverty	Armut
greenhouse gas emissions	Ausstoß von Treibhausgasen
cost of production	Produktionskosten
rise in global temperature	ein weltweiter Temperaturanstieg
robotised production	computergesteuerte Produktion/Fertigung
shareholder	Aktionär
supremacy	Vormachtsstellung, Überlegenheit
sustainability	Nachhaltigkeit, Zukunftsfähigkeit
sweatshop	ausbeuterischer Betrieb
trade	Handel
trademark policy	Markenpolitik
undernutrition, malnutrition	Unterernährung; Mangelernährung
unemployment	Arbeitslosigkeit
workforce	Arbeiterschaft
working conditions	Arbeitsbedingungen

Science and Technology

The dawn of science in the modern sense of drawing factual conclusions from empirical, experimental or statistical data can be dated back to ancient Greece, when scholars aimed to explain the world on the basis of observation and elaboration. During the Renaissance, science experienced a rebirth, and in the wake of the Industrial Revolution it evolved to become what it is today: the basis of our modern way of life.

Gaining background knowledge

The emergence of today's technology-oriented societies can only be understood by studying the Industrial Revolution. The full extent of these changes cannot be presented in this context. Various informative sites can be found online, e. g.:

- https://www.bbc.co.uk/history/scottishhistory/enlightenment/features_enlightenment_industry.shtml (accessed on 1 April 2022)
- https://www.history.com/topics/industrial-revolution/industrial-revolution (published on 29 October 2009, accessed on 1 April 2022)

Chances and Risks

Scientific research aims to explore and explain the world around us and improve the means by which we cope with it. Technology, in turn, is the practical outcome of this research, resulting in the tools and machines we use to make our lives (seemingly) easier. Every new technology, however, harbours risks as well as opportunities and creates new kinds of dependencies unknown before. One simple example will suffice to prove this point: At the end of the 19th century, the first automobiles were produced; eventually they would replace horse-drawn vehicles and other means of individual transport. In contrast to older technologies, cars need fossil fuel. Demand for cars increased during the 20th century, production became cheaper, and today almost every household in Western societies owns at least one car.

The increasing use of cars has had various consequences:

- more demand for fossil fuels: increased drilling for oil on land and at sea,
- demand for larger roads: expansion of highways, parking lots, etc.,
- consequences: growing destruction of natural habitats and resources,
- increasing mobility: the former luxury of owning a car has become a must; some jobs cannot be done without a car, one is expected to own a car; public transport systems aim to meet general mobility needs,
- cars produce exhaust fumes, dramatically increasing the amount of carbon dioxide and other climate-changing fumes released into the atmosphere.

Once limited to the so-called developed countries, cars are now in increasing demand in developing countries such as India and China. This development will further increase the amount of atmospheric pollution and have an effect on the global climate. Recently a lot of research has been done in the field of hybrid and electric mobility.

Of course, the invention of the car has improved our lives in numerous ways by making transport and mobility easier and cheaper. The example of the car represents a simple model of how you should view technological developments: always consider their positive as well as negative potential. One such ambivalent area of current scientific research is genetic engineering.

Genetic engineering

Genetic engineering is being applied in different areas, such as reprogenetics, prenatal diagnostics, human and animal cloning and agriculture.

- After the discovery of DNA, scientists have succeeded in analysing animal and human DNA sequences and seek to establish how genes determine our bodily functions, appearance, etc. searching for causes of inherited diseases.
- positive effect: knowing about genetic reasons for certain defects can save people's lives, once cures and treatments have been developed
- ambivalent effects: Genetic engineering (i. e. altering animal or human DNA by implanting or changing specific genetic material) can be used to improve plants/animals/humans to be less prone to diseases, parasites, etc.; genetically modified food can be grown more intensively (i. e. starvation might be combatted more efficiently in developing countries), but it is largely unknown whether modified corn or other plants might also cause changes to our DNA or metabolism
- possible negative effects: natural plant variants can be contaminated with the new genetic material and become extinct; cloning and manipulating animal DNA might lead to similar effects; natural selection processes might be interfered with, thus humans might actually change evolutionary development; the eradication of unwanted DNA in humans might lead to the development of a new caste system of improved and unimproved humans; the latter might eventually no longer be able to find jobs or insurances willing to take them; disabled people will be excluded even more from society; natural evolutionary processes might be halted and/or altered completely

The effects of genetic engineering on our everyday lives might turn out to be more far-reaching and irreversible than we can imagine today. Consequently, there is an ongoing debate on whether everything that can be done should be done. Because new developments emerge so quickly, laws and regulations are often slow to follow, which is also a result of the complexity of these innovations. Consequently, many inventions have already been achieved before ethical questions and possible negative effects can be considered. Science is often ahead of people's ability to use the new technology sensibly.

Keyword

Cloning: the process by which an organism or a cell is copied. Cloning human beings is illegal in most forms and in most countries. However, research on it continues and the first clones of a species close to a human being, two monkeys, were reportedly born in China in 2018.

Visions of the Future

Humankind has always dreamed about the future and keeps seeking to create the world it wants to live in. People have always aimed at new challenges and tried out new ideas. In literature, these attempts have been formulated in utopias and dystopias, positive and negative visions of the future. Technological innovation has fuelled the creation of dystopian visions of societies, often in the form of a science fiction novel. Prominent examples are Huxley's *Brave New World*, Orwell's *Nineteen Eighty-Four* and Ishiguro's *Never Let Me Go*. However, broadly dystopian ideas are also present in popular fiction like *The Hunger Games* by the American novelist Suzanne Collins.
Meanwhile, some social movements are still actively seeking new and positive ways of living with each other, sharing space, goods and skills in community projects and living. In the aging societies of the West, this is proving very important. Increasingly, ideas like urban gardening might also change the city space to create a more liveable environment.

Mary Shelley, *Frankenstein* (eA)

A note on the author and the work

Mary Wollstonecraft Shelley (1797–1851) was the daughter of one of the first feminist activists, Mary Wollstonecraft, and the political philosopher William Godwin. Her father gave her a wide-ranging but somewhat informal education. At the age of 17, Mary eloped with the married poet Percy Bysshe Shelley to France, accompanied by her stepsister Claire. On her return to England, Mary was pregnant, but her daughter, born prematurely, died.
In summer 1816 the couple set out on a trip to Switzerland, with Claire and with two of Shelley's friends, staying near Lake Geneva. In 1818, they moved on to Italy. Two other children died, and only the couple's fourth child, a boy, survived. In 1822, Percy Shelley drowned in a storm off the Italian coast, and Mary returned to England. She remained true to her mother's ideas of feminism and to her father's political philosophy and always showed an open-minded attitude despite the hardships and setbacks she endured. The final decade of her life was full of writing and editing but also marked by illness. She died at the age of 53.
Mary Shelley started writing the story of Frankenstein and his unorthodox scientific experiment during a stay in Switzerland in the cold, wet summer of 1816. As a way of countering boredom, the party – Mary, Percy Shelley and two friends, one of them the poet Lord Byron – started a competition for the best horror story. Mary Shelley's figure, the scientist Victor Frankenstein, creates life out of stolen body parts. Then, terrified at what he has created, he leaves his "creature" alone to cope with its destiny. The being, which has no name and receives no moral education from its creator, turns violent and is finally hunted down by its creator. Mary's story won the competition. A striking piece of early science fiction, *Frankenstein* is a fine example of a dystopian Gothic novel. As such, it reproduces themes from the Romantic literature popular at the time.

The story addresses the potential of science to destroy rather than to support and sustain human beings. It was written at a time of rapid scientific progress and industrialisation. The novel asks the question: What happens if humans decide to play God? This question remains a poignant one today with advances in genetic engineering, artificial intelligence and nuclear science as well as robotics threatening traditional values and beliefs.
The full title of the novel is *Frankenstein; or, The Modern Prometheus*[1]. The story was first published anonymously in London in 1818, whereas the second edition from 1821 showed Shelley's name. Ever since the first publication of the novel, the name "Frankenstein" has often been used incorrectly to refer to the creation rather than its creator.

Plot and structure

Frame story by Captain Robert Walton

The novel has a frame story in the form of letters by Captain Robert Walton to his sister in which Walton tells her about an expedition to the North Pole, where he rescued Victor Frankenstein. Half frozen from having been out on the ice, Frankenstein sees that Walton shares the obsession that has almost destroyed him. He tells him the story of the creature he had pursued and that had been seen earlier by Walton's sailors.

Victor's story

Having grown up in Italy, Victor Frankenstein studies chemistry in Ingolstadt, Germany and is fascinated by the idea of alchemy. He is a fervent student and particularly interested in giving life to non-living matter. He collects body parts from local graveyards and assembles a seemingly well-chosen human body, forming a creature some 2.4 m in height. When the creature wakes, Victor discovers that it is ugly, has watery eyes, a deathly skin colour and visible muscles and blood vessels.
On his return from meeting his friend, Henry Clerval, the creature has disappeared. Victor falls seriously ill and only recovers because Henry nurses him. Four months later, Victor's father informs him of the murder of his brother William in Geneva. Near the crime scene Victor observes the creature and suspects that it is responsible for the deed. But he sees no way of telling the truth, hence William's nanny, Justine, is accused of the crime and hanged. Victor flees to the mountains. While he is hiking near Mont Blanc, the creature approaches and talks to him.

The creature's story

After his creation by Frankenstein, the creature turns to the wilderness. Noticing that people run away from him, he hides from them. But, living in the woods near a poor family's cottage, he develops positive feelings for them and secretly helps them. He learns their language and even teaches himself how to read from books he discovered in the forest. One day, he sees his reflection in the water and realises how hideous he

[1] Original title, today often shortened. In Greek mythology, Prometheus is the Titan god of fire, who creates humans by forming them from clay. He is also credited with bringing fire – a symbol for civilisation and technology – to humanity.

is and why humans have reacted to him with horror. He stays near the family, hoping to become friends with them, and enters their house when only the blind father is present. When the rest of the family returns, the son attacks him and he flees, enraged. Giving up hope of ever being accepted by human beings, he decides to find his creator in Geneva. He believes that Frankenstein will help him.
On his way, the creature saves a child from drowning, only to be shot at by the child's father, who misunderstands his harmless intentions. This event marks a turning point, making the creature swear revenge against humanity in general. On arriving in Geneva, the creature talks to Frankenstein and demands that he create a female companion for him because, as he argues, he has the same right to happiness as any other being in the world. He promises to disappear into the wilderness with his mate if Victor agrees. Otherwise, he will kill his remaining family and ruin Victor.

Frankenstein's story continued

Frankenstein reluctantly agrees to the creation of a second being and on the Orkney Islands starts to work on a female. But, fearing that she might be even more evil than his first creation and that together they might breed a new race, he destroys the unfinished creation at a moment when his first creature is looking though the window.
Falling asleep in his boat, Frankenstein is blown to Ireland, where he is arrested for the murder of his friend Clerval, who has been strangled by the creature. Frankenstein has a mental breakdown, is put into prison, proven innocent of the crime and released. Returning to Geneva with his father, where he plans to marry and to kill the creature, who, however, strangles his future bride. To revenge these deeds, Victor chases the creature through Europe into the arctic region of the North Pole. However, the creature always stays a step ahead. After collapsing, Victor floats towards Walton's ship and is rescued.

Captain Walton's conclusion

After Captain Walton's ship has been freed from pack ice, he decides to turn south. Frankenstein vows to go off by himself, despite his weak condition: he is determined that the creature must die, but before he can fulfil his pledge, he dies. In his last words, he makes Walton promise to kill the monster for him. The creature is seen on board the ship mourning over Victor's body: the death of his creator has not brought him peace, he says, and his crimes have made him more miserable than Frankenstein ever was. He tells Walton that he will kill himself so that no one need ever know of his existence. Walton watches the creature disappear for good, drifting away on an ice floe. It is never seen again.

Reception and analysis

Frankenstein's initial reception in 1818 on the one hand appreciated its craft and workmanship, praising its imagination and its inventive expression. On the other hand, critics dismissed the novel's subject matter as unethical and repulsive; that the author should be a woman, as it was later revealed, made matters even worse in some eyes. The story, however, proved very popular, particularly as a play, even prompting Shelley to revise the text in 1831, casting the scientist in a less favourable light. The story has also found its

way into innumerable films: the silent era already saw at least three screen adaptations, and the 1931 version with Boris Karloff in the role of the creature still stands out. Since the mid-1920s, the book is generally deemed a literary success and has received many – including feminist and psychoanalytical – readings. The horror of a creature without any kind of moral principle continues to fascinate us, and the idea that creators must assume responsibilities for their inventions remains topical even today.
In her novel, Shelley invokes supernatural elements, especially in association with the creation and life of Frankenstein's monster. The setting is isolated and eerie. The scenes of action (e.g. the Alps and the Arctic) reflect Romantic interests in the wild and undiscovered elements of nature. The deep exploration of human emotions is also new to literature, as is the attraction shown for characters that break traditional social boundaries. Following their lofty ideals and their own curiosity, they are driven into dangerous situations. Thus, at a time when the ideas of the Enlightenment and the ideal of scientific knowledge are becoming popular, the author warns against the obsessive pursuit of scientific knowledge. This was also a time when rationalism and order in the arts was being contested by thinkers like Percy Shelley, who stressed individual experience over objective principles.
The novel likewise contains a lot of symbolism, including darkness (standing for emptiness and despair), light (representing hope and learning) and fire, which both creates and destroys. Electricity, a discovery of the 1800s, promises new scientific possibilities. Galvanism – the stimulation of muscles through electrical current – is seen in the same way, but in her preface to the 1831 edition, Mary Shelley warns that scientific experiments can be taken too far.
This conflict between the opportunities and dangers of scientific discovery has endured to the present day, when Shelley's *Frankenstein* has been invoked to criticise scientific breakthroughs, with cloned animals rejected as "Frankensteinian" and genetically modified crops called "Frankenfoods" (a word coined in the early 2000s).

The Media

Keyword

The Media: a collective term that denotes means of mass communication, particularly referring to newspapers, radio, TV and the internet. Communication through these media is characterised by the fact that it is public, reaches a broad audience, is not bound to a particular place and time and that it is largely unilateral, i.e. the audience does not normally interact with the sender of the messages it has received.

In the following chapter diverse aspects of the media will be presented. The central issues are:

- various forms of the the media and their prime functions
- the concept of "media literacy"
- the role of the media in contemporary society
- advertising as an example of a text that makes an appeal to the reader.

Types of Media

Newspapers

- printed publications that appear regularly (most commonly daily or weekly) and that are issued in an inexpensive form, affordable for a broad audience
- normally cover a wide range of up-to-date topics from politics, economics and sport to culture and entertainment, also featuring a certain amount of advertising
- The first newspapers were published in the early 17th century.
- Due to the growing availability of information on the internet, however, the number of printed newspapers has been steadily decreasing.
- One can distinguish between the so-called **quality press**, i. e. newspapers in which well-researched information is offered at a high level of credibility (e. g. *The Times*, *The Guardian*) and the **tabloids** (Am. **yellow press**), in which sensational stories are combined with eye-catching headlines and images (e. g. *The Sun*, *The Daily Mirror*).

Radio

- invented in the late 19th century, originally referred to as "the wireless"
- from the 1920s onwards, more and more radio stations started broadcasting and radios became affordable for an ever growing audience
- "Golden Age" of radio: between the 1930s and the mid-1950s, when radio programmes included not only music, news and advertisements but also shows and radio plays
- with the advent of television, the popularity of the radio started to decline

TV

- first introduced to the general public in the late 1930s
- did not become widely available and popular until after World War II
- originally based on a limited number of state-owned broadcasting stations
- the number of private channels, funded either by advertising or by subscriptions, has increased in the last few decades
- most recently, streaming television has enjoyed a growing audience

Advertising

- Advertising is a vital financial aspect of all forms of the media.
- It is a form of communication that makes an appeal to the reader or viewer and as such tries to persuade her or him to carry out an action (to buy the advertised product or to use the advertised service).
- With the advent of the "new media" (primarily the internet), new advertising opportunities opened up for companies. Nowadays, online advertising – e. g. in the form of pop-ups, banners and advergames (free online games that advertise a certain product) – is a growing market, whereas the rate of advertising in the traditional media has been steadily declining.

[2] Original title, today often shortened. In Greek mythology, Prometheus is the Titan god of fire, who creates humans by forming them from clay. He is also credited with bringing fire – a symbol for civilisation and technology – to humanity.

- One way of describing the effects which a particular ad might have on the receiver is the **"AIDA"** principle: the ad should first catch **A**ttention, then arouse **I**nterest, create a **D**esire for the advertised product or service and finally lead to **A**ction, i. e. the purchase of that particular product.
- Advertising is often criticised for promoting ideal images of people, thereby putting consumers under psychological pressure by making them feel inadequate.

The internet

- term derives from the longer "interconnected networks"
- system of computer networks which enables users to publicise and access information on a global scale
- originally developed to allow some American universities to exchange data quickly
- was made accessible to a broad public and commercialised in the 1990s
- by 2021, the number of internet users worldwide had risen to 4.9 billion, i. e. 60 %, more than half the global population[3]
- in many areas, the internet is mostly accessed via mobile phone
- **advantages**, e. g.
  - makes it possible to communicate with people over long distances in real time, thereby turning the world into a **"global village"**
  - easy access to almost every kind of information imaginable
- **disadvantages**, e. g.
  - the **degree of credibility** of the information available is **not always clear**
  - the rate of **criminal activities** via the internet (from the violation of privacy to internet fraud) has been steadily rising
  - some countries try to suppress information that collides with their own ideologies, employing **censorship** (e. g. China)

The mass media fulfil a number of **functions**. Originally, its primary use was the transmission of **information** to the broadest possible audience, which made the media a vital means of **education**. Public **entertainment** soon came to be seen as equally **important**. With the advent and ever-growing popularity of online social networks such as Facebook, Instagram and Twitter, forging and maintaining **social relations** independently of time and place has also become a crucial function.

Keyword

Media literacy: This term refers to the ability of a recipient to analyse and evaluate the messages they receive through the media. Thus, one is expected to question the information one is given, e. g. by asking who is the actual creator/sender of the message, what is their aim in sending this message, how does the message try to catch my attention, what is the point of view presented in the message? Ultimately, media literacy is also vital in producing one's own messages.

[3] Source: https://www.statista.com/statistics/273018/number-of-internet-users-worldwide (accessed on 1 April 2022)

The Influence of the Media on Society and Personal Life

- Being **the prime source of information**, the media can influence a whole society's opinion about certain topics.
- With the help of more or less open forms of **censorship**, public opinion can be controlled; this was most famously fictionalised by George Orwell in his novel *Nineteen Eighty-Four*, in which a totalitarian regime represses its people by – amongst other means – **controlling** and **manipulating** the **information** communicated through the media.
- It is still being debated whether **images of violence** presented on **TV** and in **computer games** facilitate adolescent violence.
- In consumer societies, **advertisements** determine to a high degree what is considered to be a desirable lifestyle. This can be seen as a form of **indoctrination** and **social control**.

INFO "Fake news"

"Fake news" refers to false stories appearing as genuine news items on the internet or other media. It is usually created to influence political opinion or as a joke or provocation. Recently, fake news has been used to manipulate public opinion and even, it seems, to affect election results.

Keyword

Social Networking Services (SNS): Social networking services such as Facebook, Instagram and Twitter are online platforms that enable users to build or maintain social and business relationships via a wide variety of communication tools. Users usually create individual profiles and share experiences and opinions by posting texts, photos and videos. These virtual communities allow them to be connected regardless of where they live and across boundaries such as social status, profession, age and gender. Among the benefits of these platforms can be listed the strengthening of interpersonal relationships, increased freedom of self-expression and sense of belonging as well as simplifying grassroots organisation.
In the past few years, however, social networks, in particular Facebook, have come under increased scrutiny. Firstly, the business models of the companies are often based not only on selling advertising space but also their users' data for marketing purposes. In 2018, an investigation uncovered that the British firm Cambridge Analytica had illegally harvested the personal data of millions of Facebook users and resold it for political advertising, potentially even the Brexit vote and Donald Trump's 2016 presidential campaign. Facebook has also become the battleground for systematically disseminating misinformation, often used by lobbying groups and intelligence agencies to try and manipulate elections abroad. In September 2021, leaked documents revealed that Facebook Inc. (now Meta Platforms) was fully aware of the negative impact that its platforms had on the health of its teenage users as well as their product's propensity to help spread misinformation.

The Digital Revolution

While the Industrial Revolution changed the way people worked and lived together, the so-called Digital Revolution has done the same by digitalising large aspects of the formerly analogue world. This process started soon after WW II and increasingly accelerated from the moment when data storage facilities became smaller and smaller and when wireless technologies were introduced.
The year 2002 is generally seen as a turning point because since then more data has been stored in a digital than in an analogue way. It was the invention and spread of the internet that have made this process possible. Today, more than half the world's population is continuously online, thanks to the usage of computers and smartphones. This interconnectivity means that everyone who is connected to the internet has the world's information at their fingertips and can communicate worldwide.
The notion of privacy will have to be closely monitored, as more and more people give personal data to a few big companies such as Apple, Google or Amazon. Physically tracking or locating a person has become easy, as smartphones continuously show their position through GPS and wireless technologies.
Digitisation has entered all areas of life: communication, homes, banking, work and industry. The Internet of Things (IoT) – as found in a smart home – means that objects and machines are online and have hardware with sensors that interconnect them and communicate autonomously – i.e. without human interference. The IoT is not without hazards, so far as privacy, data storage and security are concerned. In fact, cybersecurity is an increasingly important issue. People have made themselves dependent on the exchange and storage of data, and hacking into data systems, whether personal, corporate or governmental, has become a real threat to modern society.

Glossary – Science and Technology

genetic engineering	Gentechnik, -manipulation
fossil fuels	fossile (endliche) Brennstoffe (z. B. Öl)
renewable energy non-renewable energy	regenerative (erneuerbare) Energien nicht erneuerbare Energien (Öl, Kohle, Gas)
carbon dioxide (CO_2)	Kohlendioxid
methane	Methan
(exhaust) fumes	Abgase
to contaminate	etw. vergiften, verseuchen
fuel rod	Brennstab (im Kernkraftwerk)
half-life	Halbwertzeit (die Zeit, die es dauert, bis ein radioaktives Material die Hälfte seiner Strahlkraft einbüßt; bis zu mehreren Mio. Jahren)
power station, power plant	Kraftwerk
global warming	globale Erwärmung

climate change	Klimawandel
to have an adverse effect	eine nachteilige Wirkung auf etwas haben
to emit, emission	ausstoßen/emittieren, Ausstoß/Abstrahlung
water supply	Wasserversorgung
drought	Dürreperiode
flooding	Überflutung
soil	Boden, Erde
landfill	Mülldeponie
deforestation	Waldrodung
oil spillage/spill/pollution	Ölverschmutzung/-pest
incineration	Verbrennung
to evaporate, evaporation	verdunsten, Verdunstung
precipitation	Niederschlag
greenhouse effect	Treibhauseffekt
(radioactive, chemical, ...) waste	(radioaktiver, chemischer, ...) Abfall
to reprocess something	etwas wiederaufbereiten
raw materials, natural resources	Rohstoffe, natürliche Rohstoffe
energy-efficient	Energie sparend
subsidise	subventionieren
biodegradable	biologisch abbaubar

Glossary – The Media

primary function	Hauptfunktion
public	öffentlich/Öffentlichkeit
unilateral	einseitig
advent	Aufkommen
spread	Ausbreitung
access	Zugang/Zugriff
credibility	Glaubwürdigkeit
censorship	(politische) Zensur
internet fraud	Internetbetrug
literacy	Lese- und Schreibfähigkeit
indoctrination	Indoktrination / ideologische Beeinflussung
inclination	Bereitschaft

William Shakespeare (erhöhtes Anforderungsniveau)

The World that Made Him: The Elizabethan Age

Keyword
The Elizabethan Age: named after Queen Elizabeth I, born 1533, crowned 1558, died 1603 (reign of 45 years)

Politics and Economics

- England emerged as a world power; exploration of New World (Drake, Raleigh)
- international trade → the rise of capitalism
- strongest naval force (defeat of the Spanish Armada in 1588)
- internal problems: constant clash between Catholics and Protestants
- establishment of a Protestant Church with Elizabeth as head of the Church of England

Culture

Keyword
The Golden Age: term used for the Renaissance in Britain at the time of Elizabeth I
- freedom of spirit → imagination
- Greek and Roman thought
- domestic study of the Bible, widely read and heard
- opened new worlds of history and poetry, stimulated English culture
- cultural flowering: theatre, music, poetry, art, architecture
- writers: William Shakespeare, Christopher Marlowe, Edmund Spenser
- architect: Inigo Jones (introduced Italianate architecture to England)
- composers: Thomas Tallis, William Byrd

The era was dominated by contrast: life for ordinary people could be hard, but economic growth also meant better conditions for many.
negative aspects:
- harsh criminal laws (e. g. whipping and hanging for minor offences)
- illiteracy
- short life-expectancy
- no rights for women

positive aspects:
- public provision for the poor (possible because of economic growth)
- few beggars

The Elizabethan World Picture

Elizabethans still saw the Earth as the centre of the universe (geocentric world view) and therefore as the nucleus around which everything else revolved.
The guiding principle of this world view was universal order, which formed two ideas that crucially shaped Elizabethan society and thought: the **Great Chain of Being** and the **correspondence of microcosm and macrocosm**. Their world view was this a fixed and highly constructed one, deeply rooted in Christianity and concepts such as divine providence.

God

Angels

Man
(existence, life, feeling and understanding)

higher animals
(having touch, memory, movement and hearing)

animals like ants
(having touch, memory and movement)

animals like shellfish
(having touch)

} sensitive class (existence, life, feeling)

plants
(existence and life; vegetable class)

elements, liquids, metals
(mere existence; inanimate class)

The Great Chain of Being

To Elizabethans, everything that existed was organised in a cosmic order. In this system, everything and everyone has a designated place, as if on a very large ladder: the Great Chain of Being. This hierarchy was based on importance, which in turn was determined by the relative proportion of spirit and matter: the more spirit something or someone had, the higher was its/their place in the chain. At the top of this system sat God, followed by angels, humans, animals, plants and minerals. Each part of the chain was in turn hierarchically structured from most to least important. Each link also had a 'primate' - in the human chain, for instance, this was the king. Being higher in the chain meant natural or God-given authority to rule over those beneath one's position.
As long as all the elements stay in their designated place, the hierarchy and therefore the order of being remain intact. However, if this order is disturbed, the chain is broken

and chaos reigns. The attempt to changing one's place on the chain is therefore doomed. Romeo and Juliet, the "pair of star-cross'd lovers" (Prologue), are such a case. The couple falls in love across social boundaries and is bound to fail. Therefore, any attack on the balance has to be rectified - as in a disease of the body - to restore the original balance of the universe.

The corresponding planes

Different segments of the chain are reflected in other segments. This means there is universal interdependence, i. e. there are correspondences.

Corresponding planes

- divine and angelic
- universe (macrocosm)
- commonwealth / body politic
- man (microcosm)
- lower creation (animals, plants, ...)

The planes were connected by an immense network of correspondences.

> **Keyword**
> **Correspondences:** Since the planes were interconnected with each other, order and disorder in one plane had the same repercussions in the other planes as well. For instance, the sun governs the other planets as the father rules his children. Elizabethan literature abounds with examples of this idea: for example, King Lear's madness is mirrored in the thunderstorm he walks in, and on the night Macbeth murders the king, horses are seen eating one another. In the same sense, debates between king and council in the body politic are mirrored in the microcosm as commotions in a person's mind.

Elements and humours

Since the human being was seen as a microcosm (literally, a "little world"; cf. John Donne: "I am a little world made cunningly / Of elements"), it reflected the structure of the world as a whole, the macrocosm. The world was composed of four "elements" (earth, water, air, fire), the qualities of which were based on the notions of hot and cold, dry and moist.
Correspondingly, the human body was composed of four substances called "humours", with characteristics corresponding to the four elements. Imbalance among the humours, i. e. when they did not exist in proper proportion to each other, caused illness.

element	humour	common quality
earth	melancholy	cold and dry
water	phlegm	cold and moist
air	blood	hot and moist
fire	choler	hot and dry

Elizabethan Theatre

Theatres in Elizabethan London were venues of mass entertainment.

Performing Shakespeare

Like most companies, Shakespeare and his men performed in theatres situated outside the City of London, on the Southern banks of the River Thames. The quarter was known for its many pubs and brothels. Theatres also acted as venues for bear-baiting, a brutal entertainment popular with Elizabethan in which a bear is tied to a stake and killed by dogs.

Because audiences, who were allowed to smoke, drink and eat in the theatre, were often rowdy, this entertainment was frowned upon by religious people as well as those in power. Common complaints included the accusation that

- the theatre was disorderly,
- the immoral characters on stage corrupted the audience, particularly young people,
- the stories told were depraved and primitive instead of religiously inspiring,
- it kept people away from work and prayer,
- it attracted criminals, for example pickpockets.

After touring through different locations like the Rose Theatre, Shakespeare had his own playhouse built in 1599, the *Globe Theatre*. It is a round, wooden structure with the stage protruding into the audience. Performances were held in the middle of the day, as the Globe had no artificial lighting. Elizabethan theatre also used very few props; instead, actors created the setting by describing it ("word scenery"). They did, however, wear highly elaborate costumes to embellish the characters they were portraying. Women were not allowed on stage, as it was deemed inappropriate for them by the fiercely religious government. Instead, their roles were acted by young men. This fact was frequently exploited by Shakespeare in comedies such as *Twelfth Night,* in which a man played a woman disguising herself as a man.
The Elizabethan theatre was attended by people from all social ranks: Poorer people stood in the space right in front of the stage ("pit"), while those who could afford it took a seat in the circle around the stage. The distance between the actors and the audience was minimal and spectators often interacted with the actors on stage. This had a strong influence on how Shakespeare wrote his plays as there are comic scenes that are purely written to entertain the masses as well as monologues by the protagonists explaining their thoughts and decisions.

Elizabethan Poetry
Sonnets

Keyword
Sonnet form: originally from Italy, 14th century
Sonnets were made popular by Francesco Petrarca (in English: Petrarch).
The fashion of sonnet writing spread to France and England.

Important Elizabethan sonnet writers:
- Thomas Wyatt (introduced sonnets to England, translations from Petrarch)
- Sir Philipp Sidney
- Edmund Spenser
- John Donne
- William Shakespeare

The Italian (Petrarchan) sonnet

	rhyme scheme	
octave/octet	a b b a	quatrain
	a b b a	quatrain
turn		turn
sestet	c d e	tercet
	c d e	tercet

Characteristics of the sonnet
- addressed to a beloved
- 14 lines
- clearly defined rhyme scheme (the most common is given above)
- divided into an octet and a sestet
- turn after the octave

The turn after the octave is a shift in thought or feeling, often indicated by "but" or "yet".

Variations in the rhyme scheme within the conventional structure are justified by the function they serve.

The English (Shakespearean) sonnet

	rhyme scheme	
octave/octet	a	quatrain
	b	
	a	
	b	
	c	quatrain
	d	
	c	
	d	
turn		
sestet	e	quatrain
	f	
	e	
	f	
		turn
	g	couplet
	g	

The turn in the English sonnet occurs after the third quatrain. Ideally there should be "three turns of the screw" in the three quatrains, before the point is driven home in the couplet. The couplet therefore offers a conclusion or a summary. However, one should still be aware that there can be the traditional turn after the octave.

Shakespeare's sonnets

- Shakespeare wrote 154 sonnets.
- Sonnets 1 to 126 are addressed to a young man.
- Sonnets 127 to 154 are addressed to a "dark lady".

Main themes: love, beauty, transience, old age, death

The **basic metre** is iambic pentameter, but Shakespeare does not use it slavishly. Metre is used functionally, e.g.
- regular metre: harmony, peace, tranquillity, balance, stability, etc.
- irregular metre: disharmony, confusion, parody

Shakespeare's Plays

The universal appeal

By 1592 William Shakespeare had managed to establish his reputation as a playwright in London. Due to his success, other writers envied him enormously.
A remarkable feature of Shakespeare's time is the complete lack of what we know today as copyright regulations. Authors could not protect their work from being adapted freely or even copied as a whole. Shakespeare himself was engaged in this process of "play-doctoring", modifying existing plays for his acting company. As a consequence, his authorship of a number of plays has been questioned.
From about 1595, however, Shakespeare no longer cooperated with other authors and became the respected playwright with the reputation he has had until today.
The fascination of his plays has not been lost over the more than four centuries since their first appearance. It can at least partly be attributed to the universal appeal of the topics he deals with. Love, happiness, envy, jealousy, treachery, humour – all of these profoundly human emotions and forms of behaviour enter easily into every spectator's heart.
Unfortunately, the dating of the plays, and therefore the order in which they were written, is difficult to determine. Shakespeare did not issue a printed collection of his dramatic works since no copyright existed. *Richard II*, however, appeared in six printed editions from 1597 to 1623, and *Romeo and Juliet* had five printed editions in the same time span. If all the plays had been printed and published in Shakespeare's lifetime, they would have been used by countless actors and authors. As a result, only an approximate order can be suggested. Shakespeare's opus can thus be broadly divided into four periods:

Timeline

Period 1 (1590–1595): The first period is clearly the one that least shows Shakespeare's literary genius. The style and imagery of the plays are rather simple. Although he does use rhyme, there is also a lot of prose. It is a time of experimentation with the genre.

Period 2 (1595–1600): During this period, which is marked by improved characterisation and style, Shakespeare wrote some of his best comedies and history plays, among which are *Henry IV* and *Henry V*. He also wrote his sonnets during this period.

Period 3 (1600–1608): Many scholars consider this to be the most important period. Shakespeare wrote great tragedies like *Hamlet* and the so-called "problem plays"/"bitter comedies".

Period 4 (1608–1613): In this period Shakespeare wrote his romances, which deal with the topic of losing and regaining happiness. The plots are rather melodramatic, but they also display an idyllic atmosphere. Shakespeare's last play was *The Tempest*.

Period	Comedies	Tragedies	History plays
1590–1595	*The Comedy of Errors* *The Taming of the Shrew* *Two Gentlemen of Verona* *Love's Labour's Lost*	*Titus Andronicus*	*Henry VI*
1595–1600	*A Midsummer Night's Dream* *The Merchant of Venice* *The Merry Wives of Windsor* *Much Ado About Nothing* *As You Like It* *Twelfth Night*	*Romeo and Juliet*	*King John* *Richard II* *Henry IV* *Henry V*
1600–1608	*Troilus and Cressida* *Measure for Measure* *All's Well That Ends Well*	*Julius Caesar* *Hamlet* *Othello* *Timon of Athens* *King Lear* *Macbeth* *Antony and Cleopatra* *Coriolanus*	
1608–1613	*Pericles* *Cymbeline* *A Winter's Tale* *The Tempest*		*Henry VIII*

Source: Wilhelm Rotter and Hermann Bendl, *Your Companion to English Literary Texts.* München: Manz, 1991. S. 182 ff. (gekürzt)

Shakespeare's language

The language Shakespeare used is not easy to understand because it differs from the English spoken today. Some words have changed their meaning since the Elizabethan Age, others have been dropped altogether and certain grammatical peculiarities need to be explained. We must also keep in mind that the lines Shakespeare makes his characters speak were intended to be performed on stage. In order to achieve a combined dramatic and artistic effect, he frequently employed blank verse, which is a fixed rhythmical pattern of iambic pentameters, as in this example from *Macbeth:*

Tomórrow ánd tomórrow ánd tomórrow

Especially for the less serious or comic characters, however, Shakespeare used prose, whereas verse is spoken by the noble ones.
Shakespeare's impact on the English language has been immense. He coined more than 500 neologisms (new words), and his works are still appreciated worldwide as

examples of true linguistic genius. It should be kept in mind, though, that Shakespeare never intended his plays to be read as books; they were to be performed on stage. This is where the beauty of their language is most evident.
The following table lists some examples of characteristic vocabulary and grammar used in Shakespeare's plays:

Shakespeare	**Modern English**
thou	you (used for children, subordinates, ordinary people and friends; Juliet in *Romeo and Juliet*, however, addresses Romeo as "you".)
ye, you	you (plural); form showing respect
thee	you (object form)
thy/thine	your (determiner) / your (determiner before vowels)
mine	my (determiner) before vowels
doth	does
hath	has
thou canst	you can
thou wilt	you will
I have writ	I have written
I would	I wish
Why call you ...?	Why do you call ...?
The guests are come.	The guests have come.

Hamlet (eA)

William Shakespeare is believed to have written *The Tragedy of Hamlet, Prince of Denmark,* usually abbreviated to *Hamlet,* sometime between 1599 and 1601. It is one of his plays that has known continuous success, the tragic role of the Prince of Denmark being interpreted and adapted in countless ways to this day. Even during Shakespeare's own time, the tragedy proved highly popular and was performed regularly.

Questions of morality: 'divine order' vs 'human order'

Perhaps it is the key issue at the centre of *Hamlet,* namely the **place of the individual within a divine and social order**, that echoes through the ages. Informed about his father's – the king's – murder in rather dubious circumstances, Hamlet is not only forced to verify the allegation against Claudius, his uncle, without raising suspicion, but also to make the crucial choice of whether to avenge his father. In order to find out the truth, Hamlet simulates madness and has actors put up the murder as a play. However, having assured himself, he is stalled by the question of whether it is right to kill Claudius.
It is this ethical question that takes centre stage for most of the play. Unlike a medieval morality play, *Hamlet* does not impose an idea of right and wrong on the audience but leaves the matter open to debate. It lays bare the prince's conscience, verbalising his

thoughts, fears and resolutions, particularly in the soliloquies, thus involving its spectators in his dilemma. Hamlet effectively becomes a **play of inaction** as its protagonist fails to make a choice since, as he points out to Rosencrantz and Guildenstern, "there is nothing either good or bad, but thinking makes it so" (II, ii). Accordingly, Hamlet's only notable actions either occur off-stage – fighting the pirates – or are forced upon him in death, namely killing Claudius and avenging his father.

Hamlet was conceived during a time of **significant political chaos**. The Wars of the Roses, a bloody conflict of two families fighting over the throne, had been settled little more than a decade ago, and the monarch's – particularly a female one's – position was uncertain. In addition, religious tensions were bound up with the ruler's beliefs, often costing lives and livelihoods. Accordingly, intrigue and suspicion prospered at the royal court of Queen Elizabeth. This is duly mirrored in the play, in which – with the exception of Hamlet's and Horatio's friendship – all relationships are at least to some degree strategic alliances. For instance, Claudius uses Rosencrantz and Guildenstern to try and find out whether Hamlet knows anything about the murder. This paranoid atmosphere is also the reason why Hamlet cannot discuss his suspicions about his father's death and which forces him to pretend madness.

However, it is not only fear for his own life that lets Hamlet hesitate. He is also very aware that he is putting **private interests before public ones** in seeking revenge. This is a fatal flaw in various Shakespearean protagonists (e. g. Macbeth and Lear) and was a very real threat in the eyes of the Elizabethan public. As prince, Hamlet primarily has to fulfil a role that ensures the continuation of power and the state. He is not free to speak his mind or to fall in love with a woman of his choice, as is expressed by Laertes when he warns Ophelia that Hamlet's "will is not his own [...], for on his choice depends / The safety and health of this whole state" (I, iii). This warning gives the audience an insight into Hamlet's situation in terms of the political restrictions on his personal affairs. It also establishes Ophelia's position in society. She is considered too 'common' for marriage into the royal family, so the state (in this context, the king) must forbid this marriage for the greater good of the country. Both lovers' free will is restricted by their birth, and it is little wonder that Hamlet regards the court as a "prison" (II, ii).

Like everyone else, Hamlet is thus bound to his social rank as well as his place in the **Great Chain of Being**. He knows that acting out of personal motivation and killing his uncle in revenge would lead to chaos: Claudius is, after all, the king, a position that usually carried God's grace with it. Hamlet's revenge plot therefore threatens not only human order but also the divine plan.

Finally, *Hamlet* also asks of its audience the troubling question of who is **the better monarch**: a rightful one or one that is able to govern. On the one hand, Elizabethans' various ideas of divine order favoured a hereditary succession to the throne – i. e. usually of the deceased monarch's oldest son. On the other hand, the nation had seen a large number of conflicts arise out of this rule. Hence, British scholars of the time frequently discussed the book *The Prince* by the Italian historian Niccolò Machiavelli, which favoured a monarch that governed by force and, if necessary, by dishonest and immoral means in order to provide stability. These two conflicting ideas are obvious over the course of the play. While Hamlet's indecision and melancholy mark him out to be clearly unfit for kingship, Claudius remains an unsympathetic character throughout the play. Moreover, while the ending nominally restores order to the Danish kingdom, in Fortinbras, they effectively crown the enemy.

"Get thee to a nunnery!": the role of women in Hamlet

Despite having a female monarch, Elizabethan society was highly **patriarchal**: women were largely dependent on men and usually confined to the house as well as to providing a number of children to their husbands. They were also subjected to a very strict behavioural code, as is made obvious by the lengthy double sermon of both Laertes and Polonius in Act 1, Scene 3. Delivered in the shape of brotherly love on the one and fatherly wisdom and unshakeable assurance on the other hand, these rules enforce silence and repress female sexuality. The latter point is starkly illustrated by Hamlet demanding of his mother Gertrude that she subdue her libido (cf. III, iv). Likewise, his joke in the play-within-the-play scene, referring to the female genitalia as "[n]othing" (III, ii) – indeed a common synonym in Shakespeare's time –, reveals the usual position of women in Elizabethan society: silenced, belittled and best not seen at all.

Ophelia therefore cannot have a will of her own but is determined by where she comes from and by her **predetermined role** in society, especially by her gender. Her earlier scene with her brother (I, iii) depicts her as a rather independent, witty person. However, she is put under so much pressure and her emotions are manipulated from so many directions that she eventually descends into madness.

While it can be argued that both Ophelia's and Hamlet's madness – pretended or not – mainly served as a spectacle and humorous relief to the Elizabethan audience, their conditions are fundamentally different. To the people of Shakespeare's time, Ophelia suffered from pathological **hysteria**, regarded as a typical 'female' illness, that ultimately causes her to lose her mind and makes her speak nonsense. Hamlet, on the other hand, is affected by **melancholy**, a fashionable condition in Renaissance England, particularly among intellectuals and men of high standing. Furthermore, his words are not merely nonsense but often constitute witty wordplay, leading Polonius to observe that if "this be madness yet there is method in't" (II, ii).

Modern Adaptations

Shakespeare's works have often reached the cinema or TV screen. One has to differentiate here between straight versions and modern adaptations. Concerning storyline, characters and setting, a straight version keeps close to the original by adopting the text and usually historical costumes and stage set as well. Moreover, the characters keep their original names.

An adaptation – generally also in some way or other a modernisation of the play – is typically based on the original but may present storyline, characters and setting in a different manner. It may be put in a contemporary setting or an historical setting later than Shakespeare's time – e g. Richard Loncraine's 1995 version of *Richard III* or Julie Taymor's 1999 film *Titus*, with their references to recent European fascism. Likewise, the characters can be transplanted into different social or ethnic groups (as in the 1948 musical *Kiss Me, Kate* or in Baz Luhrmann's 1996 Californian *Romeo & Juliet*). Such modernisations often also aim at developing a market for a potential audience that might be attracted by the lightness of a musical version or an animated cartoon such as *The Lion King* (1994/2019), a loose adaptation of the Hamlet story. In such modern presentations the original poetic language, with its distinct metric scheme, is either not adopted at all or strongly abridged.

The catalogue of *Hamlet* versions currently runs to about 50 films. They range from very close straight versions to more or less loose adaptations that only adhere to the rough storyline. The first theatrical release of the story was in 1948, in which Laurence Olivier directed and also starred as the prince. The black-and-white film won four Oscars and is iconic to this day, even if it cut out political aspects of the play in favour of psychological ones. Franco Zeffirelli deliberately cast action star Mel Gibson in the titular role for his 1990 version, focussing less on the contemplative nature of the play and more on its action. In 1996, Kenneth Branagh attempted a definitive version of *Hamlet*, again both as director and actor. His film does not cut a single line from the text and thus runs to four hours, even portraying scenes that only occur offstage in the text. Set in the 19th century, the movie uses a vibrant, exquisite setting and an all-star cast. Although it proved a failure at the box office, critics regard the film as one of the best Shakespeare adaptations of all time. Finally, Michael Almereyda's version (2000) may be the most accessible to modern audiences. It translates the setting into the big-city "Denmark Corporation" and stars Ethan Hawke as the prince, who delivers his "To be or not to be" monologue in a video rental shop while cardboard signs scream "Action" at him.

Methoden der Textarbeit

Anforderungen von Aufgaben mit Textbezug

Alle im Abitur gestellten Aufgaben sind textbasiert. Sie können auch Bildmaterialien sowie audio-visuelle Materialien umfassen, auf die sprachlich reagiert werden muss. Zu den typischen Aufgabenformaten, die bei fiktionalen sowie nicht-fiktionalen Textvorlagen im freischriftlichen Teil gestellt werden, zählen die Zusammenfassung, die Analyse und der Kommentar bzw. kreative Aufgaben, die unterschiedlich ausgeprägt sein können (vgl. Hinweise zu den Operatoren, S. 102 f.). Neben diesen freischriftlichen Aufgaben werden auch neue Aufgabentypen zur Mediation vorkommen, die im Einleitungskapitel bereits thematisiert wurden. An dieser Stelle erhalten Sie Hinweise zu den üblichen schriftlichen Aufgaben, die weiterhin Teil der Abiturprüfung sind.

Aufgabenarten und Anforderungsbereiche

Aufgabenart	Anforderungsbereich
u. a. *summary* Operatoren: *describe, outline, state, summarise*	**I – comprehension, orientation, context** – Wiedergabe der zentralen Aussagen eines Textes – ggf. auch Einordnung des Textes in einen bekannten Kontext, aber üblicherweise ist die Aufgabe rein auf Basis des Ausgangstextes zu beantworten
u. a. *analysis* Operatoren: *analyse, examine, compare, explain, contrast*	**II – analysis** – Anwendung von Fachmethoden: textanalytische Verfahren, exakte Arbeit am sprachlichen Detail, Belegen und Zitieren, problemlösende Argumentation – gezielte Anwendung von Kenntnissen und Wissen – z. B. soziokulturelles Wissen oder Wissen über Sprache
u. a. *comment* Operatoren: *comment, discuss, justify, evaluate* ——— u. a. *write* Operatoren: *write, imagine, continue, find*	**III – comment, evaluation, re-creation of text, creativity** für die analytisch-interpretierende Aufgabenstellung: – Bewertung der Textvorlage auf Basis der vorher gewonnenen Erkenntnisse, Einordnung des Textes in einen größeren Zusammenhang – persönliche Stellungnahme, eigene Meinung für die produktionsorientierte/kreative Aufgabenstellung: – Umsetzung, Bewertung, Reflexion der Problematik des Ausgangstextes bzw. der Analyse in einem kreativen Kontext: z. B. Perspektivwechsel (Sicht einer Figur) – Füllen von Leerstellen (Weitererzählen, neues Ende) – Textsortenwechsel (Brief an Protagonisten, Leserbrief, Brief an *agony aunt*, Tagebucheintrag, Dialog usw.)

Die Bedeutung der Operatoren[1]

Für die Formulierung der Aufgaben gibt es klare Vorgaben. Verben für die Arbeitsanweisungen (= Operatoren) müssen in ihrer exakten Bedeutung verstanden werden. Eine ungefähre Ahnung, was gefordert ist, reicht keinesfalls aus. Die folgende Operatorenübersicht ist der Website des Ministeriums entnommen. Die mittlere Spalte definiert die genaue Wortbedeutung der Anweisung, die dritte Spalte gibt jeweils ein Beispiel für eine mögliche Aufgabenstellung.

Operatoren	Definitionen	Beispiele
	(schwerpunktmäßig) Anforderungsbereich I	
describe	give a detailed account of something	Describe the soldier's appearance. Describe the situation ...
outline	give the main features or the general principles of a text/topic, omitting minor details	Outline the author's views on love, marriage and divorce and point out how ...
state	specify clearly	State briefly the main developments in the family described in the text.
summarise, write a summary	give a concise account of the main points	Summarise the information given in the text about the hazards of cloning.
	(schwerpunktmäßig) Anforderungsbereich II	
analyse, examine	describe and explore in detail certain aspects and/or features of the text and how they are presented	Analyse the views on class held by the two protagonists. Examine the author's use of language ... Examine how the author characterises ...
compare	show similarities and differences	Compare the attitude of the two characters towards war.
explain	show causes and effects in a given context	Explain the protagonist's obsession with money. Explain XYZ's attitude towards ...
contrast	emphasise the differences between two or more things	Contrast the author's idea of human aggression with the theories of aggression you have read about.

[1] Quelle: https://www.nibis.de/uploads/mk-bolhoefer/2021/EN_2021Abi_Operatoren.pdf (verändert)

(schwerpunktmäßig) Anforderungsbereich III		
comment	state clearly your opinion on the topic in question and support your views with evidence	Comment on the suggestion made in the text that a "lack of women in the armed forces demonstrates a weakness in the role of women in society".
discuss	investigate by giving reasons for and against	Discuss the implications of globalisation as presented in this text.
justify	present reasons for decisions, positions or conclusions	You are the head boy / head girl of your school. Justify a decision taken by the pupils' council when you meet with your headmaster.
assess/ evaluate	consider in a balanced way points for and against something	Evaluate the author's view of the impact of the American Dream ... Assess the importance of standards in education.

Kreative Aufgaben

Der **Anforderungsbereich III umfasst auch kreative Aufgaben**, für die jedoch keine allgemein verbindlichen Operatoren formuliert werden können. Folgende Aufgabenstellungen sind möglich:

- Write a letter, email to a friend / to the the editor / of complaint / of enquiry ... .
- Write a dialogue / the dialogue between X and Y / a script (film, play ...) based on / XYZ's diary entry ... .
- Write an article (for ...) / a report (for ...).
- Continue the story ... / Find a suitable ending ... / Imagine you are XYZ. Continue/Tell the story ... from her/his point of view ... .

TIPP zum Punktesammeln

Befassen Sie sich intensiv mit den Operatoren. Nur wenn Sie genau wissen, was in der Aufgabenstellung gefordert ist, können Sie eine gute Lösung schreiben.

Grundlegende Hinweise zu den Aufgaben: *summary, analysis, comment*

Summary

- Hier soll gezeigt werden, dass der **Textinhalt** verstanden wurde.
- Aus diesem Grund ist es entscheidend, sich von der Textvorlage zu lösen und in eigenen Worten die Hauptinhalte wiederzugeben; das heißt auch, dass weder Passagen übernommen noch Zitate integriert werden dürfen.

- Sprachlich ist Folgendes zu beachten: Bei Zusammenfassungen von **fiktionalen Texten** ist durchgehend das **Präsens** zu verwenden (bei Vorzeitigkeit kann vereinzelt das *present perfect*, bei Nachzeitigkeit das *will future* eingesetzt werden, auf keinen Fall aber eine Vergangenheitsform).
- Bei **nicht-fiktionalen Texten** (z. B. Zeitungsartikel) sind die Hauptaussagen des Autors ebenfalls im Präsens wiederzugeben; nur in Einzelfällen ist es zulässig, für Ereignisse, die in der Vergangenheit tatsächlich stattgefunden haben, das *past tense* zu verwenden.
- **Autorenbezug herstellen:** Besonders bei **nicht-fiktionalen Texten** ist es wichtig, immer klarzustellen, wer welche Aussagen trifft (vor allem bei Zeitungsartikeln, in denen verschiedene Meinungen wiedergegeben werden).
- Je nach Operator kann eine pointierte oder umfassende Zusammenfassung verlangt werden (vgl. Operatoren, S. 102 f.).

Analysis

- Inhaltlich soll hier gezeigt werden, inwiefern die **Form des Textes** dessen Inhalt, Aussageabsicht oder die Haltung des Autors beeinflusst.
- Hier wird verlangt, dass die sprachliche Form des Textes genauer untersucht wird (z. B. im Hinblick auf Sprachebenen, stilistische Mittel, Erzählhaltung etc.) und dass daraus Rückschlüsse auf den Textinhalt bzw. dessen Wirkung gezogen werden; auch hier wird der Text im Präsens verfasst.
- Für eine sprachliche Analyse genügt es nicht, lediglich Stilmittel zu identifizieren und aufzulisten; es kommt vor allem darauf an, deren Wirkungsabsicht zu erkennen.
- Typische Analyseaspekte sind bei **fiktionalen Texten**: *point of view, character analysis, analysis of atmosphere/setting, analysis of tone,* usw.
- Typische Analyseaspekte bei **nicht-fiktionalen Texten** sind: *the use of language/structure, the intention or attitude of the author, the intended effect on the audience (i. e. in speeches), the use of language to achieve the text's aim (e. g. to convince, to provoke, to educate, etc.),* usw.
- **Autorenbezug herstellen:** Es ist sinnvoll klarzustellen, welche Aussageabsicht dem Autor oder dem Erzähler oder einer der Figuren zuzuordnen ist und welche Wirkungsabsicht damit verfolgt wird.

Comment (Evaluation)

- Inhaltlich soll hier gezeigt werden, dass der Textinhalt reflektiert werden kann.
- Diese kritische Auseinandersetzung mit dem Text kann in unterschiedlicher Form gefordert werden:
  - persönlicher *comment*: Hier wird eine persönliche Stellungnahme zum Material verlangt, die fachlich-argumentativ begründet sein muss und in der Regel auch Hintergrundwissen erfordert; das reine Feststellen der eigenen Meinung reicht nicht; sie muss erläutert werden und fundiert sein.
  - argumentativer *comment*: Hier wird in der Regel eine sachlich-distanzierte Gegenüberstellung von Vor- und Nachteilen bzw. Pro- und Kontra-Argumenten verlangt, die in einem abwägenden und schlüssigen Fazit enden muss.

- *comment* aus der Sicht einer anderen Person: Unter Umständen ist gefordert, dass Sie sich in die Situation einer Figur des Textes oder einer anderen Person versetzen, um aus deren Vorstellung heraus den Inhalt zu kommentieren; hier kann es sinnvoll sein, auch die Sprache / den Ausdruck dieser Figur zu übernehmen, um den Kommentar authentischer wirken zu lassen (insbesondere bei kreativen Aufgaben wird diese Form häufig verlangt).

Hinweise zu kreativen Aufgaben

Typische Formen

- formeller oder persönlicher Brief, E-Mail
- Tagebucheintrag, *blog entry, interior monologue*
- eine Geschichte erzählen (ein Ende für einen Text verfassen, eine Geschichte zu einem Bild erfinden, die Erzählperspektive wechseln etc.)
- einen Artikel schreiben, einen Leserbrief verfassen
- einen Dialog zwischen zwei Figuren eines fiktionalen Textes entwickeln etc.

Wichtige Aspekte für die Bearbeitung

- Zentral ist, dass Sie auf das Material eingehen und dieses einbeziehen. Unabhängig davon, welche Art von kreativer Produktion verlangt wird, sollte der Ausgangstext oder das Ausgangsbild nie aus den Augen verloren werden.
- Der selbst produzierte Text muss den formalen Anforderungen entsprechen (z. B.: Adresszeile, Anrede, ggf. Betreff, Datum, Abschlussformel bei Briefen) und muss als Brief, E-Mail, Zeitungsartikel o. Ä. klar erkennbar sein.
- Sprachlich sollte der Text den Ton der Vorlage bzw. der Figur treffen: Ein Brief aus der Sicht eines Kindes kann nicht in stilistisch gehobenem Englisch verfasst werden, ein Brief an einen Redakteur nicht mit Umgangssprache durchsetzt sein.
- Hier ist es also entscheidend, dass man das eigene Sprachrepertoire durch ein anderes ersetzen bzw. ergänzen kann, damit der Text glaubwürdig wird.
- Auch hier ist es wichtig, dass der Inhalt nicht zu oberflächlich bleibt (auch ein Tagebucheintrag eines Jugendlichen sollte emotionale Tiefe zeigen und nicht lediglich beschreibend sein).
- Insgesamt sollte der Text so verfasst werden, dass er die Lesenden überzeugt und authentisch wirkt.

Literarische Texte

Narration

Keyword
Narrative texts: Narrative texts can have many forms, among them short story, novel, fairy tale, satire, parable, legend, etc.
The ones that are most relevant for your final exam are the short story and the novel.

When asked to analyse a narrative text, you will have to focus on particular elements that are characteristic of short stories or novels.

Elements of narration

Plot

INFO Elements of a complete plot

exposition → rising action → climax / turning point → falling action → ending

A **plot** need not necessarily be complete (there may be an open ending).
The **sequence** need not necessarily be chronological.
There may be foreshadowing or flashbacks or there may be reverse narration (umgestelltes Erzählen).
In particular, an excerpt from a longer text, which is the most common sort of text in the final exam, may not contain all the elements of the plot.
Certain **key events** within the action of a story will increase the tension; they will create suspense, rising to a climax or turning point. After that there will be falling tension or relief.

INFO Tension curve

rising tension → climax or turning point → falling tension or relief

Theme

The **theme** of a story is always abstract. Themes can be love, poverty, racism, childhood, etc. The **subject matter** of a story is the concrete realisation of a theme.

<u>Example:</u>
Two stories may have the same theme: racism. The subject matter of one may be the murder of an African American, of the other the bullying of a black schoolgirl.

Characters

When asked to characterise a figure from a narrative text, you must be aware of different aspects. There are key questions that can guide you.

<u>Direct characterisation</u>
- What does the narrator say about the character?
- What do other characters say about the character?
- What does the character say about himself/herself?
- How objective is what they say? Be aware of words with negative or positive connotations.

Indirect characterisation
- How does the character act?
- What does the character say?
- What kind of language does he/she use?

It might help to fill in a table with the following headings:

Character's outward appearance	Character's language	Character's actions	What the character says	Other characters' statements (or actions)
...	...	...	...	...

Narrator / Point of view

INFO Narrator

The narrator is either a first-person or a third-person narrator.
The first-person narrator is NOT the author!

limited point of view	**unlimited/omniscient point of view**
first-person narrator	third-person narrator (neutral omniscience, God-like knowledge of all the facts)
third-person narrator (one character's point of view, "selective omniscience")	third-person narrator (several characters' points of view)

Modes of presentation

Narratives can be presented in two ways: the panoramic and the scenic mode. **Panoramic** presentation is used to pay great attention to detail, immersing the reader in the events, while **scenic** presentation condenses the action and can summarise the events of several years into a few lines.

Interior monologue is a particular kind of scenic presentation in which the thoughts and feelings passing through a character's mind are depicted. In **reported thought**, thoughts are presented as reported speech.

This is closely connected with the concepts of **narrated time** and **narrating (or acting) time**:

narrated time longer than narrating time	usually summary of events
narrated time identical with narrating time	e.g. direct speech
narrated time shorter than narrating time	e.g. stream of consciousness, interior monologue, detailed description of a scene, comparable to slow motion in a film

INFO Function of mode of presentation and point of view

A neutral, omniscient narrator, who observes the action and the characters from above and who uses a panoramic mode of presentation, is more detached and thus creates a distance between the reader and the action. On the other hand, a narrator who takes a character's point of view creates immediacy and directly involves the reader in what happens.

Setting

The place and time where the action is set is called the setting. It is especially important for *atmosphere* and *symbolism*.

Atmosphere

Atmosphere is created by means of setting, objects, colours, light and darkness but also by reference to a character's mood or the use of language.

Symbolism

Symbols are part of the setting of the narrative. They are objects, characters or even actions that suggest something beyond their mere meaning. For example, the colour white often symbolises purity.

INFO Established symbols

These are conventional symbols which have long been used and have a certain, traditional significance that everybody knows. Examples of established symbols: a rose, a cross, the colour white.

INFO Created symbols

Something becomes symbolic within a certain context because it is closely connected to an event, a situation or a character.

INFO Symbols

Symbols are NOT metaphors!
Symbols are a factual physical part of the story. Metaphors or similes are figures of speech without an actual representation in the narrated world.

Examples:
She was a rose, so beautiful. → metaphor
She was like a rose, so beautiful. → simile/comparison
They fell in love when they first met in her father's rose garden. → symbol

Language and style

In order to determine the style of a text, it is necessary to examine aspects such as register, diction (choice of words), tone and also sentence structure.

Register is the level of language used in a particular situation. It may be formal, neutral, informal, or vulgar. There may be a lot of slang words, even taboo words as well as technical terms or jargon.

The **tone** may be ironic, sarcastic, sad, humorous, serious, playful, angry, etc., depending on the emotional attitude it expresses. This depends on the choice of words, level of speech, rhythm, sentence length, etc.

Stylistic devices will be considered at length in the chapters on drama and non-fictional texts (p. 116 f. and 121 f.).

Poetry

Poetry focuses on the **aesthetic function** of language; it appeals to the senses. It is to be enjoyed for its beauty, its cleverness, its wit, its impact.
This is achieved by
- the sound of words,
- the rhythm of the words and phrases,
- the choice of words,
- the structure of the sentences,
- the composition of the poem,
- the visual arrangement of words and lines,
- and, above all, by means of imagery.

In your final exams, however, you will be asked not so much to enjoy the poem but to examine its meaning and the effect of the language the speaker uses.

How to proceed

Questions to be asked

- Who is the speaker of the poem?
- Where is the speaker?
- Does the speaker address somebody?
- Does the speaker contemplate something?
- Does the speaker describe something or somebody?
- Does the speaker tell a story?
- Does the speaker explain something?
- Does the speaker argue against or in favour of something?
- What is the speaker's attitude? What is he/she saying?
- How is the poem composed? Is it structured by a rhyme scheme, by the division into stanzas or by some other device?
- Is there a correspondence between the structure of the poem and the structure of the speaker's thoughts?
- What is the significance of the title?
- What words does the speaker use? What do they mean?
- What is the structure of the sentences? Simple? Complex?
- What poetic devices does the speaker use?
- And what is the effect of all this? What is the experience of reading the poem?

In order to understand and describe poetry, you need to be familiar with its most important elements.

Elements of poetry

INFO Speaker and author

The speaker of the poem is NOT the author. Poems may be autobiographical, but you must still refer to the "speaker in the poem".

Poems are composed of **stanzas** and **lines**.
Stanzas may have a certain **rhyme scheme.**

Rhyme

Rhyme schemes

pair rhyme	a a b b
alternate rhyme	a b a b
embracing rhyme	a b b a

Types of rhyme

masculine rhyme (one syllable)	kiss/this
feminine rhyme (two syllables)	dreary/weary
true rhyme	kiss/this, dreary/weary
slant rhyme assonance (same vowel) consonance (same consonant)	 comb/coat hope/heap

Lines and rhythm

Lines may have a certain rhythm. The smallest unit that determines rhythm is the foot, consisting of at least one stressed and one or two unstressed syllables. The pattern of stressed and unstressed syllables is called **metre.**

A sequence of stressed and unstressed syllables is not something artificial. It is the natural rhythm of the English language. It is the poet's skill to choose words in such a way that this pattern constitutes a regular metre.Types of foot:

foot	stresses	example
iamb/iambic	–/ (da-**dum**)	compare
trochee/trochaic	/ – (**dum**-da)	lovely
spondee/spondaic	// (**dum dum**)	drop dead
anapest/anapestic	– –/ (da-da-**dum**)	lemonade
dactyl/dactylic	/ – – (**dum**-da-da)	whispering

The number of feet or stressed syllables in a line determines its metre. The most common types are shown here:

number of feet	metre	example
1	monometer	"And **find** / What **wind**" (John Donne, "Song", ll. 7 – 8)
2	dimeter	"Why **dost** thou **thus**" (John Donne, "The Sun Rising", l. 2)
3	trimeter	"**Go**, Soul, the **bod**y's **guest** / Upon a **thank**less **er**rant" (Sir Walter Raleigh, "The Lie", l. 1 f.)
4	tetrameter	"**Bus**y old **fool**, un**ru**ly **sun**" (John Donne, "The Sun Rising", l. 1)

5	pentameter	"If **mu**sic **be** the **food** of **love**, play **on**" (William Shakespeare, *Twelfth Night,* l. i)
6	hexameter	"And **in** your **dread**ful **verse** in**grav'd** the **pro**ph**e**cies" (Michael Drayton, „Poly-Olbion", l. 33)

INFO Most important metre in English poetry

Iambic pentameter:
"But **thy** e**ter**nal **sum**mer **shall** not **fade**" (Shakespeare, Sonnet 18).

Types of lines

end-stop lines	The meaning requires a pause at the end of the line.	"Shall I compare thee to a summer's day**?**" (Shakespeare, Sonnet 18)
run-on lines (enjambement)	The meaning requires no pause between the lines.	"When yellow leaves, or none, or few, do **hang** **Upon** those boughs which shake against the cold" (Shakespeare, Sonnet 73)
caesura	The meaning requires a pause in mid-line.	"Let me not to the marriage of true minds Admit **impediments**; **love** is not love" (Shakespeare, Sonnet 116)

TIPP Watch out!

The word *imagery* is an abstract noun. There is no plural. You can only talk about single *images*.

Imagery

A writer or speaker using language beyond its dictionary meaning makes use of **imagery.** All figurative use of language is imagery. Imagery appeals to all the senses; it is meant to stimulate the reader's or listener's imagination.

Important types of imagery are: metaphor, simile/comparison, personification and symbol (cf. p. 109 f.).

Drama

When asked to analyse a dramatic text, you will have to focus on particular elements that are characteristic of plays.

Elements of drama
Plot

INFO Elements of a dramatic plot

exposition → rising action → climax or crisis → falling action → dénouement or catastrophe

The action is presented to the audience on stage or on a screen directly. There is no narrator. Yet one can identify the same elements of plot as are found in narration.
In tragedy, the opponents of the hero gain the upper hand in the falling action, which ends in the catastrophe. Comedy has a happy ending, in which conflicts are resolved (dénouement).

Stage directions

The dramatic text consists of **two kinds of text:** the more important kind of text is spoken by the characters (i. e. dialogue, monologue, soliloquy and asides).
The **stage directions** are the second kind of text. They give instructions concerning the stage design, about sounds to be heard, visual effects, the characters' outer appearance and actions and also the way some of the dialogue has to be spoken.
The following visual and acoustic elements will have to be considered in your analysis of stage directions. They will help to characterise the dramatis personae, to create a specific atmosphere or they will function as symbols (cf. p. 109 f.).

concerning the actors		concerning the stage	
visual	**acoustic**	**visual**	**acoustic**
size facial expressions gestures costumes	voice intonation language of the play non-verbal noises	scenery stage design lighting props	music background noise sounds

Characters

The characters are not mediated via a narrator but present themselves through action, interaction and dialogue and, of course, their outward appearance on stage (see above). There are **flat** characters, types that act in a predictable way and do not develop over the course of the action, and **round** characters that appear and act lifelike and non-stereotypical and often undergo some form of inner development during the play.

Language/Dialogue/Communication

When analysing the language of a play, you have to keep in mind that it works on two levels:

1. the inner system of communication, i. e. the communication among the characters
2. the outer system of communication between the playwright and the audience

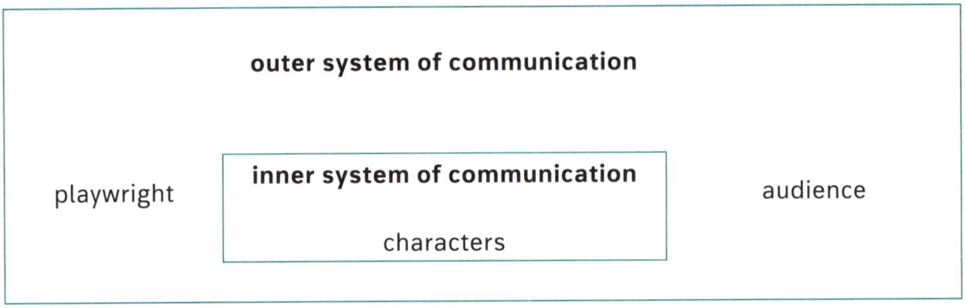

Dramatic irony

Dramatic irony is an important effect that is created by these two levels of communication. It arises when there is a sharp contrast between what the audience knows and what a character knows or utters. Dramatic irony often serves to great comic effect as well. Shakespeare, for example, puts it to great effect in his comedies when he introduces cases of mistaken identity.

Example:

In Shakespeare's Macbeth, King Duncan praises the peaceful atmosphere at Macbeth's castle, whereas the audience knows that Duncan is going to be murdered.

Aside

In an aside, an actor speaks to the audience in order to provide information on his thoughts and feelings or intentions. The other characters on stage supposedly do not hear what she/he says.

TIPP

As many of Shakespeare's plays are written in verse, you may approach their language in the same way as poetry.

Language and style

Important stylistic devices

device	definition	example
alliteration	repetition of a sound (usually a consonant) at the beginning of neighbouring words	"From forth the fatal loins of these two foes" (Shakespeare, *Romeo and Juliet,* Prologue)
allusion	direct or implied reference	Poetry is great. Just think of the most famous writer of sonnets in English.
analogy	establishing a resemblance between two things that are basically unlike	The heart is simply a pump propelling the blood round the body.

anaphora	neighbouring sentences starting with the same word(s)	"We shall not flag or fail. We shall go on to the end. We shall fight in France" (W. Churchill)
antithesis	contrasting ideas using a parallel syntactic structure	"It's a story that hasn't made me the most conventional candidate. But it is a story that has seared into my genetic make-up the idea that […]" (B. Obama)
assonance	repetition of internal vowel sounds in neighbouring words	How now, brown cow?
blank verse	poetry without rhyme but with a regular metre: iambic pentameter	"The king has happily received, Macbeth, / The news of thy success, and when he reads" (Shakespeare, *Macbeth*)
chiasmus	the reversal of word order in two parts of a sentence	"Fair is foul, and foul is fair" (Shakespeare, *Macbeth*)
climax	an enumeration of arguments that become stronger	Friendship, affection, love.
ellipsis	incomplete sentence	A good choice!
enumeration	list of arguments	Macbeth is disloyal, greedy and obedient to his wife.
euphemism	replacing an unpleasant expression with a more agreeable one	"Civilising" Australian Aboriginals meant forcibly removing the children from their families.
hyperbole	exaggeration	I've told you a thousand times.
inversion	reversal of word order	Not only did he like chocolate, he also ate a lot of it.
metaphor	indirect comparison without "like" or "as"	Love is a red, red rose.
metonymy	name of a thing or concept is replaced by a part of it or by s.th. associated with it	"wheels" for "car" / "turf" for "horse-racing"
onomatopoeia	word that imitates the sound that it stands for	Bang! Swoosh! Ding-dong.
paradox	an apparent contradiction	This statement is true and false at the same time.
parallelism	same syntactic structure of two or more sentences	"One small step for man, one giant leap for mankind." (Neil Armstrong)
personification	inanimate objects / abstract ideas presented as if human beings	The flowers are begging for water.

rhetorical question	a question that does not require an answer	Do you think I'm stupid?
simile	comparison using the words "like" or "as"	Your love is like a red, red rose.
telling name	a name that represents character traits	"Doolittle": she is too little, or: she does too little (Shaw, Pygmalion)

Glossary – Analysing Literary Texts

the narrator tells of / shows / relates / reveals
the narrator takes xy's point of view
the narrator is omniscient
the story is told in the first-person/third-person form
the narrator uses / employs / makes use of metaphors/similes/comparisons
this metaphor shows / stands for / suggests
the narrator speaks in an ironic/satirical/detached/matter-of-fact/serious tone
the story deals with / treats of / concentrates on / focuses on ...
atmosphere is created
tension/suspense is created/built up
the poem is written/composed
the poem is read/spoken/recited
the recital of a poem
the poem is by Shakespeare / it is a song by Genesis
the speaker of the poem / the poetic I / the poetic persona
the poem consists of / is composed of / is arranged in stanzas
the comedy ridicules/mocks/satirises
the exposition sets the action in motion
the action moves towards and culminates in a turning point
the play has a simple/complex/tight plot
it has a happy/unhappy ending
the main/major/minor character(s) is/are
the protagonist is in conflict with an opponent
the antagonist fights the protagonist
the spectator/audience follows the play
the play is performed/produced/staged
the scenery is shifted
actors perform/play/enact
an actor enters / makes an entrance / exits / makes her/his exit

Sach- und Gebrauchstexte

Argumentative Texts: How to Deal with (Political) Speeches

Keyword
(Political) speeches: aim at convincing *(überzeugen)* the audience of the speaker's position, winning them over to his/her side. Very often, the speaker tries to persuade *(überreden)* the listener by appealing to his/her feelings. In some cases, the orator may even attempt to manipulate *(manipulieren)* his/her audience.
You should always keep in mind that the speaker wants to present his/her opinion / conviction / point of view as positively as possible.

When asked to analyse a political speech, you will have to focus on the topic as well as characteristic features.

How to proceed

Reading the text

1. Read the speech (or, more likely, an extract from it) as a whole, trying to identify the main topic (reading for gist).
2. Re-read the speech/extract several times, paying close attention to certain characteristic features of such speeches. Mark words or phrases in the text and take notes (intensive reading).

Pay close attention to

- key words and phrases
- references to historical events
- the use of symbols, key words, slogans
- references to famous people
- references to works of literature
- stylistic devices (see below)

Questions to be asked

When it comes to analysing a speech, you should always ask yourself the following questions:

- What is the main topic of the speech?
- What is its political, historical and social context?
- What do I know about the speaker (biography, political orientation)?

Elements of a (political) speech

Structure

Speeches can usually be divided into an **introduction**, a **main part** and a **conclusion**. These parts serve different purposes:

INFO Introduction to a speech

In the introduction the orator announces the topic/purpose of the speech and explains its importance. He/She also wants to attract the audience's attention so that they will follow the speech closely and accept his/her opinion.

There are several ways to make listeners interested:

- The speaker can open by telling the audience **something about their personal history / recent experience**, thereby underlining the fact that the topic of the speech is of personal importance to them. By relating a **little story** to the audience, the speaker will also appear more human and less remote.
- Another common way of starting a speech is to **open it with a question** that refers to the main topic and which will be answered later in the speech. By asking the audience a question, the speaker actively involves them, indirectly asking them to think more deeply about an issue.
- A speaker may **present visual material to the audience,** e.g. pictures, concrete objects or a short extract from a film. This also helps to attract the audience's attention: listeners will become curious about how the object or visual material is related to the content of the speech.

INFO Main part of a speech

In the main part of the speech the orator needs to keep the audience interested and to make sure that they can follow the train of thought.

Again, there are several ways to do this. The following techniques are particularly effective:

- **using short and simple sentences**, developing the argumentation step by step and ensuring that the audience can follow,
- quoting reliable sources/experts, referring to statistics and **providing the audience with facts and necessary background information**, which shows that the speaker is well-informed and has researched the subject,
- **pointing out problems** but also providing solutions to them, thus showing that the speaker is competent, and
- **including personal experiences** and vivid, specific events, again aiming for a personal relationship with the audience, often using personal pronouns like "we", "us", "our".

Towards the end of a speech the speaker might
- take up a question posed at the beginning of the speech,
- appeal once more to both the audience's heads and hearts,
- ask for support, giving the listeners the feeling that their support is of major importance, and
- develop a vision for the future.

Language and style

There are certain stylistic devices which are often used in speeches. They aim at making the speech more lively and interesting.

Important stylistic devices

analogy	A resemblance is established between things which are dissimilar.
simile	This is a direct comparison using the words "like" or "as", e.g. *He fought like a lion in the battle.*
metaphor	This is an indirect comparison without using the words "like" or "as", e.g. *He was a lion in the battle.*
alliteration	A consonantal sound is repeated in two or more adjacent words, e.g. *We will win; "We must understand that ties of trade bind nations in closest intimacy"* (Warren G. Harding: Inaugural address, 4 March 1921).
repetition	Repeating certain words or phrases puts emphasis on their meaning, e.g. *"The answer to the slavery question was already embedded within our Constitution – a Constitution that had at its very core the ideal of equal citizenship under the law; a Constitution that promised its people liberty, and justice"* (Barack Obama: *A More Perfect Union)*
parallelism	Two or more parts of a sentence (or two or more sentences) have the same (or similar) syntactic structure. Like repetition, parallelism serves to emphasise the parts of the sentence in question, intensifying the force of the statement and encouraging the audience to think about its meaning, e.g. *"Let us be our sister's keeper. Let us find that common stake we all have in one another, and let our politics reflect that spirit as well."* (Barack Obama: *A More Perfect Union)*
antithesis	Two ideas are opposed to one another, using a parallel syntactic structure to achieve the desired effect, i.e. establishing a contrast, e.g. *"It's a story that hasn't made me the most conventional candidate. But it is a story that has seared into my genetic make-up the idea that this nation is more than the sum of its parts – that out of many, we are truly one."* (Barack Obama: *A More Perfect Union)*

rhetorical question	A rhetorical question is one to which no answer is expected; instead, the listener is asked to think about the question and its relevance, e.g. *"How long should this suffering continue?"*
irony	Irony is the use of a statement in which the literal meaning is very different, often even the opposite of the intended meaning; usually, the recipient is made aware of the intended meaning through context or verbal and non-verbal cues, e.g. *hugging oneself in a thunderstorm, saying, „Lovely weather!"*

Glossary – Vocabulary for Analysing Speeches

By telling the listeners something about himself he attempts to establish a personal relationship with his audience.	Er bemüht sich, eine persönliche Beziehung zu seinen Zuhörern aufzubauen, indem er seinem Publikum etwas über seine persönliche Geschichte erzählt.
She attempts to win her listeners over to her side.	Sie versucht, das Publikum auf ihre Seite zu ziehen.
He draws a comparison between ... and ...	Er zieht einen Vergleich zwischen ... und ...
He puts emphasis on the meaning of his words by using parallelism/ repetition in line X.	Durch den in Zeile X verwendeten Parallelismus / die in Zeile X verwendete Wiederholung verleiht er seinen Worten Nachdruck.
He refers to well-known historical events such as ...	Er bezieht sich auf allgemein bekannte historische Ereignisse wie z. B. ...
He wants to call/draw the audience's attention to the fact that ...	Er möchte die Aufmerksamkeit des Publikums auf die Tatsache lenken, dass ...
His frequent use of rhetorical questions is intended to show that ...	Sein häufiger Gebrauch rhetorischer Fragen soll verdeutlichen, dass ...
His use of metaphorical language is intended to make his speech more lively and interesting.	Sein metaphorischer Sprachgebrauch soll seine Rede interessanter und lebendiger machen.
In line X he directly criticises his political opponents.	In Zeile ... kritisiert er offen seine politischen Gegner.
The frequent use of personal pronouns such as "we", "us" and "our" gives the audience the impression that he does not regard himself as superior to them but as one of them.	Der häufige Gebrauch der Personalpronomen „wir", „uns" und „unser" soll dem Publikum das Gefühl geben, dass er sich als einer von ihnen und nicht als eine höher gestellte Person sieht.
The speaker appeals to the audience's emotions by ...	Der Redner / Die Rednerin spricht die Gefühle des Publikums an, indem er/sie ...

The speaker begins by ...	Der Redner / Die Rednerin beginnt mit ...
The speaker makes frequent use of metaphors/similes/symbols/examples to point out / to underline that ...	Der Redner / Die Rednerin macht regen Gebrauch von Metaphern/Vergleichen/Symbolen/Beispielen, um herauszustellen / zu unterstreichen, dass ...
The speaker tries to convince his/her audience of his/her point of view by ...	Der Redner / Die Rednerin versucht sein/ihr Publikum von seinem/ihrem Standpunkt zu überzeugen, indem er/sie ...
The speaker aims to convince/persuade/manipulate the audience.	Es ist das Anliegen des Redners / der Rednerin, das Publikum zu überzeugen/überreden/manipulieren.

Expository Texts: How to Deal with Essays

Keyword

Essay: There are various kinds:

a) essays which reflect the author's opinion on a certain topic (**comment**)

b) essays in which the author weighs up the pros and cons of a particular subject (**argumentative essay**)

c) essays in which a topic is presented in a clear and logical way and which do not contain the author's opinion (**expository essay**)

How to proceed

First you have to find out which kind of essay you are being asked to analyse.
For details on how to analyse **comments** you can refer to the section on **political speeches** above.
Here we will focus on the **argumentative essay.**

Structure

- In the **introduction** the author expresses the main idea of the essay. Instead of giving a personal opinion, she/he might choose to provide the reader with some background information or start with a question which will serve as a guideline and be answered in the course of the essay.
- For the **main part** of the essay, the author can decide on a dialectical or an enumerative approach.
- In an **enumerative approach** the author will enumerate all the aspects of the topic in a neutral way. A **dialectical approach** can either present all the arguments in favour of a position before focusing on the counterarguments (or vice versa), or it can present the pros and cons alternately. The latter is usually considered more skilful.
- Each **new aspect** is usually presented in a new paragraph. The various **arguments** can be backed with examples from real life, established facts, an expert opinion or

other reliable sources. These pieces of evidence are very important as they enable the author to make his/her argument convincing and thus to persuade the reader.
- In the **conclusion** the author sums up the arguments, frequently also restating his/her own opinion and referring to what could happen in the future.

Glossary – Vocabulary for Analysing Essays

The author discusses the pros and cons of …	Der Verfasser / Die Verfasserin diskutiert die Vor- und Nachteile von …
The author gives his/her personal opinion on the problem of …	Der Verfasser / Die Verfasserin äußert seine/ihre eigene Meinung zum Thema …
He/She believes / is convinced / presumes that …	Er/Sie glaubt / ist überzeugt / nimmt an, dass …
She/He wants to persuade the reader …	Sie/Er möchte die Lesenden überreden …
One can easily follow his train of thought.	Man kann seinen Gedankengang leicht nachvollziehen.
At the end of her essay she draws / comes to the conclusion …	Am Ende ihres Essays kommt sie zu dem Schluss …
His/Her arguments are (not) convincing/well-chosen.	Seine/Ihre Argumente sind (nicht) überzeugend/gut gewählt.
The main topic of the essay is …	Das Hauptthema des Berichts ist …
The tone of this essay is humorous/neutral/ironic/serious.	Der Ton des Berichts ist humorvoll/neutral/ironisch/ernst.
The author uses real examples to convince her readers.	Die Verfasserin verwendet reale Beispiele, um ihre Leserschaft zu überzeugen.
The author's choice of words shows/emphasises that he is for/against …	Die Wortwahl des Verfassers zeigt/unterstreicht, dass er für/gegen … ist.
In the introductory paragraph of her essay, she asks a rhetorical question, which serves as a thread.	Im einleitenden Abschnitt ihres Berichts stellt sie den Lesenden eine rhetorische Frage, die sich wie ein roter Faden durch den Bericht zieht.
The author uses adjectives with positive/negative connotations to support his/her point of view.	Der Verfasser / Die Verfasserin verwendet Adjektive mit einer positiven/negativen Konnotation, um seinen/ihren Standpunkt zu verdeutlichen.
Her attempt to persuade the readers backfires / works very well.	Ihr Versuch, die Leser zu überreden, misslingt/gelingt.

Narrative Texts: How to Deal with Reports

> **Keyword**
> **Report:** This is a special kind of newspaper article.
> It provides answers to the five "W" questions *(Who? What? Where? When? Why?),* as well as the *How* question. Its aim is to inform its readers and NOT to manipulate or influence them.
> A report deals with current events and only contains facts.

Sometimes students have problems when it comes to differentiating between a *report* and an *article,* which can also deal with current events but which is usually a mixture of both fact and opinion.
The style of an **article** is usually more personal and its main aim is to entertain the reader. This is ensured by using many adverbs and adjectives to make the article lively and by addressing its readers directly, often by asking them a hypothetical question, e. g. *How would you feel if you discovered that someone had stolen your brand-new car?*
The main characteristics of a **report** are outlined below.

Elements of a report

Structure

- To arouse the reader's curiosity, reports have **headlines** containing basic information without providing too much detail.
- The basic information is generally provided in the first paragraph, which serves as an **introduction.**
- The **main body** of a report consists of a number of paragraphs, which contain one piece of information each.
- The last paragraph serves as a kind of **conclusion.**

Language and style

- A report is written in a factual style and neither reflects the author's personal opinion nor contains any kind of speculation.
- Individual paragraphs are relatively short and consist of short sentences, aiming to ensure that the reader understands the information presented.
- Experts – or people who have first-hand experience of the topic in question – are often quoted, but no authorial comment is given on what they say.

Glossary – Vocabulary for Analysing Reports

The report [title] written by [author] deals with / is about / relates to / describes ...	Der Bericht [Titel] von [Verfasser] beschäftigt sich mit / handelt von / berichtet von / beschreibt ...
The topic(s) of the report is (are) ...	Das Thema / Die Themen des Berichts ist/sind ...
In the introduction the reader learns about / gets to know ...	In der Einleitung erfährt der Leser / die Leserin ...
The report can be divided into ... paragraphs.	Der Bericht kann in ... Absätze gegliedert werden.
The report consists of ... paragraphs.	Der Bericht besteht aus ... Absätzen.
It is the author's aim to inform the reader about ...	Es ist das Anliegen des Autors / der Autorin, die Lesenden über ... zu informieren.
The 2nd/3rd paragraph contains information on ...	Der zweite/dritte Absatz enthält Informationen über ...
The author quotes an eye-witness/ expert who says that ...	Der Autor / Die Autorin zitiert einen Augenzeugen/Experten, der sagt, dass ...
The author describes how ...	Der Verfasser / Die Verfasserin beschreibt, wie ...
The author does not give his/her personal opinion on the topic/problem/question but merely relates facts.	Der Verfasser / Die Verfasserin äußert nicht seine/ihre eigene Meinung zum Sachverhalt / Problem / zu der Frage, sondern gibt Fakten wieder.
The factual style of writing shows that it is the author's aim to inform the reader and not to entertain him/her.	Der sachliche Sprachgebrauch verdeutlicht, dass es das Anliegen des Autors / der Autorin ist, die Leser zu informieren und nicht, sie zu unterhalten.

Visuelle Materialien

Any kind of picture can be considered a type of text: it contains information that can be read and interpreted. This requires knowledge of the language of pictures, which is different for each medium: a cartoon must be approached differently from a photograph, for example. A complete account of every kind of visual material cannot be offered here, but some central aspects will be listed and explained.

INFO A note on visual texts in the Abitur

Pictures have often been used in the Zentralabitur. They generally appear as additional material illustrating a certain text and picking up its issues or introducing new aspects for the student to react to. During the written exam, visual texts are limited to printable material; oral exams may occasionally also feature short video sequences.

Common Types of Pictures Used

- **photographs:** often illustrate an issue or problem; their aesthetic qualities should be considered
- **advertisements:** mostly use photographic material combined with text to promote a certain product/service; the intention of the ad must be considered and reflected on; political ads also belong to this category
- **cartoons:** reflect an issue from a critical point of view; the cartoonist's intention to criticise a social or political problem plays a central role
- **works of art:** rarely used; can reflect a society's state of mind and ideals during a certain period (e.g. early American paintings); their aesthetic qualities are essential to an understanding of their message
- **film stills:** a special type of photograph which enables the viewer to analyse the composition of a scene and its meaning/intention
- **films/videos:** this may include formats such as movie scenes, vines and vlogs; for legal reasons these are not likely to be shown in the Abitur but are used in the class-room for film analysis as well as comprehension tasks and as central study texts
- **statistics:** used to prove or explain a certain issue scientifically

Steps for Approaching Visual Material

Step 1: Describe the picture and its content. Do not begin by analysing or interpreting it, but state clearly and briefly what can be seen in the picture. The central question to be answered is, "What type of picture are you dealing with and what can be seen?"
Step 2: Analyse the content and form. The method of analysis depends on the picture. Ask yourself: "What information does the picture convey?" and (except for statistics) "Why was the picture created in this way and not differently?" End by stating what the picture aims to reveal, illustrate, criticise or otherwise convey.

Step 3: Interpret and evaluate the meaning or importance of the picture and the possible intention(s) of its creator. You may ask yourself whether the picture gives a truthful reflection of a certain issue or aspect, whether it distorts or exaggerates reality or whether it is meant to manipulate the viewer.

INFO A note on tasks given to discuss pictures in the Abitur

Many tasks in the Abitur that involve the use of pictures do not specifically ask for an analysis or interpretation but imply that this must be provided. Usually, visual materials have been used to illustrate an issue already introduced in a longer text. In such cases, you will be asked to react to the picture and relate it to the text or to a certain general topic discussed in class.

Examples of Types of Picture

Cartoons

When analysing cartoons, pay attention to the following aspects:
context: the circumstances in which it was created: when and in what type of magazine or newspaper it was published (historical, political context), connection to a particular article or reference to a current topic, position of its creator
content: the details of what it shows:
- **target:** who or what is it aimed at, what issue does it discuss/criticise?
- **message:** what point does the cartoon aim to make or what ideas does it propose?
  - Has the cartoonist taken sides? Is he/she biased?
  - Is the cartoon's humour ironic, satirical, aggressive ...?

style: How is this message put across? Consider visual and textual elements.

visual elements	textual elements
Do visual items display incongruities by means of size, contrast, exaggeration, distortion, personification, etc.?	Has the cartoonist used labels/speech bubbles/captions? What words are made up to convey sounds? (onomatopoeia)
What facial features are used to convey expressions?	Does the cartoon use formal or informal language?
Do the images have symbolic meaning?	Does it play with words?
Does it use contrasts to convey certain issues of the main topic?	Does it use technical or specific terms?
Note: Almost every form of humour is based on incongruity. Things that are juxtaposed or compared in a strange way make us laugh.	

Key elements of cartoons

- **visual metaphors:** Cartoons use simplified visual symbols to carry meaning. The viewer can usually quickly decode them without any effort, e.g. when seeing a grey, dissolving shape one can imagine that this represents smoke.
- **caricature** (noun/verb): usually an exaggerated drawing or picture of a well-known person that makes them seem ridiculous but also easy to recognise
- **onomatopoeia** (noun): a word that sounds similar to the thing it describes, for example "hiss", "bang", "pow" (adj: onomatopoeic)

Advertisements

When analysing ads, pay attention to the AIDA principle (see below) and ask how the ad achieves the following points:
Attention: Ads aim to attract the consumer's attention quickly, for example by showing an appealing, provocative or shocking image or message.
Interest: This initial attention must be kept, thus the ad must create a further interest in the product.
Desire: Once the consumer is interested, the advertisement must spark a desire to buy the product which is advertised.
Action: The desire to own or use the product must lead to action by the consumer; he/she must seek ways to buy or access the product.

These aspects apply to all ads in general even if they do not directly aim to sell a specific product. Campaign ads in politics aim to "sell" a programme or candidate, whereas campaigns published by organisations such as Greenpeace seek to make viewers change their way of living or become politically involved. One must always consider the context in which an ad tries to affect its audience.

Photographs

When analysing and interpreting photographs, it is important to remember that even if a photograph shows a real environment at a certain time, it is still a fabrication of sorts. All photography is influenced by a) the photographer's choice of perspective, frame and timing and b) the camera itself, which can only show a limited view.
Photographers make choices when taking a picture in order to convey a specific effect or impression of their object. So a photograph must be considered in the same way as a painting – always ask yourself why the photographer chose this specific object, perspective, frame (what can and cannot be seen), moment in time and rendition (e.g. colour, black and white, sepia).

Modern means of digital photography have also led to increasing manipulation. Thus, even though we still tend to believe that pictures show reality, it can no longer be taken for granted that a photograph shows an aspect of the real world and/or has not been digitally altered.

Glossary – Vocabulary for Analysing Visual Material

viewer	Betrachter
picture, image	Bild
painting, drawing	Gemälde, Zeichnung
photograph/photo	Fotografie (Vorsicht: nicht Fotograf)
photographer	Fotograf
portrait	Porträt
landscape painting/photograph	Landschaftsgemälde/-fotografie
bird's eye view	Vogelperspektive
worm's eye view	Froschperspektive
incongruity	Widerspruch, Widersprüchlichkeit
background	Hintergrund
foreground	Vordergrund

Basic phrases for a description

In the picture/advertisement one can see ...
In the foreground/middle ground/background ...
The theme / topic / main motif of the advertisement is ...
It's an image of ... (place, person, scene)
The picture shows ... (place, person, scene) close up / from a medium/long distance view.
You look at ... (place, person, scene) from ... (above/behind/...)
The picture was taken in/at ... (place)
Above/On top of ... one can read / it says / one can see a short text ...

Basic phrases to express intention/message/aim

The picture/advertisement is aimed at / is meant to attract / is intended to / appeals to a / shows a/an (exaggerated, illustrative, provocative, unrealistic, flattering/beautified) depiction/image of ...
It expresses/criticises/suggests/reveals/claims/manipulates/influences ...

Basic phrases to express stylistic means / how aims are achieved

The photographer/painter/cartoonist achieves his/her aim by presenting ... in an objective / artistic / exaggerated / limited / digitally manipulated way/style.
By using contrasts / incongruities such as ... / differences in colour/focus, ... the artist/photographer/cartoonist illustrates/emphasises/shows ...
The perspective / point of view suggests that ...
The motif was chosen deliberately because it illustrates the issue well / evokes emotions / stands for / represents a larger, more complex issue ...

Die sprachliche Leistung im Abitur

Die integrative Sprachbewertung

Mit der **integrativen Sprachbewertung** entfallen sowohl die früher getrennte Bewertung von Ausdrucksvermögen und Sprachrichtigkeit als auch die entsprechenden Fehlerindex-Tabellen.
Nun gibt es nur noch eine Gesamtzensur für die sprachliche Leistung, wobei sich die Bewertung an klar umrissenen Kriterien orientiert. Hierbei hat sich ein grundlegender Wandel vollzogen. Wurden früher insbesondere die fehlerhaften Äußerungen einer Klausur als Bewertungsgrundlage herangezogen, so steht jetzt eine sogenannte **Positiv-Korrektur** im Vordergrund. Zwar werden die Mängel der sprachlichen Leistung nach wie vor rot markiert, jedoch sollen besonders gelungene Teile einer Klausur in grüner Farbe hervorgehoben werden. Beispiele für eine positive, grüne Markierung wären etwa der richtige Gebrauch von Präpositionen, Gerundien oder Konnektoren (zur Satzverknüpfung).
Es wird bewertet, ob und in welchem Umfang die Verstöße gegen die sprachliche Richtigkeit die Kommunikation zwischen der/dem Schreibenden und der/dem Lesenden der Klausur beeinträchtigen und ob die Häufigkeit den Gesamteindruck des Textes bestimmt, inwiefern die Fehler störend wirken und ob sie auf eine Nichtbeherrschung grammatischer Regeln schließen lassen.
Zur integrativen Leistungsbewertung im sprachlichen Bereich werden folgende Kriterien betrachtet:

Texterstellung

- Ist der Text übersichtlich gegliedert und für die Leserschaft damit leicht zu erfassen?
- Ist der Textumfang angemessen?
- Werden sogenannte *linking words* (Konnektoren) zur Verknüpfung von Satzteilen und Ideen sinnvoll und abwechslungsreich eingesetzt?
- Ist das Ausdrucksvermögen anspruchsvoll und wird evtl. das Risiko von möglichen Fehlern akzeptiert, um einen flüssigen und idiomatisch ansprechenden Text zu produzieren?
- Werden textsortenspezifische Formulierungen verwendet (z. B. wird eine private E-Mail anders formuliert als ein Leserbrief)?
- Werden Zitate sinnvoll integriert (treffend gewählt, nicht zu lang)?

Syntax

- Wird der Satzbau variiert oder werden hauptsächlich gleiche Strukturen verwendet?
- Wird auch komplexerer Satzbau beherrscht oder werden bei den Versuchen, nicht nur einfache Strukturen zu verwenden, viele Fehler gemacht?

Lexik

- Sind sowohl der allgemeine als auch der themenspezifische Wortschatz reichhaltig?
- Wird der Wortschatz treffsicher eingesetzt?

Grammatik

- Ist die Fehlerzahl eher gering und beeinträchtigt sie die Kommunikation eher nicht, oder führt eine Häufung zu einer eingeschränkten Verständlichkeit?
- Deuten die Fehler auf eine Unkenntnis oder Unsicherheit hinsichtlich relevanter grammatischer Regeln hin?

Kommunikative Relevanz typischer Fehler

Die folgenden Beispiele zeigen **Fehler, die die Kommunikation beeinträchtigen** und somit zu Abzügen führen. Die Auflistung ist nicht vollständig, sondern vermittelt einen exemplarischen Überblick:

- korrupte Syntax durch Fehlerhäufung
- falsche Bezüge
- uneinheitlicher bzw. falscher Tempusgebrauch (vgl. *summary*)
- falscher Tempusgebrauch bei eindeutigen Signalwörtern (z. B. *last year*)
- fehlende Umschreibung mit *to do* bei Frage und Verneinung
- falsche Präpositionen in *phrasal verbs*
- Germanismen
- falscher Gebrauch von Infinitiv und Gerundium
- *contact clause* im nicht notwendigen Relativsatz
- *that* im nicht notwendigen Relativsatz

Folgende Fehler beeinträchtigen die Kommunikation nicht oder nur in geringem Umfang:

- Rechtschreibfehler, wenn deutlich wird, welches Wort gemeint ist
- falsch gesetztes oder fehlendes Apostroph (**Peters bike; its/it's*)
- fehlerhafte Partizipialkonstruktionen
- Flüchtigkeitsfehler wie gelegentliches Fehlen des *3rd-person singular present -s* oder Plural-s
- ungebräuchliche Präposition bei klarer Aussageabsicht (z. B. **typical for*)
- *progressive* anstatt *simple* (z. B. **The author is dealing with …*)
- fehlerhafte Zeichensetzung

Operatoren für das Fach Englisch[1]

Die Liste der Operatoren gibt einen Überblick über die wichtigsten Arbeitsanweisungen, die in den Prüfungen vorkommen.

[1] Quelle: https://www.nibis.de/uploads/1gohrgs/za2021/2018_Erlass_ZA_Bewertung_FS.pdf (Zugriff: 01.04.2022, gekürzt)

Anforderungsbereich I

describe	give a detailed account of
outline	give the main features or general principles of a text; leave out minor details
state	specify clearly
summarise	give a concise account of the main points

Anforderungsbereich II

analyse	describe and explore in detail certain aspects of the text and how they are presented
compare	show similarities and differences
contrast	emphasise the differences between two or more things
examine	describe and explore in detail certain aspects of the text and how they are presented
explain	show causes and effects in a given context

Anforderungsbereich III

comment	state clearly your opinion on the topic in question and support your views with evidence
discuss	investigate and give reasons for and against
justify	present reasons for decisions, positions or conclusions
assess/evaluate	consider in a balanced way points for and/or against something

Aufgabenarten

Es können auch Aufgaben gestellt werden, die eine **kreative Lösung** erfordern, um dem Anforderungsbereich III zu genügen. Denkbar sind u. a. das Schreiben eines Briefes oder einer E-Mail an einen Freund oder an die Herausgeberin einer Zeitung, ein Schreiben zur Erlangung von Informationen oder auch ein Beschwerdebrief.
Weiterhin sind Aufgabenstellungen möglich, die das Verfassen eines Artikels, eines **Berichtes**, eines **Drehbuches,** eines **Tagebucheintrags** oder eines **Dialogs** erforderlich machen.
Das Schreiben einer **Fortsetzung** oder eines **alternativen Endes einer Geschichte** ist ebenso eine mögliche Aufgabenstellung wie die **Schilderung einer Begebenheit** aus einer anderen Perspektive, um nur einige mögliche Beispiele zu benennen.

Strukturiertes Vorgehen in der Abiturprüfung

Bei der Bearbeitung der Aufgaben in der Abiturprüfung empfiehlt sich ein systematisches Vorgehen in klar definierten Einzelschritten:

Lesen Sie sich zunächst den Text in Ruhe durch und unterstreichen Sie mit Bleistift Wörter, die Sie nicht kennen und die Sie im Wörterbuch nachschlagen möchten. Konzentrieren Sie sich dabei auf solche Wörter, die bedeutungsrelevant und zentral für Ihr Verständnis des Textes sind. Verlieren Sie keine wertvolle Zeit mit dem Nachschlagen von Füllwörtern. Schlagen Sie dann die wichtigsten Wörter nach und lesen Sie den Text ein zweites Mal – nun zügiger – durch. Wenden Sie sich danach den Aufgaben zu: Lesen Sie zuerst alle Teilaufgaben genau durch. Machen Sie sich nochmals klar, dass die Bearbeitung der *comprehension task* (Anforderungsbereich I) weitgehend am Ausgangstext orientiert erfolgen soll, gegebenenfalls unter Einbindung vorhandenen Hintergrundwissens. Die *analysis* (Anforderungsbereich II) erfordert die detaillierte Betrachtung von Einzelaspekten unter Anwendung Ihrer Kenntnisse aus dem Bereich Zitieren und Argumentieren. In der *evaluation* (Anforderungsbereich III) wird schließlich nach Ihrer persönlichen Einordnung und Bewertung gefragt.

Konzentrieren Sie sich anschließend auf die erste Teilaufgabe und kennzeichnen Sie gezielt unmittelbar relevante Textpassagen mit einem Marker. Machen Sie sich auf einem separaten Blatt stichpunktartige Notizen zur Bearbeitung der ersten Aufgabe und verfahren Sie so mit allen weiteren Teilaufgaben. Strukturieren Sie nun Ihre Stichpunkte durch Nummerieren und prüfen Sie unmittelbar vor dem Ausformulieren noch einmal die Aufgabenstellung, um sich rechtzeitig zu vergewissern, dass Ihre Bearbeitung auf den Kern der Frage abzielt. Nehmen Sie sich genug Zeit für diese Vorarbeiten (etwa ein Drittel der Zeit ist nicht zu viel), da Sie mit gut vorsortierten Inhalten umso schneller schreiben und sich dabei stärker auf die sprachlichen Aspekte im Englischen konzentrieren können. Es wird als positiv im Sinne der Textkohärenz bewertet, wenn Sie sich bemühen, Ihre Antworten zu den einzelnen Teilaufgaben sprachlich miteinander in Verbindung zu setzen. Betrachten Sie nicht jede Aufgabe als isolierten Einzelaspekt, der jeweils mit einem Satz für Leser ohne Vorwissen eingeleitet wird.

TIPP zum Punktesammeln

Gehen Sie professionell vor und lesen Sie Ihre gesamte Arbeit vor der Abgabe noch einmal gründlich durch. Planen Sie dafür etwa 15 bis 20 Minuten ein. Bei diesem Arbeitsgang werden Ihnen selbst ganz sicher sprachliche Fehler auffallen. Achten Sie besonders auf die Bezüge bei den Pronomina, das *-s* in der 3. Person Singular Präsens, die Zeitenfolge sowie Rechtschreibung und Zeichensetzung.

TIPP zur Zeitplanung

1. Schritt: Text lesen, bedeutungsrelevanten Wortschatz klären	20 Min
2. Schritt: Fragen lesen, Stichpunkte machen und vorsortieren	20 Min
3. Schritt: Fragen unter Verwendung der Gliederung beantworten	80 Min
4. Schritt: Korrekturlesen	15 Min

(Diese zeitlichen Richtlinien gelten für Grundkurse; bei Prüfungen im Leistungskurs verlängern sich die Zeiten entsprechend.)

Wortschatzerschließung

Viele scheinbar unbekannte Wörter lassen sich problemlos ableiten. Hierzu kann man den Kontext oder andere bekannte Wörter aus derselben Wortfamilie zurate ziehen. In manchen Fällen helfen auch fächerübergreifend die Kenntnisse in anderen Fremdsprachen oder der Muttersprache. Insbesondere auf das Lateinische bzw. Französische kann man hier häufig zurückgreifen.

Textgestaltung

Kohärenz, Adressatenorientierung, Leserleitung

Kohärenz

TIPP zum Punktesammeln

Bemühen Sie sich, Ihren Text kohärent, also auch sprachlich zusammenhängend, zu gestalten. Schaffen Sie sinnvolle inhaltliche Verknüpfungen zwischen Satzteilen, Sätzen und Sinnabschnitten. Verwenden Sie dazu die sogenannten **Konnektoren,** die als Verbindungsglieder zum besseren Textverständnis beitragen.

Hier ist eine Liste der wichtigsten Konnektoren, geordnet nach ihrer Funktion im Satz.

Reihung von Argumenten

and	und
first(ly)/second(ly)/third(ly)	erstens/zweitens/drittens
furthermore/moreover	außerdem / darüber hinaus / überdies
in addition to	zusätzlich zu
not only ... but also ...	nicht nur ..., sondern auch
as well as	sowie
finally	schließlich

Gegensatz

but	aber/sondern
although	obwohl
however	jedoch
despite the fact that	trotz der Tatsache, dass
in spite of	trotz
nevertheless/nonetheless	nichtsdestoweniger

even so	selbst dann
on the contrary	im Gegensatz dazu
on the one hand, ... on the other hand,	einerseits ..., andererseits
unlike	anders als
whereas	während/wogegen/indessen
while/whilst	während (dagegen)
yet	dennoch

Bedingung

if	falls/wenn
unless	wenn nicht
otherwise	ansonsten

Folge

because	weil
since	da
so	daher
consequently	folglich
as a result	demzufolge
therefore	daher/deshalb
due to	infolge
according to	zufolge
that is why	deshalb

Vergleich

like	wie
in comparison to/with	im Vergleich zu
similarly	ähnlich
equally	gleichermaßen

Zielgruppenorientierung

Schneiden Sie Ihren Text genau auf den Adressaten zu und drücken Sie sich präzise aus. Bewegen Sie sich in der Abiturklausur auf einer neutralen Sprachebene, vermeiden Sie also Stilbrüche wie Slangwörter und *spoken English*. Auch *contracted forms (they're, he's got)* sind nur in privater Kommunikation angebracht.

Lesendenleitung: *Writing a paragraph/comment*

Hier soll insbesondere der *argumentative comment* näher betrachtet werden, in dem Argumente für und gegen eine Behauptung erläutert werden. Die Form des *comment,* der eine These stützt bzw. nur antithetisch arbeitet, ist ein Teilbereich eines *argumentative comment.*

TIPP zum Punktesammeln

Entwickeln Sie in Ihrem Text eine für die Lesenden nachvollziehbare Argumentation.

Ein *comment* folgt einer klaren Struktur: Er beginnt mit einem *topic sentence* zur Einleitung, in dem eine Aussage zum Thema gemacht wird. Anschließend führt er das Argument aus (**These**), geht über zur Darstellung der Gegenargumente (**Antithese**), um mit einer **Schlussfolgerung** bzw. der **Darstellung der eigenen Meinung** abzuschließen. In jedem Teil sollten spezifische Formulierungen zur logischen Verknüpfung eingesetzt werden, um den Lesenden die Redeabsicht zu signalisieren.

Eine Sicherheit ausdrücken

The fact is that ...	Es ist eine Tatsache, dass ...
It cannot be denied that ...	Man kann nicht leugnen, dass ...
It goes without saying that ...	Selbstredend ...
Undoubtedly, ...	Zweifellos ...
I am convinced that ...	Ich bin überzeugt davon, dass ...
It is indisputable/obvious that ... There is no doubt that ...	Es ist unbestreitbar / offensichtlich / nicht zu bezweifeln, dass ...
It is inevitable that ...	Es ist unvermeidbar, dass ...

Eine Vermutung ausdrücken

Apparently, ...	Anscheinend ...
They will probably ...	Sie werden wahrscheinlich ...
It seems highly likely that ...	Es scheint äußerst wahrscheinlich, dass ...
It may be the case that ...	Es kann sein, dass ...

Einen Zweifel ausdrücken

It is doubtful whether ...	Es ist zweifelhaft, ob ...
I wonder if ...	Ich frage mich, ob ...
There is no proof/evidence that ...	Es gibt keine Beweise, dass ...

Einen Sachverhalt betonen

In order to stress that ...	Um hervorzuheben, dass ...
to emphasise	betonen
I would like to make it clear that ...	Ich möchte klarstellen, dass ...

Eine Meinung ausdrücken

In my opinion, ... / In my view, ...	Meiner Meinung nach ...
My thoughts on the subject are ...	Meine Meinung zu diesem Thema ist ...
Personally, I think that ...	Ich persönlich denke, dass ...
As far as I am concerned, ...	Was mich angeht ...
From my point of view, ...	Aus meiner Sicht ...
I assume that ...	Ich vermute, dass ...
I am (not) convinced that ...	Ich bin (nicht) überzeugt davon, dass ...
I cannot help thinking that ...	Ich kann nicht umhin zu denken, dass ...
I get the impression that ...	Ich habe den Eindruck, dass ...
I am afraid that ...	(abschwächend) Ich fürchte, dass ...
Honestly, ... / To be honest, ...	Ehrlich gesagt ...
I cannot judge whether/if ...	Ich kann nicht beurteilen, ob ...
I am in no position to say ...	Es steht mir nicht zu, zu sagen ...

Einen Widerspruch einräumen

in contrast to ...	im Gegensatz zu ...
On the contrary, ...	Ganz im Gegenteil ...
whereas	(gegenüberstellend) während
I strongly object to ...	Ich spreche mich deutlich gegen ... aus.
One could argue that ..., but ...	Man könnte argumentieren, dass ... , aber ...
Although it is true that ... it would be wrong to claim that ...	Obwohl es wahr ist, dass ..., wäre es falsch zu behaupten, dass ...

Zustimmung ausdrücken

Fortunately, ...	Glücklicherweise ...
I entirely agree with / I share the opinion that ...	Ich stimme vollkommen mit ... überein.

I support his view.	Ich unterstütze seine Meinung.
I share her views.	Ich teile ihre Meinung.
I am of the same opinion (as) ...	Ich bin der gleichen Meinung (wie) ...
I approve of his/her opinion.	Ich bin mit seiner/ihrer Meinung einverstanden.
I take your point about ...	Ich akzeptiere Ihre Meinung über ...
I am in favour of ...	Ich bin für ...
He rightly mentions that ...	Zu Recht betont er, dass ...
I will not object to ...	Ich widerspreche ... nicht.
It cannot be justified that ...	Es gibt keine Rechtfertigung für ...
Nobody would disagree with that statement.	Niemand würde dieser Behauptung widersprechen.
This statement is very convincing.	Diese Aussage ist sehr überzeugend.
I have to admit that the author ...	Ich muss zugeben, dass der Autor / die Autorin ...

Ablehnung ausdrücken

It is only partly true that ...	Es entspricht nur teilweise der Wahrheit, dass ...
I disagree completely with ...	Ich muss widersprechen.
I see things differently.	Ich sehe den Sachverhalt anders.
I must/have to disagree on this matter.	Ich bin in dieser Angelegenheit anderer Meinung.
One cannot possibly accept that ...	Man kann unmöglich akzeptieren, dass ...
I must object to ...	Ich muss ... widersprechen.
I have to criticise strongly that ...	Ich muss scharf kritisieren, dass ...
I doubt whether ...	Ich bezweifle, dass ...
This statement entirely contradicts ...	Diese Behauptung widerspricht ganz und gar ...
However, ...	Jedoch ...
It is not as simple as it seems.	Es ist nicht so einfach wie es scheint.
Unlike the author, I think ...	Anders als der Autor / die Autorin glaube ich ...
I cannot share the author's view on ...	Ich kann die Meinung des Autors / der Autorin über ... nicht teilen.

Einen Grund angeben

As/Since ...	Da/Weil ...
In view of the fact that ...	Angesichts der Tatsache, dass ...
The reason for this lies in ...	Der Grund dafür liegt bei ...
This causes confusion.	Das sorgt für Verwirrung.
That is why ... / Therefore / For this reason ...	Aus diesem Grund ... / Deshalb
Given that ...	In Anbetracht der Tatsache, dass ...
That was caused by ...	Das wurde verursacht durch ...

Eine Folge darstellen

Consequently, ... / As a consequence, ...	Folglich (am Satzanfang)
In view of this statement, ...	In Anbetracht dieser Behauptung ...
in order to	um zu
as a result of	als Folge von

Vergleiche anstellen

to be comparable	vergleichbar sein
compared to / in comparison with	im Vergleich zu
to be different from	sich unterscheiden von
distinguish between (A and B)	(A von B) unterscheiden
to be considerably better than	wesentlich besser sein als
to get more and more difficult	immer schwieriger werden
Nowadays, it is less and less common ...	Heutzutage ist es immer weniger üblich ...
superior/inferior to	überlegen/unterlegen
The former ..., the latter	Der erstere ..., der letztere ...
They have little in common.	Sie haben wenig gemeinsam.
They are equal in price.	Sie haben den gleichen Preis.

Beispiele anführen

for example/instance	zum Beispiel
Let me give you an example.	Lassen Sie mich ein Beispiel anführen.
such as	wie (zum Beispiel)
Look at ...	Sehen wir uns einmal ... an.

Conclusion

To sum up, ... / To summarise, ...	Zusammenfassend kann man sagen ...
I come to the conclusion that ...	Ich komme zu dem Schluss, dass ...
in short	kurz gesagt
To put it in a nutshell ...	Um es auf einen Nenner zu bringen ...
I can support the author's view on ...	Ich kann die Ansicht des Autors / der Autorin über ... unterstützen.
All in all, I believe that ...	Insgesamt glaube ich ...

Autorenintention

An mehreren Stellen in Ihrer Abiturklausur werden Sie Ihre eigenen Aussagen in Relation zur Autorenmeinung setzen müssen. Dafür empfiehlt es sich, eine Reihe von sprachlichen Ausdrücken parat zu haben, z. B.:

He/She points out / argues that ...	Er/Sie weist darauf hin / führt an, dass ...
He implies/claims/states that ...	Er behauptet, dass ...
He/She believes/suggests ...	Er/Sie glaubt/schlägt vor ...
He/She lays emphasis on ...	Er/Sie betont ...
His/Her idea was to ...	Er/Sie wollte ...
He/She writes with the intention of *(+ gerund)* ...	Er/Sie schreibt mit der Absicht, ...
His/Her aim is to ...	Sein/Ihr Ziel ist es ...
His/Her attitude towards ...	Seine/Ihre Einstellung gegenüber ...
When he/she says/writes ..., he/she means that ...	Wenn er/sie sagt/schreibt ..., meint er/sie ...
According to the author, ...	Dem Autor / Der Autorin zufolge ...

Verweise und Zitate

Um Ihre Aussagen zu belegen, fügen Sie geeignete Zitate aus dem Originaltext in Ihre Antworten ein. Setzen Sie diese in englische Anführungszeichen – diese beginnen und enden oben. Da es sich in der Abiturklausur um einen relativ kurzen Ausgangstext handelt, genügt als Quellenangabe die Zeilennummer in Klammern direkt hinter dem Zitat.

Beispiel zu Shakespeare, Romeo and Juliet:
In his speech Prince Escalus speaks about the Montagues and the Capulets as "enemies to peace" (l. 1) and finishes by even menacing them with "pain of death" (l. 23).
Verwenden Sie nicht das ganze Zitat, können Sie die ausgelassenen Passagen mit eckigen Klammern kennzeichnen. Genauso können Sie ein Bezugswort in eckigen Klammern einfügen, wenn dies aufgrund der Satzkonstruktion notwendig ist.

Die wörtliche Übernahme von Formulierungen aus dem Ausgangstext bzw. einem anderen Text ohne entsprechende Kennzeichnung ist nicht zulässig und wird negativ bewertet. Da mit Zitaten Aussagen belegt oder gefestigt werden, stehen sie normalerweise nach der entsprechenden Behauptung. Diese sollten Sie zunächst mit eigenen Worten paraphrasieren. Nehmen Sie dabei Ihr einsprachiges Wörterbuch zur Hilfe, um nach Synonymen zu suchen.

Textstruktur und Absätze

Formalia

TIPP zum Punktesammeln

Achten Sie darauf, dass Sie formale Nachlässigkeiten vermeiden. Hier Punkte zu verschenken, ist unnötig.

Zunächst eine generelle Bemerkung: Die Lesenden Ihrer Englischprüfung werden Ihnen grundsätzlich wohlgesonnen sein und werden Sie gerecht bewerten wollen. Dazu ist es natürlich gerade in einer Fremdsprache eine wichtige Voraussetzung, dass Ihre Handschrift gut lesbar ist, sowie dass die Buchstaben und die Wortgrenzen deutlich erkennbar sind, damit die Leser nicht raten müssen, ob Sie nun das für den jeweiligen Kontext passende Wort benutzt haben oder nicht. Wenn Sie also wissen, dass Ihre Handschrift schlecht lesbar ist, bemühen Sie sich zu Ihrem eigenen Vorteil darum, besonders groß und deutlich zu schreiben! Reduzieren Sie nachträgliche Ergänzungen auf ein Minimum. Lassen sich diese nicht vermeiden, nummerieren Sie sie fortlaufend und deutlich und listen Sie den eingefügten Text entweder jeweils am Seitenende oder nach Abschluss des Textes in chronologischer Reihenfolge auf.
Rücken Sie zur besseren Lesbarkeit zwei bis drei Zentimeter ein, wenn Sie einen neuen Absatz beginnen. Erlauben Sie wie gefordert die Hälfte der Seite als Rand für Korrekturzeichen und Bemerkungen der Lehrkraft.

Satzzeichen

Natürlich sollen Sie in der Englischprüfung im Abitur zeigen, dass Sie mit komplexen Satzgefügen umgehen können. Vermeiden Sie allerdings Schwerfälligkeit! Allzu lange Sätze mit vielen Nebensätzen machen Ihren Text schwer lesbar und erhöhen die Wahrscheinlichkeit, dass Sie sich in Ihrer Satzkonstruktion verzetteln. Achten Sie auf sinnvolle Strukturierung durch Satzzeichen; sie helfen dem Leser / der Leserin, Ihren Gedanken zu folgen und sich in Ihrem Text zurechtzufinden. Wechseln Sie ab: Verwenden Sie nicht nur Punkt und Komma, sondern auch Strichpunkt oder Gedankenstrich. Auch durch den Einsatz von Fragen können Sie Ihre Texte ansprechender gestalten.
Interpunktion wird in den Bewertungskriterien nicht aufgeführt und in der Schule großzügig gehandhabt. Bedeutungstragende Satzzeichen, z. B. bei *non-defining relative clauses,* werden jedoch verlangt.

Ausdrucksvermögen / Verfügbarkeit sprachlicher Mittel

Klarheit und Präzision

Die Formulierung der Abituraufgaben folgt klar definierten Regeln. So kommen als Arbeitsanweisungen nur bestimmte Verben in Frage, die sogenannten **Operatoren**. Eine Aufstellung der Operatoren finden Sie auf den Seiten 103 und 132 in diesem Buch.
Lesen Sie die Formulierung der Fragen genau und machen Sie sich klar, welche Art der Antwort von Ihnen im konkreten Fall erwartet wird. Der Operator drückt deutlich aus, was von Ihnen verlangt wird.
Nachdem also die Art der Fragestellung aufgrund der Formulierung mittels der Operatoren klar definiert ist, können Sie Ihre Antwort entsprechend ausrichten. Achten Sie beim Verfassen auf Fehlerquellen, die leicht vermieden werden können. Im Folgenden werden einige typische Fehlerquellen genannt und erläutert. Diese Hinweise mögen auf den ersten Blick selbstverständlich erscheinen, doch durch die notwendige Konzentration auf den Inhalt oder das Arbeiten unter Zeitdruck schleichen sich oft unnötige Fehler ein.

Textökonomie

Schreiben Sie nach dem Grundsatz der Textökonomie „Jeder Satz ein Statement". Vermeiden Sie Wiederholungen im Wortschatz und umständliche inhaltliche „Schleifen". Zum einen leidet darunter der Stil und zum anderen wird die korrigierende Person diese Taktik wahrscheinlich durchschauen.
Vermeiden Sie die Formulierung von Allgemeinplätzen.
(Beispiel: *It is well-known that Europe is suffering from many problems these days.)*

Stellen Sie sicher, dass die sprachlichen Bezüge korrekt sind: Wählen Sie also bewusst die passenden Personal-, Possessiv-, Demonstrativ- und Relativpronomen, um Ihre Leserschaft eindeutig durch den Text zu führen. Verwenden Sie zusätzlich **signal words** *(Firstly, secondly, thirdly, ...)* als Gliederungssignale, um den Text sinnvoll zu strukturieren. Achten Sie auf die Verwendung der Zeiten! Wenn Sie im **past tense** beginnen, müssen Sie diese Zeitebene auch durchgängig beibehalten.

Wortschatz

Der in Ihren Texten verwendete Wortschatz sollte sachlich und stilistisch angemessen sein. Demonstrieren Sie, dass Sie über einen differenzierten allgemeinen Wortschatz verfügen, und variieren Sie in Ihrem Ausdruck.

Ausdrucksmöglichkeiten im Wortfeld „sagen"
to say, to tell, to relate, to describe, to let somebody know, to state, to speak, to talk, to answer, to respond, to reply, to inform, to advise, to recommend, to brief, to update somebody, to promise, to lie, to whisper, to shout, to scream, to yell, to report, to repeat, to argue, to converse, to allude to something, to articulate, to suggest, to demand, to insist, to urge, to ask, to question

Achten Sie dabei besonders auf gängige Fehlerquellen. Die Beispiele sollen Sie für die Problematik sensibilisieren, aus Platzgründen werden jeweils nur einige genannt.

Seien Sie in Alarmbereitschaft bei potenziellen **false friends.**
Hier ist eine Liste der gängigen Fallen:

deutsch	**englisch**	**false friend**
bekommen	to get	*nicht:* become
die Kritik	criticism	*nicht:* critic – die Kritikerin / der Kritiker
die Politik	politics	*nicht:* policy – persönliche Strat*egie, außer in Begriffen wie* foreign policy – Außenpolitik
sensibel	sensitive	*nicht:* sensible – vernünftig
meinen/ glauben	to think	*nicht:* mean – bedeuten *(oder Adj.* mean – gemein)
aktuell	current	*nicht:* actually – in der Tat
also	so	*nicht:* also – auch
Chef	boss	*nicht:* chef – der Küchenchef
engagiert	committed	*nicht:* engaged – verlobt; besetzt
eventuell	possibly	*nicht:* eventually – schließlich
Handy	mobile phone (AE: cell phone)	*nicht:* handy – handlich, praktisch
Konfession	denomination	*nicht:* confession – die Beichte
Konkurrenz	competition	*nicht:* concurrence – Übereinstimmung
konsequent	consistent	*nicht:* consequently – folglich
mobben	to bully	*nicht:* mob – das gemeine Volk
prägnant	concise	*nicht:* pregnant – schwanger
prinzipiell	fundamentally, basically, in/on principle	*nicht:* principally – hauptsächlich
Prospekt	brochure, leaflet	*nicht:* prospect(s) – die Zukunftsaussichten
Protokoll	minutes	*nicht:* protocol – die Etikette (außer bei EDV)
Publikum	audience	*nicht:* public – die Öffentlichkeit
rentabel	profitable	*nicht:* rentable – zu mieten
Rückseite	back	*nicht:* backside – Hinterteil
spenden	to donate	*nicht:* to spend – ausgeben

Verwendung der richtigen Präposition nach Verben oder Adjektiven
Orientieren Sie sich hier nicht am Deutschen, das kann leicht zu einem falschen Ergebnis führen.

Collocations
Bestimmte Wörter treten immer in einer **festen Verbindung** auf, einer **Kollokation**. Der Austausch eines der Bestandteile ist nicht möglich. (Beispiele: *a quick shower, strong tea, to drive so. crazy, fully aware)*

Darüber hinaus wird von Ihnen die Verwendung eines angemessenen **thematischen Wortschatzes** erwartet. Prägen Sie sich die Glossare zu den lehrplanrelevanten Themen der vorangegangenen Kapitel ein, um den thematischen Wortschatz bei Bedarf zur Verfügung zu haben (vgl. Kapitel „Basiswissen", S. 18).
Zu guter Letzt sollten Sie über einen präzisen **fachmethodischen Wortschatz** verfügen. Das Handwerkszeug dazu bekommen Sie im Kapitel „Methoden der Textarbeit" (S. 102) dieses Buches, wo Sie geeignetes Vokabular zum Thema finden. Sie sollten sich sowohl Vokabular für literarische Texte als auch für Sach- und Gebrauchstexte aneignen.

Differenzierte Satzgestaltung

Neben der Gewandtheit im Wortschatz wird natürlich auch Ihr Können im Bereich Syntax bewertet. Wechseln Sie also je nach Kontext ab zwischen Parataxe und Hypotaxe, d. h. einer Reihung von Hauptsätzen bzw. komplexen Satzgefügen mit Nebensätzen. Verbinden Sie diese entsprechend mit Konnektoren (s. Liste S. 135); erwähnen Sie Bezüge in temporaler, kausaler, konzessiver, konditionaler und resultativer Hinsicht.

Übersicht über die möglichen Konjunktionen

temporal	while, before, after, until
kausal	since, because, as, for
konzessiv	(al)though, while/whilst, whereas
konditional	if, unless
resultativ	so (that)

Integrieren Sie Partizipial-, Gerundial- und Infinitivkonstruktionen sowie Passivkonstruktionen. Wechseln Sie zusätzlich durch Inversion sowie gelegentliche Verwendung von (rhetorischen) Fragen mit anderen Satzformen ab.

Eigenständigkeit (Paraphrase)

In der Abiturklausur werden Ihr Textverständnis und Ihre Ausdrucksfähigkeit bewertet. Ihr Ziel muss es deshalb sein, dem Korrektor ein umfassendes Bild von Ihrer Ausdrucksfähigkeit im Englischen zu geben. Greifen Sie dabei häufig auf längere Textpassagen des Originaltexts zurück, kann die Eigenständigkeit der Leistung nicht ausreichend bewertet werden. Denken Sie also daran, Zitate nur zum Belegen Ihrer eigenen Thesen zu verwenden.

Sprachliche Richtigkeit (Fehlerschwerpunkte vermeiden)

Orthografie, Grammatik

Orthografie

Rechtschreibfehler passieren leicht als Flüchtigkeitsfehler beim Schreiben. Um dem entgegenzuwirken, sollten Sie sich eine funktionierende Zeitplanung aneignen, die Ihnen genug Spielraum lässt, nach Abschluss der produktiven Phase den Text noch einmal durchzulesen und eventuelle Rechtschreibkorrekturen vorzunehmen. Achten Sie dabei besonders auf Interferenzen mit dem Deutschen.

Grammatik

Wie bereits zu Eingang des Kapitels erwähnt, kann in diesem Rahmen keine umfassende Grammatikwiederholung stattfinden. Gehen Sie also Ihre individuellen Problempunkte selbst an.
Trotzdem können an dieser Stelle einige gängige Fehlerquellen genannt werden, auf die Sie ein besonderes Augenmerk legen sollten:

Verben

Sehen Sie sich vor der Prüfung noch einmal die Liste der unregelmäßigen Verben an und prägen Sie sich die Formen ein, die keinem gängigen Schema folgen, z. B. *lie, lay, catch.*

Denken Sie darüber hinaus auch an *phrasal verbs,* deren Bedeutung zum Teil nicht aus den Bedeutungen der Einzelwörter erschließbar ist, z. B. *turn down* (etwas ablehnen).

Adverbien

position of adverbs in the sentence: Adverbien können im englischen Satz an verschiedenen Stellen stehen, die oft nicht mit dem Deutschen übereinstimmen. Sie können folgende Positionen einnehmen: Satzanfang oder -ende sowie vor und nach dem Verb, das sie näher bestimmen (bei zusammengesetzten Verbformen nach dem Hilfsverb).

Beispiele:
Unfortunately, *the turnout for the country's first free election was very low.*
They had counted the votes ***carefully.***
Nevertheless, *the bad news weighed* ***heavily*** *on them.*
I ***often*** *wonder what became of him.*
My sister ***also*** *came.*
We must ***also*** *consider the opposite case.*

Beispiele für Prüfungsaufgaben

Die Beispielaufgaben sind vom Umfang und vom Schwierigkeitsgrad her teilweise für Leistungskurse, teilweise für Grundkurse konzipiert.
Um den verschiedenen Vorgaben für die beiden Kursarten gerecht zu werden, wurden überwiegend Texte ausgewählt, die den Vorgaben beider Kursarten entsprechen. Von Fall zu Fall werden Aufgabenstellungen ergänzt oder angepasst. Eine gute Möglichkeit, sich auf diesen Teil der Prüfung vorzubereiten, sind die TED talks: www.ted.com.

Aufgaben mit Beispiellösungen

Hörverstehen

Beispielklausur: *Immigration in Britain*

You can listen to the audio file by scanning this QR code:

Source: http://www.marketplace.org/2013/08/08/world/britains-immigration-crackdown-sparks-anger
(published on 8 August 2013, accessed on 1 April 2022)

You will hear a radio programme called *Marketplace,* dealing with the topic of immigration in Britain. While listening, tick the right answer (a, b, c, or d). Do not tick more than one answer. You will hear the recording twice. You have 2 minutes to look at the task. You will have 30 seconds to finalise your answers after the second listening.

1. The British government is planning to reduce illegal immigration because
a) illegal immigrants are too expensive.
b) residents living in Britain legally don't get enough jobs.
c) illegal immigrants are known for their drug abuse.
d) British citizens have racial views.

2. The billboard carried by a van in the northeast corner of London
a) made most people who saw it smile.
b) diverted other drivers' attention.
c) caused a lot of anger.
d) was created by illegal immigrants

3. Neemal Patel claims that
a) black people have raided a supermarket.
b) black people were asking for a place to live.
c) the official's behaviour was illegal.
d) some of the black people refused to give their names.

4. Immigration minister Mark Harper says that
a) the billboard campaign must be stopped. ☐
b) the officials acted legally. ☐
c) black people have to be checked. ☐
d) immigration status must be controlled. ☐

5. James Goddard from Ilford complains that
a) the reporter's English is rather poor. ☐
b) only a few people in Ilford speak English. ☐
c) nobody speaks English accurately. ☐
d) in Ilford it is dangerous to walk along the street. ☐

6. According to Goddard, life in Ilford has changed because
a) whites are now a minority. ☐
b) the press only reports about positive aspects of immigration. ☐
c) the media ignore the immigrants. ☐
d) the white people have left the immigrants behind. ☐

7. James Goddard's reaction to the billboard campaign shows that
a) he is in favour of it. ☐
b) he wants to see another campaign like that. ☐
c) he likes the idea of stirring up trouble. ☐
d) he is against campaigns like that. ☐

Lösungen

1. b	5. b
2. c	6. a
3. c	7. d
4. b	

Beispielklausur: *British Asians are Living in Fear*

You can listen to the audio file by scanning this QR code:

Source: https://www.bbc.co.uk/sounds/play/p01hn2xg (accessed on 1 April 2022)

You will hear a radio programme dealing with the topic of Asians in Britain. While listening, complete the table below. Write your answers in the boxes. You do not have to write complete sentences. There is one example answer (0). You will hear the recording twice. You have 90 seconds to look at the table. You will have 2 minutes to finalise your answers after the second listening.

0	The Runnymede Trust made a survey and argues that, due to race and religion, 60 % of members of ethnic minorities are worried about ... (Give two examples.)	*a) personal safety* *b) discrimination in education services (and the workplace)*
1	As a means to stop the harassment, one woman says she had to ... (Give two examples.)	*a)* *b)*
2	Being British, she says, has always been ...	
3	The leader of a Meena women's project says the massive media coverage has led to ... (Give two examples.)	
4	The fear of Asians to leave their homes and their immediate area has been creating ...	
5	The Runnymede Trust claims that even the British government has been using racist rhetoric, telling ethnic minorities to ...	
6	A survey has shown that the colour of people's skin has had a negative impact on ... (Give two examples.)	*a)* *b)*
7	It is feared that a change will only happen in something like ...	

Lösungen

1. a) change her (personal) appearance
   b) stop wearing certain clothes
2. a part of their lives
3. a) a sense of concern
   b) anxiety
4. enclaves
5. go home
6. a) their life chances
   b) their security
7. 50 years

Beispielklausur: *Mum's Cooking Makes Jobs*

You can listen to the audio file by scanning this QR code:

Source: https://www.bbc.co.uk/sounds/play/p018zgpl
(accessed on 1 April 2022)

You will hear a radio programme dealing with the topic of Asians in Britain. While listening, complete the table below. Write your answers in the boxes. You do not have to write complete sentences. There is one example answer (0). You will hear the recording twice. You have 90 seconds to look at the table. You will have 2 minutes to finalise your answers after the second listening.

0	The speaker's mother has always wanted to start a food business but did not do it because of ... (Give two examples.)	*a) lack of confidence* *b) lack of formal qualifications (and language barriers)*
1	Things started to change when the speaker ... (Give two examples.)	*a)* *b)*
2	Together with some friends, the idea of home delivery made him ...	
3	In the South Asian community, after the children have left the house, women consider themselves ...	
4	Women of these ethnic minority backgrounds are not usually found in the statistics and do not claim ...	
5	They are so scared that they lack everything, so they do not even start ...	
6	Irene motivated herself to be a part of 'Mummy's Cooking' because she thought she ... (Give two examples.)	*a)* *b)*
7	How she was going to be perceived was something that she at first ...	
8	That training would be for young people only is what Irene considered ... at first.	

Lösungen

1. a) was studying at university
   b) had to eat bad food there
2. found a company with friends
3. too old
4. unemployment benefit
5. the process of getting benefit
6. a) was a good candidate
   b) could be independent
7. feared
8. a barrier

Kombinierte Aufgabe – Sachtext und Politische Rede

Part 1: Mediation

AUFGABENSTELLUNG

Together with your English partner school, you are participating in an international project on climate change. Your task is to write an article on the results of the Glasgow Climate Change Conference 2021 (COP 26) to be published on the project's website. Write this text using the article below and focussing on the perspective of the African nations.

Materialgrundlage

M1 Andrea Böhm, „Klimaschutz oder grüner Kolonialismus? – Eine Kolumne von Andrea Böhm", *ZEIT online,* 06.01.2022, https://www.zeit.de/politik/ausland/2022-01/cop-26-globaler-sueden-klimawandel-gerechtigkeit-5vor8 (Zugriff: 01.04.2022, gekürzt).

Hilfsmittel

Den Prüflingen stehen einsprachige sowie für den schulischen Gebrauch geeignete zweisprachige Wörterbücher der Allgemeinsprache (Deutsch–Englisch/Englisch–Deutsch) zur Verfügung.

M1 „Klimaschutz oder grüner Kolonialismus?" *Andrea Böhm*

[...]

Die Konferenz in Glasgow im vergangenen November, in Deutschland schon fast wieder vergessen, hat in Staaten des globalen Südens enorme Verbitterung hinterlassen. Erneut wurde ihre zentrale Forderung abgebügelt: Klimagerechtigkeit.

Natürlich war COP26 kein totaler Reinfall. Der schrittweise Abschied aus der Kohleenergie steht im Abschlusspapier, über 140 Regierungen haben den Schutz und die Wiederaufforstung der Wälder versprochen, über 100 Länder wollen bis 2030 den Methanausstoß um ein Drittel reduzieren und alle sollen ihre Klimaziele bis zur nächsten Konferenz nachbessern. Was in Glasgow nicht passierte: die Verantwortung für die Erhitzung unseres Planeten ehrlich zu benennen und Rechenschaft abzulegen.

Dass die Ärmsten am wenigsten zur Erderwärmung beigetragen haben, aber schon seit Langem den höchsten Preis zahlen, ist längst eine Binsenweisheit. Bloß empfindet sie in unseren Breitengraden kaum jemand als Skandal. 23 reiche Staaten mit heute zwölf Prozent der Weltbevölkerung (darunter die USA, Deutschland, Kanada und Japan) haben seit Beginn der Industrialisierung die Hälfte aller CO_2-Emissionen ausgestoßen.

Die andere Hälfte verteilt sich auf über 150 andere Länder – und wird angeführt von China, das inzwischen fast 14 Prozent der Emissionen verursacht hat. Subsaharaafrika ist für gerade mal 1,85 Prozent verantwortlich, wird aber schon seit Jahrzehnten weit dramatischer von den Folgen der Klimakrise getroffen als Europa. Gleiches gilt für die kleinen Inselstaaten, denen buchstäblich der Untergang droht.

Deswegen fordern ärmere Staaten seit Jahren einen Fonds für Schäden und Verluste (*loss and damage*) gefüllt von den Hauptverursachern des Klimawandels. Aus diesem Fonds sollen von Dürren, Fluten, Hungersnöten oder Unwettern Betroffene im Zusammenhang mit der Erderwärmung unterstützt werden. Der Außenminister von Bangladesch, AK Abdul Momen, hat das Konzept unlängst mit dem Vorgehen gegen die Tabakindustrie in den Neunzigerjahren verglichen, als sich die US-Regierung von den Konzernen vor Gericht einige der Milliarden Dollar zurückholte, die durch die Gesundheitsschäden des Rauchens entstanden waren.

Die Entwicklungsländer fühlen sich verprellt

Nun, der Fonds wurde in Glasgow nicht beschlossen, vor allem aufgrund des Widerstands der USA und der EU, die fürchten, für Klimaschäden haftbar gemacht zu werden. Auch bei anderen Zahlungen fühlen sich Entwicklungsländer verprellt. 100 Milliarden US-Dollar jährlich ab 2020 wollten Industrienationen für Klimaprojekte im globalen Süden bereitstellen, um beim Übergang zu grüner Energie und bei der Anpassung an die Krise zu helfen – zum Beispiel durch Frühwarnsysteme oder Küstenbefestigungen. Die Summe wird frühestens 2023 zum ersten Mal erreicht.

Zum Vergleich: Der Hilfsfonds für die Opfer des Hochwassers in Rheinland-Pfalz und Nordrhein-Westfalen ist auf 30 Milliarden Euro angelegt.

Viel des internationalen Geldes wird laut einer Studie von Oxfam auch gar nicht als Zuschuss geleistet, sondern als Kredite, die oft mit Zinsen zurückgezahlt werden müssen. Soll heißen: Was vonseiten der Industriestaaten als Hilfe angeboten wird, ist für die Empfänger oftmals eine Schuldenfalle.

Natürlich gibt es auch kleine Lichtblicke: So gaben die EU, Großbritannien, Deutschland und Frankreich während der Glasgower Konferenz bekannt, Südafrika mit 8,5 Milliarden Euro beim Ausstieg aus der Kohle helfen zu wollen.

Prima. Aber es mindert nicht die Wut unter Politikern wie Aktivistinnen auf dem Nachbarkontinent über europäische und US-amerikanische Heuchelei. In Glasgow versprachen westliche Industrienationen, die Finanzierung weiterer Projekte zur Öl- und Gasförderung zu stoppen. Im Ausland, aber nicht daheim. Großbritannien subventioniert weiter seine Erdölindustrie, die USA wollen ihre Inlandsproduktion sogar noch steigern.

Kein afrikanisches Land sieht seine Zukunft in fossilen Energieträgern

Und während westliche Staaten sowie internationale Finanzinstitutionen den Geldhahn für Erdgasförderung in afrikanischen Ländern zudrehen, stempelt sich die EU Atomkraft und Gas klimafreundlich. Der Vorwurf des "grünen Kolonialismus" afrikanischer Aktivisten mag in europäischen Ohren harsch klingen, verständlich ist er allemal: Hier warten Abermillionen darauf, dass endlich Strom aus der Steckdose kommt. Gerade Afrika braucht Erdgas für seine wirtschaftliche Entwicklung – als Übergang. Denn kein afrikanisches Land sieht seine Zukunft in fossilen Energieträgern. Kenia oder Sambia beziehen schon heute über 50 Prozent ihrer Energie aus nachhaltigen Quellen. Das Ölland Nigeria, das 2050 mehr Einwohner haben wird als die USA, will seine Stromproduktion bis dahin verachtfachen – überwiegend mit Solarenergie. Zur Absicherung braucht es, wie gesagt, Erdgas. Und mehr finanzielle Hilfe.

Die Forderung nach einer gerechteren Beteiligung und Entschädigung durch Industriestaaten wird nach Glasgow nicht leiser, sondern lauter werden. Immerhin: Die Deutschen sehen ihr Land in der Verantwortung. Über 70 Prozent erklärten in einer Umfrage des Instituts für Demoskopie Allensbach im vergangenen Sommer, dass die Industrieländer eine "große" oder "sehr große" Verantwortung für die Klimakrise in Entwicklungsländern tragen.

Die Frage ist, was daraus folgt. Zum Beispiel ein Vorstoß der Ampel-Regierung für einen *Loss-and-damage*-Fonds. Die nächste Klimakonferenz findet im November 2022 in Ägypten statt.

Part 2: Politische Rede

AUFGABENSTELLUNG Writing

1. Outline the main points in Kamala Harris's speech.
2. Imagine you are a member of a journalist club in your school. Write an article expressing your own views towards the possibility of change in the USA, referring to Kamala Harris's visions and to information you have gathered during your English lessons.

Materialgrundlage

M2 „Senator and Vice-Presidential Nominee Kamala Harris' 2020 Democratic National Convention (DNC) speech on August 19", 19.02.2020, General Counsel, Austin; https://www.rev.com/blog/transcripts/kamala-harris-2020-dnc-speech-transcript (Zugriff: 01.04.2022, gekürzt)

M2 Kamala Harris: 2020 Speech at the Democratic National Convention (extract)

Aug 20, 2020

That I am here tonight is a testament to the dedication of generations before me, women and men who believed so fiercely in the promise of equality, liberty, and justice for all. [...]

My mother instilled in my sister Maya and me the values that would chart the course of our lives. She raised us to be proud, strong Black women, and she raised us to know and be proud of our Indian heritage. She taught us to put family first, the family you're born into, and the family you choose. [...]

And even as she taught us to keep our family at the center of our world, she also pushed us to see a world beyond ourselves. She taught us to be conscious and compassionate about the struggles of all people, to believe public service is a noble cause, and the fight for justice is a shared responsibility. [...]

I accept your nomination for Vice President of the United States of America.

I do so committed to the values she taught me, [...] and to a vision passed on through generations of Americans, one that Joe Biden shares. A vision of our nation as a beloved community, where all are welcome, no matter what we look like, no matter where we come from, or who we love. A country where we may not agree on every detail, but we are united by the fundamental belief that every human being is of infinite worth, deserving of compassion, dignity, and respect. A country where we look out for one another, where we rise and fall as one, where we face our challenges and celebrate our triumphs together.

Today, that country feels distant. Donald Trump's failure of leadership has cost lives and livelihoods. [...] And while this virus touches us all, we got to be honest. It is not an equal opportunity offender. Black, Latino, and Indigenous people are suffering and dying disproportionately. And this is not a coincidence. It is the effect of structural racism, of inequities in education and technology, healthcare and housing, job security and transportation. [...]

So we're at an inflection point. The constant chaos leaves us adrift. The incompetence makes us feel afraid. The callousness makes us feel alone. It's a lot, and here's the thing. We can do better, and deserve so much more. We must elect a president who will bring something different, something better, and do the important work. A president who will bring all of us together, Black, White, Latino, Asian, Indigenous, to achieve the future we collectively want. We must elect Joe Biden. [...]

Right now, we have a president who turns our tragedies into political weapons. Joe will be a president who turn s our challenges into purpose. Joe will bring us together to build an economy that doesn't leave anyone behind, where a good paying job is the floor, not the ceiling. [...]

That's the vision that our parents and grandparents fought for. The vision that made my own life possible. The vision that makes the American promise, for all its complexities and imperfections, a promise worth fighting for. So make no mistake, the road ahead is not easy. We may stumble. We may fall short, but I pledge to you that we will act boldly and deal with our challenges honestly. We will speak truths, and we will act with the same faith in you that we ask you to place in us. We believe that our country, all of us, will stand together for a better future. [...]

In this election, we have a chance to change the course of history. We're all in this fight. You, me, and Joe, together. What an awesome responsibility. What an awesome privilege. So let's fight with conviction. Let's fight with hope. Let's fight with confidence in ourselves, and a commitment to each other, to the America we know is possible, the America we love. And years from now, this moment will have passed, and our children and our grandchildren will look in our eyes. And they're going to ask us, "Where were you when the stakes were so high?" They will ask us, "What was it like?" And we will tell them. We will tell them not just how we felt. We will tell them what we did. [...]

Erwartungshorizont

Überprüfte Kompetenzen	
Mediation	Strategien
Aufg. 1)	Zusammenstellen der wichtigsten Inhalte, Verfassen eines Internetartikels mit passender Überschrift, Verwendung von thematisch passendem Vokabular
Schreiben	
Aufg. 1)	Zusammenfassen der wichtigsten Inhalte
Aufg. 2)	In einem Artikel die eigene Meinung darlegen und begründen und sie in Beziehung zu den Aussagen des Textes setzen

Beispiellösung

Part 1: Mediation

<u>North vs. South: The Climate Injustice of COP 26</u>

The conference in Glasgow may seem a success story for a lot of states in the Northern hemisphere: 140 countries signed a treaty to phase out of fossil fuels, to protect forests and to reduce methane emissions by a third.

However, in her review of COP 26 in the German newspaper "ZEIT", Andrea Böhm points out that it has left many nations in the South feeling bitter, as the conference once again failed to address one pressing issue: climate justice. While 23 states with 12 % of the world population are responsible for half of all CO_2 emissions, these suffer comparatively little from the effects of climate change. On the other hand, sub-Saharan nations, for ex-

ample, which contribute less than 2 % of global CO_2 emissions, are hit particularly hard by climate change. Hence, these southern nations demand that those mainly responsible for CO_2 emissions create a special fund to pay for the damages caused by climate change. Due to resistance from the US and the EU, COP 26 failed to implement this fund. In addition, financial aids promised by these richer nations for climate projects in the global south not only appear relatively small compared to money that is spent on climate-related damages nationally. A lot of these payments are also planned as loans, making further debt likely.
Another injustice has led some African activists to speak of "green colonialism": While the EU labels natural gas as climate-friendly within its sphere, it has stopped financial support for its exploitation further south. This decision hits African nations hard since they rely on gas for their economic growth, even though some of these states already gain over 50 % of their energy from sustainable sources and no African country sees its future in fossil fuels.
In any case, the calls for more climate justice are growing louder even in Western nations such as Germany. Luckily, COP 27 is just around the corner.

Part 2: Politische Rede

Aufgabe 1

The text is from Senator Kamala Harris's acceptance speech, given at the Democratic National Convention on 20 August 2020 after her nomination as democratic vice presidential candidate for the forthcoming election. As the first woman of colour to run for vice presidency of the USA, she emphasises her pride in her Indian heritage and her gratitude to her mother, who brought her up to be compassionate and conscious of other people's problems.
Harris touches upon liberty, equality and justice for all: this is the "shared responsibility" (l. 21 f.) she and Joe Biden accept. She pictures the USA as a "beloved community" (l. 29) where everybody is welcome, irrespective of ethnic heritage or sexual orientation. Everyone deserves respect; every individual is of inestimable value.
Harris calls on her fellow Democratic Party members to show unity and loyalty to Joe Biden and herself in the task of reversing Trump's white-supremacy policy, which has politically polarised and socially divided the country. She holds out the prospect of Joe Biden as a healing and unifying head of state, building an economy that provides jobs for all and in this way re-establishes the "American promise" (l. 75). But at the same time she admits that this may be a path of trial and tribulation.
Harris ends her speech by emphasising her belief in the country standing together to achieve a better future for all American citizens and by again invoking Democratic Party unity. Underlining the opportunity to change the course of history by winning the Presidency, she calls the election a "fight" (l. 89) which should be undertaken confidently and convincingly.

Aufgabe 2

Kamala Harris gave a very interesting and inspiring acceptance speech as vice presidential candidate of the USA. In her speech, held before the Democratic National Convention on 20 August 2020, Harris mentions politically charged issues she wants to address during Joe Biden's and her term of office. These include the situation of minorities – for example people of colour or homosexuals. Furthermore, she pursues the idea of a "united" America as a country every American can love.

The latter is a noble and ambitious aim in a politically polarised society, where the Democratic Party nurtures ideas of equality, while conservative Republicans are often unwilling to give up on latent ideas of white supremacy. The Democrats will have a hard fight to enact their intended bills.

The situation is compounded by the fact that there is now, after the election, a standoff in the Senate between Democrats and Republicans. But this tricky situation might be resolved by Kamala Harris herself, as she will have a 'casting vote' as vice president when it comes to a 50:50 situation for and against a bill.

The Democrats might, then, be able to legally change situations for certain social groups. History shows, however, that laws can be implemented but are not necessarily observed by people who oppose them. Racism will not be removed by law alone: profound social and cultural change must occur, above all in countering the fear that drives self-aggrandisement, racism and violence.

As racist actions are often carried out covertly, it is hard to take adequate measures against them. To my mind, the vision of peaceful coexistence among groups of people with a widely different experience of everyday life, like WASPs and those from the LGBTQ community, may be difficult – or even impossible – to realise in today's societies.

Harris's speech is powerfully written and touches on topics of major importance for individual and social life in the USA. Her appeal for change in US society is positive and her ideas are contagious. Let us hope that she will succeed in achieving her political goals.

Sachtext – Politischer Zeitungsartikel

AUFGABENSTELLUNG

1 Point out the different measures the LAPD uses to fight crime. (30 %)

2 Explain the pros and cons of the concept of "predictive policing" (ll. 34 f.) on the basis of the given article and compare it to the police's work in the films you have seen. (30 %)

3 For many young people becoming a police officer is a dream job. *The Guardian* has invited young people like you to debate the new measures of policing in a conference held in London. As you have dealt with fictional films which show police work and the problems officers face, you want to take part in it. In order to apply for participation in the conference, you have to write an essay outlining your idea of a modern police force. In your essay you should also refer to this article and to material studied in class. (40 %)

Materialgrundlage

Nate Berg, „Predicting crime, LAPD-style", *The Guardian*, 25.06.2014, https://www.theguardian.com/cities/2014/jun/25/predicting-crime-lapd-los-angeles-police-data-analysis-algorithm-minority-report (Zugriff: 01.04.2022, gekürzt)

Hilfsmittel

Den Prüflingen stehen einsprachige sowie für den schulischen Gebrauch geeignete zweisprachige Wörterbücher der Allgemeinsprache (Deutsch–Englisch/Englisch–Deutsch) zur Verfügung.

"Predicting crime, LAPD-style" *Nate Berg*

[...]

The Los Angeles Police Department, like many urban police forces today, is both heavily armed and thoroughly computerised. The Real-Time Analysis and Critical Response Division in downtown LA is its central processor. Rows of crime analysts and technologists sit before a wall covered in video screens stretching more than 10 metres wide. Multiple news broadcasts are playing simultaneously, and a real-time earthquake map is tracking the region's seismic activity. Half-a-dozen security cameras are focused on the Hollywood sign, the city's icon. In the centre of this video menagerie is an oversized satellite map showing some of the most recent arrests made across the city – a couple of burglaries, a few assaults, a shooting.

On a slightly smaller screen the division's top official, Captain John Romero, mans the keyboard and zooms in on a comparably micro-scale section of LA. It represents just 500 feet by 500 feet. Over the past six months, this sub-block section of the city has seen three vehicle burglaries and two property burglaries – an atypical concentration. And, according to a new algorithm crunching crime numbers in LA, and dozens of other cities worldwide, it's a sign that yet more crime is likely to occur right here in this tiny pocket of the city.

The algorithm at play is performing what's commonly referred to as predictive policing. Using years – and sometimes decades – worth of crime reports, the algorithm analyses the data to identify areas with high probabilities for certain types of crime, placing little red boxes on maps of the city that are streamed into patrol cars. "Burglars tend to be territorial, so once they find a neighbourhood where they get good stuff, they come back again and again," Romero says. "And that assists the algorithm in placing the boxes. [...] A really good officer would be able to go out and do the same, but this somehow makes the average guys' ability to find the crime a little bit better."

Predictive policing is just one tool in this new, tech-enhanced and data-fortified era of fighting and preventing crime. As the ability to collect, store and analyse data becomes cheaper and easier, law enforcement agencies all over the world are adopting techniques that harness the potential of technology to provide more and better information. But while these new tools have been welcomed by law enforcement agencies, they're raising concerns about privacy, surveillance and how much power should be given over to computer algorithms.

P. Jeffrey Brantingham is a professor of anthropology at UCLA who helped develop the predictive policing system that is now licensed to dozens of police departments under the brand name PredPol. "This is not Minority Report," he's quick to say, referring to the science-fiction story often associated with PredPol's technique and proprietary algorithm. "Minority Report is about predicting who will commit a crime before they commit it. This is about predicting where and when crime is most likely to occur, not who will commit it."

[...] Jennifer Lynch [senior staff attorney at the Electronic Frontier Foundation (EFF)] worries that there's too much submissive acceptance of these technologies by the public, without consideration of exactly how this data is collected and used. She says that predictive policing, with its claims of reducing crime, will be given something of a free pass.

"What starts to happen is people think the results that come out of that must be accurate because there's technology involved," Lynch says. "But what we forget is that the information that went in may have been the subject of bias, may have been based on inaccurate assumptions about people, may have been collected in certain communities more than other communities. The problem is technology legitimises somehow the problematic policing that was the origination of the data to begin with."

[...] "We're pretty careful about what people do here," Romero says. "I care about civil liberties and freedom. And I know that our constitution was not written to protect us from gang members and thieves and thugs; it was written to protect us from the government and overreach of the government."

But concerns persist. Gary T Marx, professor emeritus of sociology at the Massachusetts Institute of Technology, says technology such as predictive policing creates "categorical suspicion" of people in predicted crime areas, which can lead to unnecessary questioning or excessive stopping-and-searching. And as data-driven policing expands, Marx worries that analysis and decision-making by machine will lead to what he calls "the tyranny of the algorithm". "The Soviet Union had remarkably little street crime when they were at their worst of their totalitarian, authoritarian controls," Marx says. "But, my god, at what price?"

Lösungshinweise

Aufgabe 1

Measures used by LAPD to fight crime: CCTV (closed circuit television) surveillance; satellite map of LA showing recent arrests; zoom-in facility governed by "predictive policing" algorithms; conventional armed policing

Aufgabe 2

Predictive policing

- pros: crime tends to concentrate in hotspots which are identifiable by algorithms, which can process far more data far more quickly than the average police officer; this enables police to focus on these areas
- cons: people believe technology too easily; algorithms are only as reliable as the information fed into them; focus on a particular area can easily lead to focus on the particular people or ethnic group that live in that area; predicting crime is not the same as detecting or preventing crime and can even be counterproductive.

  The film "Crash", for example, is concerned more with the way the particular experience, background and circumstances of the individual police officer can affect their work. But the film is set before the "digital revolution", so has nothing directly to do with the scenario of the "predictive policing" article. The police in "Crash" are out on the streets and in their patrol cars and have to survive there in their job, with their colleagues and in their personal lives. They are more affected by problems like racism and xenophobia, criminals in the family and so on – i. e. personal problems.

Aufgabe 3

Here are some ideas for your application:

- purpose of policing is to make life safe for all citizens – a basic need of society;
- but this cannot be at the cost of equally basic liberties;
- policing can only be as fair as the laws governing society;
- fair policing presupposes fair and just laws and law courts;
- and this principle must also govern the means the police use to maintain and protect people's safety;
- there's no inherent reason why high-tech digital methods should not be used to analyse and even "predict" crime patterns, but one has to be careful here: the reason for surveillance of all kinds is always suspicion, and suspicion will soon interpret an action as illegal or threatening even if it is not so;
- after all, everyone is made of good and evil and there is an inherent human tendency to accuse anyone who is however slightly different from what we ourselves consider the norm.

Cartoon – Globalisation

AUFGABENSTELLUNG

Globalisation – a fair chance for everyone?
With an international group of university students, you are preparing a weekend seminar on the effects of globalisation. You do these preparations via email.
You are responsible for the opening session and have been given the task of choosing a cartoon for it. You have found the cartoon at hand. Explain how it will best suit the purpose of introducing the issue and why it can be given to the participants as a means for stimulating their awareness.
After describing the cartoon, analyse what the students can learn from it and plan your seminar session, giving your partners some ideas of the main points you want to make.
Write this email.

Copyright: Popa Matumula/toonpool.com

TIPP zur Beschreibung von Bildmaterial

Auch bei Aufgaben, in denen das Material nur eingebettet ist, ist es sinnvoll, dieses an der entsprechenden Stelle im Text zu beschreiben. In unserem Beispiel ist es notwendig, die Beschreibung des Bildes in der Einleitung aufzugreifen, um anschließend darauf eingehen zu können. Bei der Betrachtung von Bildern ist es ebenso wie bei Texten entscheidend, die Position des Fotografen, Künstlers, Karikaturisten etc. zu berücksichtigen. Bei jedem Bild sollte man sich die Frage stellen, mit welcher Absicht es angefertigt worden ist, und sollte dies sprachlich in der Darstellung berücksichtigen.

Beispiellösung

Dear Sarah and Everyone,

I am looking forward to doing this weekend seminar with you on this absolutely controversial subject. In preparation for next week, I have found the cartoon attached to this email. I think it will suit nicely because it addresses one of the core issues of globalisation and the criticism about it: the growing differences in the distribution of wealth on this planet. I think I will use it after the introduction as an eye-opener displaying it via our projector so that everyone can see it on the wall.

The students will first notice the big wave that comes from the right and has "GLOBALISATION" written on it in capital letters. I might cover this caption at first because otherwise they will not describe what they see but enter into a discussion straight away. Two men can be seen, one riding on the wave like a seafaring captain and the other threatened by the huge wave – more like a tsunami, with the power to kill the person on the beach. Looking closer, the students will see that the man on the beach holds an empty bowl in his hands and the few clothes he is wearing suggest that he is one of the poor of this world. The man in the boat has Caucasian (Western) features, and the boat he is steering bears the words "THE RICH" as its name. The cartoon evidently has to do with the vast difference rich and poor. If I then reveal the caption "globalisation", the topic of the cartoon will become clear to the students.

So, there is a lot to describe and to think about in this cartoon. But what do I intend the students to learn from it? They will be able to understand that there is an enormous difference in the effects of globalisation for people in the Northern hemisphere and those in the South, whether from Sub-Saharan, Latin American, or East Asian regions. They will understand that their own everyday experience of globalisation is positive because they belong to those on top of the wave but that the effects for those smothered by the wave of globalisation are different and even life-threatening. The white boatman is happy, thinking he is safe: he gains power and wealth from globalisation, he shares in global trade and global goods, and it has great advantages for him. But the poor person is exploited, has no resources, cannot afford the goods he produces and will not survive. However – and this is a big point in the cartoon – the wave, like all waves, will break, and the bigger the wave the greater the force it releases. What will this force do with the white man's little boat? The cartoon's answer is pretty obvious.

Interpreting the cartoon is, I think, the first main point of the session. From there, we can go on to a discussion of global trade. Here we can get a bit more personal, asking questions like: Where do you personally notice the effects of globalisation? Where do the products you use come from? What negative effects of globalisation do you know about? Have you ever been to countries that suffer negative effects from globalisation? Those are the main points I would suggest for discussion, and they should amply fill the time at our disposal. Please give me some feedback. Do these ideas make sense to you? See you at lunchtime in the cafeteria tomorrow after Mr. Clooney's class.

Best,
Jens

Aufgaben mit Bewertungskriterien

Kombinierte Aufgabe – Mediation und Writing

Part 1: Mediation

Aufgabenart

Zielgruppengerechte Sprachmittlung – keine Übersetzung! Für die Aufgabe stehen 60 Minuten Zeit zur Verfügung. Es darf ein Wörterbuch verwendet werden. Nach Ablauf der Bearbeitungszeit wird der zweite Prüfungsteil ausgehändigt.

AUFGABENSTELLUNG

Your English partner school is planning an international work experience programme, which also welcomes applications from German students. The programme's supervising teacher found the article below online and has asked you for a contribution to the school's homepage. Write this text, summarising the article's key information.

Materialgrundlage

M1 Roland Preuß, „Anonyme Bewerbungen: Inkognito zum neuen Job", *Süddeutsche Zeitung*, 17.04.2012, https://www.sueddeutsche.de/karriere/anonyme-bewerbungen-inkognito-zum-neuen-job-1.1334284 (Zugriff: 01.04.2022, gekürzt)

M1 „Anonyme Bewerbungen: Inkognito zum neuen Job" *Roland Preuß*

[...]

Ein Pilotprojekt zeigt nun auf, wie mehr Chancengleichheit in die Personalabteilungen einziehen kann. Eineinhalb Jahre lang haben fünf Unternehmen und drei öffentliche Arbeitgeber anonymisierte Bewerbungen getestet, unter ihnen die Deutsche Post, L'Oréal und das Bundesfamilienministerium. An diesem Dienstag stellt die Antidiskriminierungsstelle des Bundes in Berlin die Ergebnisse vor. In dem Bericht, der der *Süddeutschen Zeitung* vorliegt, kommen die Autoren [...] zu dem Schluss, dass anonyme Bewerbungen denen, die sonst unter Pauschalurteilen leiden, zugutekommen.

[...]

Bei dem Großversuch mit gut 8500 Bewerbungen hatten die Arbeitgeber zunächst auf Angaben wie Foto, Name, Alter und Geschlecht verzichtet. Mal mussten die Aspiranten einen Online-Fragebogen ausfüllen, mal wurden verräterische Zeilen geschwärzt. Für die Vorentscheidung zählten also nur die Fakten wie Abschlüsse und Berufserfahrung. Erst vor dem Bewerbungsgespräch durften die Chefs Namen und Zeugnisse sehen. Dann aber haben die Bewerber nach Einschätzung der Forscher bereits die entscheidende Hürde überwunden, denn im persönlichen Gespräch wucherten Klischees weniger.

„Das Projekt hat gezeigt, dass anonymisierte Bewerbungen den Fokus auf die Qualifikation lenken", sagt die Leiterin der Antidiskriminierungsstelle des Bundes, Christine Lüders. Zudem habe sich das Verfahren als praktikabel erwiesen. Laut Bericht sehen die Personalverantwortlichen das neue Verfahren „durchgängig positiv", nur das Schwärzen von Unterlagen wird als aufwendig kritisiert. Auch die Jobsuchenden befürworten das Verfahren überwiegend, allerdings glaubt ein gutes Viertel von ihnen, dass ihre Chancen bei herkömmlichen Bewerbungen höher sind.

Vier Arbeitgeber des Pilotversuchs haben sich bereits dafür entscheiden, weiter auf anonymisierte Bewerbungen zu setzen, darunter der Geschenkedienstleister Mydays und das Bundesfamilienministerium. [...]

Part 2: Literarischer Text – Zadie Smith, *White Teeth*

Aufgabenart

Analyse und Interpretation eines literarischen Textes im Rahmen eines situativen Kontextes. Für diesen Prüfungsteil stehen ca. 240 Minuten (auf erhöhtem Niveau) zur Verfügung.

AUFGABENSTELLUNG

You are taking part in an international seminar on the situation of black immigrants in Great Britain. The basis of your studies is Zadie Smith's novel. In order to sum up the results of your group, you have been asked to write an article to be read by the other participants.

1 In your article you contrast the situation of immigrants in England with the situation of people of colour in America.

2 You interpret the author's intention when writing this passage and her possible personal opinion on the matter of immigration.

Materialgrundlage

M2 Zadie Smith, *White Teeth*, London: Hamish Hamilton, 2000. S. 326 f. (346 Wörter)

M2 White Teeth (excerpt) *Zadie Smith*

The following text is an extract from the novel "White Teeth" by Zadie Smith, which is set in contemporary London. The story focuses on three families with different cultural backgrounds whose lives become intertwined because of their children. One of the characters (Irie Jones, l. 8) has an English father and a Caribbean mother. She has fallen in love with a boy called Millat Iqbal, whose parents are from Bangladesh.

This has been the century of strangers, brown, yellow, and white. This has been the century of the great immigrant experiment. It is only this late in the day that you can walk into a playground and find Isaac Leung by the fish pond, Danny Rahman in the football cage, Quang O'Rourke bouncing a basketball, and Irie Jones humming a tune. Children with first and last names on a direct collision course. Names that secrete within them mass exodus, cramped boats and planes, cold arrivals, medical checkups.

It is only this late in the day, and possibly only in Willesden, that you can find best friends Sita and Sharon, constantly mistaken for each other because Sita is white (her mother liked the name) and Sharon is Pakistani (her mother thought it best – less trouble). Yet, despite all the mixing up, despite the fact that we have finally slipped into each other's lives with reasonable comfort (like a man returning to his lover's bed after a midnight walk), despite all this, it is still hard to admit that there is no one more English than the Indian, no one more Indian than the English. There are still young white men who are angry about that; who will roll out at closing time into the poorly lit streets with a kitchen knife wrapped in a tight fist. But it makes an immigrant laugh to hear the fears of the nationalist, scared of infection, penetration, miscegenation, when this is small fry, peanuts, compared to what the immigrant fears – dissolution, disappearance. Even the unflappable Alsana Iqbal would regularly wake up in a puddle of her own sweat after a night visited by visions of Millat (genetically BB; where B stands for Bengaliness) marrying someone called Sarah (aa where 'a' stands for Aryan), resulting in a child called Michael (Ba), who in turn marries someone called Lucy (aa), leaving Alsana with a legacy of unrecognizable great-grandchildren (Aaaaaaa!), their Bengaliness thoroughly diluted, genotype hidden by phenotype. It is both the most irrational and natural feeling in the world.

Annotations:

8 to hum: summen; **10 to secrete:** to hide; **14 Willesden:** an area in North West London;
33 miscegenation: Rassenmischung; **36 unflappable:** unerschütterlich;
46 diluted: verdünnt; **46 f. genotype/phenotype:** genetische Veranlagung / äußere Erscheinung

Bewertungskriterien und Erwartungshorizont
Teil 1: Sprachmittlung

Dieser Teil wird in Abhängigkeit von Qualität und Klarheit der sprachlichen Vermittlung integrativ bewertet. Es erfolgt keine getrennte Wertung von Sprache und Inhalt.

Sprachmittlung
Die Schülerin / Der Schüler stellt im Rahmen der geforderten Textsorte zielgruppengerecht und sprachlich angemessen die wesentlichen Punkte des Textes dar: – pilot scheme that included the German mail service and companies like L'Oreal tested anonymous applications for 18 months – proved that otherwise disadvantaged applicants profit from this process – applicants either blacked out details like name, gender and age or completed an online application; these details were only provided to the potential employer shortly before interviews – process put greater focus on an applicant's qualifications instead of clichés – while a quarter of the applicants believed to have a better chance with a regular application, four of the five participating employers decided to continue with the anonymous application process

TIPP zum Punktesammeln

In Mediationsaufgaben wird generell erwartet, dass das Material nicht wortwörtlich übersetzt, sondern sinngemäß einbezogen wird. Dies erfordert einen souveränen Umgang mit der englischen Sprache, sodass deutsche Ausdrücke und Redewendungen nicht wörtlich übernommen, sondern in richtiges Englisch umgesetzt werden. Auch die kulturellen Unterschiede können bei diesem Aufgabentyp von Bedeutung sein, sodass beachtet werden muss, ob typisch deutsche Gepflogenheiten ggf. geklärt werden sollten oder ob es, wie in diesem Fall, darauf ankommt, auf im englischen Sprachraum bekannte Themen zurückzugreifen.

Teil 2: Schreibaufgabe

Aufgabe 1

Diese Aufgabe gehört zum Anforderungsbereich II.

TIPP zum Punktesammeln

Es wird hier erwartet, dass Sie einen Artikel verfassen, der den vorliegenden Text mit vorhandenem landeskundlichen Hintergrundwissen verknüpft. Beachten Sie die geforderte Textsorte! Wichtig ist auch hier eine geeignete Überschrift! Denken Sie auch daran, dass ein adressatenorientierter Text verfasst werden muss.

Aufgabe 1
In einem zielgruppengerechten Artikel werden Parallelen zwischen der Situation von Immigranten in Großbritannien und der der Afroamerikaner in den USA erarbeitet. Folgende Aspekte könnten erörtert werden:
– While immigrants have decided to move to a different country in order to live there, people of colour in America did not choose to live in the US – they were forced to live and work there as slaves.
– People of colour in the US were treated as second-class people for centuries; immigrants also often face prejudice and discrimination.
– Both immigrants and people of colour face everyday discrimination in education, jobs, housing, etc. This makes it difficult for them to accept the host society as their own; both groups tend towards ghettoisation and cultural isolation.
– While immigrants have the chance to blend in with their new surroundings, so long as they do not look too foreign (see names in the excerpt), people of colour cannot shed their skin – their heritage is always visible and they are therefore perceived as different; this also applies to many immigrant groups, whose members are visibly different.
– Despite being American citizens, people of colour in the US have long been outsiders in American society; with a growing number of prominent black representatives (e.g. President Barack Obama), this role is changing.

Aufgabe 2

Diese Aufgabe gehört zum Anforderungsbereich III – *Interpretation*.

Aufgabe 2
Die Schülerin / Der Schüler interpretiert im Rahmen der geforderten Textsorte den Textauszug im Hinblick auf die mögliche Aussageabsicht der Autorin Zadie Smith. – Smith wants to reveal how immigrants feel about living in Britain; she wants to **arouse empathy** for first-generation immigrants who are afraid that their children will lose their cultural identity.
– She points out that immigration has already led to a mix of cultures and states that "we have finally slipped into each other's lives with reasonable comfort" (ll. 20–22). With this comment, one gets a positive, consoling impression of immigration. It becomes evident that **integration is possible.**
– But Smith is also conscious of the **dangers of assimilation.** She describes the loss of cultural identity and parents' fear that integration into British society might mean their children **giving up their cultural heritage.**
– But Smith comments on this by saying, "[i]t is both the most irrational and natural feeling in the world" (ll. 47 f.). Here it becomes clear that, while she understands this feeling, **she is not afraid that cultural roots will be lost completely.**
– In this respect, Smith seeks to convey the positive aspects of immigration by showing the possibility of living together. She takes on a **critical and insightful** perspective, which enables the reader to understand that (first-generation) immigrants are just as afraid of a cultural and genetic mixing as are British nationalists.

Aufgaben zur Sprachmittlung mit Beispiellösungen oder Bewertungskriterien

Sachtext – *Gun debate*

AUFGABENSTELLUNG

You are doing an exchange year at an American high school in Massachusetts. During a social studies project about violence, your exchange partner has given a presentation about shootings at German schools and their consequences. You have discovered the following article on *ZEIT online* and would like to use it for a presentation about American teachers arming themselves. Write that part of the presentation that deals with this article.

Materialgrundlage

Martin Klingst, „Wir zielten liegend“, in: *ZEIT online,* https://www.zeit.de/2014/01/usa-schule-bewaffnete-lehrer (Veröffentlichung: 27.12.2013, Zugriff: 01.04.2022, verändert)

Wir zielten liegend *Martin Klingst*

Vor einem Jahr richtete ein Amokläufer in einer Grundschule in Newtown, Connecticut, ein Blutbad an. Am Morgen des 14. Dezember 2013 zog der offenbar psychisch gestörte Adam Lanza mit einem halb automatischen Sturmgewehr durch Flure und Klassenzimmer und tötete zwanzig Kinder und sechs Schulangestellte, ehe er sich selbst tötete. Der Bericht der Staatsanwaltschaft ist ein erschreckendes Dokument des Waffenwahns.

Das Massaker erschütterte Amerika. Präsident Obama hielt eine aufwühlende Rede, die Nation vereinte sich im Schmerz. Wie Obama plädierten zwei Drittel der Amerikaner für ein Verbot von Sturmgewehren, acht von zehn waren für eine schärfere Kontrolle von Waffenverkäufen. Demokratische und republikanische Senatoren arbeiteten an einer gemeinsamen Initiative. Doch die mächtige Waffenlobby NRA mobilisierte gegen jede Einschränkung des Waffenbesitzes und setzte mit ihren gut vier Millionen Mitgliedern die Politik in Washington unter enormen Druck. Ein nationales Waffengesetz scheiterte schon im ersten Anlauf.

Die Schuldirektorin Nancy Anderson hat ihre geladene Smith & Wesson immer dabei. Mal steckt sie in ihrer rosafarbenen Handtasche, mal im schwarzen Anorak, auf dem groß „Security“ steht. Und in einem halben Dutzend über das gesamte Schulgelände verteilten Safes werden weitere Schusswaffen aufbewahrt. Nur Anderson und eine Handvoll speziell ausgebildeter Kollegen besitzen dafür einen Schlüssel. Von der Öffentlichkeit kaum bemerkt, haben sich Hunderte von Schulen in Amerika bewaffnet. Jedes zweite Elternpaar glaubt inzwischen, seine Kinder seien dadurch sicherer.

Im Sommer versuchte der Justizminister des Bundesstaates Arkansas der Schulleiterin Anderson und zwölf weiteren Direktoren die Bewaffnung zu untersagen.

Was sie täten, sei „ungesetzlich", sagte er. Der Schul- und Polizeiausschuss des Parlaments gab zunächst dem Justizminister recht. Doch dann trat Nancy Anderson in den Zeugenstand und sagte voller Empörung: „Für Polizisten fehlt meiner Schule das Geld, ist das Leben armer Kinder darum weniger wert?" Der Ausschuss revidierte sein Urteil.

Doch für viele Menschen im Süden Amerikas wie in den Weiten des Mittleren Westens erscheint die Debatte über ein strengeres Waffengesetz wie von einem anderen Stern. Viele lernen schießen, bevor sie schreiben können. Nancy Anderson ging bereits als kleines Kind mit dem Großvater auf die Jagd. Die Eltern betrieben auf dem Land eine Tankstelle samt Lebensmittelladen. Neben der Kasse habe stets eine geladene Flinte gelegen. „Waffen", sagt die Schulleiterin, „gehören zu unserem Haushalt wie Messer und Gabel." Eine Waffe zu besitzen ist in diesem Amerika Teil der Geschichte, der Identität und der Weltanschauung.

Für sie gibt es darum nur eine richtige Antwort auf das Massaker: „Gegen einen schlechten Menschen mit einem Gewehr hilft nur ein guter Mensch mit einem Gewehr."

Anderson, unterstützt von ihren Schülern, Eltern und Lehrern, machte darum sofort mit, als die Waffenlobby NRA als Konsequenz aus dem Amoklauf von Newtown bewaffnete Sicherheitskräfte forderte. Am besten schützten sich Schulen durch Polizisten oder einen privaten Wachdienst, steht in einem 225-Seiten-Report der NRA, „notfalls" aber auch durch im Schießen besonders geschulten Lehrern. „Die Entscheidung darüber sollte jede Schule für sich treffen."

Nancy Anderson versteht nicht, warum die Lehrergewerkschaft entsetzt „Bücher statt Gewehre!" ruft. Natürlich hat sie von den Einwänden etlicher Sicherheitsexperten gehört und weiß, dass Lehrer im Umgang mit Waffen längst nicht so geübt sind wie Polizisten. Doch Anderson hält dagegen. „Ich bin kein schießwütiges Cowgirl", sagt sie. „Ich bin aber auch hier, um all diese Schüler zu schützen."

Das Argument, je weniger Waffen, desto weniger Morde, zieht bei ihr nicht. In Andersons Welt, die sie mit der Hälfte der Amerikaner teilt, wird völlig anders gedacht. Hier sagt man: Je mehr Gewehre in den richtigen Händen, desto größer die Sicherheit! Ein Jahr nach dem Amoklauf von Newtown muss man darum nüchtern feststellen: Obama hat den politischen Kampf einstweilen verloren, die anfangs breite Unterstützung für ein nationales Waffengesetz ist längst geschwunden. Zwar schufen eine Handvoll Bundesstaaten striktere Vorschriften und verbieten inzwischen Mitarbeitern von Unternehmen wie Starbucks in ihren Filialen das Tragen von Schusswaffen. Aber die Gegenwehr der Waffenlobby ist erfolgreicher.

Vierzig Stunden mussten Anderson und die anderen Gesetze büffeln und schießen üben. „Wir warfen uns auf den Boden und zielten liegend aus der Hüfte", erzählt die Direktorin. Im Februar werden Anderson und ihre Kollegen an einer besonderen Übung teilnehmen, um ihre Stressresistenz zu testen. In einer Schule werden darum Szenen wie in Newtown nachgestellt.

Quelle: http://www.zeit.de/2014/01/usa-schule-bewaffnete-lehrer
Dieser Text wurde aus didaktischen Gründen leicht gekürzt und verändert.

Beispiellösung

Dear Class,

Last week Benjamin told us about violence at schools in the context of our social studies project and presented the way my country, Germany, deals with school massacres and the measures that have been taken. I would like to look at the fact that quite a few American schools have armed themselves and give you some information about their reasons. I found an interesting article on this topic in a well-known daily newspaper from Germany, "ZEIT online".

So let's start with some important background information. After the terrible school massacre at Newtown Connecticut in 2013, in which a mentally disturbed young man killed 20 students and six teachers, the nation was shocked. Taking sides with President Obama, two-thirds of American citizens wanted a ban on assault rifles, and eight out of ten favoured stricter controls on rifle sales.

But the National Rifle Association (NRA), a powerful lobby with more than four million members, immediately stepped in. As you know, the discussion about gun control is not new in America, and the NRA used all its traditional arguments, reminding the public of their right under the 2nd Amendment to own a gun and pressuring the government to back down. They demanded more armed security guards in schools and went so far as to suggest that teachers should also be armed, even offering to give them firearms training courses.

But what does an "armed school" mean? Nancy Anderson, the head teacher in Arkansas on whom the article focuses, pointed out that financial restrictions prevent many schools from hiring armed security guards and argued that this was discrimination against the poor. She is seen as a hero for her cause and joined an NRA-sponsored 40-hour training programme in order to learn how to handle dangerous situations with the help of guns – which in her school are kept in safes at different places in the building. Her beliefs are shared by many Americans, especially in the South and Mid-West, where guns belong to the cultural tradition. Many grow up with guns as part of their everyday life. To put it in a nutshell: Ms Anderson thinks that she can protect her students adequately now that her school is armed. She strongly believes that guns help protect people from evil; hence it seems logical to assume that safety increases with the number of guns in the right hands. Protecting the weak against the bad calls for strong measures, and arming teachers can certainly be labelled a strong measure. Already every second parental couple believes that this can increase their children's safety.

Now that you have heard why many schools in America choose to defend themselves with guns against possible violence, it is up to you to decide how you feel about the question. By the way, the teachers' union is asking for "books instead of guns" and I have to say, that even if I don't believe that schoolbooks hold all the answers, in this I totally agree with them.

Sachtext – *Migration*

AUFGABENSTELLUNG

With an international group of university students, you are preparing a weekend seminar on current population developments in big cities.
You take part in the opening session of this international project, and you have been given the task of talking about different aspects of migration to major German cities. Using the notion of "good/bad migrants" from Sadigh's article, write an email to your professor and your fellow students, giving them an idea of the main points of your presentation.

Materialgrundlage

Parvin Sadigh, „Die guten, bösen Einwanderer", in: *ZEIT online,* 20.06.2013, http://www.zeit.de/wirtschaft/2013-06/einwanderung-migration-mythen-fakten/seite-5 (Zugriff: 01.04.2022, gekürzt)

„Die guten, bösen Einwanderer" *Parvin Sadigh*

[…] Mythos 5: Es gibt genug Parallelgesellschaften in deutschen Städten. Kommen mehr Einwanderer, ist der gesellschaftliche Zusammenhalt gefährdet.

Jeder kennt die Straßenzüge in Berlin-Neukölln, Hamburg-Wilhelmsburg oder Duisburg-Marxloh: Straßen, in denen alle Läden türkisch sind und Frauen mit Kopftuch herumlaufen. Diese Bilder werden oft mit der Vorstellung verknüpft, hinter den Wohnungs- und Moscheetüren habe sich eine autonome fremde Gesellschaft gebildet, die ihren eigenen Regeln folgt.

Der Historiker Jochen Oltmer findet jedoch schon das Wort falsch. Parallelgesellschaft sei ein Kampfbegriff, sagt er. Meist seien damit nur türkische-muslimische Communitys gemeint. Die Elite, die in Dahlem oder Blankenese unter sich bleibt und deren Mitglieder sich gegenseitig Vorteile verschaffen, wird nicht so bezeichnet. Freiwillig ist die Konzentration der ungebildeten, armen Einwanderer in bestimmten Stadtteilen ohnehin nur bedingt. Sie brauchen bezahlbare Wohnungen. Und natürlich leben nicht nur Türken und Muslime in Neukölln. Eigene Schiedsgerichte oder Schulen gibt es sehr selten. Die meisten türkischstämmigen Einwanderer nutzen die deutschen Institutionen und arbeiten in deutschen Firmen.

Tatsächlich aber nutzen Einwanderer soziale oder ethnische Netzwerke, denn es nützt ihnen. Der Politikwissenschaftler Thomas Meyer spricht von einer „hilfreichen Schleusenfunktion". Bereits hier lebende Verwandte oder Freunde erklären, zu welcher Behörde die neu Eingewanderten gehen müssen, wie man eine Wohnung findet. Sie sprechen die gleiche Sprache und sorgen für ein wenig Geborgenheit in der Fremde. Oltmer sagt, diese Netzwerke seien charakteristisch für Migration, sogar verantwortlich für ihr Ausmaß. Man denke an Kolonien in New York wie Little Italy, Little Germany oder China Town.

Nur wenn das Netz sehr groß ist, die Einwanderer einheitlich aus einer ungebildeten armen Schicht kommen und sie sich von der Mehrheitsgesellschaft diskriminiert fühlen, kann das für sie zur Falle werden, sagt Meyer. Die neuen Migranten lernen nicht Deutsch, können ihren Kindern in der Schule nicht helfen, sie konsumieren nur türkischsprachige Medien. Eine Spirale entsteht, die die Einwanderer am Aufstieg und an der Integration in die Mehrheitsgesellschaft hindert. Wer arbeitslos ist, verkehrt nur noch mit Arbeitslosen, der Hilfsarbeiter mit Hilfsarbeitern.

Besteht also die Gefahr, dass sich neue Kolonien bilden? Neue Einwanderer in Deutschland kommen zu 60 Prozent aus europäischen Ländern. Polen, Rumänen und Bulgaren nutzen natürlich ihre Netzwerke. Spanische Studenten ziehen in eine WG mit befreundeten Spaniern. Doch diese Netze werden sich nicht zu sogenannten Parallelgesellschaften verfestigen. Die meisten der aktuellen Einwanderer sind gebildet – und „je höher der Bildungsgrad, desto größer ist die Tendenz, dass sich Kolonien wieder auflösen", sagt Oltmer. Auch die Gefahr, dass sich sogenannte Parallelgesellschaften von ungebildeten Bulgaren und Rumänen bilden, sei nicht sehr groß. Viele der Einwanderer bleiben nicht lange in Deutschland, sagt Oltmer, und sie sind zu wenige, um eigene Kolonien zu bilden.

Bewertungskriterien

Formale Aspekte

E-Mail-Form, um Information bezüglich eines Themenkomplexes (Einwanderung) an den Professor und an Studienkollegen weiterzugeben:

- Sprachregister: gepflegtes Englisch (aber nicht zu formell, aufgrund des Adressaten)
- Einleitung (um Anlass, Kontext und Adressat zu nennen) sowie Quelle (Erklärung, was *ZEIT online* ist)
- Hauptteil bestehend aus für die Fragestellung wesentlichen Aspekten aus dem Text

Inhaltliche Aspekte

- Einleitung – Adressat: Professor und Studienkollegen
- Kontext: E-Mail zur Vorbereitung einer Präsentation zum Thema Einwanderung
- Verweis auf Quelle und Gesamtkontext des Textauszuges
- Hauptteil
- Assoziationen in Bezug auf Alltagsbilder mit vermeintlichen Parallelgesellschaften aus Neukölln, Hamburg etc.
- tatsächlicher Ist-Zustand: es wird nur der ärmere, bildungsferner Teil der Migranten mit diesem Begriff bezeichnet, nicht die gebildete Elite, äußere Faktoren wie Mietpreise spielen eine Rolle
- Bedeutung der Netzwerke, Vergleich zu den USA
- Gefahr nur bei zu großem, einheitlichem Netz und Gefühl der Diskriminierung: kaum Spracherwerb, soziale Kontakte bleiben im bekannten Umfeld, kein Aufstieg
- Gefahr neuer Kolonienbildung ist gering, da Anteil der gebildeten Migranten höher ist
- Schluss mit Bezug zum Kontext

Original-Prüfungsaufgaben 2021 gA

Quelle der Aufgabenstellung

Niedersächsisches Kultusministerium
Hinweis: Die Musterlösungen zu den Aufgaben sind nicht amtlich, sondern wurden von den Autoren des Bandes „FiNALE-Prüfungstraining" erstellt.

Hinweise:

Die zentrale schriftliche Abiturprüfung im Fach Englisch besteht aus einer kombinierten Aufgabe:

Prüfungsteil 1:	a)	**Hörverstehen**
	b)	**Sprachmittlung**
Prüfungsteil 2:	**Textaufgabe**	

Hilfsmittel:

Den Prüflingen stehen für die Prüfungsteile 1b und 2 einsprachige sowie für den schulischen Gebrauch geeignete zweisprachige Wörterbücher der Allgemeinsprache (Deutsch–Englisch/Englisch–Deutsch) zur Verfügung.

Ablauf und Bewertung der Prüfung:

Ausgabe der **Aufgaben für den Prüfungsteil 1a**	
Prüfungsteil 1a:	**Hörverstehen**
Gewichtung:	20 %
Einlesezeit:	keine
Bearbeitungszeit:	30 Minuten
	Abgabe sämtlicher Unterlagen des **Prüfungsteils 1a**
Ausgabe der **Aufgaben für den Prüfungsteil 1b** und der zugelassenen **Hilfsmittel**	
Prüfungsteil 1b:	**Sprachmittlung**
Gewichtung:	25 %
Einlesezeit:	keine
Bearbeitungszeit:	60 Minuten
	Abgabe sämtlicher Unterlagen des **Prüfungsteils 1b**
Ausgabe der **Aufgaben für den Prüfungsteil 2**	
Prüfungsteil 2:	**Textaufgabe**
Gewichtung:	55 %
Prüfungszeit:	210 Minuten
anschließend:	Abgabe sämtlicher Unterlagen des **Prüfungsteils 2**

Hinweise zum Prüfungsteil 1

- Jedes einzelne Blatt ist mit dem Namen zu versehen. Der Prüfungsteil 1a ist ohne Hilfsmittel zu bearbeiten.

Hinweise zum Prüfungsteil 2

- Von den zwei Aufgaben ist eine auszuwählen und zu bearbeiten.
- Bei jeder Teilaufgabe ist die inhaltliche Gewichtung angegeben.

gA Listening Comprehension

AUFGABENSTELLUNG

You will hear each recording twice. After each listening you will have time to complete your answers. **25 BE**

Task 1: Book Reviews **5 BE**

You will hear five excerpts from radio reports in which the host reviews audiobooks. Match each book review (1 to 5) with one of the headings (A to G) by putting the corresponding letter into the correct box. For each book review there is only one answer which sums up the overall idea best. There are two more headings than you need.

Headings	
A	Stealing to survive
B	A cruel new parent
C	Downfall of a nation
D	Territorial expansion
E	Frustration upon arrival
F	History from a female perspective
G	Hope in the face of financial difficulties

Book Review	1	2	3	4	5	6
Heading						

Source: Audio File Magazine, May/June 2015.
Audio 1: https://soundcloud.com/audiofilemagazine/ross-poldark-by-winston-graham-read-by-oliver-j-hembrough (00:05–00:23); Audio 2: https://soundcloud.com/audiofilemagazine/one-for-the-murphys-by-lynda-mullaly-hunt-read-by-nora-hunter (00:05–00:24); Audio 3: https://soundcloud.com/audiofilemagazine/the-book-of-aron-by-jim-shepard-read-by-michael-goldstrom (00:05–00:29); Audio 4: https://soundcloud.com/audiofilemagazine/jacksonland-written-and-narrated-by-steve-inskeep (00:05–00:24); Audio 5: https://soundcloud.com/audiofilemagazine/capital-dames-which-is-written-and-narrated-by-cokie-roberts (00:04–00:27). (All audio files accessed on 1 April 2022.)

Task 2: Lunch

13 BE

You will hear a BBC report about how lunch breaks have changed.
While listening, fill in the missing information. You need not write complete sentences. Unless otherwise specified, name one aspect.

1	Role of lunch breaks in the past (Add two.)	• enjoy food and drink • ____________ • ____________
2	Reason for the return of lunch breaks in a Singapore institution	
3	Purpose of lunch breaks in the banking district of London in the past	
4	Changes in what is consumed (Name two.)	• ____________ • ____________
5	Reason why business lunches have changed	
6	Role of "Marks and Spencer"	
7	Reason why new kind of lunches are considered "democratic"	
8	Changes in the kind of food that can be purchased for lunch	
9	Way the food is usually consumed	
10	Result of an international study on the effect of extended lunches	
11	Assessment of the current situation by the interviewee (Name *one* aspect.)	

Source: BBC News World Service, "Why Lunch is No Longer On A Worker's Menu", 25 March 2017, http://www.bbc.co.uk/programmes/p04y01d3 (00:26–04:24) (accessed on 1 April 2022).

Task 3: A New Idea for Travelling

7 BE

You will hear an interview with the British adventurer Alastair Humphreys.
While listening, tick the correct answer (a, b, c or d). There is only one correct answer.

1. Having travelled the world, Alastair Humphreys turned to

a	package tours.	☐
b	survival training.	☐
c	nature preservation.	☐
d	unspectacular activities.	☐

2. Humphreys says that the week's experience was

a	relaxing.	☐
b	manifold.	☐
c	dangerous.	☐
d	monotonous.	☐

3. For Humphreys, the advantage of a microadventure is that it is

a	romantic.	☐
b	exclusive.	☐
c	inexpensive.	☐
d	uncomplicated.	☐

4. His contribution to the microadventure concept is to have

a	popularized it.	☐
b	commercialized it.	☐
c	come up with the idea.	☐
d	placed more focus on sports activities.	☐

5. Humphreys' concept motivates people to

a	live healthier lives.	☐
b	take random trails.	☐
c	cycle along motorways.	☐
d	explore the places around them.	☐

6. For Humphreys, spending a night outside

a	unites the family.	☐
b	provides a new perspective.	☐
c	makes you feel insignificant.	☐
d	helps you understand the world.	☐

7. Humphreys' main message is that you should

a	take more but shorter holidays.	☐
b	take a break from working too much.	☐
c	go on environmentally friendly holidays.	☐
d	enjoy ordinary things that fit in with your life.	☐

Source: BBC Radio 4, "Why microadventures are the way to holiday", 31 January 2018, http://www.bbc.co.uk/programmes/p05wpv38 (00:00–04:05) (accessed on 1 April 2022).

Lösungen

Task 1: Book Reviews

1	2	3	4	5
E	B	A	D	F

Task 2: Lunch

No.	BE	*Lösungsvorschlag:*
1	2	*two of the following:* • recharge batteries • socialise with colleagues • make contacts
2	1	people/traders (complained of) feeling overworked
3	1	entertain clients / cement (lucrative) contracts
4	2	*two of the following:* • no big lunches • lunches barely consist of anything at all • drinking (alcohol) is gone • smoking is gone
5	1	business lunches can be seen as a bribe / business can be fined / (business people) can lose (their) job
6	1	launched pre-packed sandwiches (as a convenience meal at lunchtime to save time)

7	1	everybody (regardless of status or income) will buy it / consumed by all classes
8	1	food more exotic/costly/expensive / wider variety of food
9	1	quick in-and-out/eat-at-the-desk (experience)
10	1	French are more productive (than their UK counterparts) / long lunches increase effectiveness of work/productivity
11	1	good that lunch culture has changed /// now sometimes gone too far (the other way) /// you have to be able to establish rapport/personal relationships / sit down and talk over a meal (not just about dealing with mathematics)

Task 3: A New Idea for Travelling

1 d
2 b
3 d
4 a
5 d
6 b
7 d

gA Sprachmittlung

Katja Borowski, „Wenn Grundschülern die Worte fehlen“ (2017)

AUFGABENSTELLUNG

Students at your American partner school are doing a project on volunteer work in elementary schools. Your exchange partner has asked you about examples from Germany. You have come across the article below about reading mentors.
Write him/her an email, presenting the reasons for this initiative and its impact on students and mentors.

Materialgrundlage:

Katja Borowski, „Wenn Grundschülern die Worte fehlen“, in: Frankfurter Allgemeine Zeitung, 24. August 2017, zitiert nach: https://www.faz.net/aktuell/rhein-main/lesepaten-fuer-kinder-wenn-grundschuelern-die-worte-fehlen-1565325.html (Zugriff: 01.04.2022, gekürzt); © Alle Rechte vorbehalten. Frankfurter Allgemeine Zeitung GmbH, Frankfurt. Zur Verfügung gestellt vom Frankfurter Allgemeine Archiv.

Hilfsmittel:

Den Prüflingen stehen einsprachige sowie für den schulischen Gebrauch geeignete zweisprachige Wörterbücher der Allgemeinsprache (Deutsch–Englisch/Englisch–Deutsch) zur Verfügung.

Bearbeitungszeit: 60 Minuten

„Wenn Grundschülern die Worte fehlen“ *Katja Borowski*

„Wenn ich weiß, dass die meisten Kinder nur noch einen Grundwortschatz von 2000 bis 3000 Wörtern haben, wenn sie eingeschult werden, obwohl 5000 Wörter normal wären, und wenn ich außerdem weiß, dass es in jeder Klasse mindestens zwei Kinder gibt, die nicht richtig lesen, schreiben oder sprechen können, dann muss ich sagen: Eigentlich hätte jede Grundschulklasse einen Lesepaten bitter nötig“, sagt Petra Köster. Seit November 2012 baut Köster für den bundesweit agierenden Verein „Mentor – Die Leselernhelfer“ ein flächendeckendes Netz an ehrenamtlichen Lesepaten in Darmstadt und dem Landkreis Darmstadt-Dieburg auf. [...]

Obwohl es in der Region inzwischen 135 ehrenamtliche Mentoren beziehungsweise Lesepaten gibt, aus allen gesellschaftlichen Schichten, von der Hausfrau über Studenten und Berufstätige bis hin zu Rentnern, und Köster eigentlich stolz auf ihre Arbeit sein könnte, sieht sie auch Defizite. Es mache sie traurig, dass manche Schulen eine Zusammenarbeit ablehnten, weil sie meinten, sie hätten es nicht nötig. Oder weil sie befürchteten, die Lehrer noch mehr zu belasten. [...]

Alle Lesepaten steckten viel Herzblut und noch mehr Zeit in ihr Ehrenamt. Die Berufstätigen unter ihnen opferten häufig sogar ihre Mittagspause, um ihren Schützlingen vorzulesen und sie behutsam beim eigenen Lesen, Schreiben und Sprechen zu korrigieren. Das habe positive Auswirkungen auf den Deutschunterricht, berichtet Köster, aber auch auf andere Fächer – beispielsweise bei Textaufgaben in Mathematik. „Viel wichtiger als das Lesen ist aber, dass die Paten mit den Kindern erzählen und lachen und sich ihrer Nöte annehmen“, sagt Köster.

[...]

Marion Aufleger kann ihr da nur zustimmen. Die Direktorin der Darmstädter Schillerschule arbeitet schon lange mit Lesepaten zusammen. Sie sagt: „Bildung und Erziehung funktioniert nun einmal über ‚Beziehung‘. Das Wichtigste ist, dass jemand einfach für die Kinder da ist, weil ihnen im Alltag die Großeltern und andere Bezugspersonen fehlen. Alles andere ergibt sich dann meist von allein.“ Aufleger und Köster wissen, dass in den meisten Familien kaum noch vorgelesen, geschweige denn über Bücher gesprochen wird. Dabei brauchen selbst Kinder, die schon etwas lesen können, immer noch regelmäßig einen Ansprechpartner, um das Gelesene zu reflektieren und Zusammenhänge sowie unbekannte Wörter nachzufragen. „Ein Computer kann mir da in der Regel nicht weiterhelfen“, sagt Köster.

[...] Neue Mitstreiter, sowohl bei den Schulen als auch bei den Lesepaten, findet Köster normalerweise über Mundpropaganda, Aushänge an Schulen, die bundesweite Internetseite „Ehrenamtsuche“ und Zeitungsberichte.

So fand auch Brigitte Alberti zum Verein. Die ehemalige Chefsekretärin wollte ihr Rentnerdasein nicht nur mit Kochen, Lesen und Rückenschule verbringen. Eines Tages las sie in der Zeitung über die Lesepaten. Sie kontaktierte den Verein und fragte, ob es auch in ihrer Nähe eine Schule gebe, an der sie aktiv werden könne. „Und so kam ich zur heutigen Klasse 4a der Andersenschule in Darmstadt-Eberstadt. Die betreue ich seit dem ersten Schuljahr“, sagt Alberti. Einmal wöchentlich übt sie mit Kindern das Lesen, Vorlesen und Verstehen von Texten. Und zwar einzeln oder in Gruppen. Nicht nur die unruhigen und lernschwächeren Schüler kämen dran, sondern auch die guten, „damit die sich nicht langweilen, wenn die anderen mal länger an einer Aufgabe knobeln".

[...]

Bei aller Wertschätzung weiß Alberti aber auch um ihren Vorteil gegenüber Eltern und Lehrern: Sie muss keine Autorität sein, und sie muss keine Noten vergeben. Klassenlehrerin Anke Thiem schätzt sie „als herzensgute, verständnisvolle Ersatz-Omi, wie sie sich jedes Kind wünscht". Sie sei eine große Entlastung für die Lehrer im Unterricht und bei kleineren Ausflügen, auf die sie die Klasse hin und wieder begleite. Zudem kenne sie die Geburtstage aller Kinder und bringe ihnen manchmal sogar kleine Geschenke aus dem Urlaub mit.

[...]

(572 Wörter)

Beispiellösung

Hi Jean,

A while ago, you asked me about examples for volunteer work in elementary schools for your project. I found an article about reading mentors from 2017 in the German newspaper "Frankfurter Allgemeine Zeitung", which I think will be interesting for you.
The problem in Germany is that children often start school with half of the vocabulary that they should usually have a grasp of, and at least two children per class can't read, write or speak properly. They often lack close personal relationships in their daily lives, and therefore they can't reflect on what they read, experience and learn, nor can they ask for unknown vocabulary. Computers just can't take that role!
These are some of the reasons why an initiative of reading mentors was founded. It is a nationwide network with local groups in various regions, one of which is in Darmstadt and was initiated in November 2012.
Marion Aufleger, the director of a local elementary school, says that it's relationships that make education possible. Mentors not only read to their "foster children" but also remember their birthdays and sometimes bring them souvenirs from their holidays. The reading mentors come from all walks of life. Often they are retired and want to get more out of their time, like Brigitte Alberti, a former secretary. She has been coaching a class for four years and is seen as a sort of substitute grandma. The class's form teacher very much appreciates her involvement during lessons and on short school trips.
However, students seem to benefit the most from this volunteer work. When committed reading mentors work with them, positive effects for the children can be seen in their German lessons as well as in their performance in other subjects. More importantly, they have someone to laugh with and to confide in.
Well, I hope this was a helpful contribution to your project. If you have any questions, just let me know.

Best wishes,
XXX

gA Aufgabe I mit Beispiellösung

Alison Allen-Gray, *Unique* (2004, excerpt)

AUFGABENSTELLUNG

1. Sum up the excerpt. (30 %)
2. Compare Dominic's situation with that of the clones in *Never Let Me Go*. (30 %)
3. You are taking part in a literature workshop on "Visions of the Future." You have been asked to contribute an article for the workshop's website, discussing the statement that "narrative fiction expands the ability of readers for ethical contemplation" by Amit Marcus[1], a literary scholar. Write the article, referring to the text at hand and materials studied in class. (40 %)

Materialgrundlage:

Alison Allen-Gray, *Unique*, Oxford: Oxford University Press, 2004, S. 110–112 (gekürzt)

Hilfsmittel:

Den Prüflingen stehen einsprachige sowie für den schulischen Gebrauch geeignete zweisprachige Wörterbücher der Allgemeinsprache (Deutsch–Englisch/Englisch–Deutsch) zur Verfügung.

Prüfungszeit: 210 Minuten

Unique *Alison Allen-Gray*

Dominic, the protagonist, discovers that he had an older and academically brilliant brother called Nick, who died before Dominic was born. As his parents have never told Dominic about his brother's existence, he tries to find out more about him. After meeting Nick's former university professor Imogen Holt, he is staying with his brother's friends Becky and Giles.

[...]

Giles took me back to his house, a tall, old-fashioned terraced place with huge windows. I don't remember falling asleep but I'll never forget the waking on that first day of my new life.

My eyes opened onto a room full of dim, unfamiliar shapes. I struggled in my mind, stretching to reach the clues floating just outside my memory. Something had happened, something vast and unstoppable, but what?

I saw the outline of a man slumped in a chair near the bed. For long, fearful moments, I didn't know who he was, but as my eyes grew accustomed to the charcoal shades, I remembered Giles. And then I remembered why I knew him. My brother's best friend. And with a sudden sickening rush, all the new facts of my life came back.

[1] Amit Marcus, „The Ethics of Human Cloning in Narrative Fiction", in: *Comparative Literature Studies* 49, 3 (2012), 405–433. S. 405

I sat bolt upright and Giles woke.

“It’s all right, mate, you’re with me. It’s Giles,” he said. “You’re quite safe.”We looked at each other a while in the dimness.

At last, I managed to whisper, “Is it true, what Imogen said?”

“Yes, it’s true.”

“I feel so different,” I said. “I don’t know who I am any more.”

Giles went to draw back the curtains from two tall windows. Sunlight drenched the room. I felt the warmth of it.

“You are who you’ve always been.”

He came to sit on the bed and, for the first time, he met my eye, smiled a different kind of smile. I suddenly thought that he would have smiled at Nick like this.

“I don’t feel as if I am.”

A fly buzzed in the hot room.

“What time is it?” I asked.

“Umm … eleven.”

“Giles, did you know what I was?” I said. “From the very first time you saw me?”

He looked up and the worry in his face made me panic. He was worried for me the freak, the unnatural being. Afraid for what would become of me.

“The first time you came to Grenville Hall?”

“Yes. Did you know already – about what Imogen had done?” I remembered his face peering up at me in the gloomy stairwell. He’d looked as if he’d seen a ghost.

“It was a shock seeing you,” he said, “because you’re so like him. To look at, I mean. But no – I didn’t know about what Imogen had done, but …”

“But you guessed?”

He sighed. “It wasn’t such a hard guess to make. Gene therapy and the ethics of cloning were all part of what Nick was studying. And Imogen was – still is – one of the most brilliant geneticists in the world.”

He sprang off the bed as if he wanted to get rid of the whole idea. “I thought, no, this is bizarre, it just isn’t possible that Imogen would have done this to Nick. But of course I knew that it was theoretically possible. She could have done it. I just couldn’t quite accept that she would have done it, knowing the penalty she would face if she was found out. I’d almost convinced myself that it was just an uncanny likeness, just coincidence. Lots of brothers look very alike. And then … when we saw the birthmark …”

“That proved it,” I whispered.

“Beyond doubt.”

“Becky knew it was proof too, didn’t she?”

“Yes. It was a shock. Like me, she knew what was possible in theory, but she’d never in a million years have believed that Imogen would have actually gone ahead and done it.” […]

I suddenly felt trapped in the bed. I threw back the covers and went to stare out of a window overlooking an ancient church. Gravestones were sticking up out of the long grass. […]

“I wish I’d never found out about it! It hasn’t helped, me finding out the truth, it just makes it worse!”

“Makes what worse? What do you mean?”

“The whole thing with me and my father. When you said that just now about Imogen ‘doing that to Nick,’ it sounded as if it was a dreadful thing to do. It’s all right, I know you didn’t mean it to make me feel bad. But it is a dreadful thing to do. Imogen did it because she wanted to see if she could. That’s bad enough. But my father did it because he wanted to replace Nick. Except it didn’t work. I’m a duff copy. But he’ll never stop trying to make me like Nick. He’ll never accept that I just can’t fit into the mould. There's nothing I can do to please him, ever. I don't want to see him again!" [...]

(757 words)

Annotations

48 f. Grenville Hall – a residence building at the university Dominic's brother went to

104 duff – inferior, cheap

Beispiellösung

Aufgabe 1

In this extract from Alison Allen-Gray's novel "Unique", published in 2004, the author explores questions of identity and self-worth in the face of human cloning.
Dominic, the protagonist, wakes up after spending the night at Becky's and Giles', two friends of his deceased brother Nick. He has just found out that genetics professor Imogen Holt has cloned him and calls this first morning the waking up into his new life. Dominic talks to Giles about this revelation and admits that he no longer feels sure of his own identity. Giles tells Nick that, at first, he and Becky believed Dominic to be Nick's twin brother but that they realised that he must be the result of a cloning experiment by Holt when they saw that Dominic even had the same birthmark as Nick.
Dominic is both saddened and angered by finding out the truth. He feels that Holt used him as a guinea pig for her scientific curiosity. More significantly, he is hurt by the fact that his father purely wanted to have a copy of his son Nick, about whose existence their parents had never told Dominic. This realisation plunges Dominic into a complete identity crisis, and he decides never to see his father again.

Aufgabe 2

On the surface, both Allen-Gray's "Unique" as well as Kazuo Ishiguro's novel "Never Let Me Go" deal with a similar issue, namely the ethical and individual consequences of cloning. Accordingly, the protagonists in both novels are clones. All of them are initially unaware of this fact and find out about it in the course of their teenage years. Likewise, for the clones in both novels, this revelation casts doubt on their sense of self and makes them feel unsure about their individuality, as for instance in Dominic's admission: "I feel so different [. ...] I don't know who I am any more" (ll. 28 f.).
Apart from these facts, the novels portray very different situations. The cloning in "Unique" takes place as an illegal university experiment (ll. 60–63). Giles tells Dominic about his and Becky's disbelief once they found out about Holt's experiment (ll. 81–84). Giles talks about the moral implications and science's fault – "it just isn't possible that Imogen would have done this [...], knowing the penalty she would face if she was found out" (ll. 66–72) –, whereas Dominic adds that the blame lies with his father because he wanted a replacement for his deceased son. This knowledge plunges Dominic into a deep identity crisis. He feels so different ("I don't know who I am any more", ll. 28 f.) and regards himself as a "freak" (l. 46).

In "Never Let Me Go", on the other hand, cloning is legal and also, arguably, serves selfish ends, as the clones are bred as organ donors. The novel shows several characters in the same situation. They can therefore share their experience of growing up in the boarding school Hailsham. It is one of their teachers, Ms Lucy, who hints at their purpose in life, of which they are completely ignorant until their teenage years. The students have been cloned systematically and officially to be organ donors for their 'originals', who – unlike Dominic – they do not know and in the course of the story try to find. The clones are not regarded as fully human, nor is there any family around them with which they could grow up. They are believed to have no moral understanding nor feelings. Dominic in "Unique", on the other hand, is certainly regarded as fully human by both his creator as well as his father.

He has no such purpose as the clones in "Never Let Me Go". He is free to move around and live his own life once he has angrily decided to liberate himself from his father's wish ("There's nothing I can do to please him, ever. I don't want to see him again!", ll. 107–109). In "Never Let Me Go", Kathy and her friends accept their fate after finding out about it. There is no real fight against this nor against the system that made them, even when they realise that they will die with their third or fourth "donation". Unlike in "Unique", it is not they themselves but society that treats them with disgust and locks them away in a sort of prison.

Aufgabe 3

Is it easier to read a scientific text on human cloning or is it indeed, as Amit Marcus says, rather "narrative fiction [that] expands the ability of readers for ethical contemplation"? Is it better to focus on the factual and the informative or is it easier – and perhaps more worthwhile – to understand and follow the identity crisis of a fictional character like Dominic in the novel "Unique" or Kathy in the novel "Never Let Me Go"? Non-fictional texts about scientific developments may tell us about facts – they do this efficiently and inform us in scientific language about the background, the procedure and the outcome of a scientific experiment –, but do we understand the moral implications?

Fictional literature serves this idea of considering moral questions much better in that it is far more accessible. Novels try to entertain their readers, while scientific texts often use very complex language in order to explain complex details. Fictional language is easier to understand; a narrator speaks to us in a voice that we know from our own lives. However, not all fictional texts are easily accessible and all of them need to be interpreted in order to gain a good understanding of them. In the excerpt from Allen-Gray's "Unique", for example, there is no direct reference to cloning, and the reader has to guess what Dominic's revelation really was. Likewise, we may wonder whether the clones in Ishiguro's "Never Let Me Go" are brought up or even genetically engineered to be docile or whether this is a realistic, perhaps even desirable reaction to their fate. It must also be noted that magazines like "National Geographic" or "Nature" also address morally difficult subjects in a widely accessible way and may contribute as much to such a discussion as a good novel. Narrative texts are, however, far better at showing what effects certain scientific developments may have on an individual. They tell us about the development of characters, their feelings, their doubts, their crises, their hopes and their fate. As readers of fiction, we are able to slip into a character's thoughts, follow them in their conflicts and their problems. We get a chance to feel empathy for a character and to identify with them. When reading Dominic's words and doubts about his identity in the novel "Unique", we share his suffering from not knowing who he is. Narratives are thus able to introduce conflicting moral standpoints, whereas scientific texts stay more one-dimensional and often do not show the issue in its complexity. On the other hand, ethical questions are not the only component of narrative fiction. A narrative may also be more interested in telling an exciting, fantastical story rather than concern itself with moral issues.

Arguably, narrative fiction is less realistic and therefore less credible than its scientific counterpart. It is less useful at telling us, for instance, if and in what form human cloning will be possible in the future. On the other hand, it has the capacity to create a multitude of utopian and dystopian versions. And unlike scientific texts, fictional literature can evaluate technological advance (as in the excerpt from "Unique") or remain ambiguous about it while still pointing out possible consequences (as in "Never Let Me Go").

Ultimately, scientific literature can only tell us about what is; it is tied to facts and has little room to speculate. Narrative texts, on the other hand, can tell us about what may be; they offer us space to experiment with an idea of ourselves – as humans and as individuals. In this sense, it is much more appropriate for "ethical contemplation" than science.

gA Aufgabe II mit Beispiellösung

Kiley Reid, *Such A Fun Age* (2019, excerpt)

AUFGABENSTELLUNG

1 Describe the situation in the grocery store. (30 %)

2 Examine the way Emira reacts to the treatment by the other people in the store. (30 %)

3 The creators of the blog "Don't Stereotype Me!" have invited readers to send in guest entries, commenting on the following statement by the American psychologist Virginia Satir: "We must not allow other people's limited perceptions to define us." Write this blog entry, also referring to the text at hand and materials studied in class, such as the movie Crash and the short story "The Child." (40 %)

Materialgrundlage:

Kiley Reid, *Such a Fun Age*, 2019, New York: Putnam, 2020, S. 9–14 (gekürzt)

Hilfsmittel:

Den Prüflingen stehen einsprachige sowie für den schulischen Gebrauch geeignete zweisprachige Wörterbücher der Allgemeinsprache (Deutsch–Englisch/Englisch–Deutsch) zur Verfügung.

Prüfungszeit: 210 Minuten

Such a Fun Age *Kiley Reid*

Emira Tucker, a young African-American woman, is in a grocery store together with Briar, the child of the Chamberlains, a rich white family.

[...]

"Excuse me, ma'am." Footsteps followed and when Emira turned around, a gold security badge blinked and glittered in her face. On top it read Public Safety and the bottom curve read Philadelphia.

Briar pointed up at his face. "That," she said, "is not the mailman."

Emira swallowed and heard herself say, "Oh, hi." The man stood in front of her and placed his thumbs in his belt loops, but he did not say hello back.

Emira touched her hair and said, "Are you guys closing or something?" She knew this store would stay open for another forty-five minutes – it stayed open, clean, and stocked until midnight on weekends – but she wanted him to hear the way she could talk. From behind the security guard's dark sideburns, at the other end of the aisle, Emira saw another face. The gray-haired, athletic-looking woman, who had appeared to be touched by Briar's dancing, folded her arms over her chest. She'd set her grocery basket down by her feet.

"Ma'am," the guard said. Emira looked up at his large mouth and small eyes. He looked like the type of person to have a big family, the kind that spends holidays together for the entire day from start to finish, and not the type of person to use ma'am in passing. "It's very late for someone this small," he said. "Is this your child?"

"No." Emira laughed. "I'm her babysitter."

"Alright, well..." he said, "with all due respect, you don't look like you've been babysitting tonight."

Emira found herself arranging her mouth as if she'd ingested something too hot. She caught a morphed reflection in a freezer door, and she saw herself in her entirety. Her face – full brown lips, a tiny nose, and a high forehead covered with black bangs – barely showed up in the reflection. Her black skirt, her slinky V-neck top, and her liquid eyeliner refused to take shape in the panels of thick glass. All she could see was something very dark and skinny, and the top of a small, blond stick of hair that belonged to Briar Chamberlain.

"K," she exhaled. "I'm her babysitter, and her mom called me because –" "Hi, I'm so sorry, I just ... hi." From the end of the aisle, the woman came forward, and her very used tennis shoes squeaked against the tile floor. She put a hand to her chest. "I'm a mom. And I heard the little girl say that she's not with her mom, and since it's so late I got a little nervous."

Emira looked at the woman and half laughed. The sentiment felt childish, but all she could think was, You really just told on me right now?

"Where ..." – Briar pointed to one side of the aisle – "Where these doors go?"

"One second, mama. Okay ..." Emira said.

"I'm her sitter and her mom asked me to take her because they had an emergency and she wanted me to get her out of the house. They are three blocks away." She felt her skin becoming tight at her neck. "We just came here to look at the nuts. Well, we don't touch them or anything. We're just ... we're really into nuts right now, so ... yeah."

For a moment, the security guard's nostrils expanded. He nodded to himself, as if he'd been asked a question, and said, "Any chance you've been drinking tonight, ma'am?" Emira closed her mouth and took a step back. The woman next to him winced and said, "Oh, geez." [...]

All at once, on top of the surreptitious accusations, this entire interaction seemed completely humiliating, as if she'd been loudly told that her name was not on a guest list. "You know what – it's cool," she said. "We can just leave."

"Now wait a minute." The guard held out his hand. "I can't let you leave, because a child is involved."

"But she's my child right now." Emira laughed again. "I'm her sitter. I'm technically her nanny ..." This was a lie, but Emira wanted to imply that paperwork had been done concerning her employment, and that it connected her to the child in question.

"Hi, sweetie." The woman bent and pressed her hands into her knees. "Do you know where your mommy is?"

"Her mom is at home." Emira tapped her collarbone twice as she said, "You can just talk to me." [...]

"Okay, ma'am?" The security guard widened his stance to match hers. "You are being held and questioned because the safety of a child is at risk. Please put the child on the ground – "

"Alright, you know what?" Emira's left ankle shook as she retrieved her cell phone from her tiny purse. "I'll call her father and he can come down here. He's an old white guy so I'm sure everyone will feel better." [...]

(797 words)

Annotations

23 **Briar's dancing** – The woman has watched Emira and Briar dance in the frozen-food aisle before.

36 f. **you don't look like you've been babysitting tonight** – When the Chamberlains call her earlier in the story, Emira is at a party.

39 **to ingest** – to eat or drink, to swallow

51 **K** – okay

62 f. **to tell on s. o.** – to give information on s.o.'s bad behaviour or secrets

66 **mama** – a nickname Emira uses for Briar

82 **surreptitious** – done secretly or quickly

Beispiellösung

Aufgabe 1

In this excerpt from Kiley Reid's novel "Such a Fun Age", published in 2019, the young African-American woman Emira is babysitting Briar, her white neighbors' daughter. Briar's parents have called her in from a party at short notice, and it is late at night. Emira and Briar walk and dance through the rows of a local supermarket, attracting attention. They are stopped by the shop's security guard, who questions Emira whether Briar is her child. As Emira tries to explain the situation, pointing out that she is Briar's babysitter, another customer interferes, admitting that she informed the guard because she feared for the child's safety. As the confrontation continues, Emira becomes more and more unsettled. The security guard, smelling alcohol on Emira's breath, neither accepts any of her explanations, nor does he let her leave the place. In order to finally get out of this awkward situation, Emira offers to call Briar's father, insinuating that she has been made a suspect because of the color of her skin.

Aufgabe 2

In spite of her innocence and her de-escalating behavior, Emira feels increasingly trapped in the excerpted situation. Her emotions thus transform from surprise to downright fear. When Emira is first addressed by shop security, she is surprised and apprehensive. She swallows and offers him an innocent and neutral "Oh, hi" (l. 10), followed by a question that is supposed to show that she is articulate and polite ("Are you guys closing [...] on weekends", ll. 13–17). In the course of the encounter, Emira also refers to her babysitter job as an official employment (ll. 92 f.) in order to make her caring for Briar more legal and to show that she is harmless. This continually places her on the defensive, a feeling that is encouraged by the guard's intimidating behaviour ("The man stood in front of her and placed his thumbs in his belt loops, but he did not say hello back", ll. 10–12; "The security guard widened his stance", ll. 108 f.).

When the "gray-haired, athletic-looking woman" (ll. 21 f.) gets involved, Emira continues to become more and more insecure but outwardly pretends to be at ease. This is shown by some physical reactions: she touches her hair (l. 13), she laughs (l. 34), she consciously arranges her mouth (ll. 38 f.) and finally laughs again (ll. 60 f.).

After the guard's "Ma'am" (l. 26), Emira studies him and believes that privately he must be a nice person, only to be taken aback when he asks her if this was her child (l. 33). Her natural, yet defensive answer "I'm her babysitter" (l. 34) is not accepted because she does not look like one in the guard's eyes. Emira then becomes particularly aware of her identity as an African-American woman – "[h]er face – full brown lips, a tiny nose, and a high forehead covered with black bangs" (ll. 42–44) – particularly in contrast to Briar (ll. 49 f.). She sees a sort of blurred image of herself: she "caught a morphed reflection in a freezer door" (l. 40 f.) and "all she could see was something very dark and skinny" (ll. 47–49). She is thus anxious to avoid being stereotyped, for example as uneducated ("she wanted him to hear the way she could talk", ll. 18 f.) or as aggressive.

As the situation continues, Emira feels increasingly uncomfortable and frightened, particularly at the white woman's far-fetched implication of child theft (ll. 56–59). Emira still wants to explain why Briar and herself had come to the shop (for "nuts", l. 74), but she also feels the skin of her neck tighten (ll. 70 f.).

Yet, the guard's humiliations continue, accusing Emira of possibly having been drinking (l. 78). Emira, unable to deny this, is silenced and steps back (ll. 79 f.). She feels disgraced and compares this to not being accepted as a guest because she is not on the list (ll. 84–86). As a consequence, she tries to flee out of this vortex of accusations and offers to "just leave" (l. 87).

The situation worsens as this is denied to her by the guard, pointing to the child (ll. 89 f.). When the other customer starts talking to Briar instead of directly to Emira (ll. 102–104), she tries to assert herself and regain some authority (ll. 105–107). However, her body reacts physically again as her ankle shakes (ll. 113 f.).

To put an end to this, Emira sees no other way than to call out the stereotypes that she believes to be the cause of her ordeal. She offers to call Briar's father, who is "an old white guy" (ll. 116 f.), sarcastically saying that she is "sure that everyone will feel better" (l. 117).

Aufgabe 3

Virginia Satir is absolutely right when she says that "[w]e must not allow other people's limited perceptions to define us". Thank you for letting me write this entry as a guest to your blog "Don't Stereotype Me!".

Every day, people are defined by what others see in them – they are reduced to their age, their size, their skin color, their ethnicity. They are not looked at as individual human beings but as part of a particular group of people, judged on their outward appearance and on stereotypes that linger at every corner. We all struggle not to be determined by the prejudices people have about us but by what we truly do and are. Even literature and films give us ample proof of this problem, as I've recently learned in my studies.

In Kiley Reid's "Such a Fun Age" (2019), for example, we find that stereotypes often lead to racist discrimination, as when African-American babysitter Emira, taking care of a white child, is put into a humiliating situation just because of her skin color. She is made to feel insecure and lacks self-esteem to free herself from what people see in her. She is completely powerless against the limited perceptions of those accusing her and frustrated by constantly being misunderstood. A similar instance of distrust based on the color of someone's skin can be found in the film "Crash", where Jean demands the locks in her house to be changed again because the previous locksmith was Hispanic.

Stereotypes can also put pressure on people to conform to other people's expectations. The character of Jamal in the movie "Crash", for example, is expected to perform in a particular way: the producers think he should speak more "black" because they do not want his character to appear too well-educated. In the same movie Officer Hansen completely misjudges Peter. Expecting him to draw a weapon simply because he is African-American, Hansen shoots him. In Andrea Lee's short story "The Child", the pregnant young woman Karen is feeling judged by the inappropriate behavior of the drunk man on the underground but likewise regards him as the stereotypical African-American dropout.

If this problem of "limited perceptions" is so ubiquitous, what can we do about it in our daily routine, at work, at parties or in public? Sadly, not very much but show that one is an individual and not a stereotype. This is extremely hard and will often be done in vain. One can try to explain the situation like Emira does in the supermarket. Will this help? No, it won't if the people involved are bigots and unable to see past their prejudices. Emira's only chance is to confront her adversaries with their own racism by implying that they will believe Briar's father simply because he is white. Tragically, the text also reveals how well she has internalised these stereotypes about African-Americans herself.

In other situations, it might be better to just give in, not to fight. Obviously, this is no solution, but in some cases, it might be the only way to get out of a bad situation physically unharmed.

In 2021, I saw empowerment and an emancipation from stereotypes when an African-American poet – Amanda Gorman – was chosen to read her words at the inauguration ceremony of President Biden. Young, black and strong in her message to the world watching her, she described leaving stereotypes behind as a hill everyone has to climb, but she also offered hope by what and by how she said it.

So, people will always stereotype us. Let us not let them limit us to what they see in us but always keep telling and showing them what and who we are.

Original-Prüfungsaufgaben 2021 eA

Hinweise:

Die zentrale schriftliche Abiturprüfung im Fach Englisch besteht aus einer kombinierten Aufgabe:

Prüfungsteil 1:	a)	**Hörverstehen**
	b)	**Sprachmittlung**
Prüfungsteil 2:	**Textaufgabe**	

Hilfsmittel:

Den Prüflingen stehen für die Prüfungsteile 1b und 2 einsprachige sowie für den schulischen Gebrauch geeignete zweisprachige Wörterbücher der Allgemeinsprache (Deutsch–Englisch/Englisch–Deutsch) zur Verfügung.

Ablauf und Bewertung der Prüfung:

Ausgabe der **Aufgaben für den Prüfungsteil 1a**	
Prüfungsteil 1a:	**Hörverstehen**
Gewichtung:	20 %
Einlesezeit:	keine
Bearbeitungszeit:	30 Minuten
anschließend:	Abgabe sämtlicher Unterlagen des **Prüfungsteils 1a**
Ausgabe der **Aufgaben für den Prüfungsteil 1b** und der zugelassenen **Hilfsmittel**	
Prüfungsteil 1b:	**Sprachmittlung**
Gewichtung:	25 %
Einlesezeit:	keine
Bearbeitungszeit:	60 Minuten
anschließend:	Abgabe sämtlicher Unterlagen des **Prüfungsteils 1b**
Ausgabe der **Aufgaben für den Prüfungsteil 2**	
Prüfungsteil 2:	**Textaufgabe**
Gewichtung:	55 %
Prüfungszeit:	240 Minuten
anschließend:	Abgabe sämtlicher Unterlagen des **Prüfungsteils 2**

Hinweise zum Prüfungsteil 1

- Jedes einzelne Blatt ist mit dem Namen zu versehen. Der Prüfungsteil 1a ist ohne Hilfsmittel zu bearbeiten.

Hinweise zum Prüfungsteil 2

- Von den zwei Aufgaben ist eine auszuwählen und zu bearbeiten.
- Bei jeder Teilaufgabe ist die inhaltliche Gewichtung angegeben.

eA Listening Comprehension

AUFGABENSTELLUNG

You will hear each recording twice. After each listening you will have time to complete your answers. **23 BE**

Task 1: Street Trees **7 BE**

You will hear a podcast on trees in Detroit.
While listening, answer the questions. You need not write complete sentences. Unless otherwise specified, name one aspect.

1	What are the advantages of street trees according to the presenter? (Name two.)	• ______ • ______ • make streets look nicer
2	What did a study say about the effect of planting eleven more trees per block?	
3	What was the paradoxical situation in Detroit between 2011 and 2014?	
4	What was the aim of Christine Carmichael's campaign?	
5	According to Christine Carmichael, what were some people in disadvantaged neighborhoods worried about?	
6	What would change these people's attitude towards street trees?	

Source: Jason G. Goldman, "Do-Gooders Should Survey Communities First", *Scientific American*, 22 January 2019, https://www.scientificamerican.com/podcast/episode/do-gooders-should-survey-communities-first/ (accessed on 1 April 2022)

Task 2: Border **6 BE**

You will hear a radio report about life on the Mexican-American border with the cities of El Paso on the American side and Juárez on the Mexican side.
While listening, tick the correct answer (a, b, c, or d). There is only one correct answer.

1. According to the female presenter, how do young locals see the border?

a	as a sad reality	☐
b	as separating families	☐
c	as having little importance	☐
d	as separating different cultures	☐

2. How does Antonio Villaseñor-Baca perceive the border?

a	as a protective measure	☐
b	as a necessary measure	☐
c	as an annoying measure	☐
d	as a threatening measure	☐

3. Why are some children from Juárez able to attend an American school?

a	The school is run privately.	☐
b	The American school is in Mexico	☐
c	They take part in a special program.	☐
d	They have an American and a Mexican passport.	☐

4. What is said about the connection of the two border cities?

a	They are twin cities.	☐
b	They are interdependent.	☐
c	Their police forces cooperate closely.	☐
d	El Paso dominates Juárez financially.	☐

5. Why can Kenia Guerrero cross the border faster?

a	She holds a Green Card.	☐
b	She uses the commercial lane.	☐
c	She only has a small backpack.	☐
d	She has bought a special document.	☐

6. What has made crossing the border more difficult for Kenia?

a	a change in politics	☐
b	rising drug trafficking	☐
c	increased illegal migration	☐
d	the introduction of body scans	☐

Source: Billy Cruz, "Young People Adapt To A Changing Life At The Texas-Mexico Border", *npr: National Public Radio*, 20 July 2018, https://www.npr.org/2018/07/20/630076251/young-people-adapt-to-a-changing-life-at-the-texas-mexico-border (00:05–03:06) (accessed on 1 April 2022)

Task 3: Ship

12 BE

You will hear an interview with Sam King, one of the passengers of the *Empire Windrush*, a ship that took about 500 people from Jamaica to Great Britain in 1948.
While listening, fill in the missing information. You need not write complete sentences.
Unless otherwise specified, name one aspect.

1	Why the economic situation in Jamaica was so serious in 1948	
2	What Sam King's father wanted his son to do	
3	Why Sam King had spent time away from Jamaica	
4	What Sam King realized when back in Jamaica	
5	What Sam King says about the fare for the passage (Name *one* aspect.)	
6	What the journey of the *Windrush* led to	
7	Why some middle-aged passengers found it hard to leave Jamaica	
8	What some travellers did when learning a woman was on board illegally	
9	Why Sam considered the food on board bad (Name *one* reason.)	

10	How people spent their time on board (Name two activities.)	• __________ • __________
11	What some younger passengers worried about	

Source: BBC World Service – Witness History, "The Voyage of the Empire Windrush", 26 June 2011, https://www.bbc.co.uk/programmes/p00h8xkq (00:20–04:43) (accessed on 1 April 2022)

Lösungen

Task 1: Street Trees

No.	BE	*Lösungsvorschlag:*	
1	2	*two of the following:* • good for human health • scrub pollution from the air • good for biodiversity	• provide habitat for wildlife • reduce stress • (have been linked to) reductions in crime
2	1	reduce heart-related conditions (as if people became one-and-a-half years younger) / improve health	
3	1	(on the one hand) offer of free trees / Detroit is city of trees (on the other hand) people didn't want trees	
4	1	get more residents to accept free trees	
5	1	(they) create (an additional) burden of care / extra work	
6	1	involve them (more) in the decision-making process / avoid planting certain trees (size/flowers/fruit/sap)	

Task 2: Border

1 c
2 c
3 d
4 b
5 d
6 a

Task 3: Ship

No.	BE	*Lösungsvorschlag:*
1	1	coconuts were destroyed (in 1944) / coconuts needed time to grow again after hurricane / whole structure of farming was undermined
2	1	to take over the farm / to plant bananas
3	1	volunteered during World War II / served in Royal Air Force in Britain
4	1	(he knew) he wouldn't stay

5	1	28 pounds, 10 shillings /// the average man didn't have 28 pounds, 10 shillings /// equivalent to about three cows /// too expensive for average people
6	1	new wave of migration / a quarter of a million West Indians would follow
7	1	had (to leave their) families/children and wives
8	1	clubbed together and paid to buy her a ticket / bought her a ticket
9	1	old, tinned food (mashed potatoes) /// same food served over and over again
10	2	*two of the following:* • playing dominoes • milling around • boxing competitions • dances • mentally getting ready to land
11	1	finding a job (in England)

eA Sprachmittlung

AUFGABENSTELLUNG

Your US exchange partner has to give a presentation in class about a German tradition and decides to talk about travelling journeymen, as he/she saw one in your hometown last summer. He/She asks you for some help.
Using the information in the text, write an email in which you present the tradition of travelling journeymen and the situation now.

Materialgrundlage:

Andrea Döring, „Mit Stock und Hut auf der Walz – eine alte Tradition lebt“ (2018), wgr/©dpa (gekürzt)

Hilfsmittel:

Den Prüflingen stehen einsprachige sowie für den schulischen Gebrauch geeignete zweisprachige Wörterbücher der Allgemeinsprache (Deutsch–Englisch/Englisch–Deutsch) zur Verfügung.

Bearbeitungszeit: 60 Minuten

„Mit Stock und Hut auf der Walz – eine alte Tradition lebt“ (2018)

Andrea Döring, dpa

[...]

Hut, Stock und ein Bündel – der freundliche junge Mann mit den langen Rasta-Locken ist unschwer als Wandergeselle zu erkennen. An einer Raststätte an der A61 in Rheinland-Pfalz fragt er nach einer Mitfahrgelegenheit. Bis Worms passen die Pläne zusammen, und das kleine Bündel, auch Charlottenburger genannt, hat locker Platz im Kofferraum.

Konstantin Schäfer stammt aus Saarlouis und ist Zimmermann. Gerade kommt der 24-Jährige von einer Feier in der Eifel. Jetzt ist er auf dem Weg zu seinem bislang letzten Arbeitgeber im südhessischen Heppenheim. Der soll ihm in seinem Wanderbuch noch ein Zeugnis ausstellen.

Das Wanderbuch, der knotige Stock, auch Stenz genannt, und das Bündel gehören zur Grundausstattung jedes Wandergesellen dazu. Stolz trägt Schäfer den traditionellen schwarzen Hut, einen Ohrring, ein weißes Hemd, darüber eine Weste mit acht Perlmuttknöpfen, ein Jackett und weite Schlaghosen. Seine Kluft ist schwarz. Das weist ihn als Zimmermann aus, denn jedes Gewerk hat seine eigene Farbe.

Wer Meister werden wollte, musste vom Spätmittelalter bis zur beginnenden Industrialisierung auf Wanderschaft gehen. Arbeits- und Lebenserfahrung sollten die jungen Männer sammeln. In ungefähr 35 Handwerken ist das bis heute möglich: Bäcker, Betonbauer, Bootsbauer, Goldschmiede, Köche, Landwirte, Maurer und Schneider gehören etwa dazu.

„Es ist wunderbar, wenn junge Menschen Erfahrungen sammeln. In der Bäckerei habe ich Wandersleute allerdings noch nie gesehen“, erzählt Peter Görtz, Inhaber einer großen Bäckerei-Kette in Ludwigshafen und Umgebung. „Ich würde sofort 20 nehmen.“

Maternus Burauen von der IG Bau und erster Sekretär der Conföderation Europäischer Gesellenzünfte (CCEG) schätzt, dass derzeit etwa 450 bis 550 Gesellen auf der Walz sind. Eine offizielle Statistik gibt es nicht. Aktuell seien schätzungsweise zehn bis zwanzig Prozent der Wandersleute Frauen. [...]

Seit 2014 gehört die Walz in Deutschland zum immateriellen Kulturerbe der UNESCO. Wer sich auf sie begeben will, muss einige Regeln beachten: Er muss in einem Handwerk einen Gesellenbrief erlangt haben, unverheiratet sowie schuldenfrei sein. Die Wanderschaft dauert zwei oder drei Jahre – und einen Tag. In dieser Zeit darf man sich seinem Heimatort bis auf 50 Kilometer nicht nähern. Ursprünglich war dies als Marktkontrolle für die Meister gedacht – ihre Gesellen sollten woanders ihr Glück finden und ihnen keine Konkurrenz machen.

„Ich hatte Fernweh“, sagt Schäfer. Seit fast zwei Jahren ist er schon unterwegs. Durch Holland, Belgien, Frankreich, Österreich, die Schweiz und Israel führte ihn bereits sein Weg. „Viele unterschiedliche Arbeitstechniken habe ich kennengelernt, aber wichtiger als die handwerkliche ist die Erfahrung mit Menschen und die Selbsterkenntnis“, sagt er.

„Beim Österreichischen Hospiz in Jerusalem habe ich am Eingangsportal Schusslöcher zugespachtelt“, berichtet er. Welche Arbeitgeber Schäfer nach seinem Besuch in Heppenheim findet, ist offen. Der Geselle will nach Norwegen. „Die zahlen gut“, hofft er. Der Lohn richtet sich nach den ortsüblichen Tarifen. Üblich ist oft auch Kost und Logis.

In Worms am Dom ist die gemeinsame Fahrt zu Ende, es bleibt noch der Weg bis Heppenheim. Dort hat sich Schäfers zwischenzeitlicher Arbeitgeber und früherer Altgeselle Jerome Schmitt bereits mit 25 Jahren selbstständig gemacht. „Ich habe ihn unter meine Fittiche genommen, habe ihm beigebracht, wie das Leben auf der Landstraße funktioniert, wie man Arbeit findet, als ich vor zwei Jahren selber noch unterwegs war“, berichtet Schmitt. „Wer auf Wanderschaft geht, hat schon ein gewisses handwerkliches Know-how. Man lernt mehr im Bereich des Menschlichen“, erzählt er. „Wichtig ist das vor allem bei problematischen Kunden. Man ist pragmatisch und zielorientiert, wirft nicht so schnell die Flinte ins Korn“, sagt er zum Wert der alten Traditionen. „Man gibt sein Wort, man lässt sich festnageln.“

Festnageln ist dabei im buchstäblichen Sinne gemeint. „Man wird auch heute noch mit dem Ohrläppchen an einen Balken genagelt. Dann bekommt man Ringe an die Ohren. Ursprünglich waren die dazu da, die Beerdigung zu bezahlen, wenn man unterwegs stirbt“, sagt Schmitt. Im Zeitalter von Piercings und Tattoos wirkt das aber gar nicht mehr so archaisch. Und ganz modern erscheint auch die Idee der Walz, an verschiedenen Orten zu leben und zu arbeiten.

(638 Wörter)

Beispiellösung

Dear Mike,

I think I can help you with your presentation on traveling journeymen. I recently came across a fascinating article, written by Andrea Döring in 2018 and entitled “Mit Stock und Hut auf der Walz – eine alte Tradition lebt”.
The tradition of taking to the road dates back to the Middle Ages and is still practiced by some craftspeople today. They travel within Germany or even abroad and work in different places to acquire more knowledge of their craft. In former times craftsmen had to be on the road in order to get their master diploma. The goal of such a journey was and still is to gain work and life experience.
Travelling journeymen and -women wear traditional clothing and carry their belongings in a bundle. They also have a walking stick and wear earrings, which, in former times, were considered as a means of payment if the journeyman died on his tour. They're also meant to keep a journal.
In addition, there are a few rules that need to be observed. Craftspeople have to be unmarried, clear of debt and they have to have a journeyman's certificate. Their journey lasts for two or three years and one day and they are banned from getting closer than 50 kilometers to their hometown. This rule was supposed to avoid any local competition.
Even nowadays, journeymen and -women of 35 crafts can take to the road. Sadly, only 10–20 % of those that do are female. On the whole, there are currently between 450 and 550 craftspersons on the road. They learn how to work pragmatically and in a goal-oriented fashion as well as how to handle inconvenient customers. When working in

other places, they are paid standard local wages and normally they receive board and lodging for free.
If you need any more information, just ask. I'll keep my fingers crossed for a great presentation!

Best,
XXX

eA Aufgabe I mit Beispiellösung

Sophie Mackintosh, *Blue Ticket* (2020, excerpt)

AUFGABENSTELLUNG

1. Sum up the excerpt. (30 %)
2. Examine the atmosphere created in the text. (30 %)
3. You are taking part in an international project entitled "Facing Life's Crossroads", dealing with the choices young people are confronted with. You have to hand in an article for the project website in which you discuss the following statement by the writer Roy T. Bennett: "You are not the victim of the world, but rather the master of your own destiny. It is your choices and decisions that determine your destiny".
   Write the article, also referring to the text at hand and materials studied in class, such as the novel Never Let Me Go and the story "Two Kinds". (40 %)

Materialgrundlage:
Sophie Mackintosh, *Blue Ticket*, New York: Doubleday, 2020, S. 9–12 (gekürzt)

Hilfsmittel:
Den Prüflingen stehen einsprachige sowie für den schulischen Gebrauch geeignete zweisprachige Wörterbücher der Allgemeinsprache (Deutsch–Englisch/Englisch–Deutsch) zur Verfügung.

Prüfungszeit: 240 Minuten

Blue Ticket *Sophie Mackintosh*

Calla is a 14-year-old teenager living in a dystopian society. She has just reached puberty and therefore has to go to "the lottery," which determines whether she will have children or not.

[...]

The lottery station was a lot like the clinic: two storeys of pale brick, a flat roof. When we pulled up, the emissary outside was smoking a cigarette, but he threw it into the road when he saw us. Congratulations, he said to me. He led us inside to where the others waited.

The floorboards were wooden, varnished aggressively. Countless feet had scuffed that floor. It pooled the reflections of all the lights – spotlights from the ceiling, a lamp on the desk where a man in a dark suit sat on an orange plastic chair, watching us, legs crossed. He could have been a doctor, but he wore no white coat, no white plastic gloves. There were four other girls in their own dresses sitting in a row on a wooden bench, flowers both real and fake pinned to chests. They were not the girls from my school. One wore velvet, two wore tulle, and the other wore satin like me. I took a shine to the girl in satin. Same species.

We lined up, waiting to pull our tickets from the machine, the way you would take your number at the butcher's counter. The music popular that year played from speakers on the ceiling. Just gravity enough. Just ceremony enough. Not necessarily such an important thing, after all.

My name was called first. They watched me as I walked the length of the room, towards the machine inside its cloaked box. I put my hand in it. I was apprehensive but ready for my life to be decided. I closed my eyes and thought about my father with the wine bottle to his eye. The machine was silent as it discharged a sliver of hard paper into my hand. It was a deep cobalt. Congratulations, the possible doctor in the dark suit said to me.

The other girls followed, each taking their own ticket from the machine in turn. Almost a full house! he exclaimed at the end, reading a piece of paper spat out from the machine. We huddled and compared tickets. They were all blue, except for one, which was white. The girl with the white ticket was escorted into a separate room by the doctor and another emissary. We watched the three of them walk through an unlit doorway. When the doctor came back he clapped his hands twice. You have been spared, he said with a terrible benevolence. [...]

The bathroom of the lottery house was filled with yellow light, the veins of my thin neck standing out underneath it. I was a plucked chicken with badly applied eyeshadow, but the locket was around my throat now. There was a long, low mirror above the sink, a wicker chair in the corner and two bathroom stalls painted peach. In the mirror I watched the other girls leaning against the wall. Toes flexing. Eyes raised to the ceiling, moving to the door when the girl with the white ticket came in to join us, then back to the ceiling. There was a dying flower arrangement at the corner of the sink, gaps of oasis showing through pink carnations. The music came through in here too, speakers in the ceiling or underneath the sink.

At first I kept looking at the girl who had drawn the white ticket, the other girl in satin, though hers was pale blue and dirty at the hem where it dragged. Her eyes were red. I had the urge to take her arm and run with her somewhere, out to the woodland where I used to smoke with the other girls in my class between lessons, beyond the broken barbed wire of the school perimeter where the teachers could not see us. But I did not touch her; I made myself stop looking.

Inside the cubicle I spent some time reading the names and dates scratched on the door. With the safety pin that held on my fake peony corsage I engraved Calla, Blue Ticket, a smiley face and the date underneath. The swell of relief, smooth and natural as a muscle. I would never have children. And I was glad. I had been a child myself, not so long ago. I did not want to put any other puny creature through that. [...]

An emissary handed us each a bottle of water, a compass and a sandwich from the table, wrapped in a napkin. We did not get to pick the filling. The bottle given to the white-ticket girl was larger than ours, I noticed, and she received two sandwiches. It was happening immediately, the diverging of our paths, no time to spare.

Go, the doctor said to us. To the place of your choice. Walk into it. Anywhere but here. Congratulations.

I met my father's gaze. I had a city in mind. He looked back at me and nodded his head.

We walked out together into the cool night. The adults stayed in the light, for coffee and refreshments, to debrief with the doctor. We might see our parents again, we might not. Some of the girls halted at once when we got outside. They didn't know where to go. New and bewildered as the fawns I saw at the edges of the trees, in the dusk. The girl with the white ticket, though, she walked directly into the woods, the lights of our torches bouncing off the satin until she was gone into the dark. We were not so different.

I put the compass in the palm of my hand. North or south, east or west. The flicker of the needle, the splintered light of the moon on its glass casing. I knew I could do this [...]. My life was out there, ahead of me. I had to run to it, now that the shape was cast. (967 words)

Annotations

4 **we** – Calla and her father

37 f. my father with the wine bottle to his eye – Earlier in the story, her father holds an empty wine bottle to his eye like a telescope with which he can see into the future.

40 **cobalt** – here: the colour blue

60 **locket** – Girls and women keep their white or blue ticket in a locket (a small piece of jewellery that opens to show a small picture or object).

Beispiellösung

Aufgabe 1

The excerpt taken from "Blue Ticket", written by Sophie Mackintosh in 2020, deals with Calla, a 14-year-old girl who lives in a dystopian society in which "the lottery" determines whether a girl will have children or not.
Calla is accompanied to the clinic-like lottery station by her father. She is one of five girls who have to draw a ticket from a machine. Calla gets a blue ticket, which means that she will not have any children. She feels relieved about this result.

Calla carefully observes the one girl that received a white ticket and who is treated differently. She is taken to a separate room and receives more food and water than the other girls. Calla feels a lot of compassion for her but makes no contact with her.
Before the girls leave, all of them are equipped with compasses as well as some food and water. The doctor congratulates them and urges them to go. The girls leave the lottery without saying goodbye to their families and walk into the forest and into the night, each on their own. Calla feels confident now that the decision about her future has been made.

Aufgabe 2
The excerpt from "Blue Ticket" depicts a cold, nightmarish setting. The lottery station is a clinic-like building (ll. 2 f.) that conveys a sterile and inhospitable feeling, supported by uncomfortable furniture like the "orange plastic chair" (l. 14) and "the wooden bench" (l. 19). On the one hand, the rooms are spotlessly clean, as shown by the "floorboards [...], varnished aggressively" (ll. 9 f.). On the other hand, the station is obviously old and run-down: the doors in the toilets have been scratched with names and dates for years (ll. 89 f.) and the nearly withered flowers (ll. 68 f.) likewise point to decay.
The omnipresent use of light suggests that the girls are under constant observation. There does not seem to be any dark corners because the lights are everywhere ("reflections of all the lights – spotlights from the ceiling, a lamp on the desk", ll. 11–13). Accordingly, Calla feels like "a plucked chicken" (l. 59) under the unforgiving lights in the bathroom. Playing popular music constantly ("Just gravity enough. Just ceremony enough. Not necessarily such an important thing, after all", ll. 29–31) also seems to comply with the goal of evoking a feeling of familiarity, making the girls feel safe or perhaps rather complacent. Nevertheless, this cannot hide the fact that they are permanently regulated ("We lined up [...] the way you would take your number at the butcher's counter", ll. 25–27; "The girl with the white ticket was escorted into a separate room", ll. 49 f.) and under observation ("They watched me as I walked the length of the room", ll. 32 f.). The brightness of the lottery station is contrasted by the darkness of the nightly woods, which the girls are sent out into (ll. 121 f.). This represents a mysterious and challenging future, which likewise turns out to be intimidating ("bewildered", l. 120), particularly since the girls go into it each on their own. Being separated from their families and sent away at night seems both unnecessary and cruel.
A closer look at the language shows that there are many words with negative connotations, creating an unwelcoming, hostile atmosphere. Calla compares getting her ticket to "tak[ing] your number at the butcher's counter" (ll. 26 f.); the machine just "sp[its] out" (ll. 46 f.) the blue ticket so crucial for her future journey through life. The comparison to the butcher's implies that the girls are symbolically lead like lambs to the slaughter. This gives the setting a nightmarish atmosphere. This sense is further heightened by cryptic statements made by the lottery's staff, e. g. when the doctor congratulates the girls with the blue tickets that they "have been spared [...] with a terrible benevolence" (ll. 54 f.). This utterance leaves the reader as much as the girls in the dark about the fate they avoided and so reinforces the secretive atmosphere. The setting and the language used to describe it thus create a mysterious and unsettling scene. This makes obvious the helplessness and fear Calla and the other girls face at this pivotal moment.

Aufgabe 3

Roy T. Bennett once wrote: "You are not the victim of the world, but rather the master of your own destiny. It is your choices and decisions that determine your destiny". His statement clearly expresses the fact that every individual is self-determined, that everyone is responsible for their own future as well as the choices and decisions they make. But are we? Particularly as young people, we face a multitude of options in our lives. We choose friends, career paths, a place to live, the groups and partnerships we enter. But are our choices truly our own or merely the result of outward factors like laws, our culture and expectations of our family? In our times there appears to be so much space for us to develop our selves. There is a wide variety of paths – career and personal – we may choose from and so much flexibility to change them. But this may also be an illusion. So many people in this world have far fewer opportunities, perhaps because they live in poverty, in repressive societies or because they are antagonised for being different. We may all be able to choose, but not everyone gets the same options.

Since literature is so good at exploring possibilities and ideas about ourselves, let us look at a few narrative texts. In Amy Tan's short story "Two Kinds" (1989), protagonist Jing-mei decides not to follow the path set out for her by her mother. As a child, Jing-mei is eager to please her, but as she grows older, she realises that a career as a musician is not her personal goal. For this reason, she gives up playing the piano and thus deeply disappoints her mother. By doing so, Jing-mei seizes her chance to fulfil her own dreams and dismissing her mother's. However, the short story also shows that Jing-mei cannot really cope with this disavowal and only comes to terms with her internal conflict after her mother has died. Amy Tan therefore shows us that we may be self-determined but that it may still be difficult to free ourselves from the expectations of others.

Dystopian fiction may also offer us a worthwhile perspective into the difficulties in becoming masters of our own destiny. In Sophie Mackintosh's novel "Blue Ticket" (2020), a machine determines if girls will have children or not. It is easy to see that Calla, the protagonist, is largely unable to make her own choice. She and the other girls are subjects of a state system that has mapped out a large part of their future for them. The excerpt may end on a positive note, with Calla looking into the darkness with self-confidence about reaching her destination. To the reader, however, it is clear that she does not even realise how much her choices have been narrowed down. Her path into the future is, to a large part, a matter of luck, namely the colour of her ticket.

The clones in Kazuo Ishiguro's novel "Never Let Me Go" are "victim[s] of the world" to an even greater degree. Bred as organ donors, all meaningful choices are made for them and their fate is predetermined. When they learn of their purpose, they fail to rebel and instead resign themselves to their destiny.

With these sketches in mind, one may come to the conclusion that the truth of Bennett's statement strongly depends on the environment people live in. We always make our decisions within a certain social framework. In most cases this system will not be as repressive as the ones in "Blue Ticket" or "Never Let Me Go", but expectations, laws and also luck will always determine the options we may choose from. In most cases, we may be as oblivious as Calla to the ways in which our choices have been preselected. And perhaps this is all for the better if we want to be happy.

eA Aufgabe II mit Beispiellösung

Karla Cornejo Villavicencio, "Waking Up from the American Dream" (2021)

AUFGABENSTELLUNG

1 Outline the information about the author's parents. (30 %)
2 Analyze the stylistic means the author uses and their effect on the reader. (30 %)
3 Having come across the blog "The American Dream Today – Myth or Reality?" you have decided to leave a guest post assessing whether the American Dream is achievable in contemporary society.
Write this blog entry, also referring to the text at hand and materials studied in class, such as the movie Crash and the short story "The Child". (40 %)

Materialgrundlage:

Karla Cornejo Villavicencio, „Waking Up from the American Dream“, in: *The New Yorker* 18. Januar 2021, zitiert nach: https://www.newyorker.com/magazine/2021/01/25/waking-up-from-the-american-dream (Zugriff: 01.04.2022, gekürzt)

Hilfsmittel:

Den Prüflingen stehen einsprachige sowie für den schulischen Gebrauch geeignete zweisprachige Wörterbücher der Allgemeinsprache (Deutsch–Englisch/Englisch–Deutsch) zur Verfügung.

Prüfungszeit: 240 Minuten

"Waking Up from the American Dream" (2021)

Karla Cornejo Villavicencio

[...] My parents were not tony expats. At home, meals could be rice and a fried egg. We sometimes hid from our landlord by crouching next to my bed and drawing the blinds. My father had started out driving a cab, but after 9/11, when the governor revoked the driver's licenses of undocumented immigrants, he began working as a deliveryman, carrying meals to Wall Street executives, the plastic bags slicing into his fingers. Some of those executives forced him to ride on freight elevators. Others tipped him in spare change.

My mother worked in a factory. For seven days a week, sometimes in twelve-hour shifts, she sewed in a heat that caught in your throat like lint, while her bosses, also immigrants, hurled racist slurs at her. Some days I sat on the factory floor, making dolls with swatches of fabric, cosplaying childhood. I didn't put a lot of effort into making the dolls – I sort of just screwed around, with an eye on my mom at her sewing station, stiffening whenever her supervisor came by to see how fast she was working. What could I do to protect her? Well, murder, I guess.

Our problem appeared to be poverty, which even then, before I'd seen "Rent[",] seemed glamorous, or at least normal. All the protagonists in the books I read were poor. Ramona Quimby on Klickitat Street, the kids in "Five Little Peppers and How They Grew[".] Every fictional child was hungry, an orphan, or tubercular. But there was something else setting us apart. At school, I looked at my nonwhite classmates and wondered how their parents could be nurses, or own houses, or leave the country on vacation. It was none of my business – everyone in New York had secrets – but I cautiously gathered intel, toothpick in mouth. I finally cracked the case when I tried to apply to an essay contest and asked my parents for my Social Security number. My father was probably reading a newspaper, and I doubt he even looked up to say, "We don't have papers, so we don't have a Social."

It was not traumatic. I turned on our computer, waited for the dial-up, and searched what it meant not to have a Social Security number. "Undocumented immigrant" had not yet entered the discourse. Back then, the politically correct term, the term I saw online, was "illegal immigrant[",] which grated – it was hurtful in a clinical way, like having your teeth drilled. Various angry comments sections offered another option: illegal alien. I knew it was form language, legalese meant to wound me, but it didn't. It was punk as hell. We were hated, and maybe not entirely of this world. […]

I never called myself a Dreamer. The word was saccharine and dumb, and it yoked basic human rights to getting an A on a report card. Dreamers couldn't flunk out of high school, or have D.U.I.s, or work at McDonald's. *Those* kids lived with the pressure of needing a literal miracle in order to save their families, but the miracle didn't happen, because the odds were against them, because the odds were against all of us. And so America decided that they didn't deserve an I.D.

The Dream, it turned out, needed to demonize others in order to help the chosen few. Our parents, too, would be sacrificed. The price of our innocence was the guilt of our loved ones. Jeff Sessions, while he was Attorney General, suggested that we had been trafficked against our will. People actually pitied me because my parents brought me to America. Without even *consulting* me.

The irony, of course, is that the Dream was our inheritance. We were Dreamers because our parents had dreams.

It's painful to think about this. My mother, an aspiring interior designer, has gone twenty-eight years without a sick day. My dad, who loves problem-solving, has spent his life wanting a restaurant. He's a talented cook and a brilliant manager, and he often did the work of his actual managers for them. But, without papers, he could advance only so far in a job. He needed to be paid in cash; he could never receive benefits.

He often used a soccer metaphor to describe our journey in America. Our family was a team, but I scored the goals. Everything my family did was, in some sense, a pass to me. Then the American Dream could be mine, and then we could start passing to my brother. […]

When I was a kid, my mother found a crystal heart in my father's taxi. The light that came through it was pretty, shimmering, like a gasoline spill on the road. She put it in her jewelry box, and sometimes we'd take out the box, spill the contents onto my pink twin bed, and admire what we both thought was a heart-shaped diamond. I grew up, I went to college. I often heard of kids who had inherited their grandmother's heirlooms, and I sincerely believed that there were jewels in my family, too. Then, a few years ago, my partner and I visited my mom, and she spilled out her box. She gave me a few items I cherish: a nameplate bracelet in white, yellow, and rose gold, and the thick gold hoop earrings that she wore when she first moved to Brooklyn. Everything else was costume jewelry. I couldn't find the heart.

I realized that, when my mother found the crystal, she was around the same age I am now. She had probably never held a diamond, and she probably wanted to believe that she had found one in America, a dream come true. She wanted me to believe it, and then, as we both grew up, alone, together, she stopped believing, stopped wanting to believe, and stopped me from wanting to believe. And she probably threw that shit out. I didn't ask. Some things are none of our business.

(987 words)

Annotations

1 tony – here: well-off

17 lint – fine fibres that come off the surface of cloth

20 to cosplay – here: to pretend to have

28 Rent – rock musical about poor artists

41 to gather intel – to collect useful and secret information

62 Dreamer – person who has been in the US illegally since coming to the country as a minor and who is given the temporary right to live and study there when meeting certain conditions

64 to yoke – here: making one the prerequisite for the other

66 D.U.I. – abbreviation for: Driving Under the Influence (= driving while significantly impaired by alcohol or other drugs)

Beispiellösung

Aufgabe 1

In her article "Waking Up from the American Dream" (published in "The New Yorker" on January 25, 2021), Karla Cornejo Villavicencio details her family's life as immigrants in the US.

Because they are regarded as "illegal" and therefore lack the necessary documents, the author's parents are deprived of well-paid and safe jobs. In spite of working hard, they are forced into menial jobs without career opportunities and remain poor.

The author's mother seems to be a seamstress. She is bullied by her racist bosses (who are also immigrants) and exploited to do long shifts seven days a week, closely supervised. Unable to afford childcare, the mother has to take her daughter to work, even though the conditions there are unhealthy.

Villavicencio's father originally worked as a taxi driver until his driver's licence was revoked due to a political decision. As a consequence, he is forced to pick up menial jobs, for example as a deliveryman, in which he and his work are not valued and which convey to him a feeling of being excluded and discriminated against.

In the end, the author's parents lost all hopes of ever achieving any of their dreams as their ambitions were stifled. Her mother has been working for twenty-eight years and has proved that she is a reliable worker but cannot move up because of missing papers.

Similarly, Villavicencio's father would have made a skillful manager and cook but is permanently excluded from pursuing his dream. As a consequence, both parents are setting all their hopes on their Dreamer children by supporting them wherever possible.

Aufgabe 2

Reading the article, it is striking that the author consistently uses different stylistic devices to convey the desperate situation of undocumented immigrants to the US by way of her own family's history.

Villavicencio's perhaps most eye-catching stylistic device is the symbol of the "crystal heart" her mother once found in her husband's cab (ll. 109 f.). At first, this heart embodies the American Dream she and her daughter share but later lose or cast off when their situation does not improve.

The family's hopelessness is expressed via the ironic exaggeration that only "murder" (l. 26) could protect the author's mother from her bosses. Villavicencio also uses irony to point out that her parents could hardly have consulted her on whether to emigrate to the US (ll. 81–83).

The parallelism of the father's words – "We don't have papers, so we don't have a Social" (ll. 46 f.) – makes obvious the fact that it always comes back to this problem, that having no papers prevents them from enjoying personal freedom. The degree to which undocumented immigrants are excluded is brought home by means of personification: "America decided that they didn't deserve an I.D. The Dream [...] needed to demonize others in order to help the chosen few" (ll. 72–76).

The author also applies similes to make situations more relatable to the reader. For instance, she compares the pain of being stigmatised by the state and society with "having your teeth drilled" (ll. 55 f.), evoking a very painful feeling. Similarly, she describes the air at her mother's workplace with breathing lint (l. 17) and hints at the cheapness of the crystal heart by comparing it with spilled gasoline (ll. 110–112).

When scrutinising the words of the text, it becomes obvious that several words are written in italics in order to emphasise certain aspects. Drawing the reader's attention to words like "illegal alien" (l. 57), "We were hated" (l. 60) and "*Those* kids" (l. 67) helps them understand the feeling of being different and being treated as inferior and unwanted.

The author also conveys a degree of annoyance and anger by drastically changing the register of speech. She writes that she felt "punk as hell" (ll. 59 f.) about being called an illegal alien, and regarding the crystal heart, she guesses that her mother "probably threw that shit out" (ll. 138 f.).

Metaphors can also be discovered in the text. It is the father's soccer metaphor which describes their family as a team that tries to help their daughter to score the "goal" of realising the American Dream (ll. 103–108). Another metaphor interprets the family's attempts to get documented as a "journey" (l. 103).

The key sentence "She wanted me to believe [...], and then [...] she stopped believing, stopped wanting to believe, and stopped me from wanting to believe" (ll. 134–138) shows the contrast between hope for the American Dream and the hard reality the family permanently faces. The repetition of the word "stopped" also brings home the finality of the mother's decision.

Finally, the author also makes use of comic relief: "everyone in New York had secrets – but I cautiously gathered intel, toothpick in mouth. I finally cracked the case" (ll. 39–42). By delivering such a cliché of detective habits, she makes the text more accessible.

Aufgabe 3

In the past few months I've been pointing you to Rodrian's great blog "The American Dream Today – Myth or Reality?", which I've been following for quite a while now. Today I'd like to contribute some thoughts of my own on the question whether the American Dream is achievable today.

As everybody knows, living the American Dream has always been a pursuit for many for about the last 250 years. From the first settlers to immigrants today, many have consistently tried to achieve "rewards" like happiness and riches. The American Dream is a great promise, raising and nourishing hope, particularly for people who come from humble beginnings and try to rise through hard work to prosperity. Hollywood holds some of the most famous 'rags-to-riches' stories, such as Madonna and Tom Cruise.

Karla Villavicencio's article "Waking Up from the American Dream" paints a very different picture. Her family's success has been continually hampered by the fact that they are undocumented immigrants. They are refused well-paid jobs which prevents them from developing their potential to the full. Keeping these people away from climbing the social ladder shows that there is inequality and also discrimination against them. The trafficking of illegal immigrants as depicted in the movie "Crash" also points out how the American Dream of poor people is exploited.

Ethnicity always plays a role. "Crash" is full of examples of the stereotyping and discrimination daily faced by immigrants: actor Jamal is asked to speak with a stronger African-American accent in order to appear less intelligent, Jean doesn't trust the Hispanic locksmith and Officer Ryan targets predominantly African-American citizens. Julius Lester's short story "The Child" also depicts racism towards the old, drunk man.

Clearly, the role of education is vital because it's the key qualification to better jobs and a satisfying life. The requirements for getting a good education are quite different among immigrants, which one may realise when having a look at some of the characters of the texts mentioned above. Karla attends college, whereas Karen in "The Child" is unable to finish school. Consequently, Karla has better opportunities to take up a well-paid and prestigious profession.

Undoubtedly, family background is significantly important as well. Profound support and consistently strengthening one's child is an essential quality parents should permanently provide. This is the case with Daniel in "Crash", trying to enable upward mobility for his family in order to achieve better living conditions. But not all parents have the same opportunities to support their children, as Villavicencio eventually realises when she finds out that her non-white classmate's prosperity is founded on the fact that their families have the necessary legal documents.

What all three narratives have in common is the crushing of hopes and the following disillusionment when the characters realise that they will not achieve their desired goals. Even though some of them like Karla's parents have useful talents and have proven that they are skillful workers, they are not given the chance to climb the ladder of success

in order to make a fortune and to find happiness. Similarly, “Crash” shows that racism keeps the cycle of violence going when Officer Hansen shoots Peter and when the film ends in another racially charged scene.
To be honest, to me the American Dream seems to be a purely theoretical social construct. The ideal of the ‘self-made man/woman’ who rises ‘from rags to riches’ can only be reached by a small number of people due to political regulations. The poorer one’s social background is, the fewer the chances are to improve one’s station. Poor education and strict state regulations often prevent occupational advancement and there is very limited support for upward mobility from the American government. Undocumented immigrants in particular have very little opportunity to make it to the top, as the idea of integration has been widely been abandoned and the effects of the “America first” policy are still noticeable. Resentment towards ethnic minorities and undocumented immigrants further exacerbates this problematic situation.

Stichwortverzeichnis